### *This was not a dream . . .*

Mac could not escape the creature that held him so effortlessly in its front claws. With his arms pinned to his sides,
the gun he held was useless.

Horrified, Lanie watched the creature draw him close
and lower its mouth to his neck. She saw the fangs pierce
the skin, but it was the sound of blood being sucked from
Mac's body that catapulted her into action. Lying on the
ground where it had fallen was the search lamp. She
grabbed it and turned it back on. The sudden brightness of
the beam pierced the night and the creature reared back,
releasing its hold on Mac.

Lanie held the beam steady with one hand and
wrapped her other arm around Mac as he fell against her.
She wasn't sure if he was alive or dead . . .

Please turn to the back of this book
for a preview of Robin T. Popp's upcoming novel,
*Seduced by the Night*

# Out of the
# NIGHT

## ROBIN T. POPP

NEW YORK   BOSTON

*Cover design by Diane Luger*
*Book design by Giorgetta Bell McRee*

Warner Books

Time Warner Book Group
1271 Avenue of the Americas
New York, NY 10020
Visit our Web site at www.twbookmark.com

Printed in the United States of America

First Paperback Printing: September 2005

10 9 8 7 6 5 4 3 2 1

To Adam, with love—I can shoulder the weight of the world as long as I know you're there to catch me should I fall.

And to Mom and Dad—Mom, for sharing her love of all things paranormal; and Dad, for being the example of perseverance that taught me to never give up on my dream.

# Acknowledgments

There are several people I have come to rely on as I undertake each writing adventure. Their creativity, friendship, and support sustain and motivate me. I would like to thank Donna Grant, Mary O'Connor, Georgia Ward, Corkey Sandman, Adam Popp, and Marlaine Loftin for brainstorming plot ideas, reading various drafts, keeping me on track, and just generally being there for me.

Also, I would like to thank Michelle Grajkowski for being such a terrific agent and having such enthusiasm for my writing.

And I would like to thank Karen Kosztolnyik for taking a chance on me and my writing. I appreciate this opportunity more than you'll ever know.

# INVICTUS

## by William Henley


Out of the night that covers me,
Black as the Pit from pole to pole,
I thank whatever gods may be
For my unconquerable soul.

In the fell clutch of circumstance
I have not winced nor cried aloud.
Under the bludgeonings of chance
My head is bloody, but unbowed.

Beyond this place of wrath and tears
Looms but the Horror of the shade,
And yet the menace of the years
Finds, and shall find, me unafraid.

It matters not how strait the gate,
How charged with punishments the scroll,
I am the master of my fate:
I am the captain of my soul.

# Out of the
# NIGHT

# Chapter
# 1

Great tongues of fire leaped from the structure, more brilliant against the night sky than any fireworks display; beautiful, mesmerizing—and deadly. Lanie Weber stood close, feeling the heat beat at her, her skin burning despite the protection of her gear.

"Lanie's crew takes left; Marcus—center. We'll take right. Let's go." The fire chief's muted voice carried to her over the roaring of the flames, and she nodded to let him know she'd heard.

With the fire hose cradled along her right arm, Lanie gripped the nozzle securely with both hands. Her second lineman braced her with his elbow, offering resistance against the pressure of the water, which tried to propel her backward as soon as the water started to flow.

Lanie adjusted the stream until a focused, narrow torrent shot forth. She concentrated on the left side of the structure, her only goal to contain the flames and protect the exposure of the house next door, because it was too late to save the one-story home. At least no one had been hurt.

Though she couldn't hear anything beyond the noise of the fire, Lanie was aware of the family's devastation. In their minds, they had lost everything, but Lanie knew what real loss was. Houses, clothes, possessions—those things could be replaced. The loss of a loved one . . .

Shying away from the thought, she turned her full attention back to fighting the blaze. After ten years as a volunteer firefighter, the heat of the flames, the acrid smell of smoke, the camaraderie of the other volunteers, even the mechanics of putting out the fire—these things were familiar to her. Tonight, of all nights, she needed the comfort of familiarity about her.

Hours later, Lanie shut off the water for the last time and eased the hose to the ground. Leaving it to the rookies, she walked to her truck, the evening's adrenaline rush long since spent. It had been a long mop-up, and the sun was already climbing high in the sky. Removing her helmet, she tossed it into the back, then opened her jacket and welcomed the cool breeze against her hot, sweaty body.

"Don't you have a flight to catch?" The chief came to stand next to her, angling his raised arm to show her the time on his watch.

"Yeah, I guess so." Her tone sounded as weary as she felt. She briefly considered canceling, but arrangements were already made.

"Thanks for coming," he added. "It would have been a lot tougher without you here."

She shrugged. "I didn't feel like sitting at home last night anyway, and three calls in a row kept me from dwelling on other things, you know?"

He nodded, wrapped an arm around her shoulders, gave her a fatherly hug, and then walked off, leaving her to climb into her truck and drive off to face her future—alone.

Truly alone, because her father was dead.

She knew the pain of his loss would hit sooner or later, but right now, she felt numb. It was like standing on the precipice of a great, bottomless chasm while the wind beat at her, pushing her until, eventually, she knew she would fall. But not yet. There was too much to do.

Arriving home, she saw the light blinking on her answering machine. Playing the message, she heard her employer's sympathetic voice urging her to take off as much time as she needed. Grateful, she showered and changed into fresh clothes, then saw that it was well after noon. She'd been too depressed last night to eat dinner and too busy fighting fires all morning for breakfast. Now there was no time for lunch.

Grabbing her duffel bag, she set the security alarm on her house and climbed back into her truck, navigating the Houston traffic until she was on the freeway headed out of town. She tried to focus on the road, but her thoughts pulled her back to a faded but never forgotten memory.

She was twelve years old, and her father had left her in the cold, sterile waiting room of the city morgue while he went in, alone, to identify her mother's body. He'd not wanted Lanie to carry the image of her mother's battered body with her for the rest of her life, wanting her, instead, to remember her mother as she'd last seen her—energetic, happy, and full of love and vitality.

Lanie *had* remembered her that way. So much so that for years, she'd suffered from the belief that her mother's death was all a huge mistake; that her father had identified the wrong body and any day now, her mother would return—because a woman so full of life would never have surrendered to death.

Now, sixteen years later, she was having to accept a loved one's death again. This time would be different, she vowed. This time, there would be closure. Yesterday afternoon, when she'd gotten the phone call from Admiral Charles Winslow about her father's accident, she'd been insistent. If her father was dead, then she wanted to see the body, and she didn't care how difficult or impossible it was to arrange. If her father's body couldn't be flown back into the United States, then she would go to South America.

Fortunately, the admiral had understood. A friend of the family for years, "Uncle" Charles was the one who'd talked her father into accepting the top secret research position earlier that year. He was also the one to suggest the private charter company that would fly her to the town of Taribu in the northern part of the Amazon, making the arrangements himself.

Bringing her thoughts back to the present, Lanie concentrated on driving. Three hours later, she steered her truck onto a narrow side road and drove for several minutes before spotting the gate with the large ANYTIME—DEY OR KNIGHT PRIVATE CHARTERS sign across the top. Pulling across the dirt lot, she parked in front of the plain white building that seemed so out of place in the middle of the endless open stretch of land. Behind it were two smaller buildings.

Getting out, Lanie was struck by the absolute silence. She found herself questioning the wisdom of driving out here alone, much less traveling alone to South America.

Trying to discount her sense of foreboding as nothing more than extreme fatigue and an acknowledged fear of flying, she took a deep breath and headed inside the building.

"Hi." A young woman, almost wearing a low-cut tank top and tight blue-jean shorts, greeted her with a hundred-watt smile and eyes as warm as spiced ginger. "You must be Ms. Weber."

Lanie tried to return her smile, but couldn't quite manage it. "That's me."

"We spoke yesterday. I'm Sandra." She walked behind a counter and picked up a thin stack of papers that she quickly leafed through. "Everything seems to be in order. I've got you flying to Taribu today with a return trip day after tomorrow—is that correct?"

Lanie walked closer so she wouldn't feel like she was yelling across the room. "That's right. Did you have any problems getting the authorization from Admiral Winslow?"

"No, you're all set." She picked up a two-way radio and spoke into it. "Mac, your charter is here." There was a crackling of some response a moment later that made Sandra smile. Then she turned her attention back to Lanie. "Mac'll be here in a second. Can I get you something while you wait? No? Okay, if you change your mind, just holler. I'll be in back." She gestured to the door behind her, replaced the stack of papers on the counter with a smile, and then disappeared through the door.

Lanie wandered to the far wall where she took a seat in one of the chairs. The clock above her showed that she had less than an hour before her scheduled departure, and conflicting emotions warred inside her: grief, depression, anxiety. She glanced out the side window, hoping to distract herself, and spotted a single white jet. Compared to the commercial planes she was used to, it was a toy— surely incapable of the long flight to Taribu. *Wherever the hell that is.* Her ignorance slammed into her like a fist. She should have shown more interest in her father's work. Maybe if she had . . .

No, he still would have gone, and in her heart she knew he'd understood. How many years had he dragged her all over the place in pursuit of his studies? The remote wilderness areas of Florida, the mountain regions of Washington, the desert plains of southwest Texas—even the impoverished farmlands of Puerto Rico.

She'd helped him research and catalog his findings to the extent that becoming a librarian seemed a natural choice of careers for her when the time came. She'd also liked the stability of staying in one place while attending college. Later, having settled in with the local fire department and taken a job with the university library, her days of traveling with her father stopped for good. She'd wanted her own life.

The creaking of a screen door being opened, followed immediately by the sound of it slamming shut, broke into her recriminations. She looked up to see a man walking toward her, tall and muscular, with broad shoulders. His features were dark, and he moved with the ease of a large jungle cat stalking its prey. Only the slight limp kept him from appearing totally predatory. As he drew closer, Lanie saw that the thick, nearly black waves of his hair fell so long, the ends brushed the back of his neck. The sun had tanned his skin to a rich, healthy glow and his dark chocolate-brown eyes seemed to miss no detail as they quickly came to rest on her.

"Ms. Weber?" His deep voice washed over her, sending chills racing down her spine and making her suddenly very conscious of her appearance.

"Yes." She fought the urge to run a hand down her hair in order to smooth the errant strands she knew must be sticking out from her head. The smoke from the fire had irritated her eyes, so she'd put on her glasses instead of her contacts and now felt as if she were staring out from behind a thick wall of glass.

"I'm Michael Knight, but folks call me 'Mac.' I'll be your pilot." His outstretched hand caught her attention, and she realized that she'd been gaping at him.

"It's nice to meet you." She took his hand and felt the warm, rough texture of it against her skin. His grip was firm and solid, giving her the impression of controlled strength. This was a man who could handle any situation and remain unfazed.

"We have a long flight ahead of us," he said, releasing her hand so he could glance at his wristwatch. "You understand that we'll have to fly to Brasilia first, since we're not technically a government aircraft. That adds about eight hours to our flight time, plus a short layover to take care of the administrative details."

She nodded, knowing that the unavoidable delays still had her arriving at the research facility long before she'd have been able to through standard commercial means.

"Fine, then let me check the flight plan once more and then we'll be on our way." He didn't even wait for her response, but turned and walked behind the counter where he flipped through several sheets of paper.

At that moment, Sandra appeared, moving immediately to his side. "There you are."

"Hey, Babycakes." For the first time since he'd walked into the room, Mac smiled, causing Lanie's breath to catch. He was gorgeous, and Lanie wondered about the nature of his relationship with *Babycakes*. Were they married? Sleeping together? Just really close friends? The speculation cast her own solitary life into sharp relief.

"Time to go."

Mac's announcement sent a spurt of adrenaline shooting through her, and she watched as he leaned down to give Sandra a chaste kiss on the cheek.

"Be good while I'm gone."

"That's no fun." Sandra smiled as she returned his hug, but then her tone grew serious when she added, "Be careful, okay?"

"You know me."

"That's what worries me."

Mac chuckled as he released her and crossed to the door, which he held open for Lanie to walk through. Outside, he stopped to put on his sunglasses and then glanced at the duffel bag in her hand.

"Where's the rest of your luggage?"

"This is it."

"Good."

His response was curt, delivered in a cool, distant tone that contradicted the warm laugh he'd just given *Baby-cakes*. Lanie tried to judge his expression, but couldn't see past the image of her own pale, unkempt face reflected in his mirrored lenses. Once again, Lanie was reminded of a predator, studying its prey, and when he moved toward her, she couldn't stop herself from taking a quick step back. His expression changed to one of obvious irritation, and she felt like a fool when all he did was take her bag.

"Follow me. Plane's over here." He walked off, seemingly unconcerned whether she trailed after him or not.

Already nervous, she refused to allow this man to intimidate her further. Hurrying so she could fall in step beside him, she tried to ease the situation with conversation.

"Admiral Winslow speaks very highly of you."

A grunt was his only response. Undaunted, she tried again.

"Have you known him long?"

He glanced at her, his look telling her that he suffered her questions only because he had no other choice. "Ten years."

"Were you in the Navy?"

"Yes."

"But you're not now."

"Correct."

Lanie sighed. She wasn't one of those people who could make conversation easily, and his lack of cooperation was frustrating.

"I'm a librarian." She cringed as soon as the words left her mouth. It made no sense; a random comment born of desperation, and she prayed that he ignored it.

"Really?" His tone revealed his complete lack of interest.

Up ahead, another fifty yards, stood the small white jet she'd spotted from the building. Seeing it up close, it still looked tiny, and another shiver ran down her spine.

"How long have you been flying private charters?"

"A year."

*One year?* Lanie almost stumbled. Did she really want to fly to a foreign country with a man who'd been flying for only one year? "How long have you been a pilot?" That was maybe the better question, she hoped.

"Ten years."

She sighed with relief as they reached the plane and she stopped beside it, waiting for him to open the hatch.

"Yo, keep moving."

Lanie jerked to her left, to see Mac staring at her from behind the plane.

"I'm sorry?"

"I said, keep moving. We don't have time to waste sightseeing."

Confused, she waved a hand toward the plane. "But isn't this—"

"Our plane?" He gave a short laugh. "Hell, no. I'm not flying a Falcon 2000 into that part of the Amazon." He leaned back and pointed to something she couldn't see, hidden on the other side. "*That's* what we're flying."

With a feeling of dread, Lanie moved to the end of the small white jet and looked beyond it. She turned to stare at Mac in absolute horror and started shaking her head. "Oh, no, no, no. I am *not* getting into that . . . that . . . what is it, anyway?"

"It's a plane—let's go."

She continued to stare. "It's a rotted-out tin can with wings—correction, one wing and a stump. Surely you don't expect me to ride in that? I mean, I can't. I won't."

"Can and will." He put a hand behind her back and gave her a gentle shove. "My instructions from Admiral Winslow are to get you to Taribu with all due haste. I believe those were your orders to him, were they not?" He glanced at her, but didn't wait for an answer as his hand continued to propel her forward.

"The only people flying into Taribu are drug dealers, DEA, and the poor souls trying to make an honest living transporting livestock and workers back and forth between the larger cities."

They were at the plane now, and Lanie saw that it truly was a rusted-out, beat-up old plane. Mac opened the hatch and threw in her bag before turning back to her. "Personally, I don't want the DEA thinking we're drug dealers or the drug dealers thinking we're DEA. So we'll go in looking like the poor souls who have to haul livestock." He waved a hand at the plane and gave her a smile, the first he'd directed her way, and it had a decidedly evil bent to it.

"All aboard."

Lanie stepped forward as he jumped on board and saw that the inside looked only slightly safer than the outside. When she felt his gaze on her, she tipped her head back, blocking the sun with her hand, and gave him a weak smile.

"I'm not going."

"You're afraid of flying," he accused her.

"Even if I was, I have serious doubts that this *thing* will actually attain an altitude high enough to constitute flying," she retorted. "But if it does, I assure you, it's not the flying I'm afraid of—it's mechanical failure and, possibly, pilot error."

This time his laugh sounded more genuine. "This is no time to be faint of heart. Man up, Weber. Time's a-wasting."

*Man up?* She didn't know what she hated more—his macho attitude or his obviously low opinion of her. Deciding it was the latter, she gritted her teeth, took a deep breath, and grabbed the sides of the open hatch to haul herself up.

Once inside, Lanie verified that it was as bad as she'd feared. Unbidden, her thoughts conjured the image of the plane doing a nosedive through the air, engines sputtering erratically and smoke billowing forth. "This thing is a death trap," she muttered, "and we're both going to die before we even make it out of Texas."

"Nice positive attitude," Mac chided, suddenly appearing from out of a cubbyhole near the back of the plane. "Here, drink this. It'll calm your nerves."

"What is it?" She stared at the small Styrofoam cup half full of light amber liquid.

"Tequila."

Lanie studied it for a long time, silently debating the merits of jumping off and running away versus staying on board. An image of her father's face came to mind and she sighed. There really wasn't a choice. Given that, maybe a little something to help her relax was a good idea. "Please tell me that you're not also planning to seek courage at the bottom of a cup, or ten?"

He gave her another one of those grins that made her think the joke was on her. "Not this trip."

Though she wasn't sure she trusted him, she didn't think he was the kind to jeopardize his job or the lives of his clients by drinking. Besides, Uncle Charles had recommended him. She accepted the cup and lifted it to her lips. The familiar tangy-sweet smell of the alcohol tickled her nose. Bracing herself, she threw back the contents and felt the burn all the way down to her stomach. Tears stung her eyes, and she blinked several times to clear them. As the cabin swam back into focus, she couldn't help but wonder if maybe two shots would be better than one. Reluctantly, she dismissed the idea and handed back the cup.

"You can sit up front, in the copilot's seat. Just don't touch anything." He pointed her in the direction of the cockpit, which, despite her fear, she found fascinating. She liked all the gauges and buttons, though she had no cluc what any of them did. Plus, the view out the front window beat staring out the small side opening hands down.

"Sit here and let me help you with the straps."

She slid into the copilot's chair and watched those tan, masculine hands pull the straps across her front. When the back of his hand brushed against her breast, she froze, trying to hide her body's immediate reaction, unsure whether he'd done it on purpose or by accident. She finally decided the contact had been unintentional, because even though *her* pulse was racing in response to it, he seemed not to have noticed at all.

After she was buckled in, he closed the plane's door and did whatever needed to be done in the back before they could take off. As she waited for him to return, Lanie felt a warm lassitude steal over her muscles, and the prospect of the upcoming flight grew less threatening.

When Mac finally joined her in the cockpit, she found herself actually smiling at him. More amazing was the smile he gave her in return. He really was rather breathtaking when he did that, she thought again, her body growing lighter and her worries vanishing into thin air.

"Well, I think we're just about ready." Mac's voice floated to her as if from far away and she tried to focus on it, but it proved to be impossible. It occurred to her that one shot of tequila had never affected her like this before and that something was wrong, terribly wrong.

Now her head felt too heavy to hold up, so she let it fall back against the seat. It took every bit of her willpower to look to the side where Mac's face wavered unsteadily.

"Wha . . . ?" Her mouth refused to ask the question her mind had no trouble screaming. *What did you do to me?*

Then there was only darkness.

# Chapter
# 2

Long hours later, Mac guided the plane across the tiny airfield in the northern Amazon of South America. The facility to which he and his passenger were headed was the headquarters for a zoological research project studying the indigenous wildlife of the area. The project was being conducted by one of the larger stateside universities, though Mac didn't know which one specifically. It didn't matter. The whole thing was a front for the U.S. military, giving them an excuse to have a covert presence in the Amazon. The sizable fee paid to key members of the Brazilian government ensured that the "university researchers" were left alone, and everyone seemed to like it that way.

Mac wasn't sure what type of research was really being done at the remote location. That information was classified, and he was no longer "in the know." Still, there was no reason to believe that Weber's and Burton's deaths were anything more than they appeared—the result of a

wild animal attack. Except, of course, that it seemed
unusually convenient that Burton should die now of all
times, and Mac wasn't the only one to think so. As soon
as someone at the research facility had contacted Admiral
Winslow with news of the deaths, the admiral had phoned
Mac and the two had immediately begun making plans. It
was imperative that Mac see the body of Lance Burton for
himself. It was the only way they could be sure the man
was truly dead.

Shutting down the plane's engines, Mac glanced at his
client, amazed and grateful that she'd stayed unconscious
for so long. He'd known the moment he saw her that she
wouldn't make the trip without a little help—she was just
that kind—so he'd slipped a couple of pain pills into her
tequila. He knew the white coloring of the Styrofoam cup
would mask any particles of the pills that hadn't fully dis-
solved. He needed to get to that research compound.

Still, he was a little surprised at how long she'd been
asleep. He'd been shooting for "relaxed," not total unconsciousness. For the fourth time he checked her pulse,
worried that he'd grossly underestimated the effects of
two pain pills administered with alcohol. Just because
they had little effect on him when he took them for the
pain in his leg, didn't mean they would affect her the
same way. Once again, he found her pulse was strong and
steady; she'd live.

He couldn't put off waking her any longer; it was time
to face the music. Pulling a tissue from the nearest dis-
penser, he wiped away the drool at the corner of her mouth,
trying to give back some of the dignity he'd stolen. She
was a mousy little thing, he thought, glancing at the
Coke-bottle glasses sitting askew on her nose.

His eyes fell to the steady rise and fall of her chest, and he felt his body tighten at the memory of his hand brushing against the full treasure hidden beneath her oversized shirt. Touching her had been an accident, but not one he could bring himself to regret, although he was surprised that his body reacted so quickly. She wasn't exactly his type.

Leaving his chair, he walked to the galley and took a bottle of water from the fridge. He moistened a small towel and then returned to his charge. She hadn't moved.

*Come on, Mac,* he thought. *Stop stalling.* Heaving a sigh, he leaned over and jostled her arm. "Ms. Weber? Lanie? It's time to wake up." There was no response. He tried again, shaking her harder, but still nothing. Reluctantly, he laid the cool, damp cloth across her forehead and was rewarded with a sharp intake of breath as her eyes snapped open.

She looked at him, blinking rapidly, as if trying to clear her vision. Then she looked around the cockpit, and when her gaze returned to his, he saw that while her eyes were still dilated, she seemed more alert.

"I'm sorry, I must have dozed off." She pushed herself up to sit straighter in the seat. A hand strayed to her head to massage her temples. "Just give me a second, and then we can leave."

Mac ignored the quick stab of guilt. "We're already there. You slept through the entire flight."

"We're in Brasilia?"

"No. Taribu."

"Already?" She raised her arm, and he saw her try to focus on the watch face. "I don't understand." She glanced around, as if the answer to the mystery lay somewhere nearby. "I knew I was tired, but . . ." She broke off as she leaned her head back against the seat and closed her eyes.

He didn't like the greenish cast to her complexion. "Are you okay?"

"I don't feel very good," she mumbled.

"Not much of a drinker?"

She started to shake her head but stopped suddenly, as if the motion made things worse. "Not on an empty stomach and thirty-six hours of no sleep. Or maybe I'm coming down with something."

Mac inwardly cringed, thinking about the six-hour drive through the jungle that lay ahead of them.

"Rest here while I get our stuff together." He walked back to the plane's small galley and scrounged through the pantry until he found crackers and a plastic bag. Going back to the cockpit, he held them out to her.

"I thought you might want these."

When he spoke, one eyelid lifted slightly so she could see what he offered. She raised a hand to take both from him. "Thanks."

Trying to ignore how weak she sounded, Mac looked out the cockpit window. They'd flown all night and the sun wasn't even a promise on the horizon. In another couple of hours, though, it would be high in the sky and hot as hell.

He looked back down at her and saw that she hadn't moved. "Look, I need to go across the way to get our rental Jeep and take care of the paperwork. Will you be okay here? By yourself?"

"As long as I'm not moving, I'm fine."

*Yeah, great,* he thought, envisioning the dirt road they'd be bouncing along shortly. *Man up, Knight. You picked the song, now it's time to dance to the tune.*

"The head—uh, sorry—bathroom is right behind the cockpit, if you need it. I suggest you try to use it before we leave. We still have a long trip ahead of us."

He opened the hatch and stepped out. The stifling humidity instantly closed around him as he made his way across the darkened airfield to the main building ahead, nodding to the airfield workers he saw along the way.

Fifteen minutes later, he'd secured transportation and had their respective bags loaded. Ten more minutes, and he'd managed to get the librarian from the cockpit chair into the passenger seat of the Jeep.

"This might get a little rough." *Understatement of the year.* He debated on whether or not to tell her about the muddy, rutted trail they had to drive on, or the bug-infested rain forest through which they would travel.

No. Some things did not get better with anticipation. "Hang on."

He started the engine and, ignoring the sense of urgency gnawing at him, kept to a moderately slow pace as he drove, doing what he could to avoid the deepest ruts. Despite his best efforts, it wasn't long before she hollered at him to stop.

Jumping from the vehicle as soon as it was safe to do so, she ran a few feet into the woods, where Mac saw her bend over. Seconds later, her body convulsed and he knew she was throwing up. Heaving a sigh, he climbed out of the Jeep, pulled a clean rag from his gear, and used some of the water from his canteen to wet it. Then he crossed to where she was hunched over and, standing behind her, wrapped one arm around her waist and pressed his other hand against her forehead until she was finished. Then he handed her the wet cloth to wipe her face.

"Thank you," she said, sounding humiliated as they walked back to the Jeep.

"Don't worry about it. Here." He gave her the canteen to rinse out her mouth and take a drink.

When she was done, she wiped the mouth of the canteen off with her shirt and handed it back to him. He stood beside her until she was settled in her seat, then stowed the canteen in the back.

"You look better," he told her as he climbed behind the wheel and started the Jeep. "Some of the color is back in your face."

"I don't understand. I've never had just one shot of anything kick my butt so bad before." She gave a self-deprecating laugh. "What was in that tequila anyway?"

He knew the second she put it all together. Her posture grew rigid as she stared at him accusingly.

"You did—you put something in the tequila. What? Damn it, what did you give me?"

"Pain pills, that's all. It shouldn't have done more than relax you."

"Based on what logic did you think that a couple of pain pills mixed with alcohol would only relax me? You're lucky it didn't kill me. No wonder I feel so lousy."

"You're a big woman; I figured you had the body weight to handle it." He glanced at her and found her gaping at him. "What?"

"You're not scoring any points here, pal."

He thought back to his last comment and sighed. "I

didn't mean that you were fat; I only meant you weren't petite."

She put a hand to her head as if it ached. "Maybe you shouldn't try to explain that part of it, okay? Diplomacy isn't your strong suit. Just tell me why you did it. I mean, we were already scheduled to leave, so why knock me out, unless . . ." He saw her look around and then back at him. "We *are* in Taribu, aren't we? Or did you take me someplace else?"

"No, we're in Taribu. And the reason I did it is because we didn't have time to wait for you to find the courage to make the flight, and I couldn't take the chance that you'd back out. So I drugged you. Sue me."

"Yeah? Well, I just might do that."

They drove in silence for another two hours before she had to stop by the side of the road again. This time, when they were both back in the Jeep, she sat up straighter in the seat, as if she felt better.

"I *am* sorry that I made you so sick," he finally offered.

She turned to study his face, and he hoped she saw the sincerity he felt. After a moment, she nodded. "I'll consider forgiving you if you can produce a mint or something."

He smiled, reached into his shirt pocket, and pulled out a pack of gum. "How's this?"

Her eyes lit up as she took it from him. "It's a start. Thanks." She took a stick and handed the pack back to him. He took a piece for himself before putting it away, and they drove in silence as the sun rose and light began to filter through the canopy of tree limbs overhead.

"I hate flying."

Her comment seemed to come out of thin air and when Mac glanced at her, he thought she looked very vulnerable sitting there, her eyes looking unusually large behind the thick glasses and wisps of light brown hair escaping from the band designed to secure them, making a halo around her head. She gave him a slight smile. "I don't like your methods, but I have to admit that was one of the easiest flights I've ever taken." She faced forward again, watching the road in front of them. "Don't do it again."

"Okay."

After that, the road grew rougher, and it became too hard to shout over the rumble of the Jeep as it bounced along. Occasionally, the haunting cries of various birds and animals hidden within the jungle could be heard. Eventually, tired from being jostled about, they stopped to stretch their legs and Mac broke out the sandwiches he'd brought along. He was relieved to see that Lanie felt well enough to eat.

Afterward, they took opposite sides of the road to answer nature's call and Mac, who had expected Lanie to balk, was pleasantly surprised when she didn't.

As Mac feared, the trip took much longer than six hours, and it was pushing midafternoon when he spotted the road that would lead them to the compound. Turning, they followed it until suddenly the rain forest opened up and they found themselves in a huge clearing. Ahead was the parking lot, and to the right was a small white-stone building with tinted front windows. The modern building looked out of place in the middle of the Amazon jungle.

The parking lot was empty, except for a single army-green utility truck parked off to one side.

"Why don't you go in and let them know we're here," Mac said as he pulled into a parking spot. "I'll get our bags and be right behind you."

He grabbed his Colt .45 from under the seat and climbed out. Moving around to the back where the bags were stowed, he glanced up and saw Lanie making her way up the front walk. He opened his pack, checked the gun to make sure the safety was on, and was about to place it in the bag when he was startled by the sound of the front door of the building crashing open. Whipping his head up, he saw Lanie running out, her face deathly white.

Forgetting about the bags, he raced to her side. "What's the matter?"

She gripped his arms, staring up at him with an expression that sent alarms tripping throughout his body. "Inside . . ."

Still holding his gun, he released the safety. Then he shoved the Jeep keys into her hand. "Go to the Jeep."

Mac wasn't sure what type of trouble to expect, but he wanted her out of the way when it started.

Rushing to the door, he bent his head close to listen. All was quiet. Gripping the handle, he slowly eased it open, and making hardly a sound, he slipped inside.

The absolute silence was the first thing he noticed. *As quiet as the proverbial tomb*, he thought as he looked about. He stood inside a small foyer, facing a security desk that was absent a guard. Beyond that was a set of double doors leading to the rest of the building.

Mac crept forward, constantly scanning the area for what had frightened Lanie. After about four steps, he found it.

Behind the desk, strewn across the floor like forgotten rag dolls, were the bodies of the missing security guard and four other men. Their unnatural gray pallor and sightless, staring eyes left no doubt that all five were dead.

A small noise behind him had Mac whipping around to confront the source, weapon leveled and ready. Lanie stood right inside the door, her eyes wide and staring at the muzzle pointed at her.

Before he could gesture for her to return to the Jeep, she recovered and moved quickly toward him. When she reached his side, she paused at the sight of the bodies.

"Who—"

He touched a finger to her lips to silence her. Though he doubted it, whatever, or whomever, had killed these men might still be lurking about the compound. The last thing he wanted to do was announce their presence—at least, no more so than the door crashing open already had, he thought ruefully.

Spotting the guard's weapon lying nearby, Mac picked it up. Checking to see if it was loaded and ready to fire, he considered giving the weapon to Lanie and then thought better of it. It would be his luck to have her accidentally shoot him in the back.

He clicked on the safety and tucked the weapon into the waistband of his pants, then gestured for her to follow him. Reaching the double doors, he leaned his head close, once again listening for sounds from the other side.

Hearing none, he pushed one of the doors open a crack and peered through. Nothing. Opening it farther, he quickly stepped through, gun ready and body tensed for action.

The hallway appeared empty. He moved forward, the sound of Lanie's breathing echoing in the silence. When he reached the first door, he motioned for her to stand beside him against the wall as he reached for the handle and slowly turned it. Swinging the door inward, he again braced for an attack. Again, nothing happened. Carefully, he stepped into the doorway and then slowly into the room. It was someone's office, neat, undisturbed—and empty.

Back in the hallway, they moved to the next door and repeated the process, slowly working their way through the entire building. By the end of their search, they'd located the security office, the kitchen, offices, and residence rooms. All looked normal and undisturbed.

The last room, the medical lab, was a different story.

"What have you gotten yourself into this time, Knight?"

Lanie turned at the sound of Mac's muttered question, having asked herself a similar one only moments before. "What do you think happened?"

"I have no idea, and that's the God's honest truth." He shook his head as he looked around.

She wondered if he saw it the way she did—metal gurneys knocked askew and medical instruments scattered across the floor. In Lanie's imagination, the attackers had heedlessly shoved things aside in their pursuit of the four men, whose bodies now rested crumpled against the far wall, as if, after being murdered, they'd been carelessly tossed there and forgotten, like so many bones discarded after a meal.

*Such a violent end to life*, Lanie thought, and yet the question of how, exactly, they had died remained a mystery to her. For all the show of violence, there was very little blood and no obvious wounds.

Still struggling to make sense of it all, she saw Mac reach into his shirt pocket and pull out a phone. As he punched in a number, he turned to her, looking worried. "Are you okay?"

She nodded, finding his concern surprising, yet touching, until it occurred to her that he was probably worried about her falling apart and adding to his problems. He had no way of knowing that she was a trained EMT and had seen far worse than this at some of the traffic accidents she'd attended. It was the unexpected shock of finding the bodies and the fear that the murderer lurked inside that sent her running from the building initially.

"Admiral, this is Knight," she heard Mac say moments later. "We've got a problem."

Lanie walked over to the body lying closest to her and examined it as she listened to Mac describe what had happened.

"No," she heard him say after a pause. "Heading back through the jungle at this hour would be unwise. We'll stay here; just get that team to us ASAP." She glanced up and saw him looking at her. "She's fine." He ended the call and put his phone away.

"Was that Charles?"

He nodded. "He's sending out a team."

"Good. I hope they get here soon." She rubbed her hands up and down her arms, trying to chase away the goose bumps.

"Even if they leave now, they won't get here until morning. We're on our own." He looked around the room, shaking his head. "What the hell kind of research were they doing out here, anyway? Biochemical? Weapons?"

"Maybe biochemical, but I don't think so." She sighed. "I think it was cryptozoological."

His brow furrowed as he shot her a curious look. "Come again?"

She wondered how best to explain. "Cryptozoology. Literally translated, it's the study of hidden animals. You're probably more familiar with it in the context of searching for evidence of Big Foot or the Loch Ness monster."

As expected, his expression turned to one of total disbelief. "You're kidding me, right?"

"No, it's a legitimate field of research and happens to have been my father's area of expertise. As big as this world is, there's no way that man has discovered and documented all the life-forms that exist here. As civilization spreads out and encroaches on these animals' space, they have nowhere to go—and we suddenly have sightings."

"You believe in all that shit?"

She glared at him. "Let's just say that over the years, traveling with my dad, I've seen stuff that's hard to explain any other way."

He stared at her for a moment, as if considering whether she was a harmless but crazy academic—or just plain certifiable. "So you're telling me that Big Foot killed these men?" he scoffed.

"No. To my knowledge, and admittedly I'm no expert, Big Foot doesn't drink blood."

Now she had his attention. "What do you mean?"

"Come look." Squatting beside the body closest to her, she waved her hand up and down it. "There aren't any bullet holes or stab wounds. It's unlikely that poison was used. The only evidence I can find of foul play is this." She gently pushed the head to the side, exposing the side of the neck. Dried blood was smeared across it, but two puncture wounds were clearly visible. Each hole was the size of the end of a Q-Tip, and they were spaced a little over an inch apart.

"Go on," Mac said, coming to squat beside her.

"Okay. Well, notice the pallor and dryness of the skin. The grayish cast denotes a lack of blood. Now, I figure they've been dead for several hours. If that's true, then we should see signs of lividity in the lowest levels of the body—in this case, the man's right side, since that's how he's lying. But look here." She pulled up the man's shirt. "It's the same gray color—there wasn't enough blood left to pool and discolor the skin."

At her declaration, their eyes met and Lanie wondered what thoughts raced through his head.

"Who would take the time to do something like this?" he asked.

"I guess it could have been some type of wild animal," she offered.

"No, it was human." He pointed to a bloody stain on the man's shoulder where Lanie could barely make out the imprint of a hand—a human hand.

"Well, I know this sounds far-fetched, but there might be one other explanation . . ."

"What?"

She didn't say anything, her gaze and attention focused on the two puncture marks on the victim's neck.

"Oh, hell, no. Don't even say—"

"Vampires."

He swung his head away from her, uttering a soft curse under his breath before slapping his hands against his legs and pushing himself to a standing position. "You know? For about three minutes there, I actually thought you had a brain cell."

Lanie knew it sounded crazy and wished she could laugh it off and tell him that she was kidding, but too many years with her father kept her silent.

"I don't believe any of that crap." Mac walked to the opposite side of the room, clearly agitated. He stopped at the doorway long enough to look back at her. "It'll be dark soon. I'm going to check the outside of the compound while I can still see."

He left the lab and she hurried to follow, trailing after him to the small security office they'd discovered earlier. She stood silently by the door as he systematically searched each of the cabinets. From the fourth, he extracted a hand-held search lamp that, when switched on, was so bright, Lanie had to shield her eyes from the nearly blinding light.

Apparently satisfied, he shut it off, left the office, and walked to the front of the building, Lanie following behind him. As they passed the security desk, she tried to ignore the bodies.

"I want you to wait in here," Mac said, heading for the door. "I'll be back in a few minutes."

"No, I don't want to stay by myself."

"I don't care. You'll be safer inside."

She jerked her head toward the bodies. "Like they were? No thanks; I'm going with you."

He glared at her. "Be reasonable. We've searched the entire building. There's no danger inside, but there may still be something outside. If I run into trouble, the last thing I need to worry about is keeping your butt safe."

"You worry about your butt, and I'll worry about mine."

He pointed a finger at her, his expression stern and unyielding. "Stay here."

She pushed her glasses up her nose with the tip of her index finger as she stared at him, unfazed. "Do you find that works with most people? Because I'm not buying it."

His expression grew outright lethal and despite her bravado, she found herself a little intimidated. "Fine, I won't go with you," she finally huffed.

"Very sensible of you," Mac acknowledged, pulling the guard's gun from his waistband and handing it to her. "Do you know how to use this?"

"I think I can grasp the basic concept—you point and pull the trigger, right?"

She peered down the weapon's sights at an imaginary target, perilously close to where Mac stood, her aim not quite steady as her arm wavered in the air. Mac swore again as he pressed her arm downward until the weapon was pointed at the floor. Then gently but firmly, he pulled it from her hand, checked the safety, and shoved it back into the front of his pants.

"On second thought, it might be better if I was the only one who carried a gun."

She shrugged. "Suit yourself, but then I'm going with you."

They left the building and Mac paused on the sidewalk outside. Lanie knew he was listening for anything that might sound out of the ordinary. With anyone else, she might have scoffed at the action. After all, they weren't in familiar territory—how would they know what sounded normal and what didn't?

But Mac was different. *More capable* was the description that came to mind. The way he'd handled the situation inside, had coped with finding all the bodies and yet remained calm, cool, and collected—it made her wonder what he'd done and seen in the Navy.

When he started walking, she was struck by his skills. He moved without a sound, making her own attempts at stealth sound loud and jarring by contrast.

He led them along the front, hugging the wall until they'd traveled the length of it, at which point he stopped and cautiously peered around the next corner. Apparently seeing nothing of concern, he gestured for her to follow as he continued around to the side.

Here they found a four-foot-wide stretch of ground, cleared of trees, with patches of undergrowth insidiously creeping back. It was as if the rain forest, looming dark and silent beyond the clearing, was trying to reclaim its own. Lanie kept a wary eye open, expecting something to jump out at any moment.

When they reached the back of the building, Mac again guided them close to the wall so he could see around the corner. When he gave the all-clear, they proceeded to the backyard.

Like the side, this area had been cleared of trees and brush, but a huge metal cage, like one would find at the zoo, stood in the very middle.

There appeared to be something inside, but with the growing shadows of dusk, it was impossible to tell exactly

what it was. Moving closer, Lanie made out what looked
like the statue of a gargoyle.

Unfamiliar with the different cultural beliefs of the
South Americans, she was unsure if the statue was reli-
gious or decorative, but she was intrigued by its appearance. It sat hunched on its disproportionately large hind
legs like a big cat. All four legs ended in three-toed claws,
and a row of sharp fins ran down its head and back. A
caninelike muzzle protruded from its round face, with
two three-inch fangs extending from its upper jaw. The
oval eyes appeared too large for its head and gave the
statue an almost demonic, alien appearance.

As the sun sank lower in the sky, shadows danced
across the cage, making the statue appear almost alive.
Intrigued, Lanie tried the handle of the door.

"Why would they keep a statue locked in a cage?" she
mused, more to herself than to Mac. "I want to take a
closer look." She searched for a way to unlock the door.

"Look at it tomorrow, when the light is better," Mac
ordered. "We still have half the grounds to search."

She didn't even glance at him as she dragged her foot
across the grass, feeling for a dropped key or some hidden
mechanism. "Those men have been dead awhile. Whatever killed them is gone, or we'd be dead now, too." She
paused when her toe hit something. Bending down, she
moved the grass aside and found a small remote-control
box. Picking it up, she saw an on/off switch. "I found it."

"Wait," Mac hollered at her, but it was too late. She'd
already flipped the lever. The sound of a bolt shooting
back echoed ominously in the silence, causing the hairs on
the back of Lanie's neck to prickle. She tensed, expecting

something to spring out of the cage at them. Beside her, Mac stood with his gun ready.

Time seemed to stop as in the distance a bird cawed and a gentle breeze stirred the leaves of the surrounding trees, creating a gentle rustling sound.

Lanie gave Mac a withering look for scaring her and moved past him to the cage's entrance, where she hesitated only a moment before continuing on in.

The statue was fascinating. The masonry work was so detailed and fine that it gave the piece a lifelike appearance. Intrigued, Lanie pressed a finger against it and found the rough surface cool to the touch.

"It's amazing," she breathed when Mac came to stand by her side.

"Yeah. Can we go?"

Her gaze traveled to the statue's face, mesmerized by the craftsmanship that was so exquisite she could practically see the eyes glowing red in the darkness and drops of moisture running down the long, deadly fangs.

Then the eyes blinked.

# Chapter
# 3

Lanie felt herself pushed roughly to the ground and looked up to see a nightmare come to life. Though he struggled, Mac could not escape the creature that held him so effortlessly in its front claws. With his arms pinned to his sides, the gun he held was useless.

Horrified, she watched the creature draw him close and lower its mouth to his neck. She saw the fangs pierce the skin, but it was the sound of blood being sucked from Mac's body that catapulted her into action.

Lying on the ground where it had fallen was the search lamp. Crawling over, she grabbed it and, standing so that she faced the creature, pulled the trigger. The sudden brightness of the beam pierced the night and the creature reared back, in that moment releasing its hold on Mac.

Lanie held the beam steady with one hand and wrapped her other arm around Mac as he fell against her. She wasn't sure if he was alive or dead as she struggled to support his weight.

As the creature tried to shield itself from the light, Lanie frantically cast her eyes about for something else to use as a weapon. The sudden explosion and reverberation of Mac's gun startled her as he discharged his weapon into the creature's belly.

"Again," she shouted, seeing the creature stumble back. Mac fired a second time, but the shot went wild. He grew too heavy to hold and slid to the ground.

His ashen face was in stark contrast to the blood covering his neck and clothes. His eyes were closed, and his gun rested in a grip gone slack. Fear and anger raged within her and she grabbed the gun, turning it on the creature. A Texas girl, she knew a hell of a lot more about guns than she'd led Mac to believe.

Firing one-handed would be difficult, but not impossible, and there was no way she was letting go of the light. She pulled the trigger. At this range, the creature was a hard target to miss, and she didn't stop until the clicking of an empty weapon finally registered.

The creature lay on the ground, unmoving. She knew she should check to make sure it was dead, but Mac was at her feet, bleeding to death—if he wasn't already dead.

Ears ringing from the sound of the gun, she cast the beam of the lamp over the creature one last time to make sure it wasn't moving. She didn't want to put down the lamp, but she couldn't pull Mac out of the cage one-handed. She wasn't sure she could pull him out at all. Tucking the gun into the back of her pants, she found the trigger-lock on the lamp and laid it outside the cage on the ground, shining in.

Hurrying back inside, she grabbed Mac by the ankles. He was almost too heavy for her to drag, but there was no way she was leaving him there. As soon as she had his body out of the cage, she slammed the door shut and activated the lock.

There was no time to relax. With effort, she ripped off the sleeve of her shirt and wrapped the material around Mac's neck, hoping to staunch the flow of blood until she could get him inside. Next, she lifted Mac's wrist and felt for a pulse. Thankfully, she found one. It was weak, but at least he was alive, though he wouldn't be for long if she didn't do something. He'd lost so much blood, it would take a miracle to save him.

Lanie had no idea where the nearest medical facility was and knew that even if she called for medical assistance, they couldn't get there any sooner than the team already on its way. She'd have to treat Mac herself.

Remembering the medical supplies they'd found inside the building, Lanie made up her mind. He was too big for her to use a fireman's carry, so stooping behind him, she squatted until she could leverage Mac into a sitting position and slipped her arms underneath his armpits. Locking her hands together across his chest, she stood and began the strenuous task of dragging him into the building, keeping up a constant dialogue. "Hang in there, Mac." "You're going to be okay." "Stay with me."

It felt like it took forever, and Lanie was sure that every second cost Mac a little more of his life. Finally, she managed to drag him through the halls to the lab, and there, her strength ran out. Unable to lift him onto the gurney, she left him on the floor and set to work gathering the supplies she needed, giving a silent prayer of thanks when she found the collection of bagged blood in the refrigerator.

She didn't know Mac's blood type, but knew if she found type "O," the universal donor, then it wouldn't matter. For a change, luck was with her. Mixed in with an assortment of animal blood, she found several units of human blood, types "AB" and "O."

She crossed to the sink and filled it with hot water. Then she placed the bags of "O" into the basin to warm while she searched the drawers and cabinets for the rest of the supplies she'd need. She was about to execute a very crude blood transfusion that under different circumstances she would never have considered attempting without a physician's guidance, but she knew Mac would be long dead by the time other help arrived. She was his only chance.

Praying she wasn't about to speed his way to death, she removed the warmed blood from the sink and set to work finding a vein. Working carefully, she inserted the large IV needle, secured it in place with tape, and then opened the clamp on the tubing. Almost immediately, the blood began to flow into his body.

Lanie bit her lip, knowing there were so many things that could go wrong and he might still die. As she waited for the first bag to empty, she cleaned away the blood on his neck and saw there wasn't a gaping wound as she'd feared, only two very large punctures. *Just like the other bodies*, she thought, except these holes were bigger and spaced farther apart.

She treated the wounds with antibiotic ointment, covered them with gauze, and taped it all in place.

When the first bag was empty, she clamped off the IV, hooked up a second bag, and started over again.

All through the night she watched over him, bathing his head, replacing each spent bag of blood with a fresh one. By early morning, it seemed that his breathing was steadier and the color was returning to his complexion.

Sitting on the floor next to him, Lanie finally allowed herself to relax. Placing both the guard's loaded gun and Mac's empty gun on the floor beside her, she leaned back against the wall and let her eyes close.

"Miss Weber? Wake up, ma'am."

Lanie's eyes snapped open at the sound, her hand reaching automatically for a gun that was no longer there. Alarmed, she blinked several times to bring the face of the man bending over her into focus. "Who are . . . ?" Her voice cracked, and she had to clear her throat before trying again. "Who are you?"

"Captain Sanchez, United States Navy, ma'am. I'm a physician." He made a show of setting her missing guns off to the side. "I'm here to help. Admiral Winslow sent us."

As the cogwheels of her mind finally started to turn, she nodded and relaxed.

"Are you injured? Hurt in any way?" Dr. Sanchez asked, turning to the black bag open at his side and pulling out a stethoscope to slip around his neck.

"No, I'm fine."

"Good. Maybe you need some more sleep, though?" He didn't wait for her answer, but knelt and began running his hands along Mac's arms and legs, feeling gingerly for broken bones.

"This is Captain Knight?" He glanced at her and when she nodded, he slipped the earpieces of the scope into his ears and listened to Mac's heart and lungs.

"Did you say *Captain* Knight?"

"Yes, ma'am. Captain Michael Knight. Retired, I believe."

His comment was followed by a moment of silence as he continued to listen. Next, he pulled the stethoscope from his ears and checked Mac's pulse while keeping track of the time on his wristwatch. From the outer room came the faint sounds of men shouting orders.

Seemingly satisfied, Dr. Sanchez lowered the wrist he'd been holding. Shifting his position, he peeled the bandages off Mac's neck. "Are these the only injuries?"

Lanie nodded. "He was attacked by a . . ." She hesitated. How could she tell him that the statue had come to life? "I don't know what kind of animal it was. It pierced his jugular vein, I think. Anyway, he lost a lot of blood."

"What happened to the creature?"

"I shot it."

He raised an eyebrow and gave her an appreciative look before turning his attention to the empty bags of blood and discarded tubing on the floor. "You gave him a transfusion?"

She nodded. "I didn't know what else to do. I thought he was going to die."

"Well, he's not out of the woods yet. How'd you know what to do?"

"I'm an EMT with the fire department."

He nodded and then, apparently finished with his initial examination of Mac, he turned his attention to her. "Are you sure you're not hurt?"

"Yes—just really tired."

The physician gave her a warm smile, reminding her of her father. Since arriving, she'd been too distracted to think of him, and suddenly the well of emotion she'd kept tamped down for so long threatened to bubble forth and overwhelm her. Dr. Sanchez must have seen it in her face because he stood and helped her to her feet.

"You should get some rest. I'll take over here." He held on to her hand while she worked the stiffness out of her leg muscles.

"Lieutenant Davis!"

A young man in his mid-twenties ran into the room at the doctor's shout. "Escort Miss Weber to one of the bedrooms so she can rest."

The man nodded and then led her out of the room. When they would have gone left to the residence rooms, Lanie stopped.

"I've got a bag in the Jeep." She started for the front entrance, but the lieutenant stopped her.

"You don't want to go that way, ma'am. I'll get it for you after I show you to a room."

He led her down the back hallway, stopping at the first door.

"Do I have to stay in this room, specifically?"

Lieutenant Davis gave her a puzzled look. "Beg pardon, ma'am?"

Lanie smiled. "I mean, could I perhaps stay in that room?" She'd noticed the room in their earlier search and now pointed to the third door on the other side.

He gave a final look at the door before them, shrugged, and dropped his hand to his side. "Yes, ma'am. My orders were only to take you to one of the rooms to rest. I don't suppose it matters which room you take."

She rewarded him with a smile. "Thanks. I think I'd prefer that one, then." She followed him to the other door and waited while he did a quick walk-through of the room.

"All clear, ma'am," he said, turning to her. "Try to get some sleep, if you can. We've got men all over the place; you're safe. If you need anything, just shout. I'll be posted outside."

"Thank you."

He nodded and started to leave, but stopped at the door. "Ma'am, if you don't mind my asking, why this particular room?"

She looked around at the mix of strange and familiar items lying about the place and felt her throat muscles tighten with emotion. "It was my father's."

The young man gave her a sympathetic nod, stepped through the door, and closed it, leaving her alone. For a long time, she stayed in one spot, slowly turning as her eyes traveled across the room. Books were piled on virtually every available surface, including the floor. Most of the piles contained research books, but there were several stacks of popular fiction as well. Her father had been an avid reader.

She didn't know how long she stood there, but it must have been several minutes before a knock at the door startled her from her thoughts. It was the lieutenant, delivering her bag from the Jeep. Seeing it bolstered her spirits a little, and she set it on the bed before slowly wandering about the room, continuing to take it all in.

Against the far wall was the desk her father had used. Several research volumes with yellow sticky notes bookmarking various pages sat to one side while magazines and printed articles littered the other. In the middle, a pile of used legal pads and mechanical pencils rested, as if he had just set them aside and was planning to return. Lanie trailed a finger across the surface of one of the pages, smiling when she spotted spilled pipe tobacco on the desk. She pinched the finely chopped leaves between her fingers and brought them to her nose to smell.

She used to hate the smell of his smoking, begging him to at least try the aromatic blends if he had to smoke at all. He always refused, arguing that the blends that smelled good tasted bad.

She rubbed her fingers together, letting the tobacco fall back to the desk. How she would give anything now to smell the acrid smoke from his pipe one more time.

Something tickled her cheek and when she reached up to brush it away, she found tears. She hadn't even realized she was crying, but once the waterworks started, she couldn't turn them off. She cried for both her parents, brought down too early in their lives, and for all the men here who'd died. She cried for herself, so alone now, and for Mac, who'd risked his life saving hers.

Finally, too exhausted to cry anymore, she crawled into her father's bed. She closed her eyes, remembering all the nights she'd sat curled up in a favorite chair. She'd read a book while he worked at his desk nearby, writing in his journal and smoking his pipe. The faint odor of his tobacco clung to the sheets and pillow, so she turned her head into it, letting the familiar scent envelop her and lull her to sleep.

* * *

Lanie woke feeling refreshed and confused. It took only a second, though, to recall where she was and everything that had happened. It was enough to bring her fully awake.

She strained to hear sounds from outside her room—something to indicate that she wasn't the only living creature still in the facility—that the monster, which had killed so many, hadn't returned while she slept and slaughtered her rescuers. All was quiet.

Throwing back her covers, she walked to the door and listened. She heard no sound. Because she couldn't remain in the room forever, she took a deep breath and placed her hand on the knob, turned it, and pulled open the door.

When nothing rushed to attack her, she stepped out into the hallway.

"Everything okay, ma'am?" Lieutenant Davis stood a few feet away, looking at her with polite concern.

"Yes." She gazed up and down the hallway. It was otherwise empty and appeared almost boring in its lack of ornamentation or activity. Satisfied, she turned to go back into the room, stopping in the doorway to look at Lieutenant Davis once more. "Did you stand outside my door all day?"

"Yes, ma'am." If he'd found guarding her door boring, tiring, or even insulting, he gave no indication of it. She suspected that was as much a credit to his personality as to his training, and she was grateful.

"Thank you." She gave him a smile to show her appreciation. "Would you happen to know how Mac—I mean, Captain Knight—is doing?"

He pressed the mike at his throat and spoke. "Doc, this is Davis. Ms. Weber would like to know how the captain is doing."

She watched as he stood there, his eyes focused elsewhere as if distracted, and then he nodded. "Roger."

Then he turned to her. "The captain is sleeping, but the doc thinks he's going to make it."

A wave of relief washed over her, making her almost giddy. Not wanting to embarrass herself in front of Lieutenant Davis, she thanked him again and went back into the room.

Then she caught a glimpse of herself in the mirror and gasped. She'd had bad hair and makeup days before, but this set an all-time new low. Digging in her duffel bag for her toiletry case, she hurried into the bathroom and showered. Afterward, she felt almost human again. As she took the time to fix her hair, apply a little makeup, and put in her contacts, she argued with herself that she wasn't doing this to impress Mac, who, other than saving her life, had treated her indifferently ever since she'd met him. She was doing this—just because.

Finding a fresh change of clothes, she considered burning the ones she'd arrived in and tossed them into the corner, pending a final decision. When she was finished dressing, she stared around the room, somewhat at a loss as to what to do now. Something she'd remembered before falling asleep tickled the back of her mind and she reached for the memory, finally grasping it. Her father had always kept a private journal, so somewhere in this room, she might find her father's last recorded thoughts.

She began with a search through the piles of books on the desk, but the dark brown leather journal wasn't among them. Next she turned her attention to the dresser and then to the small closet. After her first hurried search yielded nothing, she stepped back and surveyed the room, trying to imagine her father after a hard day, coming back to his room, anxious to fill the pages of his private journal with everything he'd learned.

While the desk seemed a logical place to work, he'd want to be someplace where he could hide his notes from prying eyes. Her father would have kept an ongoing record of his findings on the computer in the lab for the government, but he was still old school and didn't completely trust computers—or the government. His private thoughts and theories would have been recorded in the journal.

Lanie also knew that he never wrote in the journal without smoking, so she scanned the room, locating each ashtray. The one by the big easy chair in the room caught her attention. She hurried to it. A book called *Ancient Roman Times* rested on the side table beside the ashtray. A bookmark poked out the top at the last page her father had read. Lanie ignored it as she searched under the cushions of the chair. Nothing. Next she examined the pile of books stacked beside the chair, to see if the journal was one of them, but again, she came away with nothing. Finally, her eyes returned to the large volume on the table. It was thick enough . . .

She smiled as she lifted the front cover. There, set inside a cut-out section, lay the leatherbound volume.

Sitting down, she began to read.

> *March 6: I have arrived at the Taribu research facility. My excitement knows no*

*limit. Never in my lifetime did I hope to verify the existence of El Chupacabra, the legendary goat-sucker. Now, thanks to the government's spectacular discovery, I have two specimens to study. Oh, if only I could share this find with Lanie.*

Surprise and remorse filled her. She understood all too well what such a find would have meant to him. A life's dream come true. She hurried to read the next entry.

*March 7: I have finished my initial examination of the chupas. One is much larger than the other and I believe it to be an adult, while the smaller one must be very young. At this time, I have no way of telling male from female, nor can I ascertain the relationship between the two creatures. As they were captured together, however, I suspect them to be an adult female and her offspring.*

*The creatures appear much as described in reported sightings. They are gray-skinned with a round head, large glowing red eyes, a slightly elongated muzzle with two fangs (approx. three inches in length), and a long tubular tongue. Its preferred prey is domestic livestock, which it hunts at night, piercing the throat and sucking the blood through its tongue.*

*The adult stands at about five feet while the younger creature is not quite two feet. It has powerful hind legs that enable it to leap great distances and heights. All four limbs end in sharp three-toed claws, and there is a single row of fins running down its back.*

Flipping through the pages of the book, Lanie stopped at random to read.

*. . . the chupas become almost stonelike in the light of the sun. At first, I thought they were dead, but it's more as if they are hibernating through the daylight hours . . .*

*The statue in the cage*, she realized.

*. . . I was able to tranquilize the baby long enough to examine it more fully. The fangs are hollow and when the chupa bites down, it secretes a venom into the prey's bloodstream, much as a snake would. Until I run more tests, I can only guess that this venom-type secretion acts as an anticoagulant . . .*

*. . . I doubled-checked Juan's injury and it is fully healed. It's amazing. I had no idea the chupa venom would have such restorative powers for humans. I injected myself last night with a small dose collected from the baby chupa when I felt the onset of fever and sinus related to the common cold. This morning, I have never felt better. If the young chupa's venom can do this, what powers does the adult chupa's venom have? . . .*

Lanie turned to the last entry.

> ... *tomorrow I will try to obtain a sample*
> *from the adult. I believe the safest time will*
> *be right before sunrise, when the chupa is*
> *weakest, before the sun turns it to stone.*

Her father must have tried to collect the specimen as he'd planned, but miscalculated the adult's strength before sunrise. When Uncle Charles called to tell her of her father's death, he'd told her that her father had been killed by a wild animal. In the Amazon jungle, such an event was not unusual. Now, though, she couldn't help but think the "wild animal" that had attacked and killed her father and the other man was actually the chupacabra.

If she was right, they would have the same puncture wounds on their necks as Mac had. Lanie knew it was time to do what she'd originally come to do. She needed to see her father's body.

Putting down the book, she walked out of the room to where Lieutenant Davis stood guard.

"Everything all right, ma'am?"

"I'd like to see my father's body. Can you take me to it?"

The young man relayed her request to the man in charge, and Lanie saw him nod once as he listened on the earpiece. He glanced at her and then quickly looked away, causing Lanie to wonder if something was wrong.

"Is there a problem?" she asked as soon as it was obvious that he was through listening.

"Yes, ma'am. You see, we searched the entire facility and only found nine bodies. The five men at the front and the four back in the lab. They've all been identified; your father wasn't one of them."

Feeling they'd had a miscommunication, she tried to explain. "No, I know he wasn't one of those men. My father and another man were killed a couple of days ago. That's why I came down here—to identify his body. It's probably in the back or something."

"Yes, ma'am. We were briefed on the circumstances of Dr. Weber's and Commander Burton's deaths and their bodies apparently *were* in the back, but they're not there now."

Lanie's confusion grew. "I don't understand."

"We found two body bags in the back. The ID tags were still attached, identifying them as containing the bodies of Dr. Weber and Commander Burton, but the bags are empty. They look like they've been torn open."

"Maybe their bodies were moved to a new location?"

He gave her a sympathetic look. "No, ma'am. We searched everywhere. I'm afraid your father's body isn't on the grounds."

She felt as if she'd been hit. "It doesn't make sense. A body doesn't just disappear."

"That's the hell of it, ma'am. It's like they just walked off."

His words sent a chill over her. The statue in the cage, the chupacabra, the wounds on the dead men's necks, their bodies drained of blood—the handprint. All those images flashed through her mind in a split second, leaving her with the horrifying thought that maybe her father's body had done exactly as the lieutenant so naively suggested.

She'd mentioned vampires earlier to Mac and now thought of them again. The similarity between the chupacabra and the vampire wasn't coincidental, but the exact nature of the connection escaped her. There had been something she'd read once, long ago; forgotten— until now.

She struggled to put it together. What if the chupacabra's attack on her father and the other man somehow turned *them* into vampires? And they, in turn, had killed those nine men? Her mind wrestled with the impossibility of it, but no logical explanation sprang forth to take its place. Then another, more horrifying thought hit her.

The chupacabra had also attacked Mac.

# Chapter
# 4

"M a'am? Are you all right?" Lieutenant Davis's concerned tone barely pierced her awareness.

"I need to go." Lanie started walking down the hallway with hurried steps, not really caring if the lieutenant followed or not. All of her thoughts were focused on what she might find. The doctor had reported that Mac was doing better, she told herself.

She left the residence hallway and turned the corner. Sounds of activity elsewhere in the building were audible now, but she ignored them. By the time she reached the doorway to the medical lab, she was practically running. Not wanting to draw undue attention to herself, she stopped just shy of the door to catch her breath—and then lost it as soon as she walked into the room.

Expecting to see Mac on a stretcher, IVs running electrolytes into his still-weakened body, she instead found the gurney empty and Dr. Sanchez in deep, jovial conversation with another man who stood with his back to Lanie.

He was bared to the waist, and the pure masculine beauty of his back struck Lanie. Only a few angry red scratches marred the tanned skin. Around his neck was a white collar, which Lanie belatedly realized was a bandage.

She moved into the room, amazed. "Mac?"

The man turned, hissing under his breath as if the sudden movement hurt, and a look of confusion crossed his face. Lanie walked up to him, nodding to Dr. Sanchez, who smiled at her before crossing to the far side of the room where he sat at a small table and began writing.

Left alone with Mac, Lanie felt small and feminine before him. Up close, it was hard not to stare. He was barefoot and while he had on camo-patterned pants, they were fastened only partway, leaving an inviting "V" open at the top into which a dark trail of hair disappeared.

His abs, while not washboard, were nevertheless impressive, and rather than the rounded shoulders and sunken chest that one might find on a leaner man, Mac was all straight planes and muscle. His chest had a light covering of the same dark hair she'd spied beneath his navel, and there was nothing about his appearance to suggest he wasn't in the absolute peak of health, except for the scratches across his chest that mirrored the ones she'd seen on his back. Souvenirs from the chupacabra.

Thinking of the creature reminded her why she was there, though with the light of the afternoon sun streaming in through the windows and Mac up and about, Lanie's fears that he might be a vampire seemed suddenly absurd.

"How are you feeling?" she asked, studying his face carefully.

"Fine, uh, Lanie?" Mac's eyes grew round, and he leaned closer to her, studying her face.

His scrutiny made her feel self-conscious, so she scowled at him.

"Holy shit." He laughed. "It IS you. Damn, woman"— he raked his eyes slowly over her from head to toe and back again—"you clean up nice."

She wanted to return the compliment, but found herself too embarrassed to respond. "I can't believe you're up and around so soon. I mean, last night . . ."

She swallowed as the events from the night before came rushing back. "Thank you," she said softly, looking into his face. "You saved my life." Guilt hit her and she found it hard to hold his gaze, so she let hers fall to the floor. "I should have listened to you and never gone into that cage. If I had . . ."

"Yes, you should have," he said, his voice gruff. Then she felt the warmth of his finger as he placed it beneath her chin and tilted her head up until their gazes met. He gave her a small smile. "I understand you saved my life last night with that transfusion." The tone of his voice was softer, friendlier. "I'd say that makes us even."

As she stared into the dark depths of his eyes, the room fell away until there was only the two of them. At that moment, she felt closer to him than she had to anyone in a long time, and though she knew it was only momentary, she didn't care.

Mac felt like he was free-falling through darkened skies to an unfamiliar target. The falling didn't bother him, but he was terrified of the landing. He'd been surprised enough to wake up earlier that day to find he was still alive. He'd been further amazed, and bewildered, to discover that he was almost fully recovered. Not even Dr. Sanchez could explain the inhumanly fast healing and had taken up crossing himself every time he came near Mac.

When Sanchez told him that Lanie had killed the creature that attacked him, using his gun, then dragged him back to the lab and proceeded to save his life—he'd been astounded. But nothing could have shocked him more than learning that the *Cover Girl* model who'd just walked into the lab was actually the dowdy little librarian he'd flown down with.

He wouldn't have thought it possible for the woman to clean up so well—but damn, she looked good. Her light brown hair cascaded down about her shoulders in rich, thick waves. It glowed with a healthy sheen that wouldn't have been possible if she colored it. A fitted shirt and well-worn pair of jeans hugged her body, showing off her figure to advantage. Mac was pleased to note that while she was not overweight, neither was she too thin, as so many women tried to be these days. If she wore makeup, it was with subtle application that left one wondering if she really wore any or naturally looked that spectacular. And her eyes, he noted, no longer hidden behind thick glasses, were the color of stonewashed denim.

Oh, yeah, Ms. Lanie Weber was definitely hot, and from her embarrassed blushes and the little looks she sneaked at him, he knew the attraction was mutual.

If they'd been anywhere else, under different circumstances, he'd be tempted to see where this mutual attraction might lead, but this was Taribu and her father was dead, as were Burton and nine other men. He had enough problems to contend with; he couldn't let her distract him from what was important.

Realizing that his finger was still under her chin, he dropped his hand and took a step back, needing to put space between them. He turned to the gurney and picked up the shirt Sanchez had brought him. Though he felt her watching him, he didn't look up.

He tucked the tail down the front of his pants and heard Lanie's quick intake of breath. He looked up to see her turning around, belatedly giving him privacy, her cheeks burning a bright pink. Despite his earlier resolve, he gave a silent laugh at her reaction. She could fend off a savage beast without batting an eye, but Mac tucking in his shirt unsettled her. For someone who'd almost died the night before, he was feeling in surprisingly good spirits.

The sound of footsteps had him turning toward the door in time to see a familiar blond, GI Joe–looking man in his mid-thirties walk into the lab.

"Doc, how's our boy doing?"

"By all rights, he should be dead," Sanchez responded from his desk. "But I think he's going to live."

"Damn right he's going to live. It'll take more than some wild creature ripping out his throat to bring *this* guy down."

"Dirk Adams," Mac said, shaking hands with his old friend. "Don't tell me they put *you* in charge. What's the world coming to?"

It'd been a year since Mac had last seen Dirk. They'd first met in boot camp, and Mac had a healthy respect for the man who'd served as a member of his SEAL team a year ago.

"I was looking for an excuse to get here after I heard about Burton's death," Dirk admitted. "When the admiral told me there'd been an accident and he needed a team, I jumped at the chance."

Dirk glanced to the side and Mac remembered his manners.

"Dirk, I'd like to introduce you to Lanie Weber. Lanie, this is Captain Dirk Adams."

Dirk turned to Lanie, and the obvious appreciation and interest in his expression irritated Mac.

"Ms. Weber, a pleasure. I'm sorry I didn't have a chance to meet you earlier." Dirk shook her hand, and Mac felt that he held it a little longer than necessary. Of further annoyance was that Lanie didn't seem to mind. She gave the captain a smile that would have turned any man's head. Mac was beginning to feel like a voyeur, so he cleared his throat and asked, "How's the cleanup going?"

Dirk released Lanie's hand and was suddenly all business. "We're no closer to having any answers," he admitted. "We think the animal that attacked you is the same one that attacked the men—the neck wounds and blood loss are similar. Unfortunately, we can't find the animal Ms. Weber shot. It may have crawled out into the jungle to die. Now that you're both up and about, I was hoping you could tell me exactly what we're looking for."

Mac gave a rueful laugh. "All I remember are sharp claws and teeth. Sorry." The details of the attack were fuzzy to him, so he turned to Lanie, hoping she could fill in the blanks.

She hesitated, and Mac wondered if the memories were too painful for her. She glanced quickly at Dr. Sanchez as he crossed the room to join them. "It suddenly appeared—

out of nowhere. You pushed me aside and it attacked you. I think shining the searchlight in its eyes is what caused it to release you. After that, I only remember firing the gun until it was empty. I thought I killed it and locked it in the cage, but my concern was getting you into the lab, so I didn't take the time to check on it."

"Well, it's not there now," Dirk said. "We looked."

Mac watched Lanie closely. He couldn't help feeling that there was something more she'd left out, or didn't want to share. About to press her on it, Dirk suddenly put his hand to his ear. They all stood silently while Dirk listened. "Roger, on my way."

"Well," he said, addressing their group. "They found the security tape from the night of the attack." He met Mac's eyes. "Want to check it out?"

Mac nodded. If the attack had been recorded, then seeing the tape could answer a lot of questions—namely, who or what killed those men. After Dirk started for the door, Mac felt a light pressure on his arm and saw Lanie's hand there.

"I need to talk to you." She glanced at the other men, now a short distance ahead of them. "In private."

He saw by her expression that this was serious. "Okay."

"Are you coming?" Dirk called back to them.

Mac, who'd been staring down into Lanie's face, looked over at him. "I forgot my shoes. You go on; I'll be right behind you."

Dirk nodded and, along with Dr. Sanchez, left the lab. Mac turned to Lanie, looking at her expectantly. Suddenly she seemed unsure of herself, so to give her time to collect her thoughts, he located his shoes and socks and put them on. When he finished, he found her watching him.

"Well?"

She looked at him. "How are you feeling?"

"I thought we already went over that." He started to feel irritated. "I'm fine. Now, can I go?"

"Mac, wait. I wondered if you felt, well, different somehow?"

He shook his head. "Yeah, it was a life-changing experience for me." His tone dripped sarcasm. "I'm not the man I was."

"Stop it," Lanie snapped. "That's not what I meant."

"Then what the hell do you mean, Lanie?"

She ran her fingers through her hair, clearly worried. "I found my father's journal. In it, he talks about the work he was doing here. He was studying a creature— El Chupacabra. Have you ever heard of it?"

"No."

"It's kind of like a vampire, but whereas a vampire is human, the origins of El Chupacabra are speculative. Some believe they are aliens stranded on Earth from some earlier visit. Others think they are the result of a NASA alien/animal experiment gone awry. Still another theory is that they are transdimensional spirits or dark angels that manifest into physical form while in our dimension, children of Lucifer—"

Mac held up his hand to stop her. "Save me the lecture and get to the point."

She huffed out a breath. "Okay. Based on what I read, I believe my father and that other man—Burton?—were killed by the chupacabra they were studying. And I think the chupacabra was that thing in the cage—the gargoyle."

"So you're saying that I was attacked and almost killed by a statue?"

"No, no. It's only a statue during the day, while the sun is up. It comes to life when darkness falls, which, if you recall, is when we went inside the cage."

Mac stared at her. "I'm willing to believe that whatever attacked me is the same animal that killed your father and Burton—and probably those other men as well."

Lanie shook her head. "The chupacabra didn't kill those men," she said quietly. "Remember the handprint we saw?"

"So what, exactly, are you saying?"

"I think that when the chupacabra killed my father and Burton, it somehow turned them into vampires and *they* killed those men."

Mac stared at her. "Are you hearing yourself?"

She shook her head in resignation. "I know it doesn't sound sane, but I think there's a connection."

"Look, all of this is speculation. I want to see what's on the tape."

He started for the door, but stopped when she didn't follow.

"That creature also attacked you," she pointed out softly.

He smiled, touched that she cared. "And as you can see, I'm fine."

"That's what worries me."

He rolled his eyes and headed for the door.

"Mac," she called after him, "the bodies of my father and Burton are missing."

He stopped. "Missing? How?"

"They're gone. According to Lieutenant Davis, they're nowhere on the premises."

She looked at him expectantly and he snorted. "Honey, all that proves is that son of a bitch Burton has gotten away with murder, faked his own death, and disappeared— all so he won't have to face a prison term. Now, I'm going to watch this tape, and I think you should stay here. I suspect it'll get pretty gruesome."

He left the room and headed for the front of the building, finding that not even his bad leg bothered him as much as usual. A few seconds later he heard Lanie's footsteps as she rushed to catch up to him, but neither spoke as they continued through the hallways and made their way through the double doors to the front desk.

Mac was glad to see that the bodies had been removed and the area cleaned. Dirk stood with Sanchez and two others behind a man seated in a chair at the security desk. All attention was focused on the monitor before them. At the sound of their approach, Dirk looked back. Then his eyes fell on Lanie.

"Ms. Weber, I don't—"

Mac held up his hand to stop Dirk midsentence. "I already told her not to come. Let her stay."

Dirk studied his face and then Lanie's, perhaps wondering how hard Mac had tried to convince her. Then he nodded. "Suit yourself."

Mac put a hand at the small of Lanie's back to guide her to the front of the group. Awareness prickled through him at the contact, but he tried to ignore it. His focus needed to be on the monitor.

Standing behind Lanie, looking over her shoulder, he saw that the screen was split into quarters, with a different part of the building appearing in each of the four sections.

The picture was a blur with figures flickering in and out of view as it fast-forwarded through the days.

Periodically, the man operating the controls would slow the recording enough that Mac could see the date and time stamp in the lower right-hand corner. When it read 11:56 in the evening on the day before yesterday, the recording was allowed to proceed.

"Okay," the tech at the desk announced. "This is it."

Thankfully, there was no noise, but what they saw was bad enough. The double doors flew open as four workers, clearly terrified, burst through. Two dark forms, moving so fast that they appeared almost as shadows, followed them.

Mac watched as the shadow-figures caught each man in turn, brought him close, and held him in a macabre embrace, mouth pressed to their victim's neck. When they finished with one, the attackers flung the lifeless body away and grabbed another.

Mac saw the security guard, moving too slowly to be effective, pull his gun and fire. The dark forms did not falter, but when the last of the four workers lay dead, one of the two forms attacked the guard, whose face was turned toward the camera. His expression of stark terror was undeniable, and when his mouth opened, Mac was again grateful that they couldn't hear the man's primal scream.

After discarding the guard's body, the dark forms lingered for the briefest of moments before disappearing through the double doors.

Within seconds, the grisly images replayed in the lab. This time, when the bodies were discarded and the dark forms left, they did not reappear elsewhere—they simply disappeared.

The monitor went black as the group stood in stunned silence. Mac spared a glance at Lanie to make sure she was okay. Her jaw was clinched tight, and he thought her breathing sounded erratic, but she was tough, he decided, and would be okay.

"I'd like to see it again," he said to the technician. "But can we watch it in real time?" He wanted to get a better look at the two dark figures.

The tech glanced over his shoulder. "That *was* real time."

*Damn.* A bad feeling stole over him, but he refused to focus on it. "Can you slow it down, then?"

The tech nodded and, turning back to the desk, typed in commands at the keyboard. A second later, the entire horrifying scene replayed in slow motion, but this time when the dark forms came into view, it was evident that they were human. Mac watched closely.

"Stop the recording," he ordered after a second. "Can you rewind a bit? Okay, now go forward, but slow it way down." The tech typed in the commands to comply, and Mac studied the action on the screen. "Freeze."

The image froze and the two attackers' faces were almost facing the camera.

"Can you zoom in?" Dirk asked.

The faces seemed to jump out at the group, fuzzy but identifiable, and he felt his own blood run cold. Beside him, Lanie gasped. On the screen, bloodied yet smiling, was Lance Burton. Standing next to him was an older man who Mac assumed was Dr. Weber.

He'd seen enough. Turning, he gently guided Lanie away from the group. She might have been in shock because she allowed him to steer her outside where the bright afternoon sun could warm them and chase away the chills still racing along his spine.

"Now do you believe me?"

It wasn't the first thing he'd expected her to say, or do, in reaction to what they'd seen. He gave her a speculative look before letting his gaze drift off to stare sightlessly at the trees.

"Honey, I already knew Burton was psycho—and this isn't the first time he's murdered innocent people to get what he wants. However, it's the first time we caught him on tape."

Eyeing her skeptically, he considered how much to tell her. "Burton and I served together in the Navy; specifically, we were members of the same SEAL team. Burton was good, but not the best. He was promoted several times to a higher rank, but never as high as *he* felt he deserved. After a while, I think it got harder for him to accept that he wasn't leadership material in the military's eyes.

"We started out as equals—friends—but when I became his commanding officer, he didn't like it. The 'accidents' started out small, and frankly, it never occurred to me that they were due to anything other than bad luck." Mac traveled back in his mind to those earlier days. "I should have paid closer attention. Maybe I would have recognized the symptoms, before . . ."

He took a deep breath, aware that Lanie was listening and grateful that she didn't rush him or ask a lot of questions. "We were on assignment in Iraq. In and out—that's all we had to do, but the mission was compromised from the start. The loyalties of the men in my unit were severely tested by Burton, who seemed bent on running the show his way. He managed to divide the group.

"We were on our way in when all hell broke loose and we were ambushed. I lost seven men—ironically, the seven whose loyalty happened to be to me, not to Burton. I took a bullet in the leg. It shattered my femur and subsequently ended my military career. Only two men knew our route—me and my second in command." He shook his head, wondering exactly why he was sharing this with her. They'd only met—how long ago? Twenty-four hours?

"And Burton was your second in command." The softly spoken statement drifted to him above the sound of hundreds of insects buzzing in the trees.

"Yeah." He hadn't realized she'd come to stand so close to him until he felt her hand lightly touch his arm. Normally, he wasn't the touchy-feely type, but he didn't find her nearness intrusive.

"Are you sure it was Burton who betrayed you?"

He gave a humorless laugh. "I've asked myself that a million times over the past year. Until recently, I had no proof. Then a month ago, Rogers, one of the survivors, came forward, supposedly in a fit of conscience, and admitted that he'd overheard Burton planning the whole thing and hadn't tried to stop him. Unfortunately, Rogers died in a car wreck before anything could be proved, but his statement was enough to warrant a formal inquiry, which happens to be scheduled for next week. That's why I found Burton's death so timely." The story was more complicated than that, but he didn't feel like going into it.

"If Burton was under investigation, then what was he doing down here in the first place?"

Mac gave a rueful smile. "You have to understand, things had not progressed so far that Burton was being accused of anything. The first step was the upcoming inquiry. All the surviving members of the team were being brought in—including Burton. His backup would have flown down any day to relieve him of duty so he could fly to D.C."

Mac saw the genuine concern in her eyes—her sympathy and understanding—and hated himself for what he had to do next. "What I don't know is the extent to which your father is involved in Burton's scheme."

His words were clearly unexpected, and for a moment she simply stared at him. "How dare you," she finally said, her voice filling with indignation. "My father is—was—a good, honest man. He's a victim of whatever is going on here, and I'll thank you not to forget it." Then she stormed off.

Lanie needed a chance to think—a chance to absorb everything Mac had told her, and a chance to cool down. She kept reminding herself that he didn't know her father and therefore, his accusation was to be expected, but that line of logic wasn't comforting. His suspicions hurt and left her feeling betrayed, which, if she was honest with herself, was a projection of her own guilt. In the privacy of her own thoughts, hadn't she also wondered about the extent of her father's involvement? Because he *was* involved. She had seen him on the tape. He *had* killed. The only question that remained was, had he gotten mixed up in Burton's scheme voluntarily?

No—absolutely not. Burton might be psychotic, but her father wasn't. He would never fake his own death or voluntarily participate in the murder of others. Yet, how could she explain his appearance on the film? The two forms had moved across the room too fast for human speed, killed innocent victims, and drank their blood. It made no sense. If Burton was hoping to quietly disappear to avoid the investigation, he was certainly doing everything he could to draw attention to himself.

Which brought her back to her earlier theory.

Lanie turned to pace the length of the building and saw that while she'd been lost in thought, Lieutenant Davis had appeared. Mac had probably sent him to keep an eye on her and make sure she was safe. Irritation flitted through her. She didn't need a babysitter. She'd never needed a babysitter.

When she was growing up, her father hadn't believed in babysitters, opting, instead, to drag her across the country with him, enlisting her help with his research when it became apparent that she was more computer literate than he. She'd grown to love her hours of digging on the Internet for obscure facts and information regarding various cryptids, the animals her father sought to find. She enjoyed the challenge of proving they existed, which was the reason why the idea that vampires existed wasn't that far-fetched to her. Especially now. If the chupacabra—believed by most to be as fictitious as the Yeti, Big Foot, or even the Loch Ness monster—was real, then why couldn't vampires be real as well?

She quickened her steps, her wandering now taking on purpose and direction. She wanted to see the cage where she and Mac had found the chupacabra. Dirk Adams had reported that the creature was gone, but she felt compelled to take a look for herself.

When she rounded the corner to the backyard, she caught the outline of something lying inside the cage.

Nerves suddenly wound tight, she slowed her speed, watchful for the least sign of movement. Her mind raced back to the events from the night before. Had she really killed the creature? If so, perhaps even in death, it turned to stone during the daylight hours. That would explain why Dirk's men hadn't found the "wild animal"—they hadn't known what to look for.

She was close enough to the cage now to see that the form was, in fact, the stone gargoyle. She had to suppress the shudder that ran through her and resist the temptation to run away. Quickly glancing at the sky, she judged that she had several minutes before the sun set and darkness descended around her. If the creature had somehow survived, she did not want to be caught unawares.

Creeping forward, she split her attention between the statue and the cage door, wondering if, in her haste the night before, she had securely closed and locked it. A few steps closer and she saw that she had.

She heard Davis's footsteps coming up behind her, his gun held ready in his arms and his eyes scanning the area for a danger he couldn't see. She practically heard the thoughts racing through his head as he glanced at her.

Turning her back on him, she moved up to the cage bars so she could see the chupacabra. It didn't look nearly as frightening in the light of day as she remembered it. Of course, right now, it wasn't snarling and trying to rip out her throat.

Small, round indentations along the statue's surface caught her eye. Peering closer, she realized they were bullet holes. They looked shallow and faint, causing Lanie to wonder if the creature might still be alive and, in its hibernating state, healing itself. If that was the case, then . . .

"Ma'am, it'll be dark soon. We should go back inside."
Davis's voice was polite but firm. She ignored him. Now
that she knew what to expect, she wasn't going to miss
out on it. As the minutes ticked by, her anticipation and
excitement built. Maybe there was more of her father in
her than she realized.

Feeling safe enough with the thick steel bars of the
cage separating her from the creature, Lanie waited as
the shadows around her grew larger and the sun slipped
below the horizon.

The transformation was as sudden this time as it had
been the night before. One minute Lanie was staring at a
statue lying on the ground and the next, a living creature
was struggling to its feet. Unlike the night before, it did
not leap to attack her, and she wondered if the bullets had
left it so wounded that it was dying; its ultimate death
postponed when the sun came up, only to resume now
that night had arrived.

She felt a small measure of sympathy for it. Animals
rarely acted maliciously—reacting merely to their circumstances. She and Mac had been in the wrong place at
the wrong time last night, and she felt bad for injuring
it when perhaps it had been as frightened as she and
Mac had been. She didn't make the mistake of feeling too
sorry, however. After all, it had killed her father and
Burton—and almost killed Mac.

"What the hell . . ."

She'd almost forgotten about Davis. "That's the creature that attacked us last night. No, wait!" She put up a
hand to stop Davis from shooting it. "Don't kill it."

"What is it?"

"El Chupacabra," she replied, returning her gaze to the creature. She wished Mac were there with her. It would be hard for him to argue against cold, hard fact. "Lieutenant Davis? Would you please radio someone inside the facility and ask them to send Mac out here?"

Davis didn't reply.

A *thunk,* followed by a soft ruffling of leaves, was her only indication that something was wrong. She turned and spotted Davis, crumpled at the base of a nearby tree.

Beside his body stood her father and Burton.

# Chapter
# 5

"D ad?"

Lanie couldn't believe her eyes. Was it really him? Her heart leaped with sudden joy.

Both men stood at the forest's edge, peering at her from the shadowy depths beneath the canopy of tree limbs, their eyes glowing reddish in the dark. At the sound of her voice, her father took a step closer and she saw that he looked wan and pale; his skin almost translucent where errant beams of moonlight touched it. Yet a happy smile touched his lips as he gazed at her.

"Lanie, my child, I never thought I'd see you again—and here you are."

"They said you were dead." Her voice cracked with the strain of her emotions. She wanted to throw herself into his arms, but hesitated as images from the security recording flashed through her mind.

"No, don't come closer." His voice caught and he paused to collect himself. "I fed earlier, but still, the temptation is hard to resist."

"What?" She felt confused, and her eyes darted from his face to Burton's, which looked predatory. She didn't think her father would harm her, but she wasn't so sure about this man.

She shook her head. "I don't understand. What happened?"

"I died." Instead of sounding sorrowful, Lanie caught a hint of excitement in his voice. "It's incredible, isn't it? Two myths put to rest. Of course, no one must ever know."

"So, you really are—?"

Burton took a step closer and Lanie stopped talking, distracted by the sensation of his eyes traveling over her. Sheer willpower kept her standing in place, but fear swamped her senses. Burton's lips curled in a mockery of a grin, and she saw fangs where the canine teeth once had been. She couldn't suppress the shudder that ran through her as an unnatural silence fell.

As if playing with her, Burton crossed one arm in front of him and rested the elbow of his other arm against it so he could stroke his chin in thoughtful repose. The image was made more surreal by the talon-sharp nails that now tipped each finger.

Across the way, she heard Davis stir and gasp.

"Don't move," she warned him.

"Who are they?"

Burton chuckled. "The *who* is not as important as the *what*, I'm afraid."

"Our worst nightmare?" Lanie suggested.

Burton's laugh was more genuine this time. "I suppose that was a bit cliché. Such wit. So, Weber, this is your daughter? Maybe we should take her with us. What do you think?"

"Leave her alone," her father growled. "Or I won't help you."

Burton walked up to her, stopping inches away. He ran one sharpened nail lightly down the side of her cheek, and the light in his eyes turned to molten lava. "I wonder if her blood tastes as sweet as the smell of her fear?"

"You can't do this without my help, Lance, and I promise you, if you harm my daughter—"

Burton held up a hand to silence her father, his expression turning cold and hard. With a last long look at Lanie, he walked to the cage door. Lanie's heart lurched when she realized what he was about to do.

"No—don't!"

Displaying incredible strength, he grabbed the door and pulled it open. The metal in the lock groaned under the stress, finally submitting to the greater strength. It opened and Burton walked inside.

Amazingly enough, the adult chupacabra rose to its feet, but did not attack. For several seconds, Burton and the creature studied each other intensely. Then the chupa dipped its head and followed Burton quietly out of the cage, making no move to attack anyone. In fact, it walked straight over to her father.

A movement at her father's neck caught Lanie's attention, and she noticed a small animal clinging to his back. He smiled when he saw the direction of her gaze and turned so the moonlight fell on the small chupacabra. It was the size of a large puppy, and Lanie assumed this was the younger creature mentioned in his journal.

Amazed, Lanie watched as the adult chupa lowered its head to nuzzle the baby in an almost maternal way.

"Burton!"

Mac's sudden shout drew everyone's attention as he raced toward them, his gun drawn. Perhaps sensing his opportunity, Davis lunged to his feet, but Burton was faster and Davis's weapon went flying through the air even as Burton yanked the man in front of him like a shield.

Almost on top of them, Mac drew up short, his gun leveled, his eyes focused on the situation. Lanie understood his dilemma. If he fired at Burton, he might hit Davis by mistake. On the other hand, if he didn't fire, Burton would surely escape—most likely taking Davis with him as a hostage, in which case the young man was dead anyway.

"I should have known you'd be here, Knight."

"Release Davis and give yourself up, Burton." Mac's voice sounded like cold steel, hard and unyielding.

"And why would I do that?"

"I saw the tape. I know what you did."

"I doubt you know everything," Burton said with disdain.

"Two nights ago, you killed nine men—don't even try to deny it."

"Actually, I don't know if I deny it or not. That whole night is a little fuzzy to me. It's not every day that one gets to rise from the dead."

"Cut the crap," Mac growled. "I'm not going to let you get away with faking your own death. Come quietly now, and I'll be sure to tell the authorities that you cooperated."

"Right. You just don't get it, do you?" Burton gave a half laugh that held no humor. "That's okay. Two days ago, I wouldn't have believed it either. But now things are different. There's a whole new world of opportunity for me, and I'm not about to give it up."

"And what do you think you're going to do? That whole facility is filled with soldiers."

"Do? Why, I think I'll do whatever I damn well want to, and you'd be wise to remember that." Burton drew Davis closer to his chest and though the young man struggled, Burton held him as easily as one would a doll.

Keeping his eyes locked on Mac's face, Burton lowered his head until his mouth was inches above Davis's neck. "Leave, Professor." Burton's teeth sank into the side of his prisoner's neck, and Davis's body went suddenly rigid. From where she was standing, Lanie saw a trickle of blood escape the seam that Burton's mouth made against Davis's throat. It blazed a dark, thin trail in the moonlight. Then Davis's eyes closed, and his entire body began a spasmodic twitching.

Lanie stood as if frozen.

"I love you." The whispered words floated to her, and distracted by them, she turned away from the scene before her just as an explosion rent the air, hurting her ears. The sound of Mac's gun reverberated around the forest, and she felt the repercussions of the weapon's discharge hit her.

Almost in slow motion, she saw Mac pull the trigger again, and saw Burton's left shoulder jerk back. Burton didn't fall, though, and he didn't let go of Davis. Instead, he seemed to push off the ground with his legs and leap high into the air, up through the tree branches where he became lost from sight. Time stood still as Lanie and Mac stared above them, ready for whatever might happen. When the body came falling toward them, they almost didn't move aside in time.

Davis's body hit the ground with a resounding thud and lay there, broken—and dead. Everything suddenly started moving in real time once more.

"Are you all right?" Mac asked, standing beside her.

"I . . . I think so." She searched the branches for a sign of Burton, but saw nothing but the black of night. "Where did he go?"

She looked around for her father, but found that he, too, had disappeared. A feeling of despair settled over her until she remembered the softly whispered words. *I love you.* She fought to swallow the lump in her throat as she hurried to Davis.

Placing the flat of her fingertips to the side of his throat, she felt for a pulse and found none—not that she'd expected to. She closed the lids of the young man's eyes and rested her hand briefly against his cheek. She hadn't known him well, but no one deserved to die like that.

Killing Davis had proved to be an effective distraction, Mac thought ruefully. It had given Burton and the professor their chance to escape—and not just the two men; the creature was gone as well. Mac had recognized it immediately as the one that had attacked him; though why it was docile tonight, standing beside the professor, was a mystery.

It seemed strange that Burton would risk coming back for it, which meant he wanted it for some reason. That thought bothered Mac, a lot.

The sound of shouting voices and running feet brought him out of his reverie.

"Go inside." Mac grabbed Lanie by the arm and pushed her toward the building, his eyes searching the darkness above them. "Tell Dirk what happened. Have them take Davis's body and put it with the others."

"What about you? You can't stay out here by yourself. Burton could be anywhere, waiting to attack when your back is turned."

Mac shook his head. "No, he's gone."

"How can you be so sure?"

"I heard them moving through the forest."

A strange look flitted across her face, but all she asked was, "What are you planning to do?"

"Go after them."

Mac moved through the jungle, vaguely aware that he was making exceptionally good time. He'd never run this quickly before, not even when his leg had been healthy. He hurtled through the dense undergrowth as if he were running across short grass, grateful that the moon always seemed to be lighting his path, no matter where he went, letting him see everything clearly.

Every thought focused on finding Burton. He'd been certain that he'd hit Burton when he'd fired his gun. In his mind, he saw the replay of Burton's shoulder jerking back with the impact. Yet there was no trail of blood anywhere. Even seeing as well as he could, Mac hadn't found a single trace, but he wasn't worried yet. He knew they'd been this way. While Burton might have been trained to leave no trail, Dr. Weber had not.

What further amazed Mac were the three-clawed animal prints that he found in the dirt following alongside Dr. Weber's path of crushed plant life. The creature that had virtually made mincemeat out of him seemed to be almost domestic in the presence of Dr. Weber and Burton. Why was that?

Hours later, Mac returned to the research facility empty-handed. He found Lanie waiting for him inside and when she saw him, she hurried forward, searching him with her eyes for signs of possible injury.

"Are you okay?" Her hands strayed to touch his chest and his arms. He wasn't sure she was aware of what she was doing, and her concern warmed him for no reason he could understand.

"I'm fine."

He noticed that she was alone in the foyer. "Where's Dirk? And why isn't someone sitting up here with you?"

"They're all out searching for Burton. Did you find him? Or my father?"

"No, I lost them in the jungle."

"Well, it was dark," she offered comfortingly. "Do you think they'll come back?"

"I doubt it. Burton knows we're waiting for him. Besides, I think they got what they were after."

She nodded gravely. "The adult chupacabra."

He nodded. "But damned if I know why Burton wanted it." They had been walking toward the lab. Now Lanie grabbed the sleeve of his shirt and pulled him to a stop beside her. He could tell by the look on her face that she was lost in the pursuit of her thoughts. She didn't look at him as she turned, still holding on to his sleeve, and headed for the residence hallway.

"Where are we going?"

"My father's room—we need to talk."

He stopped walking and refused to move. "Look, I know it was a shock to think your father was dead and then suddenly discover that he's alive and working for a mercenary." He tried to gentle his tone. "I'm sorry that you had to find out the way you did, but I don't have time to *talk* about it right now. They're getting away. If we act quickly, we can head them off."

"It's a big jungle. Do you know where they're going?"

He took a deep breath and exhaled slowly. "No," he admitted.

"Then it won't hurt you to take a few minutes to listen to me. Please, Mac. This is important." When he looked unconvinced, she tried again. "I don't think our problems here are over, and if there's any way to save a few more lives before it's too late, I think we should try. Especially since it might be our lives we'll be saving."

He saw the desperation in her eyes and wondered why he even considered listening to her when he knew damn well what needed to be done. It was the added "please" that did him in.

He let her pull him down the residence hall, to the third door on the right. The room was small and cozy, almost suffocating to Mac, who noticed that the only available seating for two was the bed, looming suggestively larger than life compared to the lone reading chair in the corner and the even smaller desk chair. He decided to remain standing.

"Okay, I'm listening."

Now that she had his attention, she seemed at a loss as to how to proceed. Walking over to the desk, she picked up a small leather journal and offered it to him. "This is my father's journal. I think you should read it; maybe it will help you understand what we're up against."

Mac, who'd started to take the book from her, now offered it back with a rueful expression on his face. "I've had ten years of highly specialized training in both covert and overt military operations. I don't need some crypto-whatever the hell you call it and a librarian explaining anything to me."

"This is different, Mac. We're dealing with things most people don't even know exist. I'm talking about vampires."

He started shaking his head. The woman sounded like a broken record. "Enough already. I told you before, I don't believe that crap, and I certainly don't have time to listen to it."

He started to leave, but she ran to the door and blocked it with her body. "Didn't you see them? My father and Burton? Did they look normal to you? And the way Burton killed Davis? Do you think that was normal?"

"Being abnormal and being a vampire are two different things." He reached around her to grab the doorknob, trying to ignore the contact of their two bodies as she refused to move out of his way. He caught the faint scent of soap mixed with the lingering essence of some perfume and tried not to notice how she wet her lips when she finally realized the position of their bodies. Unfortunately for him, there was a part of his anatomy that was all too aware of these things, and he quickly took a step back to give himself space.

"I can prove vampires exist."

Mac stared down into her dark blue eyes and felt as if he were falling into a deep well. Then her words sank in, jerking him rudely back. She was a lunatic—a gorgeous, witty, alluring but certifiable nutcase. But not as crazy as he was, he thought a second later, when he found himself being led through the halls to the back of the building.

"They put the bodies in here," Lanie told him a few minutes later when they reached the research facility's storage room. Though she'd acted sure of herself up to this point, the minute they entered the room and turned on the lights, Lanie seemed to falter. He wasn't sure if she was aware of moving closer to him as she surveyed the room, wide-eyed.

"Are you okay?" he asked, amused, closing the door.

"Not really," she admitted.

Looking around, Mac saw that shelves filled with cleaning supplies and sundries lined one wall. An assortment of mops and brooms stood in a corner, along with several buckets. There was a door in the middle of the right-hand wall that led into another room.

"In there," she said, pointing to that door.

He crossed the room to it, Lanie at his heels.

"Okay," she said breathlessly. "The way I figure it, these men have been dead about forty-eight hours, which is the same amount of time that passed between the time of my father's and Burton's deaths and the night everyone was killed. So if anything is going to happen, it'll be tonight. I don't suppose you have a knife on you? Or better yet—a stake?"

About to ask if she expected the dead to come back to life, he kept his mouth shut. That was exactly what she expected to happen.

For a brief moment he gave her worries credence. How many crazy things had he already encountered on this trip? As absurd as it was, if there was even a remote possibility that she was right, Mac knew he didn't want to open that door and find himself grossly outnumbered by the living dead.

"I have this." He pulled out his gun, fully loaded. He'd taken the time to reload the clip at the Jeep when he'd returned from his search through the jungle. "The door opens in," he explained, "so I want you to stand off to the side." He pointed to a spot a short distance away from the door.

Lanie was shaking her head before he'd finished speaking. "You can't shoot them. Bullets don't affect them."

"You've been watching too much TV." He held his gun where she could see it. "This is a Colt .45 automatic. It's got enough stopping power to drop a man with a single shot."

"Yes, well. We're dealing with the undead, and despite what nonsense you think might be dished out on TV, the fact of the matter is that it's going to be hard to kill something that's already dead."

"What do you suggest?"

She looked sheepish. "Stake them through the heart? Or maybe cut off their heads?"

She said it like severing a head from its body was an easy thing, and he had to bite back the words he wanted to say.

"Just stand back, okay?"

She moved reluctantly off to the side. Taking a breath, he felt a familiar, deep calm descend upon him; the quiet before the storm. He put his hand on the knob and opened the door.

Nothing jumped out at him as the door eased open, but Mac did not relax until he'd seen every corner of the room and verified that there was nothing lurking in the shadows.

After five minutes, his caution started to take on an aura of the absurd, and Mac was glad none of the men were around to bear witness to his actions.

Seeing the ten black bags was depressing, but not frightening. It was obvious from their shape and form that they still contained the deceased. The tag affixed to each zipper, bearing the victim's identity, seemed to be the only reminder that they had once been living, breathing people.

"All clear," he announced.

Behind him, he heard Lanie come into the room. He went to stand beside her and watched her expression. Her silence was hard to interpret. He thought she was probably disappointed that her theory had been incorrect, but had she really wanted these dead men to jump up, suddenly transformed into rip-out-your-throat-and-drink-your-blood vampires?

He draped his free arm across her shoulders. "Come on." He gave her a quick hug. "Let's go. Knowing how fond you are of tequila, I put the bottle from the plane in my bag when we arrived. What say you and I go get a drink? I know I could use one."

He gave her what he hoped was a reassuring but not condescending smile, more affected by the lost, confused look in her eyes than he wanted to be.

"I was so sure," he thought he heard her mumble. "Wait, what time is it?"

"Still standing on principle?" he asked. "Don't worry, it's after five. It's safe to toss back a few."

She looked at her watch. "It's not even eleven yet. According to the security film, my dad and Burton didn't appear until after midnight. We're probably early, that's all."

He couldn't believe his ears. "You want to stay here and wait?" She nodded. "On the off chance that one, or all, of these dead men will come back to life as a vampire?" Again, she nodded.

He sighed. "Lanie, if it means you'll get off my back about vampires, I'll sit in here all night with you." And he meant every word.

She smiled her gratitude, and he left her standing by the door to walk into the outer room where the brooms and mops stood. He selected five and proceeded to break each handle into two.

"What are you doing?" Lanie asked, watching him.

Mac brought the homemade stakes over to the body bags and knelt by the first one. "You might not want to watch this."

He unzipped the first bag, ignoring the sight and smell of the corpse inside, and stabbed it through the heart with one of the broom pieces.

"Stop!" Lanie cried, running over to him. "I thought you were going to wait until after midnight."

Mac glared at her and moved to the next bag. "We only need one body to rise to prove your theory. I sure as hell am not going to sit around and wait for ten bodies to rise and *then* try to stake them." He stabbed a stake through the heart of the second victim and moved on to the third. "It's not like this is hurting them, right? They're already dead."

Davis's was the next body he came to, and for the first time he hesitated. It was easier when he didn't know the victim. He gritted his teeth, staked the body, and moved on.

Finally, there was only one corpse left. Mac didn't touch the bag, but went to stand next to Lanie as he looked back over the other bodies. "I thought they were supposed to turn to dust."

Lanie glanced at them and shrugged. "I don't know— maybe they have to be really old vampires. Old enough that had they not been turned into vampires when they died, their bodies would have disintegrated."

"Maybe," he agreed. "What time is it?"

She glanced at her watch. "It's eleven-thirty."

"Great. Now we wait."

The minutes ticked by slowly and Mac, having given his word, remained standing, ready to stake the last vampire should it appear. By one in the morning, he was wondering just how long Lanie was willing to wait to prove her theory.

One-thirty turned out to be her limit. "I guess I was wrong," she admitted. "I'm sorry I made you do all that." She waved a hand at the staked bodies. "I think I'd like that drink now."

"No problem." Feeling magnanimous, he once again draped his arm across her shoulders as he steered her out of the back room and toward the hallway door.

They were almost there when Mac heard the ripping sound.

# Chapter
# 6

W hat—?"
   "Ssshhh." Mac silenced Lanie as they both froze
to listen. Everything in him argued that he'd imagined the
sound. It wasn't a body bag being ripped open from the
inside, and the shuffling he now heard was definitely *not* a
dead guy, aka vampire, moving around.

There came a crashing noise and beside him, Lanie
jumped. Keeping her behind him, Mac pulled his gun and
turned to face whatever came out of the back room.

It happened so fast, Mac later couldn't remember thinking about it. The researcher he'd not staked burst through
the open doorway, gaunt and deathly pale, with a manic,
crazed gleam in his eyes. Snarling and hissing, he never
even paused as he raced toward them, his lips drawn back
tight against teeth that were so dingy and brown, the
pearly white fangs glowed bright by comparison.

Instinctively, Mac pulled the trigger, not stopping until what had once been the man's head lay spewed across the room. Mac stared at the still form and made a mental note—one .45 round might not affect a vampire, but eight rounds fired in rapid succession could decapitate one. It was good to know.

With the ease of long practice, he ejected the spent clip and replaced it with the spare from his pocket. He jacked a round into the chamber and waited, wondering if the corpse would stay dead this time.

Then he noticed a movement behind him and turned.

"Whoa. Easy does it." He caught Lanie with his free arm, just as her knees buckled, and eased her to the floor, not liking how pale her face had turned. Afraid she might pass out, he pushed her head down toward her knees and absently stroked her back as he returned his attention to the headless corpse lying less than ten feet away.

He couldn't have admitted to anyone how he felt at that moment. Only one thought coursed through his mind, chasing away all others, leaving him in a state of shock.

*Vampires are real! Oh, shit.*

After a couple of minutes, a soft voice broke into his thoughts. "Are you all right?"

He looked at her. "I should be asking you that question."

"I'm okay. Too much excitement and not enough blood sugar."

"I need to make sure that no one else is planning to come after us. Will you be okay by yourself?"

Slowly, almost reluctantly it seemed, she nodded. "Be careful."

His search was thorough as he double-checked the other bodies, making sure each stake was solidly in place. He didn't know the "vampire rules," didn't know what would happen if the stakes were removed, but he didn't want to find out. As far as he was concerned, the best thing would be to burn the bodies—ASAP.

He needed to see if Dirk was back and talk to him, but knew that conversation would take a while. If *he* found the whole concept of vampires hard to believe, so would Dirk. First, though, he wanted to get Lanie back to her room.

He found her where he'd left her, still sitting on the floor, turned so she didn't have to stare at the corpse. At least some of the color had returned to her face. Slipping his gun into his waistband, he crouched beside her.

"Hey, how we doing?"

"Better." She offered him a weak smile that didn't quite chase away the haunted look in her eyes. "How much tequila did you say you have left in that bottle? I don't think one shot's going to be enough."

He could relate to that. He stood, pulled her to her feet, and then slipped his arm around her waist, using the excuse of steadying her, though it wasn't entirely true. He found the warmth of her body comforting.

"Let's get out of here," he suggested, not waiting for her to reply but opening the door and propelling them both into the hallway. He pulled the door shut behind them and hoped no one would go in there before he'd had a chance to explain.

Mac kept his arm about her until they reached her room. Once inside, he made her sit on the edge of the bed while he went into the bathroom to fetch a dampened facecloth. Then, placing a finger under her chin, he tipped her face up so he could gently wipe her cheeks, hoping the coolness of the cloth would help her feel better. Their eyes met and the world faded away. For several long seconds, Mac couldn't move, lost in a sudden whirlpool of confusing emotions. The impact of such intimacy was more than he could handle, so he cleared his throat and awkwardly held the cloth out to her as he took a step back.

"Listen, I should go explain things to Dirk and make arrangements to burn the bodies. I don't want any more surprises." He studied her face, trying to judge her thoughts. "You're okay, right?"

She nodded. "I'm fine. Go do what you have to do."

He smiled, liking that she could be both feminine and tough. "Okay."

He'd reached the door when she stopped him.

"Mac? Will you come back here when you're through?"

"You bet," he said, smiling. "I promised you that drink, remember?"

Lanie watched Mac go and resisted the urge to run after him, primarily because she wasn't sure her legs would support her. Unbidden came the image of the depraved creature that had run out of the storage room. It had behaved just like the images of her father and Burton on the security tape from the night they arose. Consumed with bloodlust, she deduced, because all vampires rose needing to feed.

She shuddered at the thought. The reality of vampires was not nearly as glamorous, or romantic, as the books made out, and instead of feeling elated that her theory about the dead men was right, she felt sick to her stomach. At least they were well and truly dead now—unlike her father and Burton.

Dazed, she tried to grasp a new reality. Her father was a vampire. *A vampire!*

A surge of restless energy hit her and Lanie pushed herself to her feet. She carried the facecloth back to the bathroom and was about to hang it up, when she caught herself staring at it instead, reliving the memory of Mac caressing her face. The man was pure carnal temptation, she thought, absently lifting the cool cloth to her suddenly too-hot face once more.

He also had a girlfriend, she reminded herself harshly. Her reflection stared back at her from the mirror, looking pale and disheveled. Even on her best day, she was no competition for *Babycakes*. She didn't know why she felt the need to make the comparison, but the thought was as sobering as a cold shower.

Hanging up the cloth, she took a moment to brush her hair and apply new makeup, all the while telling herself the effort was futile. Then she went back into the room, picked up her father's journal, and sat in the big chair to read. She went back to the beginning and read the first entry several times before realizing she had no idea what it said. She just couldn't focus her attention. What was taking Mac so long?

Laying the book aside, she stood and paced the room several times until her stomach growled and she remembered how long it had been since she'd last eaten. She was a little surprised that she could even think about food, but after ten years of witnessing graphic violence and human trauma as a firefighter and EMT, not much affected her appetite anymore.

Suddenly, the thought of staying in the room another minute by herself was intolerable, so she left to go find the kitchen. In a facility located hours from the nearest town, there had to be plenty of food stored there.

The kitchen was empty when she arrived. There were clean dishes stacked and drying in the sink—evidence that Dirk's men had been in there earlier. Digging through the pantries and refrigerator, she pulled out bread, condiments, and an assortment of meats and cheeses to make a sandwich. Too hungry to wait until she was back in the room, she ate it right there, savoring every bite. Feeling better, she wondered when Mac had last eaten. It had to have been a while.

Quickly making four more sandwiches, she wrapped them in cellophane and put away the leftover food. In doing so, she noticed several sodas in the refrigerator and an unopened bag of chips in the pantry, which she took. Arms laden with food, she returned to her room.

She hadn't been back but a few minutes when Mac knocked on the door. Letting him in, she thought he looked tired.

"Everything okay?"

"Yeah. Dirk and his men are disposing of the bodies." He sighed heavily. "I was going to explain everything to him, but it sounded too unbelievable in my head when I was rehearsing it, so I didn't even try. I asked him to trust me that the bodies needed to be burned, and he agreed to take care of it." He raised his hand then and she saw the bottle of tequila he was holding. "I brought you this."

"Thanks." She smiled and then looked pointedly at the food piled on the desk. "While you were gone, I found food. I thought you might be hungry."

"You did?" His eyes lit up and he seemed genuinely pleased, which was a big relief. She didn't want him thinking she'd gone all domestic on him—men hated that, didn't they? She didn't know. An old saying flickered through her head—the quickest way to a man's heart is through his stomach—or a sharp object through his chest. Tonight, the old adage seemed unusually appropriate.

She watched Mac cross the room to the desk and stop, hand poised over the sandwiches. "Does it matter which one I take?"

"No. Take them all if you're hungry. Also, there are chips, and one of those sodas is for you."

He sat on the edge of the bed and rapidly downed the first sandwich. He was working on his second when she sat down beside him.

He opened his soda and took a long swallow, causing Lanie to marvel at the way he practically inhaled his food. She smiled, watching him eat. Finally noticing her, he waved a partially eaten sandwich at her. "Thanks."

"You're welcome."

Picking up the tequila, she looked around for glasses. There weren't any. Shrugging, she gripped the bottle by the neck and raised it in a toast to him. "Salut."

Taking a large gulp, she had to force herself not to cough, though her eyes teared up. She blinked several times to clear them and then noticed Mac watching her, an appreciative smile on his face. When he held out his hand, she gladly handed him the bottle and watched as he raised it to his mouth to take a healthy swallow. Seeing his lips wrapped around the same spot hers had been moments before seemed so intimate that she immediately felt breathless. Embarrassed, she grabbed the nearby bag of chips and opened it. If Mac noticed her reaction, he didn't say anything, and they continued to eat in companionable silence.

Then Mac suddenly jerked his head and swore.

"What's the matter?"

"I think my tooth is loose." A confused look crossed his face as he swallowed the food in his mouth and then lifted the corner of his upper lip to reveal his teeth. Placing the pad of his thumb beneath the canine, he pushed on it. When he saw her watching him, he pulled his thumb away and shrugged. "I guess that thing—what did you call it?"

"Chupacabra?"

"Yeah. I guess one of its legs hit me in the jaw last night. My tooth's loose."

Lanie thought it was possible, but part of her worried that there might be another explanation. One that Mac wouldn't want to hear. Still, she had to try.

"Mac, maybe—"

"Not now, Lanie." He heaved a great sigh. "No deep, heavy talks, okay? I'm too tired to think, much less talk, about anything." He yawned, shoved the discarded cellophane wrappers to one side of the bed, and leaned back against the headboard.

"You're going to take a nap here? In *my* bed."

He cocked open one eye and patted the spot next to him. "You're welcome to join me—I won't bite." He smiled. "Sorry, poor choice of words under the circumstances."

He gave a soft chuckle, more to himself than anything, and slid farther down on the bed until he was stretched out, his head on the pillow. He fell sound asleep within minutes.

Still staring at him, Lanie let his offer play through her mind a couple of times. Even in sleep, he emanated virile masculinity, strength, and power. So much so, it was hard to remember that he'd been attacked and near death just the night before. Now, with another night gone and the dawn of a new day upon them, it made sense that he was tired. This need for sleep was his body's way of demanding the rehabilitative rest that he needed to recover.

Her internal dialogue ground to an abrupt halt. *Recover?* One night he was at death's door. The next, he's more or less fully recovered? *No one* healed that fast.

Lanie remembered what she'd read in her father's journal about the healing powers of the baby chupacabra's venom. Was her father's theory correct? Was the adult's venom even stronger? Was it capable of healing a man on the verge of death—or, taking the thought one step further, could it bring the dead back to life?

Her father hadn't had a chance to experiment with the adult—unless one counted the attack that killed him. Her father and Burton were evidence that the adult's venom could, in fact, bring the dead back—with one drawback.

Chupacabras turned the dead into vampires.

Again, the faint memory tugged at her. Her recall of odd facts and figures was a trait she'd found useful both in the research she'd done for her father and as a librarian. She thought that if she could access the Internet, given time, she might be able to find the source of the memory that kept eluding her. Not for long, she vowed. Just because her father and the other researchers were out in the middle of nowhere didn't mean that online research wasn't possible. Somewhere in this building, there was a satellite hookup and wireless access.

Knowing she'd seen her father's laptop earlier, she did another quick search of the room. Of course, it wouldn't be out in the open; that would be too easy.

She looked in the closet and almost missed it off to the side, the black case making it hard to see in the dark. She glanced at Mac as she pulled it out, wondering if her movements might wake him. He never stirred.

She knew the laptop had a wireless Internet connection; she'd tried to teach her dad how to use it before he'd left for the facility—how long ago had it been? She shrugged off the memory as she waited for the machine to boot up.

Within minutes, she was surfing through familiar cryptozoological sites. After four hours of hitting one dead end after another, she was no closer to finding the article. She'd explored every source she could think of, even going so far as to check out the Web sites dedicated to the chupacabra cult following that contained virtually no factual data whatsoever.

Frustrated, she looked away from the screen, letting her gaze roam to the narrow opening in the curtains through which the sun now shone. The chupacabra would be stone now, she thought, remembering the cool, rough texture of its skin. It was no wonder that it reminded her of a gargoyle, she thought. Then she smiled. That was it.

One of the theories on the origins of El Chupacabra was that they were Lucifer's dark angels, traveling across the dimensions of space and time, taking the physical form of gargoyle-looking creatures while in the "human" dimension.

It was the reference to Lucifer that helped her remember what she was looking for—*Children of the Morning Star.*

Finding the article was more difficult than simply keying the name into the search engine, but at least now she remembered where to look. Soon, she found the article.

The Children of the Morning Star was a village of vampires, located somewhere in the uncharted regions of the Amazon. Hans Guberstein, an adventurer whose expedition stumbled upon it in the late 1700s, discovered it. Of the twenty-man team, only Guberstein escaped alive, carrying back with him horrifying tales of human sacrifices and demonic creatures that, from their descriptions, had to be chupacabras.

Guberstein reported that the vampires survived off the blood of the humans they hunted or who stumbled across their village. Their dead victims were staked and burned, thus preventing the victims from rising later as vampires. It was a crude means of population control.

It was hard to tell from Guberstein's report whether the chupacabras were considered pets or deities by the vampires. Their preferred food source was goat's blood, but occasionally a chupacabra fed off a human. When that happened, the corpse was allowed to rise as a vampire and become a member of the extended family.

According to Guberstein, the chupacabra-created vampire was superior to the creature that arose from a vampire killing.

Many found Guberstein's tales outlandish and believed he'd contracted jungle fever while on expedition. Furthermore, they thought the rest of his team had died from the same fever or had been killed by wild animals. The village, its vampire residents, and the creatures were all assumed to be figments of his delusional imagination.

When Lanie had first read the story, years ago, she'd considered it an interesting but fanciful tale with no basis in fact. Now she wasn't so sure.

Her gaze fell on Mac's still form. If the venom turned a *dead* man into a vampire, what did it do to a *living* man?

The chupacabra's venom restored the life it took, giving the resulting vampire certain of its own traits in return—specifically the need to survive on blood. Clearly, Mac had received enough of the venom's restorative properties to heal him. Even old injuries seemed better, she thought, remembering how his limp appeared less pronounced.

What other changes were taking place? Would he, too, need to drink blood to survive?

A flicker outside the window distracted her from the disturbing thought. Walking over to peer through the crack in the curtains, she saw Dirk and his men gathered around a bonfire and knew they were burning the bodies.

Feeling suddenly stifled in the room, she logged off

and went outside. The firefighter in her felt compelled to check that the fire was at no risk of spreading to the surrounding jungle. It wasn't that she didn't think the men knew what they were doing as much as she needed the excuse to get out of the building and do something.

"Ms. Weber." Dirk Adams inclined his head when she walked up to him a few minutes later.

"Lanie, please." She walked upwind of the smoke, wanting to avoid the stench. Doing a cursory visual inspection to assure herself that it was a controlled fire, she averted her gaze, preferring to focus on Dirk's face rather than the charred bodies being consumed by the flames.

"Where's our boy?"

Lanie smiled. Given Mac's size and personality, she wasn't sure "boy" was the right description for him. "He's sleeping. I'm not sure he's recovered from his attack," she hurriedly added, not wanting this man to think any less of Mac.

Dirk nodded, but his expression grew concerned as he studied her. "How are you doing?"

"I'm . . ." She paused, not really sure how she was doing. Dirk apparently seemed to understand because he gave her a sympathetic smile.

They stood in silence until the fire died down. Two men, one with a shovel and another holding the garden hose, stood nearby, ready to douse the last of the embers when needed. Beside her, Dirk checked his watch and Lanie thought he looked anxious. "Is something wrong?"

He glanced at her as if trying to decide what to tell her. "One of my men, Hector Munoz, is missing. He never came back from our search for Burton. A couple of the guys found what was left of his shirt lying in a patch of mangled underbrush. It was ripped to shreds and covered in blood. I sent another group out to look for him, but I don't hold out much hope. This part of the jungle is largely unknown." He fell silent for a moment, his thoughts clearly elsewhere. Then he glanced at his watch. "It's almost noon and we'll have to leave soon."

"What about your man?"

Dirk's jaw tightened as he took a breath and let it out. "I don't think there's anything left of him to find."

She nodded, understanding. Burton and her father weren't the only wild creatures lurking out there.

"You might want to wake Mac. He said he wanted to get to the airfield before dark, and if we don't leave soon, we won't make it."

Lanie returned to the room and found that Mac hadn't moved. The sound of his breathing came slow and steady.

"Mac, it's time to wake up." She spoke softly, so as not to startle him, but he didn't budge.

"Mac?" She raised her voice a little, but still he didn't stir. Laying her hand on his arm, she shook him gently—then again, but more forcefully.

Nothing seemed to penetrate his sleep. Frustrated, she crossed the room to the windows and threw open the curtains to let the sunlight in. Before she could turn around, she heard a strangled cry, followed by a loud thump. Whipping around, Lanie saw that Mac was gone, the rumpled sheets of the bed the only evidence that he'd been there.

"Mac?"

"What the hell are you doing?" His strangled yell

came from the floor on the far side of the bed where she couldn't see him. "Trying to blind me?"

Lanie looked around at the room's soft, warm glow and frowned. "It's not that bright in here."

"The hell it's not. Close the damn curtains. It's killing my eyes."

This time, she heard the pain in his voice and hurried to comply. "Okay, they're closed." She went around to the far side of the bed and dropped to her knees next to where he sat with his hand covering his eyes.

Through his parted fingers, she saw him crack open a lid experimentally before pulling his hand away. Lanie noticed that his eyes were red and bloodshot. "Are your eyes usually this sensitive to the light?"

"No," he grumbled.

Lanie added one more item to her growing list of concerns about Mac, but didn't pursue the matter with him. Instead, she changed the subject. "Dirk said we're leaving within the hour for the airfield."

Mac nodded. "Okay, let's get packed."

Lanie looked around the room, seeing all her father's things. Leaving them behind was like saying good-bye to him all over again. Mac must have realized what she was feeling because he heaved a sigh, stood up, and walked to the closet where he found one of her father's small suitcases.

"Come on," he said, laying it open on the bed. "We can't take it all, so only pack the important stuff. I'll arrange to have the rest of it shipped to you."

She wanted to hug him, but settled for a heartfelt "Thank you." The room was small and she was able to go through the contents quickly. In the end, she settled for taking her father's journal, several books, his favorite sweater, the laptop—and his pipe, which she found tucked into the pocket of his sweater.

Mac spent the majority of the ride back to the airfield thinking about all the changes to his body. What at first had seemed like a simple reaction to a rude awakening had turned out to be a legitimate hypersensitivity to sunlight. Not only was he having to wear his sunglasses outside, but earlier, with all the light streaming in through the windows, inside the facility as well.

Running his tongue across his teeth, he experimentally touched each one to see which ones had been knocked loose. Strangely, only the two upper canines moved freely. How was it possible for the animal to hit him in the jaw in such a way that only those two teeth were affected?

Mac stopped his inspection when he felt Lanie watching him. He blanked his expression but refused to meet her eyes, keeping his own fixed squarely on the road ahead. He knew she was worried about him, but not because she cared. It was because she thought he was turning into a vampire.

Mac wanted to scoff. The idea was absurd, ludicrous. Absolutely friggin' crazy. So why didn't he feel like laughing?

*Damn Burton*, he thought, *and damn that chupa— whatever the hell it was called*. Instead of driving Lanie back to the airfield and flying her home, he should be out scouring the jungle. However, being retired from the service meant he had no right to stay behind at a government facility, nor did he have the authority to order a full team of SEALs to fly down and search the jungle for him. The best he could hope for was to convince Admiral Winslow that Burton was . . .

Was what? A vampire? Mac almost snorted out loud at *that* imagined conversation.

Without the many stops they'd made on the trip out, the trip back to the airfield took much less time. Even with the time savings, though, they arrived after the sunset.

Mac pulled up to the main building, wanting to get them cleared for takeoff and under way as soon as possible. He was digging papers out of the glove compartment when Lanie spoke for the first time since they'd gotten into the Jeep.

"Where is it?"

He glanced up to see her perplexed expression. "Where's what?"

"The plane."

His gaze shot over to the stretch of tarmac where he'd parked his plane. It wasn't there. Thinking that the ground crew had moved it, he scanned the area, but still saw no sign of it. Twenty minutes later, Mac verified that the plane was nowhere on the grounds. It had disappeared.

He could think of only one man who might have need of his plane *and* was capable of taking it without anyone noticing until it was rolling down the runway.

Lance Burton.

Lance checked the dials and adjusted the plane's altitude. Damn, it felt good to be in the pilot's seat again—literally. He laughed at his own private joke, wishing he could have seen Knight's face when he discovered his plane gone. He wondered how long it would take Knight to realize who'd stolen it. Probably not long, he admitted. Knight wasn't stupid.

This time, however, his former commanding officer had no idea what he was up against. Even without looking around, Lance sensed the presence of the professor sitting in the back, watching over the dead body of Hector Munoz. The two creatures were curled up farther back in the plane, resting quietly. The psychic bond that linked the adult chupacabra to Lance and the professor was an unexpected advantage. It allowed him to control the creature's actions. It was like having his own attack dog—only on a much more lethal scale.

Dr. Weber's theory was that during an attack, the chupacabra exchanged both venom and blood with its victim and that's what caused the psychic link between them. An added advantage, in Lance's opinion, was that the link extended to all victims of the same creature, so not only was he linked to the creature itself, Lance was linked to Dr. Weber—and he'd be linked to Hector, as soon as his old friend arose from the dead.

He only hoped they reached their destination before then. The memory of the gnawing hunger that had assaulted him on his awakening still plagued him, and he knew Hector would need a lot of blood, at first, to slake his own appetite.

He didn't really anticipate any problems arriving at their destination, though. They'd flown most of the way the night before. Tonight's trip shouldn't take long at all.

Lance banked the plane, his mind moving to his plans for the future. The key to success was not lamenting what happened to him, but turning what happened to his advantage. And Lance intended to do exactly that. Things that he'd only dreamed of before now suddenly seemed very possible.

Damn, it was good to be alive, in an undead kind of way.

# Chapter
# 7

Lanie sat in the back of the plane, too tired and stressed to worry about it crashing. Dirk's jet was government issue, larger and in better shape than the one she and Mac had flown down, which also helped allay some of her fears. She gazed toward the front where Mac sat, talking to the other man. Dirk had offered them a ride as soon as he learned what happened, but now they were headed to Washington, D.C., not Houston. There simply hadn't been enough time to make the detour.

Mac had spent the first part of the trip notifying both the U.S. military and the civil authorities about the theft of his plane, although he held little hope that they'd find it—at least not with Burton still aboard. Now Mac, Dirk, and the others were sharing "war" stories, which Lanie had listened to with interest, for a while.

Unlike Mac, who seemed full of energy, Lanie was exhausted, and it didn't take long before the steady drone of the engines and voices lulled her to sleep. She awoke sometime later to find that Mac had taken a seat across from her and was on his phone, speaking in soft, warm tones. A jolt of jealousy shot through her when she realized who he must be talking to, and she quickly fought to suppress the unwanted emotion. She had no right to feel that way.

When he'd finished his conversation and hung up, he looked over at her and smiled. "You weren't asleep very long."

She gave him a small smile. "I don't enjoy flying."

"I happen to know that a couple of pain pills mixed with tequila will make you forget all about flying."

She laughed softly and shook her head. "Tempting, but I think I'll pass."

He shrugged. "If you change your mind . . ."

"Thanks. So what happens when we get to D.C.?"

"We'll make better time in this craft than in a commercial one, but it'll still be after midnight when we land, so the first thing we'll do is check into a hotel and try to get some quality sleep. Tomorrow morning, I want to meet with Admiral Winslow, and I was hoping I could talk you into going with me. I think I'm going to have trouble convincing him." For the first time, he seemed unsure of himself.

"Uncle Charles and my dad used to spend hours talking about cryptids and various theories to explain them. He might be more receptive than you think, but I'll be glad to go with you."

"Great. After we talk to him, I probably need to stick around a couple of days. There's still the matter of the inquiry, even if Burton isn't here to testify. I'll make arrangements to have you flown back to Houston. I was

going to ask Keith, my partner, to come pick you up in
that Falcon 2000 you admired back at my place."

She remembered the day they left, which now seemed
so long ago. "You know, I really don't mind taking a
commercial flight."

He gave an understanding smile. "Okay. I'll buy you a
ticket."

"I can—"

He held up his hand to interrupt her. "I insist."

She smiled. "Okay. Thank you." A big yawn stole over
her and she covered her mouth, embarrassed. "Sorry."

Amusement lit his eyes as he stood up. "I think I'm
going to leave you alone so maybe you'll be able to fall
back asleep."

She watched as he returned to the front where Dirk sat.
Soon the sound of their joking floated back to her, but
despite being tired, she couldn't seem to relax. Her mind
worried over the little changes she'd noticed in Mac—the
way he felt compelled to wear the sunglasses even indoors,
the way he'd lifted her father's suitcase full of books as if
it weighed nothing, the total absence of his limp, his two
loose teeth. She didn't like the nature of the changes; they
were too suggestive of what had happened to Burton and
her father. If her fears were justified and Mac was turning
into a vampire, she'd have to do something to deal with
the situation. The question was—did she have it in her to
put a stake through Mac's heart?

An hour after they landed at Andrew's Air Force Base,
their taxi pulled into the circle drive of their hotel. They
checked in at the front desk and found that Dirk had
already called ahead to make reservations. Apparently

Dirk was unclear about the exact nature of their relation-ship, so he'd played it safe and booked her and Mac con-necting rooms. Lanie supposed that Dirk didn't know about *Babycakes*.

The bellhop brought up what little baggage she had—her duffel bag, her father's small suitcase, and the laptop. Mac tipped him and followed the man next door, leaving Lanie to stare about the room, feeling suddenly wound tight. Before she could decide what to do, a knock sounded at the connecting door.

"I'm starving," Mac said when she opened her door. "How about a real meal? My treat."

She knew she should say no, order room service, and enjoy a nice quiet meal. The last thing she needed to do was get to know him better. It was harder to stake some-one you knew—and liked, wasn't it? "Okay."

"Great. The bar and grill downstairs is open all night—how 'bout we give that a try?" He glanced at his wrist-watch. "Will it take you long to get ready?"

"No." Lanie wouldn't have known how to take hours to primp if her life depended on it. Besides, at two-thirty in the morning, the only thing that would make her look better was sleep.

Grabbing her purse off the desk chair, she slipped the strap over her shoulder and joined him at the door. "Ready."

He stared at her in amazement and then a smile lit his face. "Let's go."

They had no trouble finding a table, and both ordered drinks as they waited for the waitress to take their food orders. Having been with Mac only under unusual circumstances, it seemed strange to suddenly find herself sitting with him in a restaurant having a normal meal.

"I am really hungry," he said, staring at the menu. "I think the only food I've had in days was those sandwiches you made, not that I wasn't damn glad to have them." He glanced at her over the top of the menu, his eyes alight with a smile. "Know what you want?"

She considered her choices, thinking that she should do the ladylike thing and order the small salad. *Screw it,* she thought.

As soon as the waitress arrived, Lanie ordered a burger and fries. After handing the waitress her menu, she gazed about the room while Mac placed his order. Once the waitress had left, they resumed their conversation.

"So you retired after the bullet broke your femur?" she asked.

"Yeah—it was a self-initiated medical retirement. I regained the use of my leg after months of physical therapy, but it wasn't one hundred percent."

"You didn't have to retire, though, did you? Wasn't there something else you could have done?"

"Special-ops soldiers don't do so well in the regular military; it's a whole different mind-set and training. If I couldn't be a SEAL, then I didn't want to be in the Navy. So I retired."

She nodded. "I understand that. What made you decide to fly private charters, as opposed to something else?"

"Like what?"

She smiled. "I don't know. Don't you special-ops guys usually start your own security agency when you quit the military?"

He laughed out loud. "You really need to check out the nonfiction section of your library more." He winked to take the sting out of his words. "Seriously, I probably could have, but I wanted something that didn't make me feel strapped down. I had my pilot's license before I ever joined the Navy, and my old high school buddy, Keith Dey, was trying to start up the private charter gig, so I agreed to be his partner. I like it—there's a freedom to be found in flying. It's hard to describe."

There were so many layers to this man, and Lanie felt like she was just beginning to see them.

"What made you become a librarian?" He grinned, reminding her of when they'd first met and she'd blurted out what she did for a living. "You seem to be into this, what was it again? Crypto—"

"Cryptozoology. It's hard to make a living as a cryptozoologist. My father was a biochemistry professor at the local university for years. He taught classes and did consulting work for various drug and chemical companies. That's how he earned a living. He did the cryptozoology on the side. The expeditions to find the various cryptids were done, for the most part, during spring, winter, and summer breaks.

"Then, as he became better known in the industry, people started paying him to do the cryptozoological stuff, and he eventually gave up the biochemistry. I, on the other hand, am not well known in the industry, and I'm not sure I'm that interested, but I knew I couldn't live off my dad forever, so I needed to find something to do that I enjoyed, but that also paid the bills." She smiled. "Becoming a librarian seemed the obvious choice. I started doing research for my dad at an early age. In fact, I knew the Dewey decimal system even before I knew how to spell Dewey decimal system."

"What about the firefighter thing?"

She gave a half laugh. "How'd you know about that?"

He shrugged. "Dr. Sanchez told me."

"Well, as you can imagine, being a librarian is not the most exciting job to have and while I liked it, I needed something more in my life. One of my librarian friends volunteers at the local station. She used to come into work and tell me about the calls that came in the night before, fighting the fires, working accident scenes. It didn't take long before I knew I wanted to be a part of it—the excitement, the danger, but most of all, helping people who really need it."

At that moment the waitress appeared with their food and reality intruded, at least for Lanie, as she watched Mac dig enthusiastically into his steak. From where she sat, the only part of it that wasn't bloodred and raw was the seared outer layer. It was almost enough to turn her stomach, but it didn't seem to bother Mac at all, and that fact set the alarm bells in her mind to ringing loudly. Was this a normal food preference for him or, like all the other changes occurring in him, had he suffered a change in palate? Did he now prefer the taste of blood?

After a while, she couldn't take it anymore. She had to know. "Do you always take your steak that rare?"

He stopped, a bite halfway to his mouth, and stared at the meat as if seeing it for the first time. "No. In fact, I usually order it medium, but tonight—I don't know—it sounded good."

He put the bite in his mouth and chewed, but his previous good mood seemed to vanish and he became thoughtful and quiet. There were a couple of times when Lanie got the impression that he was trying not to finish the steak. In the end, he left part of it untouched, and Lanie wondered what he would have done if she hadn't been there, watching. He didn't eat the vegetables or the rolls served with the meal, which she also found unusual, but this time, she wisely kept her thoughts to herself.

Throughout the rest of the meal, Mac seemed preoccupied, and they didn't talk at all as he walked her back to the room.

"I'll come get you later when it's time to go see the admiral."

"Okay." She found her key card, but before she could slip it into the lock, Mac took it and did it for her. After the green light blinked, he opened the door and followed her inside. She waited, curious about his intent, but after looking around, he went back to stand beside her at the door.

"Get some sleep, okay?" There was a moment of awkward silence as they gazed at each other. Lanie felt her heart speed up and found it difficult to breathe. Inside her, anticipation built. Then, suddenly, the moment was over and Mac put a hand on the knob and opened the door to leave.

"Where are you going?" she asked, cringing at the pathetic, almost desperate sound of her voice.

"I'm not tired, so I thought I'd go out for a while."

She wasn't sure what to think. "Do you want some company?"

"Not tonight."

"Are you sure? Because I'm not the least bit tired—"
A yawn cut off the rest of her words, undermining her
best intentions.

"Good night, Lanie."

She moved forward as he stepped into the hallway and
put her hand on the door, ready to close it. "Good night."
She didn't know how much of her was worried about
where he was going versus the fact that he was leaving
and she missed him.

"Lanie?" He reached through the opening of the door
before she shut it completely and laid his hand against her
cheek in a gentle caress. She gazed into his eyes, wondering what thoughts raced through his head; wondering if
he was as affected as she.

Then, before she realized what he was going to do, he
leaned forward and pressed his lips against hers in a kiss
that was over before she could recover.

"Keep your connecting door locked, okay?" He stepped
back out into the hallway and closed her door while she
stood in shock. By the time she could move again and
open the door, the hall was empty and he was gone.

She moved in a kind of trance as she showered and
changed into a nightshirt. She went back in her mind to
relive the exact moment when his lips touched hers, trying to re-create the sizzle that shot through her. Part of her
longed for another chance to experience those feelings
with him, while the more grounded part of her listed all
the reasons why that wasn't a good idea.

At long last, she climbed into bed and lay there, her
ears straining to hear sounds of Mac's return while her
gaze kept returning to the digital readout of the clock on
the nightstand. She tried not to think about where he was

or what he was doing, and cursed her imagination that saw him picking up women in the bar one minute and drinking their blood the next.

She finally turned on the TV for distraction and fell asleep.

When she awoke hours later, the sun was high in the sky and she felt much better. Crawling out of bed, she wondered what time Mac had finally made it back—*if* he'd made it back—and before she could stop the thought, if he'd returned alone.

Despite the fact that it was almost noon, she picked up the small in-room coffeepot and filled it with water, which she then poured into the back of the coffeemaker. It was never too late for coffee, she thought, placing the pre-packaged coffee and filter into the holder and starting the machine.

She wandered into the bathroom to shower and by the time she was done, so was the coffee. Slipping her night-shirt back on, she poured a cup and took a sip, feeling the hot liquid slide down her throat and imagining caffeine racing through her system. She immediately felt better. Carrying the cup to the bed, she sat on the end and watched TV while she drank.

The local midday news was just coming on, so she turned up the volume. She wasn't really paying attention until a story about homeless men found dead in a nearby alley caught her attention. The man reporting the story described the scene as one of "the most baffling" authorities had ever seen. The bodies were found with two puncture wounds on the sides of their necks. An interview with the medical examiner revealed that the men had lost massive quantities of blood—and yet there was little blood found at the scene.

Lanie reached out to put the coffee cup on the nearby table, almost missing it in her dazed state. The crime scene wasn't that far from the hotel, and the reporter said the victims had been killed sometime in the early morning hours.

Suddenly she had to know if Mac was in his room, yet a part of her was almost afraid of what she'd find.

Going to stand by the connecting doors, she pressed her ear against it. For several seconds, all she heard was the sound of her own breathing. Then the phone rang next door. She waited for Mac to answer it, but he never did. Finally, it stopped.

She knocked on the door, but heard no sound of movement on the other side. She knocked again, this time louder. Still, nothing.

The last thing in the world she wanted to do was open her door and barge in on Mac if he was in bed with someone else, but then reason asserted itself. Mac wasn't a hormonally driven teenager who forgot everything at the prospect of getting lucky. If he'd brought a woman back to his room, he would have closed and locked his part of the connecting doors. She had only to open her door to get her answer.

She turned the lock and eased open the door, noticing that his door was open and the room was still clothed in shadows from the tightly drawn drapes. Lanie leaned into the room far enough to see the bed and noticed a form lying there—a solitary form.

She heaved a sigh of relief. *Mac is asleep, that's all*. If he'd gotten back really late, then it made sense that he'd sleep so soundly.

The phone started ringing again. For the briefest moment, she hesitated, then she dashed across the room to answer it.

"Hello?"

"Lanie?" It was Dirk Adams's voice and it held a note of amusement. "Is Mac there?"

"He's asleep."

"Rough night, eh?" Yes, he was definitely amused. "Will you have him call me as soon as he's awake?" His tone sobered. "It's important, so the sooner the better."

"Okay." She replaced the receiver and debated on what to do. She needed to wake him.

She started for the curtains but stopped, remembering what happened the last time she'd tried that. Instead, she crossed to the desk and turned on the lamp, sending a soft, dim glow across the room.

Mac didn't stir. Walking over to the bed, she called his name softly—but got no reaction. She tried again, a little louder, with the same results. She couldn't help but wonder if he was ill. After all, that steak last night had been extremely raw—maybe he'd come down with food poisoning.

She checked his complexion and saw it had a grayish pallor. When she placed her hand against his forehead, it felt cold and clammy. The covers of the bed were pushed down around his waist and almost of their own volition, her eyes strayed over his bare chest and powerful arms. He lay on his side, facing her, so still that she had to watch carefully for several minutes before she saw the steady rise and fall of his chest as he breathed. At least he was alive.

Lanie placed her hand on his upper arm and tried to shake him awake. This time he stirred, but still did not open his eyes.

Placing her fingers against the base of his wrist, she checked his pulse. It was slow, too slow.

"That's it," she muttered to herself. "I'm calling for an ambulance."

She reached for the phone, but suddenly found her wrist caught in a powerful grip. "Mac? Are you all right?"

He didn't answer, merely stared as if he didn't really see her. There was something else about his eyes that bothered her. They seemed to glow.

Not knowing whether to be afraid or not, Lanie found herself being pulled slowly toward him. When his lips captured hers, all rational thought left her.

Mac wasn't sure at what point he realized the erotic dream was real, but his surprise was quickly replaced by pure, raw need and desire when he felt Lanie's lush body against his on the bed. With his mouth already covering hers, he rolled, trapping her beneath him as he ran his tongue across her lips, coaxing them to open. It took only a little encouragement before she did and then his tongue delved inside.

Her eager response only excited him further and he slipped his hand beneath the hem of her nightshirt to cup her breast, slowly kneading her fullness. He wanted to feel her naked body pressed against his, so he quickly pulled the nightshirt over her head and tossed it behind him.

She wrapped her arms around his neck, pulling him closer as he kissed first her mouth and then began to work his way down the column of her throat, all too aware of her rapid pulse pounding beneath the surface of the tender skin. He ran his tongue along it, causing them both to shiver and when she uttered a small cry, he shifted his weight so the hard evidence of his arousal pressed the juncture of her legs.

He wanted to take her right then and there, but a small voice cautioned him to slow down. The tension and desire in him grew, leaving him shaking with the need to possess her. His heart pounded in a primitive tempo, and he held her to him by wrapping both arms tightly around her, his mouth pressed to the base of her throat as his hips thrust against hers in an effort to satisfy the lust raging inside. When she rubbed her hips against him, the need exploded inside him. Baring his teeth, he bit down.

White-hot lights exploded behind her eyes, quickly fading as Lanie realized that Mac had scrambled away from her. Feeling exposed without his body covering hers, she looked up at him in dazed confusion. Slowly, she realized that they would not be finishing what they'd started, and she took a deep breath to keep from screaming her frustration at missing out on what had promised to be the sexual experience of a lifetime.

About to give Mac a piece of her mind for leading her on, she stopped, noticing the expression on his face. He was staring at her as if she were some type of sexual pariah. What had she done, she wondered, to make him change his mind? As the lust-crazed fog in her brain evaporated, she saw the red liquid covering his lips and seeping from the corner of his mouth. Her mind fought to make sense of what she saw, but the concept was too horrifying.

Almost in slow motion, she saw him swallow and then lick the remaining moisture from his lips.

The feel of something warm running down her neck broke the trance she was in, and she slapped a hand to her neck and felt the moisture. Almost afraid to look, she pulled her hand away, saw the blood covering her fingers, and realized what had happened.

Mac had bitten her!

# Chapter
# 8

Staring and horrified, Lanie watched Mac open his bloodstained mouth and rub a finger across his teeth. From where she sat, she saw the two elongated canines that hadn't been there the day before. Touching her neck, she felt the impression of the two punctures where the . . . fangs . . . had pierced her flesh.

She closed her eyes, suddenly faint. It wasn't a lack of blood that left her feeling light-headed, but rather the idea of Mac drinking her blood—like a vampire.

The sound of movement startled her, and she opened her eyes to see him stumble into the bathroom. Feeling vulnerable and exposed, she clutched the sheets on the bed around her and waited. From the bathroom came the sound of running water, followed by several deep breaths. She jumped when she heard the loud whack of Mac hitting the wall.

Part of her screamed to run into the other room and bolt the door behind her, but just then, Mac, looking calmer, stepped out of the bathroom, one towel wrapped around his waist and another, smaller towel clutched in his hand.

He walked over to the bed, and unable to stop herself, she shied away from him. It hurt to see the wounded look that came into his eyes, but she didn't know what to expect from him—and she was frightened.

Mac stopped and tossed her the towel. She used it to dab at her neck, but the bleeding had all but stopped.

"Lanie." His voice broke over her name and he had to clear his throat. "I'm sorry. I don't know what happened." He swallowed and clinched his hands into fists. "I never meant to hurt you."

She wanted to believe him, but it wasn't that easy, so she said nothing.

"Are you okay?"

She nodded, watching the way his mouth worked as he tried to adjust to the new teeth. After a moment, he seemed to notice that she still sat naked in his bed.

"Not to change the subject, but . . ." He paused as a thoughtful expression crossed his face. "I don't know any way to ask this without it sounding bad, but how'd you get in my bed?"

She gave him a pointed look, to which he responded with a slight nod of his head. "Right, stupid question, but, you see, I thought it was all a dream."

It was too embarrassing to sit and wait for him to tell her the whole thing was a mistake—that he'd been dreaming of *Babycakes*—so she shrugged her shoulders and pasted a casual expression on her face. "No problem. It was my fault, anyway. I came in while you were asleep and tried to wake you up."

"Why?"

For a second she was caught off guard by his question, but then she remembered why she came into the room in the first place. "I thought that maybe Burton and my father might have come to D.C."

Mac shook his head before she could continue. "That's unlikely, since half of the old unit is here this week. There'd be too many men here who'd recognize Burton. I can't see him taking that chance."

Lanie stared down at the bed and almost missed his next question as another, more horrifying thought sprang to mind.

"What made you think they were here?"

She decided to tell him the truth. "There were a couple of suspicious murders last night." Seeing the remote control on the stand beside the bed, she picked it up and turned on the TV. She flipped through the channels to an all-news station and told Mac the details as they waited for the story to replay. It didn't take long. From the corner of her eye, she watched for Mac's reaction. When the story ended, he turned to her, his expression haunted.

"If Burton and my dad didn't do this"—she paused and gave him a meaningful look—"then who did? You?"

"I don't know. I went out drinking last night—and indulged in about half a fifth more than I should have. The entire evening after the fourteenth shot is one big blur." He gave a self-deprecating laugh. "Hell, I don't even know how I got home."

He stood up, running a hand down his face. "I need to get out of here. I need to think."

Not really looking at her, he leaned down and retrieved the clothes that lay discarded on the floor. Without warning, he dropped the towel about his waist, and Lanie was treated to the full, unabashed sight of him before she could turn her head away. She waited until she heard the sound of him zipping his pants before she turned back to look at him. When she did, she found him standing with his shirt held up in front of him, an expression of shocked disbelief on his face.

"Mac, what is it?"

Slowly, almost absently, he turned the shirt around so she could see the dark brown stain covering the entire front. There was no mistaking what it was, and a myriad of thoughts raced through her head—all bad. Feeling trapped by her state of undress, she began searching through the covers for her nightshirt.

"Oh, God," Mac choked. "What have I become?" He paced across the room, swearing under his breath, and Lanie knew that there was nothing she could say to comfort him. She couldn't promise that everything would be all right when it looked like it was only going to get worse.

Suddenly he tossed his shirt onto the bed. "I *refuse* to be like *them*." Then he stormed out of the room.

For a split second she sat in stunned confusion, wondering where he'd gone. Then his words made sense. In the spirit of popular vampire fiction, Mac was going to meet the dawn—only in this case, he was meeting high noon, but the ultimate goal was the same. Mac thought he was a vampire and he was going to destroy himself.

Lanie searched through the covers for her nightshirt, damning the unfairness of it all. Mac didn't deserve this, but rather than succumb, he was going to do the honorable thing and take his own life. He didn't want to risk hurting anyone—anyone else, that is. Thinking of the homeless men, something didn't seem right. She hadn't known Mac long, but he'd proved his mettle time and again. Hadn't he pushed her out of the way of the attacking chupacabra? Thrust her behind him when the researcher had turned into a vampire and come after them? Only minutes ago, in the middle of a heated moment when she was totally at his mercy, he could have easily killed her—but he didn't. He'd pulled himself from her as soon as he realized what he'd done.

Scrambling from the bed, she looked under it for her nightshirt, but still couldn't find it. Frustrated, she ripped the covers off, letting them pile on the floor, feeling blind in the darkened room. Growing desperate, she raced to the window and threw open the curtains, letting bright sunlight flood the room. That's when she saw the huge brown stain on the wall.

Crossing to it, she noticed a brown paper bag and what looked like a take-out soup carton in the trash can by the desk. Though concern for Mac urged her to hurry, curiosity won out and she picked up the carton. The inside was covered with the same brownish red substance that stained the wall—and also Mac's shirt. Looking inside the bag, she saw another carton, this one sealed, and a small white piece of paper—the register receipt.

Pulling it out, she saw the name of DAVE'S ALL-NIGHT BUTCHER SHOP across the top and the itemized listing for two cups of pig's blood.

With the amount of blood on the wall, the carpet, and his shirt, Lanie didn't think he could have consumed very much. She pulled out the other container. It felt full.

Placing all of it on the desk, she went back to looking for her green shirt. With light filling the room, she quickly spotted it half buried in the pile of blue bedspread. The shirt was long enough to reach her mid-thigh and feeling like she'd already wasted too much time, she yanked it over her head and raced out of the room.

She reached the elevators and pressed the down button—and waited. It seemed to take forever, and growing too impatient to wait, she headed for the stairs, feeling she could run down the three flights faster than the elevator could take her.

She burst out of the exit on the lobby level winded and desperate. She ignored the stares of hotel staff and guests as she scanned the area, looking for the one person who wasn't there.

Afraid she might already be too late, she hurried outside, quickly looking up and down the sidewalk. She had no idea if Mac would burst into flames under the sun's rays or not, but she prayed she didn't find a pile of ash on the sidewalk.

When she didn't see either Mac or a pile of ashes, it occurred to her that he might have chosen someplace more private for his final moments. She looked around and noticed the opening to the alley beside the hotel. She ran the length of the sidewalk, ignoring the bite of the hot concrete on her bare feet.

When she reached the alley's opening, she stopped long enough to check for exiting cars and then dashed into it. Midway down, leaning against the wall as if in pain, with his hand over his eyes, stood Mac.

She raced to him, feeling more relieved than she wanted to admit. "Mac, it's me." She tried to grab his arms, but he shook her off.

"Leave me alone. I have to do this."

"The sun's not going to kill you," she argued, glancing up. "In fact, I'm not sure it'll even give you a decent tan today."

He resisted her efforts.

"Please, Mac. We don't even know if vampires really burn in sunlight. The chupacabra didn't; it turned to stone. So how are you feeling? Are your limbs stiff?"

Suddenly he stilled. "Lanie, so help me, if you're screwing with me—"

She smiled because he couldn't see her and reached for his arm again. This time, he didn't fight her off.

"Listen, I'm not really dressed to be outside. Can we go back to the room?"

His hand still covered his eyes. "I can't see." He didn't sound panicked; she wasn't sure he'd know *how* to sound panicked, but she could tell from his clipped tone that he was upset.

"Your eyes are sensitive to the light, that's all. You'll be fine once you have your sunglasses. Keep your eyes closed and take my arm. Here, like this." She took his hand and placed it at the crook of her elbow. "Now, just follow my lead."

Moving slowly, she guided him through the hotel's side entrance. Once they were far enough indoors, she stopped.

"It's not as bright in here; do you want to try opening your eyes?" Mac gradually pulled his hand away and blinked several times. Lanie saw immediately that they were red and irritated.

"Better?"

He gave an almost imperceptible nod and then, as if suddenly noticing her lack of proper clothing, he gave her a stern look, his eyes raking over her from head to toe. This time when he grabbed her elbow, she wasn't sure who was leading whom.

When they reached their rooms, Lanie realized she had forgotten to grab her key card. She almost laughed when Mac reached into his pocket and pulled out his. He was the perfect Boy Scout, she thought, always prepared— even when planning his own death.

"Is it too early for a drink?" she joked, trying to break the tension as she hurried over to the drapes and closed them again.

He didn't even crack a smile. "Don't you understand the severity of this situation? I'm turning into what *they* are. Just because I'm in control of my thoughts and actions at this particular moment doesn't mean that I won't morph into the thing I was when I killed those homeless men." He walked over to where his duffel bag rested on a stand inside the closet. "Go to your room, Lanie. Shut the connecting door, and don't come back in here for any reason."

She didn't like the sound of his voice. "What are you going to do?"

He pulled something from the bag as he turned to give her an exasperated look. "Would you *please* go next door? You're only making this harder."

She gasped when she saw the gun in his hand, and her thoughts started racing.

"Don't you think you're overreacting to this a little?"

"Lanie, I killed those homeless men."

"You don't know that. You told me yourself that you couldn't remember what you did last night."

He gestured to her neck. "I practically killed you."

She gave an unladylike snort. "Oh, please. I've drawn more blood shaving my legs."

He shook his head. "It's more than that. I *liked* the taste of your blood."

She eyed him skeptically. "Well, eeeuw—but still not convincing evidence that you deserve to die."

"That creature changed me when it attacked me. All my old injuries have healed, I can move incredibly fast, my night vision is better than most people's day vision, the sun hurts my eyes. I'm full of energy after dark, but once the sun comes up, it's almost impossible for me to stay awake."

Lanie held up her hand to stop his litany of changes. "Mac, I have no doubt that you've been changed because of that attack, and I think that had the chupa killed you, the venom would have brought you back as a vampire. But you didn't die. Therefore, you're not like the vampires we've seen. I mean, come on, Mac—taking a little blood in the heat of the moment is a lot different from what my father and Burton did to those researchers, or to Davis."

When he still seemed unconvinced, she pressed on. "At any time this morning, you could have killed me, but you didn't. You're in control of yourself."

He shook his head. "But for how long? Look what I did to those men."

"I'm not sure *you* killed them." She walked across the room and picked up the bag containing the empty containers of pig's blood. "Look what I found." She handed him the bag.

Mac stared at it in surprise. "Where'd you find this?"

"In the trash can—and look." She turned on the floor light in the corner and lifted the drapes until he could see the stain on the wall. "Looks to me like you tried to drink it and didn't like the taste. If you were as drunk as you say and frustrated, I can see how you might have spilled it down your shirt and then thrown it against the wall."

She took the bag from him and pulled out the full container. "This one is still full." She peeled off the lid and wanted to throw up. Inside was partially congealed dark red pig's blood. "You say you like the taste of blood? Here, drink this." She held it out to him, her gaze locked with his so he'd know she was serious. Slowly, he accepted the cup from her and raised it to his lips, but that's as far as he went. She saw the disgust on his face as he lowered the cup and set it on the desk.

"Maybe I only like human blood."

She wanted to hit him, but instead stared at him for several seconds, blinking. "Fine." She pulled her hair off to one side as she walked over to stand directly in front of him and then tilted her neck. "Have at it."

For several long seconds they stood there, and she felt his gaze on her exposed neck and prayed she hadn't misjudged his nature. When it was obvious he wasn't going to bite her, she straightened. Taking a deep breath, she placed her hand gently on the one still holding the gun. "You've gone through some changes, but you're not a killer."

"Yet."

"Yet," she agreed, slipping her hand over the barrel of the gun so she could point it away from her as she slipped it from his hand. He seemed stunned, and slightly amused, by her daring, but didn't try to stop her. "Tell you what," she continued. "If you do turn out to be a full-fledged vampire—I'll shoot you myself."

His eyes opened wide and the barest hint of a smile touched his lips. "Oh, yeah?"

"Yeah. Besides, you shooting yourself wouldn't do the trick. Based on our previous experience, if you really are a vampire, it's going to take more than one bullet to kill you. How were you planning to pull that off?"

The phone rang before Mac could respond, and he walked across the room to answer it. Lanie thought his voice sounded remarkably normal, under the circumstances.

The conversation lasted only a few minutes and from what she heard on Mac's side, he was talking to Uncle Charles. When he hung up, he turned to her. "Damn. I forgot about the reception tonight."

"What kind of reception?"

"It's sort of a bon voyage for one of the captains who's retiring. Since so many of us are in town, they decided to make a big event out of it."

"Oh."

"In fact, it's black tie. How 'bout it?"

Her heart gave a small flutter of excitement. "You want me to go with you?" She prayed she didn't sound too much like a schoolgirl who'd just been asked to the prom. Leave it to Mac to bring her back to reality, though.

"Yeah, I want you to go. I can't leave you here alone."

*Of course*, she thought. This wasn't a date. He had a girlfriend—which was a whole other issue Lanie knew she'd have to deal with soon. She *did not* have sex with other women's boyfriends.

"I'll have to go shopping."

"Fine. I'll take you."

"That's okay. I'm a big girl. I think I can handle buying an evening gown on my own."

He gave her a curious look. "I meant that I wanted to buy the dress for you."

"Oh." That took her by surprise. "Why?" Then she knew. It was a guilt gift, either for trying to rip out her throat or for almost having sex with her—or both. Lanie sighed. Maybe now was the time for that talk after all.

"Mac, what about Sandra?"

He had the audacity to look confused. "What about her?"

Lanie gave him a pointed look that, being male, he totally misinterpreted. "Oh, that. I called her from the plane earlier and told her we wouldn't be flying back for a couple of days. I'll tell her about the vampire thing later. I don't want to worry her."

Lanie heaved a labored sigh. "What about what happened this morning—*before* you bit my neck?"

He cringed at the reminder. "That's not really any of her business."

Lanie was shocked at his attitude. "You don't think your girlfriend has the right to—"

"Sister."

"What did you say?"

"Sandra is my sister."

Lanie felt herself grow red as she tried to ignore the grin spreading across his face. "You call your sister *Babycakes*?"

"Actually, Keith, my partner, started calling her *Babycakes* about five years ago, when they began dating. Now they're married, but the name sort of stuck. She hates it, which of course is why I use it."

"That's . . . nice," she offered lamely.

"So you'll go to the reception with me?"

"Are you asking me—or telling me?"

He gave her a slow, easy grin that did funny things to her insides. "Asking."

"Then yes, I'd love to go. Thank you."

He took a step toward her and it was more than she could take. "You know what? I think I'm going to run next door now and get dressed." She hurried across the room and then stopped at the door, seconds from a clean escape. "I almost forgot. Dirk phoned and wants you to call him."

Mac told himself that he wouldn't smile as she bolted through the door, but he couldn't help it. He enjoyed her discomfort because it meant that despite the fears she might have regarding his humanity, or the lack thereof, she found him attractive—as a man. If he'd doubted it, he had only to consider the little bout of jealousy she'd quickly tried to hide when she'd thought Sandra was his girlfriend. The revelation buoyed him like nothing else had so far.

Maybe, just maybe, if he got this "vampire" thing under control—or better yet, got over it completely—they could pick up where they'd left off this morning. He hoped so, because the memory of her body against his would be burned into his flesh and his mind for a long, long time.

He waited until he saw the connecting door to her room close, and then he crossed to the phone. He called the satellite phone number Dirk had given him and waited for the other man to answer. It didn't take long.

"About damn time," Dirk said when he found out who it was. "Everything okay? Your girlfriend said you were sleeping when I called earlier."

Remembering the way Dirk had looked at Lanie back at the research facility, Mac decided not to correct the misconception that she was his girlfriend. "Yeah, rough night," he said, letting Dirk interpret that any way he wanted to. "What's up? Lanie said it was important."

"We found your plane."

Mac was instantly alert. "Here in D.C.?"

"Close enough. It's still in one piece, but there was no sign of Burton or anyone else."

"Damn."

"Yeah, my thoughts exactly. What the hell is Burton doing here?"

Mac's thoughts turned to the homeless men, wondering if he was drawing the logical conclusion—or if it was wishful thinking that Burton was responsible.

"Damned if I know. Let's keep our eyes open," Mac suggested. "Thanks for the intel. Where's my plane now?"

"Old cornfield, not far from here." Dirk gave him the location. "Anything else I can do?"

Mac's mind was already thinking to the day ahead. "I don't know yet. Keep your phone on, okay?"

"Roger that."

Mac hung up and, after hearing the shower go off in the next room, knocked on the connecting doors. After a moment the door opened and Lanie stood there, a towel wrapped around her freshly washed body. Mac had to swallow a groan. Her skin still bore a fine sheen of moisture, and the smell of her soap and shampoo lingered in the air. Mesmerized, he watched a droplet of water fall from a dangling tendril of wet hair and land at the base of her throat before it rolled downward and disappeared into her generous cleavage.

Immediately his body tightened in response and he was almost overcome by the urge to rip off the towel and carry her to the bed.

Instead, he cleared his throat and took a step away from her. "I talked to Dirk and they found my plane not far from here."

Her eyes widened in surprise. "Here? Then that means Burton and my dad could be in town."

"Exactly."

Her brow furrowed. "But I thought you said he wouldn't come here."

Mac shrugged. "It doesn't make any sense." He reached into his pocket and pulled out his wallet. Digging in it, he pulled out several large bills and held them out to her. "I know I promised to take you shopping, but I need to go pick up my plane. You'll have to go without me. Take this and use it."

She shook her head. "That's okay. I have my own money—"

Mac took her hand and pressed the bills into it. "I insist. I'm bailing on the shopping spree, not the reception." He hesitated. "Plus, I feel guilty for, you know." He waved his hand toward her neck.

He realized his mistake immediately, but it was too late to take it back. He watched the flush spread from her face down her neck and saw the spark of anger light her eyes as she gripped the money in her hand. "Well, if it's a matter of easing your guilt, by all means, let me see what I can do."

It was too late to take back his words, so he merely smiled.

"I should probably run," he told her, hating the thought of leaving her. "I'll be back as soon as I can."

She nodded, but there was a worried expression on her face that he recognized. When he backed into his room, she followed him.

"Mac, if Burton and my father are in town, then it's more likely that one, or both, of them killed those homeless men."

He nodded. "The thought crossed my mind."

She bit her lip as a worried expression fell over her face. "It also means that those men—"

"I thought of that, too, so no worries, okay?"

She nodded, still looking worried. "Okay, but are you sure you don't need help with—"

"No. I'll take care of it." He waited until she walked back into her room and then he went to find a change of clothes. Exactly what did one wear to the morgue to stake a couple of corpses?

# Chapter
# 9

It was late when Lanie glanced at the clock in the taxi and mentally calculated how much time she had to achieve the impossible—make herself presentable for the reception. Taking money from her purse, she paid the cabbie when he pulled in front of the hotel and then allowed the doorman to help her out.

She hurried through the lobby to the elevator, wondering if two hours would be enough time. She couldn't remember when last she'd attended a formal affair. She hoped that Mac wasn't already upstairs waiting for her. Not just because she didn't want to feel rushed, but because she didn't want him to see all the packages she carried. Despite what she'd led him to believe, she really hadn't meant to spend any of his money, but the credit limit on her card proved unworthy of the challenge she threw at it.

She reached her room, shifted the packages to one hand, and pulled out her key card. As soon as the door opened, she dragged her bounty inside.

Exhausted from shopping, she dropped everything on the bed with a relieved sigh—everything except the dress. That she carefully hung in the closet and then waited for her heart to stop pounding. The dress was the most beautiful thing she'd ever seen—and the most expensive.

Crossing to the connecting doors, Lanie opened hers and found Mac's closed. She knocked and waited.

"Mac? Are you there?"

Visions of that morning replayed in her head as she tried the knob and found it unlocked. Pushing open the door, she poked her head inside. "Mac?"

It took about two seconds to verify that he wasn't there. The bed had been made and the room tidied—evidence that housekeeping had worked their magic—and the blood-stain beneath the window was gone—probably Mac's doing—but otherwise the room was dark and empty. Returning to her closet, she pulled the plastic wrap off the dress and stood back to admire it.

All she'd wanted was a simple black dress and shoes to match. After four stores and too many exorbitantly priced, yet astoundingly unimpressive dresses, Lanie had felt like canceling the entire evening. Then she'd seen it.

Even on the hanger, it had been eye-catching—a red so bright it was almost fuchsia, made of a fabric as smooth and cool to the touch as running water. She'd never in her life seen anything like it, and she'd been intrigued.

Taking it into the dressing room, she'd tried it on and was stunned at the vision reflected in the mirror. The cowl neck of the front draped to form a V-neckline that was lower than anything she'd ever worn before, leaving little to the imagination. The open back plunged down low, leaving her bare to the waistline, and a thin strand of small, sparkling red beads ran from one side of the dress to the other across her upper back to keep the dress from falling off. The rest of the gown fit like a silhouette, just snug enough to accentuate her curves with a slit in the skirt that ran all the way up her leg, ending a few scant inches below her hip.

It was the most revealing yet feminine outfit she'd ever put on, and she'd justified the cost of it by rationalizing how much she'd save on lingerie, which would have been impossible to wear beneath it. Her pulse raced in anticipation of what Mac might think. Would he like it? Remembering the changes he was going through and the frightening creature he could become, did she want him to?

The answer echoed as a breathless whisper in her mind. *Yes.*

Quickly showering, she got out and blow-dried her hair. Plugging in the curling iron she'd purchased, Lanie leaned closer to the mirror to check out the two tiny pin-prick marks on the side of her neck. They weren't grossly obvious, and she was able to cover them with makeup. Her lips she would paint a shiny red to match the dress—but that came last.

Smoothing perfumed lotion—also a new purchase—over her freshly shaved legs, she painted her toenails to match her lipstick.

The open-toed dress shoes she'd bought to match the dress had a higher heel than she was used to wearing, but that didn't mean much, since she normally wore flats, tennis shoes, or boots. Still, she put them on and walked around the room, trying to get used to them. It wouldn't matter how great she looked if she tripped over her own feet and fell flat on her face.

Checking the time, she saw that she was down to her final hour. Mac had still not returned, and though she knew it wouldn't take him long to shower and change, she was worried. Maybe she should have gone with him.

Trying to push her fears aside, she focused on her hair. Somehow, she didn't think leaving it loose was the way to go, but she didn't know how to fix any glamorous styles. She decided to play with it and see what she came up with.

Working her way systematically around her head, she divided her hair into sections and curled each one. She picked up her brush and then thought better of using it. She did *not* want bouffant curls. She wanted something off the neck, soft and sexy.

She crossed to the small bag containing her new earrings and pulled out another of her impulse purchases— decorative bobby pins, complete with small red rhinestones. Using the end of her comb, she lifted a strand to the top of her head and pinned it in place. She continued to pin strands to the top of her head until it was all gathered in a loose type of ponytail, with hair falling in soft curls around her head.

She gazed at her reflection critically in the mirror, turning to examine all sides. Then a slow smile spread across her face. Not bad, if she did say so herself.

The entire process had taken forty-five minutes, leaving her a total of fifteen minutes to finish dressing. Next door there was still no sound of Mac, and she was getting worried. Where was he?

She'd about convinced herself to call someone, Uncle Charles perhaps, when the phone rang.

"Hello?"

"Lanie, it's Mac. Listen, I'm sorry I'm not there—I ran into a few problems."

She knew it—she'd been right to worry. "Are you okay?"

"Yeah. Nothing I couldn't handle, but I'm running late."

"That's okay." She prayed he hadn't changed his mind altogether.

"No, it's not fair to make you wait. I called Dirk and asked him to swing by and pick you up. There's no reason for you to miss the party because I'm late. You two go, and I'll catch up with you as soon as I can."

"Oh, okay." She tried to mask her disappointment.

"Admiral Winslow will be there," he was saying. "I know he wants to visit with you."

"It'll be nice to see him again," she murmured, less than enthusiastically.

"Is everything all right?" Now *he* sounded worried, and she hadn't meant for that to happen, so she forced herself to sound positive and upbeat.

"Yes, everything's fine. I'll see you when you get there."

"You bet."

Lanie hung up the phone and crossed to the closet. It was time to put on the dress. She removed the tags with her nail clippers, and stepping out of her shoes, she unbuttoned the shirt she'd been wearing.

The material of the dress drifted over her skin like a lover's caress, sending tingles racing across her nude body.

Slipping her arms through the armholes, she adjusted the straps as best she could. As in the dressing room, she had trouble reaching the strand of beads at the back, but this time, there was no salesclerk to help her. Much as she hated to do it, she'd have to ask Dirk for help when he arrived.

Speaking of which, it was now eight o'clock. She took the new earrings from their box and put them on. The two long single strands of red crystals dangled from her ears, almost reaching her shoulders, and added the perfect touch to her outfit. She stepped into the bathroom and applied the bright red lip gloss and then examined herself one more time.

She felt self-conscious, but in a good way. Picking up her discarded clothes and other items lying around, she had just enough time to throw them on the floor of the closet before the knock sounded at the door. Glancing at the clock, she had to give Dirk credit. The man was prompt.

Taking a deep breath, she opened the door and watched with satisfaction as Dirk's mouth fell open and his eyes grew round. He quickly recovered himself, but gave her a slow, appreciative once-over. "Miss Weber? May I say you look . . ." At that point, words seemed to fail him, which caused Lanie to smile.

"Would you like to come inside?"

He gave her a lecherous smile. "No, ma'am. I think that would be an extremely bad idea."

"Let me rephrase—I need you to come inside for a moment, please."

He gave her a curious look, and after glancing up and down the hall, he stepped through the doorway and came to a stop just inside.

Turning her back to him, Lanie gestured to the beaded strand. "I need help fastening that, if you don't mind."

His fingers brushed her back as he picked up the strand to fasten it, and the contact sent more chills across her skin, causing her to consider Dirk in a whole new light. He was, after all, an attractive man, much like Mac. If she weren't so interested in Mac . . .

"There," he said, taking a step back. "Are you ready?"

"Yes." She walked over to the table where she'd set her new evening clutch and then joined him by the door, staring at him in confusion when he didn't get out of her way.

"There's a slight chill in the air," he said, as if delivering the weather forecast. "You should wear a jacket."

She gave him a funny look. "It's in the mid-eighties."

He swallowed. "The reception hall will be air-conditioned. That dress doesn't . . . look like it'll be warm enough."

"I'll be fine."

He gave up trying, offered her his arm, and escorted her down the hall. "I am so dead," she thought she heard him mumble as he followed her onto the elevator.

Mac glanced at his watch as he hurried through the corridors of the hospital. Everything he'd done today had taken longer than anticipated because all afternoon, it seemed, he'd moved in slow motion. Unfortunately, it was almost eight and he'd only just arrived at the morgue.

He'd called Lanie before going inside and knew he'd disappointed her. In retrospect, calling Dirk and asking his friend to take her to the reception might have been a mistake. Dirk had sounded a little too enthusiastic, and the

thought of them together ate at Mac, making him hurry to
finish what needed to be done.

The techs manning the morgue were away, allowing
Mac to slip inside unnoticed. Pulling the small four-inch
wooden stakes he'd purchased at the lumber store from
his backpack, he proceeded to look for the homeless men.
Not knowing which cadaver drawer held them, he systematically opened each one and checked the neck of the
body inside. Each time he spotted two puncture holes, he
hammered one of the stakes through the heart, making
sure that the top of the stake did not stick out. It was
impossible to cover the gaping hole, but at least the stake
wouldn't draw immediate attention when the body was
removed.

He only hoped that the key to killing a vampire lay in
destroying the heart, not the presence of a wooden stake,
because sooner or later, someone was bound to see the
stake and remove it.

Returning to the hotel, he went to the front desk and
found the tux that he'd ordered earlier. Taking it upstairs,
he walked into his room and immediately caught the
clean, powdery scent of perfume drifting through from
Lanie's room. Ruefully, he wondered what kind of dress
she'd found and how much of his money she'd spent.

Taking a quick shower, he ran a hand over his jaw.
He'd shaved earlier that day and thought he could stand to
do so again, but he was already so late, he decided to pass.
It took ten minutes to dress and then he was downstairs,
hailing a cab.

The ride to the reception didn't take long, and an hour
after he'd left the morgue, he was hurrying up the short
flight of stairs that led to the landing where the party was

in full swing. Musical strains from a small band drifted to him over the drone of conversation. Several couples mingled outside the great room, chatting in small groups, and he nodded to the men he recognized as he hurried past, being careful not to open his mouth too wide when he said hello. Hiding his fangs would take some getting used to, and he silently vowed to see a dentist soon about filing them down.

Stepping into the grand ballroom was an experience in sensory overload. Lights that seemed too bright to Mac shone down on at least two hundred people, some of whom were dancing in the center of the room, while others stood around, eating, drinking, laughing, and talking. Mac wondered how in the world he would ever find Dirk and Lanie in this crush of people.

Making his way toward the edge of the dance floor, he hoped to have a better view of the entire room. Dirk would be in uniform, which would distinguish him not at all from the majority of men in attendance, since this was a military affair. He thought he might have better luck looking for Lanie. He soon found that was worse because most of the women wore black gowns.

He felt his good mood deteriorate. He wondered if Dirk had his phone on him and was about to find out when a flash of red on the dance floor caught his eye. In a sea of black, the color was an attention grabber, and Mac couldn't help but look.

From his vantage point, the first thing he noticed about the woman was her bare back, provocatively framed by the drape of the dress. As her partner guided her around the dance floor, Mac noticed the long stretch of leg peeking out from the slit in the skirt. His eyes traveled upward and caught sight of her full figure before the woman disappeared from view.

Mac felt sorry for the woman's escort and hoped he was man enough to fight off the throngs of male admirers ogling her from the sidelines. There was going to be a fight before the night was out, that was certain. It was impossible to have a woman who looked like that in a room of alpha males and not expect one of them to try to establish dominance. Hell, under other circumstances, he might have been tempted to go for it himself.

He was about to resume his search for Dirk and Lanie when he noticed a young man step from the crowd, his eyes focused on the woman in red. With a sigh, Mac recognized the challenge and determination in the young man's eyes. *Let the fights begin*, he thought.

Wanting to find Lanie and Dirk before things got too out of control, he gave a final glance at the couple on the dance floor and felt the violent shock of recognition hit him.

The man facing off with the young challenger was Dirk. In stunned horror, Mac turned to look at the woman and felt his heart stop. It was Lanie.

Mac didn't know what came over him. One minute he was staring at her in stunned disbelief, the next he was standing before the young admirer, possessed by an animalistic rage.

"Bad idea," he growled at the young man, whose eyes suddenly grew wide. Mac continued to glare at him until he backed off and disappeared into the crowd. Then Mac stared angrily at the onlookers until the crowd broke and he, Dirk, and Lanie were left alone.

Then he turned on Dirk.

"About damn time you got here," Dirk snarled at him before he could say a word. "I've been doing this all evening. It's your turn. And for the record, this was your idea, remember?" He turned to Lanie. "Lanie, it's been a pleasure." With that, he gave Mac a final look, muttered "You owe me," and walked off.

Mac turned to Lanie, and even though he thought he was ready for it, the vision before him took his breath away. His eyes drank in the sight of her like a parched man who'd just been handed a cool cup of water. Though it was rude, he couldn't help raking his gaze over her, lingering longer than was polite over the generous expanse of her breasts exposed by the low neckline. The memory of her nude, in his arms, slammed into him, and for several moments he could think of nothing else.

When he finally noticed that the silence had gone on too long, he focused on her face and the faint blush kissing her checks. "You look nice."

It was so much less than he wanted to say, but about all he was capable of.

"Thank you." She offered him a tentative smile. "I'm glad you made it."

He heaved a silent, frustrated sigh as the band struck up a tune. "You're killing me, Lanie," he whispered as he pulled her into his arms to dance.

If she were to die tomorrow, she would be grateful for this moment. The look in Mac's eyes when he'd stared at her was fierce, appreciative, and primal. She found it frightening—and thrilling.

She fought the nervous laughter that bubbled up inside her. She'd wanted a reaction—and she'd gotten one.

At first, she'd thought he was angry with her, but when he held her close, she knew his anger was directed toward the other men in the room—anyone who might dare to look at her. The alpha wolf in the pack warning all the other males off with his snarl and, if necessary, his bite.

The visual of Mac biting hit too close to home, and she quickly sobered.

"How did things go at the morgue?"

"Piece of cake." He pulled her closer as he maneuvered them out of the path of another couple, but something in his tone worried her.

"So, no problems at all?"

She heard him sigh. "Only that I seemed to be in a fog all afternoon. I didn't start feeling better until dark."

She thought about it as they continued to dance, though it was hard to focus while his hand caressed the small of her back. "In a way, that makes sense. The chupacabra turns to stone during the day, going into a state of hibernation. Sunlight apparently affects you in a similar way, causing you to sleep—or at least, making you very tired."

"Beats turning into a ball of flames."

They fell silent and neither spoke for the rest of the dance. When the band finished playing and the last notes of the tune trailed off, Mac brought them to a halt. With no excuse to stay in his embrace, she reluctantly stepped back.

"I see Dirk found the admiral. They're over by the buffet. Would you mind if we went over there?"

She looked to where he indicated and saw the two. "Who's that with them?"

"Dennis Rogers."

She turned back to Mac. "The guy who came forward with testimony about Burton? I thought you said he was dead?"

"I exaggerated. Someone—Burton, I believe—tried to kill him. They failed, but Admiral Winslow thought it might be better to let them think otherwise."

"Is it safe for him to be here?"

"Probably not, but remember, they think Burton's dead and hence no longer a threat." As Mac talked, he unbuttoned his jacket and took it off. "I want you to put this on."

His request caught her off guard. "Oh, thanks, but that's okay. I'm not cold."

"Lanie, if you don't put on this jacket, I'm going to have to fight every man in here."

She stared at him, not sure if he was serious or not. "Fine." She acquiesced, not bothering to tell him it was only because she felt self-conscious wearing the dress in front of Admiral Winslow—who reminded her of her father. Let Mac think whatever he wanted.

He draped the jacket over her shoulders, and she delighted in the lingering warmth that made her feel as though he still held her close. Then he placed his hand along the small of her back and guided her toward the buffet table.

"Are you hungry?"

"A little," she admitted. "I sort of skipped dinner."

"Me, too. Let's get some food before we go over there."

He handed her a plate, taking one for himself, and as they walked along the buffet, he pointed to the various items and when she nodded, he served her. When they had all they wanted, they walked over to join Dirk, the admiral, and Rogers. Lanie didn't miss Dirk's smirk or the admiral's surprised look, which he quickly masked behind genuine pleasure at seeing her.

"Lanie, it's good to see you again. You look stunning tonight," the admiral said, giving her a hug around the plate of food. "I'm so sorry about your father. He was a good friend, and I'm going to miss him."

"Thank you," Lanie murmured, wondering how he'd take the news that her father was still alive—sort of.

"I believe you know Dirk," Admiral Winslow continued, "but let me introduce you to Dennis Rogers. He was another member of Mac's team."

"Pleasure, ma'am," Rogers said, dipping his head in a slight bow.

"Mac, I thought you were going to come by earlier today." The admiral's reprimand was gentle, but pointed.

"I ran into problems," Mac replied, his tone serious.

The admiral's smile vanished. "Could you be more specific?"

"Yes, sir. Lance Burton."

"What about him? He's dead." Rogers sounded alarmed as he looked at each of them. "Isn't he?"

"It's complicated," Mac replied.

"More so than you think," the admiral said, getting all their attention. "Patterson, Brown, and Kinsley have disappeared. Their rooms were found in shambles, and the police suspect foul play."

"When did that happen?" Mac was clearly startled by the news.

"Last night," the admiral replied.

"Who are Patterson, Brown, and Kinsley?" Lanie asked.

"They were men in our unit," Dirk answered.

Beside her, Mac's body grew tense. At first she thought he was reacting to the news, but when he cocked his head to one side, it seemed more to her as if he were listening for something, although she wasn't sure what. Then, in slow motion, he set his plate of half-eaten food on a nearby table and scanned the room. As if they communicated on an unseen wavelength, the other three men also looked around, though Lanie was sure they had no more idea what to look for than she did.

With Mac acting so strangely, her own fears rose. Wanting reassurance, she reached out to place her hand on his arm, needing to feel his strength. Without glancing at her, he covered her hand with his own.

"Mac?" This time it was Dirk asking the question, and it seemed to break the spell. Taking Lanie's forgotten plate of food from her hand, Mac set it next to his. Then he turned back to Dirk. "I don't know, but something's not right. I'm getting Lanie out of here, and then I'll be back. Keep your eyes open."

Dirk nodded.

Pulling her by the hand, Mac led her through the crowd, heading for the nearest door, which happened to be the one the waitstaff had been using all night to keep the buffet table filled with food. They had almost reached it when Mac came to an abrupt halt.

"What's wrong?" Lanie whispered, using her free hand to brace against his back to keep from running into him.

Again, he cocked his head as if he were listening and then started moving, but in a different direction this time, through the crowd toward the main doors.

Once out in the hallway, Mac didn't slow down. Lanie did her best to keep up, but his stride was longer than hers and she was wearing heels, not to mention a long skirt. When they reached the short staircase to the lower landing, she almost fell.

"Mac, slow down," she bit out, irritation pushing the fear aside. "I can't keep up." When he didn't immediately stop, she pulled back on the hand holding her.

Almost distractedly, he looked back to see what was slowing him down. Maybe it was her panting or maybe it was the glare she shot him, but instead of yanking her forward, as she expected, he stopped and came back to her side. Still holding on to her with one hand, he gently cupped her cheek with the other.

"I'm sorry, baby. Are you okay?"

"No." His endearment caught her off guard. "You're scaring me. What's going on?"

At that moment the lights flickered and went out. Lanie felt the hairs on the back of her neck prickle as alarm swept through her. She gripped Mac's hand more tightly. "Mac?" Her whisper echoed in the silence, and she opened her eyes wider, hoping to see something, anything, in the total darkness.

"Shit." Mac's muttered oath beside her was almost comforting. "I knew I should have brought my gun. Okay, put your arms through the sleeves of the jacket, so you don't have to worry about it falling off, and then hold up your skirt. We're out of here."

She felt him lift the jacket from her shoulders and help guide her hands when she couldn't find the armholes. "Thanks." She stood perfectly still, afraid to move. "I can't see a thing. How do we know which way is out?"

"No problem," he said, taking her hand. "I can see fine."

It seemed they walked a long time and Lanie, who'd been trying to keep track of where they were in the dark, was completely lost.

Suddenly the emergency lights blinked on, throwing an eerie green glow over the empty corridors. Lanie's eyes had almost adjusted when she heard the sound of women screaming and knew it had to be coming from the ballroom.

As one, they stopped.

"We have to go back," she said.

"No, it's too dangerous."

"Mac, I have to. If someone's hurt, I might be able to help."

It seemed to her that he took a long time deciding, but a part of him must have wanted to return as well, because when they started walking, it was back toward the reception.

They hadn't taken more than four or five steps, however, when a shift in the shadows stopped them. Clutching Mac's hand tighter, Lanie watched as two men stepped out of the dark.

One of them was Burton.

The other was a man Lanie had never seen before, but she was familiar with the man's pale skin and glowing eyes. This was another vampire.

No sooner had the thought formed than the two vampires rushed them. Mac, still holding Lanie's hand, tried to push her out of harm's way as he faced the men, but Burton reached him first and the punch he delivered sent Mac flying.

About to run to him, Lanie was pulled up short by the other vampire's powerful grip on her arm. He held her easily and Mac, who'd managed to get to his feet, hesitated, giving Burton time to grab him and shove him against the wall.

"Isn't this a surprise?" Burton snarled. "You know, Knight, I'm about shit full of running into you everywhere I go. You think you're going to stop me, is that it?" He gave a nasty, short laugh. "You never thought much of me, did you, Knight? Well, I've got news for you. I'm not like I was before. Death changes a man." He leaned close so that his mouth, lips curled tight and fangs protruding, was only inches from Mac's ear. "What do you think of me now?"

# Chapter
# 10

Lanie watched Mac strain to look at Burton out of the corner of his eye. Instead, his gaze locked with hers, and she knew he saw her fear. An expression of rage crossed his face, equal to the frustration she felt at not being able to help. She struggled against her captor, but he held her easily.

Then she saw something that frightened her more. Mac's eyes began to glow. In the gloom of the dimly lit hallway, they took on a reddish light—and they weren't the only pair shining like that. Two others matched his.

A growling noise, barely audible over Burton's heavy breathing, distracted her from Mac's eyes. She wondered where it came from until she realized it, too, came from Mac. Almost before her eyes, he seemed to gather his anger inside him until it burst forth. He pushed away from the wall, catching Burton off guard so that he fell back a step. In one fluid motion, Mac spun around and slammed his fist into Burton's face. The impact of that blow was so great that even after Burton hit the floor, he slid for several feet until Lanie lost sight of him behind the man holding her.

Whipping her gaze back to Mac, she found him standing a few feet away, his lips curling back to reveal his newly formed fangs. In the face of such obvious rage and promise of carnage to come, the hands holding her tightened as they dragged her back a step.

"Let her go." Mac's tone sounded lethal as he glared at the vampire clutching her.

In the distance, she heard the faint sound of running footsteps, but knew whoever it was wouldn't be able to help. This was not a battle between mere mortals. This was something more.

No sooner had she finished the thought than Mac rushed them, moving faster than her eyes could follow. One second he was several feet away; the next he'd grabbed hold of her arm and spun her from the other vampire's grip with one hand as he plowed his fist into the man's face.

When everything slowed, Mac was still holding her hand and gazing at her with such a wild intensity, she no longer knew who was more dangerous—Mac or the two vampires.

He stood with his back to them, temporarily blocking her view, yet she knew he was aware of every move they made. Finally releasing her, he turned to face them.

Lanie heard Mac's growl begin low in his throat, and though she could no longer see his face, she imagined his lips curling back farther and the two front fangs gleaming in the greenish light of the hallway. She saw Burton's feral smile fade and his eyes widen—and thought that he'd finally noticed the change in Mac.

The sound of running footsteps, louder now, came to a stop not far away. "Nobody move," Dirk's voice shouted.

Burton glared at Mac. "This isn't over."

Then in a blur of movement too fast to track, the two vampires were gone.

Lanie had a clear view of Dirk down the hall, his gun still pointed at Mac, though she could tell the sudden disappearance of Burton and the other man troubled him. As he drew closer, she waited for him to lower his gun, but he didn't.

"Put the gun away, Dirk." Mac's voice sounded rough.

"I don't think so. Lanie, step back."

Not sure why Dirk was acting that way, Lanie moved closer to Mac. "What are you doing? You can't shoot Mac."

"What's going on here?"

Lanie's focus had been on Dirk, but at his words, she turned to look at the man beside her and saw the problem. Mac looked less like himself and more like the proverbial creature of the night, fangs protruding and eyes glowing a dull orange.

Although half afraid of him herself, Lanie took the step that put her in the path of Dirk's bullet. "I can't let you shoot him, Dirk. He's not like they are, no matter what he looks like now."

She stood very still, hardly daring to breathe, while the two men contemplated each other over her shoulder. When it seemed the silent battle would go on forever, she lost her fear and grew impatient. "Oh, for God's sake. Put the gun away. And you"—she swung around to face Mac—"you need to calm down because you're scaring everyone. Right now."

Mac turned those orange eyes on her, and for a moment

she wondered if she'd been wrong about him. Maybe he was too far gone and she should have let Dirk shoot him. Then his lips relaxed and she thought she saw the hint of a smile. The relief that swept through her left her feeling weak.

When Mac's arms came up to envelop her, she went into them willingly, resting her head against his chest and wrapping her arms about his waist. He felt so strong and capable. It was hard to reconcile the vampirelike creature he'd been a few seconds ago to the caring, warm man who now stood stroking her back and whispering words of comfort. She felt him press a kiss to the top of her head before his arms pulled her a little closer.

"Someone mind telling me what in the hell is going on here?" Dirk's voice sounded closer. "Sorry, Mac. Just being careful."

Mac shifted her to one side so he could shake Dirk's hand. "I wouldn't have it any other way," Mac's deep voice rumbled in his chest beneath Lanie's head. "I'll explain everything, but later. What happened back at the reception hall?"

"They killed Rogers."

Lanie wiped the tears from her eyes and turned to stare at Dirk. "Oh, no."

"How?" Mac asked. Lanie knew he was wondering if he'd have to find a way to stake the body, to keep it from rising. He needn't have worried.

"When the emergency lights came back on, I found him on the floor with a table knife planted in his chest. They had to have come in through the kitchen, to do it so fast. Otherwise, there would have been too many people to get past. When they ran, I tried to follow, but lost them.

Then I heard the sound of voices and followed them here."

Lanie knew Dirk had questions about what he'd seen, but he'd wait until later for his answers.

"Who was that other vamp . . ." She cast a quick glance at Dirk. "Who was that other man?"

"Munoz," Dirk replied. "Hector Munoz."

"He one of yours?" Mac asked.

"Recent transfer. He's the one who disappeared in the jungle while everyone was out looking for Burton. Guess now we know what happened—he was working for Burton and went AWOL."

Lanie suspected there was more to it than that, but that conversation could also wait until later. They started walking back to the reception room, with Lanie still tucked beneath Mac's arm as he and Dirk talked.

"How's the admiral?" Mac asked.

"I think shaken, but you'd never know it. He immediately took command of the situation. I left him issuing orders."

They walked into the grand ballroom to find it mostly empty. The band had packed and left, and the waitstaff was decidedly somber as they stood around, wondering what to do. A noise outside the door caught Lanie's attention and when she turned, she saw that the police had arrived.

Efforts had already been made by the guests to preserve the crime scene. What would happen, Lanie wondered, when they discovered that the prints on the knife belonged to a dead man?

She looked around the room, unable to stop herself, knowing she wouldn't find what she searched for. The

one familiar face she would have liked to see again was
not there. It was probably just as well. She didn't like the
thought of her father being mixed up with Burton and his
schemes.

The police interviewed the remaining guests and when
it was their turn, Mac answered all the questions, avoiding
any mention of Burton and Munoz by saying that he and
Lanie had left the party early to be alone and then been
trapped in the hallway when the lights went out. There
was nothing the police could do about Burton and Munoz
anyway. It was something that he, with Dirk's help, would
have to take care of.

When they were finally allowed to leave, Dirk accom-
panied them back to their hotel. Once inside Mac's room,
Lanie, still wearing Mac's jacket, kicked off her shoes and
sat in the chair with her legs curled under her while Mac
and Dirk got comfortable, taking off their ties and unbut-
toning the collars of their shirts. Then Mac produced the
bottle of tequila.

He poured out three equal glasses, handed one to Dirk
and carried the other to Lanie. For several minutes, they
drank in silence. Mac felt the other two watching him and
could almost guess their thoughts. Dirk wanted to know
what was going on, but he wasn't going to waste his time
guessing if Mac already had an explanation. He'd wait until
Mac was ready to share—no matter how long that took.

Lanie, on the other hand, was probably wondering
how much of his humanity he'd lost in the confrontation
with Burton. Mac wasn't sure he had a satisfactory
answer for either one of them, but he knew it was Lanie's
question that he dreaded the most.

Taking a seat on the bed so he could lean back against the headboard, Mac took another swallow of the tequila and let the warmth seep down his throat. Finally, he looked at Dirk. "I'm not exactly sure where to start."

"How about with how Burton faked his own death," Dirk said.

"He didn't," Mac replied.

"Come again."

"Burton was killed by a creature called . . ."

"El Chupacabra," Lanie supplied when he hesitated. "It was in the cage at the facility."

Dirk shook his head. "I was out there. The only thing I saw in the cage was—"

"The stone gargoyle statue," Mac finished for him. "That was it. Don't ask me how it's possible, because I don't know. During the day, it turns to stone. At night, it's alive and trying to suck the blood from your body."

Dirk glanced first at Mac's face and then at Lanie's, no doubt trying to judge whether they were telling him the truth. Mac remembered how hard it was for him to accept when Lanie first tried to explain it to him.

"So you're telling me this thing killed Burton and Lanie's father." Dirk waited until they nodded before continuing on. "Then who was that I saw tonight, because it looked like Lance Burton to me."

"It was."

This was the part that Mac hated to explain. He was grateful when Lanie jumped in.

"El Chupacabra's fangs are hollow, and it secretes venom into the prey when it bites them. The venom mixes with the blood and seems to have certain healing powers in humans." She paused, and Mac knew she was about to drop the first shoe. "When El Chupacabra drinks so much blood that it kills a human, it has also injected enough venom into the human that they are able to come back to life a couple of days later." She paused and then dropped the other shoe. "As vampires."

Dirk gave a nervous laugh. "Yeah, right." He glanced from one face to the other, no doubt waiting for someone to tell him it was a joke.

"I didn't believe it either, at first," Mac admitted.

"Yeah, but come on. Vampires?"

"You remember the security recording? That was Burton and Weber—*after* they were dead—biting those men and drinking their blood."

"Vampires?" There was less laughter this time.

"And the men they killed rose a few days later as—"

"Vampires." There was no humor now in Dirk's tone, only skepticism.

"Didn't you wonder why all those researchers' bodies I asked you to burn had been staked through the heart, except for the one with its head blown off?"

Dirk glared at him. "I thought you were working through some anger issues. Didn't seem like a good time to ask a lot of questions, if you know what I mean." He heaved a sigh, ignoring the look Mac shot him. "Okay. Let's say, for the sake of argument, that I buy into this vampire theory—that explains why Burton and Weber are vampires. What about Munoz?"

"You told me you found his shirt, ripped and bloodied," Lanie said. "I think he must have found Burton and the chupacabra first." She turned thoughtful. "I think the chupacabra killed him, not Burton."

The two men stared at her and she quickly went on. "From what I've read, the creature that arises when a vampire kills a human is one step further removed from his humanity than the creature that results when a chupacabra kills a human. The vampire-created creature is, one assumes, less in control of his actions. Munoz seemed to know what he was doing at the reception hall. That's why I think it was the chupacabra that killed him."

It seemed logical to Mac, and his assessment of Lanie rose yet another notch.

"So what's the story with you?" Dirk asked finally, staring pointedly at Mac.

He'd expected the question, but wasn't sure how to respond. "The best theory we've"—he pointed to Lanie and himself—"been able to come up with is that when the chupacabra attacked me, it injected enough venom into my system that I was affected. The restorative powers helped me heal at a much faster rate."

"But there have been other changes," Dirk pressed.

"Yeah."

"What are they? The teeth, obviously," Dirk said, gazing at Mac closely. "I saw that back at the reception hall, and your eyes, they were glowing. What else?"

"I guess speed and strength," Mac replied. "Although I don't know how I compare to the vampires. We've yet to have a real showdown between us. Oh, and a sensitivity to light."

"But you can go out during the day." It was a statement, not a question. "I saw you at the airfield when you came by to make arrangements to have your plane brought over."

"I can go outside," Mac agreed, "but I'm definitely more tired during the day, and I have trouble functioning. At night, though, I'm full of energy."

"What about Burton and Weber? Can *they* go out in the day, or will they torch up like in the movies?"

Dirk was looking at Mac, who turned to Lanie. She shook her head. "We don't know the answer to that yet."

"Vampires drink blood, don't they?" Dirk continued. "I saw it on the tape. What about you?"

Mac exchanged a quick look with Lanie, who blushed and seemed to become preoccupied with studying the glass in her hand. He sighed as a fresh wave of guilt hit him. "I don't know."

Dirk stared at him, his eyes narrowing. "How safe are we"—he pointed to Lanie and himself—"in your presence?"

Mac fought his irritation because he'd already proved with Lanie that it was a valid question. "I don't think you need to stake me just yet, but I trust you'll know if the time comes." He'd sounded sarcastic, but knew Dirk would take the statement literally.

Silence fell as they each became lost in private thoughts. When Mac finally glanced around, he noticed the glasses were empty. He knew he could use a refill because what he'd had so far wasn't helping much. He climbed off the bed and grabbed the tequila bottle, refilling Dirk's glass. When he crossed the room to offer some to Lanie, she shook her head.

"What about something else to drink?" he offered. "Water? Coffee?"

"No, thanks. I'm fine."

He smiled. "Lanie, you can barely keep your eyes open. Why don't you go to bed?"

She sat up straighter and scowled at him. "I'm fine, really."

Mac decided not to push. Instead, he poured himself a drink and sat back down.

"Mac, what happened at the reception?" Lanie asked.

He stared at her, confused. Then he realized that she was referring to what had happened before Burton and Munoz had appeared. "It's hard to explain. Suddenly I felt this tingling along my spine, a sense of foreboding. I don't know. I can't explain it."

"But it was strong enough that you felt we needed to leave."

He studied Lanie's face, wondering what she was getting at. "Yes."

She waved a hand dismissively. "I don't know what it means. I just thought it was curious. There was something else I wondered about. Why did Burton stab Rogers?"

"Probably because Rogers is the one who came forward and got this whole inquiry going. Burton felt that Rogers betrayed him and wanted a little payback."

Lanie shook her head. "I mean, why stab him? Why not bite him and drink his blood?"

"Not enough time," Mac said.

"Okay," Lanie said. "That makes sense. But what about those other men—the ones Uncle Charles mentioned?"

"You think Burton's responsible for their disappearance?" Dirk asked.

"I'm wondering what these three men had in common—other than that they were all former unit members."

Mac thought about it, thinking that he might know, finally, where she was headed. "When we were on that last assignment, they served on Burton's team."

"So they were loyal to Burton?" she asked.

Mac glanced at Dirk. "I guess you could say that."

"Do you think they would have testified against Burton?"

"No," Dirk said. "They wouldn't have said anything, but I wouldn't put it past Burton to kill a friend."

"Exactly," Lanie said, sounding much more awake and excited. "He's not above killing his friends, but if he wanted them dead, he would have stabbed them—or shot them. With his training and background, I would imagine he could kill a man any number of ways—and leave the body to be found. But he didn't do that."

"What are you suggesting?" Mac asked.

"Okay, I know this sounds far-fetched, but I think Burton killed his friends or, rather, had the chupacabra kill them, because he wanted to convert them into vampires, just as he had converted Munoz."

Mac met her gaze, but his mind raced ahead. There was no point in asking why Burton would do something like that because he already knew. Burton was creating his own vampire special-ops team—a group of highly trained, lethally dangerous former soldiers who would be exceptionally hard to kill, because they were already dead.

# Chapter
# 11

Lanie could tell by the expressions on the men's faces that they'd come to the same conclusion she had. Burton was creating his own special-ops vampire team, and there was no telling what terror and destruction such a group could inflict. Someone had to stop them, and Lanie had a sinking feeling she knew who would volunteer for the job.

"We'll have to get to Burton before he has a chance to make his next move," Mac said to Dirk, proving Lanie right. With their SEAL background, she knew they thought they could take on any threat. Maybe they could.

"You think he's finished building his team?" Dirk asked.

"I don't know," Mac admitted. "He's got four now, but there's no guarantee his three latest recruits will join him. If it was me, I'd want to up my odds, give myself more of a selection. How many from the original team are still in town—or live close by?"

Dirk thought for a minute. "Four—Perkins, Smith, Couch, and Harris."

Mac rubbed his face as if he was tired, and Lanie supposed with sunrise not far off, he probably was. He wasn't the only one, she realized as a yawn stole over her.

"I don't think Couch and Perkins are the type of men Burton wants," Mac said. "Their loyalty was to the team, not to Burton specifically. Smith and Harris are probably better candidates."

Lanie saw Dirk nod in agreement while Mac glanced at his watch.

"I doubt Burton will try anything more tonight— it's almost dawn. So far, I've never seen them out during the day. They got more of the chupacabra venom than I did. If the sun doesn't destroy them, it probably makes them so lethargic that they can't function. We'll start tomorrow."

"What about Uncle Charles?" Lanie asked. "Shouldn't we tell him what's going on?"

Mac shook his head. "I think it would be better, for now, if we tried to handle this ourselves."

"I agree," Dirk said. "I'll get the addresses of where Smith and Harris are staying. After that, it's just a matter of waiting for Burton to appear."

Mac nodded, but Lanie was confused. "How do you know which man he'll go after?"

"We don't," Dirk replied. "So we're going to split up and watch both places."

"Watch? Aren't you going to call and warn these guys?"

Mac and Dirk exchanged looks, and she knew she wasn't going to like the answer.

"If we warn them, then they might say or do something to cause Burton to change his plans. If we don't stop him soon, he could do a lot more damage than killing one or two people," Mac explained.

"Besides, our plan is to get to them before Burton attacks," Dirk added.

"With each of you going to a different man's house?" Lanie couldn't believe they were going to try to take on Burton *and* the chupacabra alone. She looked to Mac for confirmation and he nodded.

"What are you going to do?" she went on sarcastically. "Sit outside their hotel rooms on the chance that Burton and the creature will show up and then run in with guns blazing?"

"Exactly—guns, plural," Mac replied. "And if you mean by blazing—a focused assault designed to terminate with extreme prejudice—then yes."

Dirk laughed. "Sounds good to me."

They exasperated her because they sounded like boys eager for their first hunting trip. "Well, I'm going with you."

The laughter stopped as both men turned to stare at her, twin patronizing expressions on their faces.

"I'm serious," she added defiantly.

"You're going home," Mac said in a flat tone.

"No, I'm not—and you can't make me." Now who sounded like a child?

"Lanie, I really think Mac's right. You should go home. Things are going to get a lot worse," Dirk said.

"I don't care. My father is here in this city, and I'm not going back to Houston until I find him."

"We don't need to worry about you while we're hunting for Burton," Dirk insisted.

Lanie turned to Mac and let him see the determination in her eyes. After a moment he heaved a labored sigh, although a wry smile touched his lips. "Okay."

"Okay?" Dirk pinned Mac with a hard stare.

"Yeah. She's right, we can't make her go back, and I'd rather know where she is than have her running around town behind our backs."

"She's going to be a distraction—one that could be costly," Dirk argued.

"Hello? *She* is still in the room. Would you mind not talking about me as if I'm not sitting right here?" She received silent, reproachful looks from the men, which only frustrated her further. "So what's our next move?"

Dirk rolled his eyes and stood up. "I'm outta here." He set his empty glass on the bedside table beside Mac, leaning close so he could mutter in Mac's ear. "She needs to stay behind."

"We'll talk about it tomorrow," Mac replied.

Dirk nodded and walked out of the room.

After the door closed, Lanie became acutely aware that she and Mac were alone. When she looked at him, she found him watching her with a heated look in his eyes that was so intense, she was reminded of the near-vampire creature he'd become when he'd faced Burton and Munoz earlier that night. That man had fought to protect her, a small voice in her head whispered. Did she really have anything to be afraid of now?

She didn't know—and what was worse, while a part of her wanted to run to the safety of her room and hide, another part wanted to play with fire.

"Go to bed, Lanie." His voice sounded huskier than normal.

She nodded, unfolding her legs to stand. She set her empty glass on the desk and headed for her room. "Good night, Mac," she said when she paused at the connecting doorway. "Thank you for tonight." She wasn't sure what she was thanking him for exactly—taking her to the reception, saving her from the vampires—or maybe something else altogether.

He merely nodded, though his eyes watched her closely.

She went into her room and closed the door, mentally kicking herself for playing it safe. Then she realized that she still wore his jacket *and* needed his help with the dress. Fate, it seemed, had made the decision for her.

She reopened the connecting door and stepped through, finding Mac with a freshly poured glass of tequila, standing by the desk. When he saw her, he paused with the glass held suspended halfway to his mouth and his eyes widened briefly in surprise.

"I forgot to give you back your jacket," she quickly explained.

He schooled his expression and gestured to the bed. "Leave it there."

She took it off and laid it on the bed, enjoying the way his gaze played over her. "I also need your help." She walked toward him in slow, easy steps, stopping just in front of him. She turned so her back was to him, and gestured vaguely with her hand. "I can't reach the fastening—would you mind?"

He didn't say anything, and it seemed she stood there a long time before she finally felt the back of his hand brush against her skin. It wasn't an accidental touch. It was a purposeful caress down the length of her back, and it sent tiny shivers through her entire body. She couldn't stop the sigh that escaped her.

She heard his quick intake of breath and then his fingers worked the fastener and disposed of it quickly, but when he might have dropped his hands, he didn't. Instead, his palms grazed her skin as he ran his hands across her back and up beneath the straps of her dress, easing them off her shoulders. Without the beaded strand to hold it in place, the entire dress slid down to puddle at her feet. She felt the warmth of Mac's mouth as he pressed it to the curve of her neck. With one hand holding her shoulder as if she might try to escape, his other slipped around to cup her breast, testing the weight of it in his palm.

His thumb flicked across her nipple, provoking another sigh, and she let her head fall back against his chest, closing her eyes so she could focus on the feel of his touch.

"I tried so hard to let you walk away," he whispered against her ear, his warm breath teasing the hypersensitive skin of her neck. "You shouldn't have come back in."

Before she could respond, he turned her around and pulled her to him, one arm supporting her back as he buried the fingers of his other hand deep in her hair. Slowly, he brought her head closer to his until their lips touched. The kiss started out slow and easy, but quickly grew to a fevered intensity. Mac kissed her with quiet desperation—and that was how she responded. Everything faded from her perception except for this single moment in time, and she clung to him as if her very life depended on it.

The sharp stab of pain on her lip startled her, and she tasted a familiar coppery liquid on her tongue that brought reality crashing down with a harshness that left her shaken.

She'd cut herself on his fangs and knew that he'd also tasted the blood. For a minute they froze with mouths tightly pressed together. Then Mac pulled back and when Lanie opened her eyes, she saw the look of regret and horror on his face.

"Go to your room, Lanie." He stepped away from her and turned around. The anguish in his voice almost broke her heart and she reached out a hand, wanting to soothe him, assure him that she wasn't hurt. The moment she touched him, he whipped back to face her, his eyes glowing red and his lips thinned to reveal his fangs, a drop of her blood still clinging to the tip of one.

Frightened, she stumbled back, almost tripping over her gown pooled around her ankles, unaware of her nudity as her entire attention focused on the creature before her. How much humanity *had* he lost?

Seeing her reaction, Mac cursed under his breath, the words sounding more like a hiss. Then, moving with inhuman speed, he rushed past her and Lanie was left alone, watching the door to the room slowly close.

Elsewhere in the city, Lance Burton paced the length of the basement, occasionally pausing long enough to slam his fist into the wall. Already, several holes marred the surface, but no one would care. The building they'd found to stay in had been condemned years ago. No one came there now, not even the homeless.

"Damn it, I should have killed him," Lance swore. "Straight off when I had the chance."

Hector Munoz stood patiently in the corner, rubbing his jaw. "I thought you said he'd be easy to handle."

"He's changed." The question in Lance's mind was—what had happened to Knight that had caused him to change? It was a mystery, and Lance didn't like mysteries.

He strode out of the room and down the length of the hallway, knowing that Hector followed him. Not many knew it, but he and Hector had been childhood friends. He was glad when Hector found them in the jungle that night; happy with his decision to have the chupacabra kill his friend. Not only did it prove, beyond doubt, the professor's theory that humans killed by chupacabras turned into vampires, but it gave Lance another like himself—a member of the undead who had a military background. Hector, he knew, would follow orders.

He gazed at the three bodies at his feet—Patterson, Brown, and Kinsley. They'd rise on the following night, and he'd know then whether they would be equally obedient.

"Stay with them, and I'll go see how the good professor did tonight."

He didn't wait for Hector to answer, but left the room and retraced his steps down the hallway, this time going to the opposite end. Walking into the last room, he found the professor fussing over the two creatures and rolled his eyes at the sight. The professor treated the things as if they were his children.

"Were you successful?" Lance asked without pre-amble.

The professor didn't jump, and Lance knew he'd felt him coming through the mind link they shared.

"Yes. I collected twenty bags tonight, and tomorrow we should do even better. As the word gets around, we'll have homeless lining up from all over the city to sell us their blood." The professor sounded tired, which Lance attributed to the coming of dawn.

"Fine." He glanced at his watch. It was only 3:00 A.M. There was still plenty of time, if he moved quickly, which he was quite capable of doing. "I'll get more money and supplies." It would be so much easier, he thought, to just lure the homeless to them and feed until they were dead, but he didn't want their bodies lying around, rotting and stinking up the joint, and he couldn't very well dump them elsewhere. The last thing he needed was to leave a trail of corpses for Knight to follow.

Part of him wondered if he'd received enough of the creature's venom to be able to convert the dead into vampires himself, as the professor had once suggested, but didn't think so. He and the professor had killed those men in Taribu and then later, after they'd arrived in D.C. and Hector rose, the three of them had fed off several homeless men. He thought that if any of the deceased had risen, he'd have heard about it by now—and so far he'd heard nothing.

He turned his thoughts back to more pressing matters. Getting money to pay the homeless was easy—for now. All he had to do was hit the nearest ATM machine. He'd never married and had no family. There was no one to mourn his passing and, more important to his immediate needs, no one to notify the bank and close his account.

Getting the blood bags and supplies was more difficult. He'd have to sneak into a different hospital this time to steal more. Soon, though, he'd have the help he needed. He wouldn't have to do everything himself.

He walked over to where several filled blood bags lay stacked on a small side table and stared at them. "I thought you said you collected twenty bags," he said, doing a quick count and coming up with twenty-five. "Where'd the extra come from?"

"I found a couple of stray dogs roaming the alley, so I filled a few extra bags—for the chupas."

Lance picked up a bag containing blood that appeared a little darker than the others and flipped it over. The word *dog* was written in pen on the label. The adult chupacabra, lying on the floor near him, lifted its head and peered up at him.

*Hunger.*

He glared at the creature and dropped the bag back onto the table. "I'll let you know when you can eat again," he told it.

"It's not healthy for her to ingest so much human blood," the professor argued. "In fact, I think it may have already caused some damage. I don't think she's well."

"Then you'd better hurry and find that substitute for the venom, hadn't you?" He glared at the professor a moment longer, then turned to the creature. *Follow me.* He ignored the professor's disapproving look and the way the creature seemed to turn to the professor for help. So far, the creature had not refused a direct command, and he wondered if there would ever come a time when it would. Like most things in nature, it was the strongest who prevailed, and Lance was determined that he would be the strongest.

He directed the creature to a remote room some distance away and told it to wait for him. There was one last thing he needed to do. He left the creature and returned to where Hector stood watching the others. With dawn so close, he saw the other man's eyelids fighting to stay up.

"Come on, my friend. It will be dawn soon, and I'm sure you're tired. It's time for you to rest. I have a room for you."

Hector followed him out and as they walked, Lance sent the other man images of moving down the hall to a nearby room while, in fact, he led the man up a flight of stairs to a room on the upper landing. Finding the room he'd prepared earlier, Lance walked in and gestured to the pallet on the floor. "This is for you."

A puzzled expression crossed Hector's face as he looked at it. "You don't want to sleep here?"

"No. I still have a few things to do before I find my rest. Sleep well. I'll see you at dusk, and we will decide then what to do about Knight."

Hector nodded and crawled onto the pallet. Lance felt a moment's guilt wash over him but quickly squelched it before the emotion leaked out and the other man picked up on it. Lance walked out of the room and headed back to where the chupa waited for him, a little thrill of excitement coursing through him. The professor had proved very helpful in answering a lot of questions about this new state of their existence, but there was one question to which neither of them had an answer. What happened if they were exposed to full sunlight?

Lance's military background required him to know all his weaknesses before going into battle, and that's what he intended to do. Hector would be asleep soon—might even be asleep already—and would not notice the slats missing from the room's window. He wouldn't realize that when the sun rose in a couple of hours, it would shine fully onto the pallet. In Lance's mind, Hector's inability to notice the trap was one of the reasons he was expendable. Lance would not tolerate any disobedience or weakness on his team.

Lance smiled to himself as he strode into the room where the adult creature awaited him. It eyed him cautiously, but did not approach. Lance had discovered, quite by accident when the creature had attacked him a second time, that he grew stronger with each infusion of venom. He was determined, now, to be the strongest of his kind—the strongest and most powerful of all vampires.

He called the creature to him and bent his neck. It was impossible for the creature to "kill" him, but still, he had to quell the tiny spurt of fear that raced through him just before the creature lowered its head and pierced his throat with its teeth.

He felt unconsciousness pulling at him, but knew that tomorrow night, he would rise again, stronger than before—

and when he did, he'd go check on Hector—or what was left of him.

Dr. Clinton Weber stroked the head of the baby chupacabra, all too aware of what Lance was doing in the next room. The man was crazy, in the worst possible sense, and part of Clint worried that the psychosis had not been there before, but was a result of the chupacabra's attack, for which he felt directly responsible.

That was one of the reasons he'd stayed with Lance— he hoped to find a cure for him. He'd convinced Lance that they needed to study the chupacabra's venom and possibly duplicate it. Lance had gone along with the suggestion, helping Clint to purchase and steal the supplies needed for a crude lab. They'd even secured a generator to provide the electricity off which they ran the various appliances and machines. Clint had been impressed with how resourceful Lance was—and how quickly he'd been able to secure the things Clint needed.

Clint's intentions in studying the venom were different from Lance's, however. Clint was hoping to analyze the venom for its healing and restorative properties. Perhaps the cure for cancer and AIDs, even their own vampire state, lay within it.

Lance, on the other hand, was interested in the venom for the special powers it gave him—the increased speed and strength, the incredible night vision, control over the chupacabras, immortality. He didn't seem to mind the price they paid in return—surviving only on blood, giving up the sunlight and their humanity. Clint fought nightly to hold on to the latter, worried that it would fade completely before he finished his work.

The baby chupacabra nuzzled the palm of his hand, and Clint realized that he'd stopped scratching the creature's head. "You like that, do you, Gem?" He smiled down at her and knew there'd been another reason he'd stayed with Lance. He'd wanted to study the creatures further. Now he felt a need to save them from Lance's abuse. Their systems were not designed to live off human blood. They could tolerate it in small doses, but Lance had been feeding the adult chupa a steady diet of human blood—specifically, the blood of the men he'd chosen to convert into vampires like himself.

Already, Clint saw deterioration in the health of the adult. He knew he had to do something to help her, and finding a synthetic venom seemed the only solution, but he worried that he might find it too late.

He gave the small chupa a final scratch, feeling the lethargy of the coming dawn slowing his thought processes as well as his physical movements. There was time, he thought, to recheck his earlier tests.

He crossed to the small refrigerator, opened the door, and pulled out two tiny vials, not for the first time grateful that Lance knew nothing about biochemistry. He set the vials in a test tube holder while he gathered the rest of what he needed.

Pulling the stopper out of the first vial, he took a dropper and extracted a small amount of liquid, which he squeezed onto a microscope slide. Then he took one of the bags of blood and, using a syringe, drew a small amount of blood from it, which he then added to the liquid on the slide. Though he'd not told Lance yet, he'd managed to create artificial venom that matched the chupa's in every way—except one. The venom contained a substance he'd never seen before, and it was that which stabilized it.

Peering through the microscope, he watched as the cells in the sample started to change shape, growing larger and healthier. Everything looked much as his own blood now did under a microscope—until he tapped the slide with his finger. The slight vibration from his finger caused a disturbance among the cells, which suddenly started to burst. Clint shook his head. The artificial venom was unstable, and he couldn't figure out why.

Sighing, he wiped the slides clean and placed them in the plastic tub of glassware to be washed later. Getting out another slide, he once again placed a drop of venom on it. This time, though, he added a drop of liquid from the second vial. He looked through the eyepiece of the microscope and watched the tiny cells of the second liquid gather around the larger venom cells. Soon, the larger cells were completely surrounded. As Clint watched, the smaller cells started to pulse as they attacked the larger cells. Within a second, the activity on the slide ended and the venom cells were gone.

Clint removed the slide, satisfied with the results. The antiserum had totally denatured the chupa's venom. Now came the real test. Picking up a sterile needle, he stabbed his finger. It took a lot of squeezing to generate the single drop of blood, which he gingerly placed in the center of the slide. He picked up the dropper and allowed one drop of the antiserum to fall and mix with the blood. He used the end of the needle to stir the two together and then placed the slide on the microscope.

The cells of his blood were healthy and plump, but as he watched, the tiny cells of the antiserum moved in as they had on the earlier slide. There was a flurry of microscopic activity, and when the attacking cells finally quieted and drifted apart, the blood cells were gone—completely destroyed.

As he disposed of the slide and stored the vials in the refrigerator once again, he thought about the implications of the antiserum. If injected into a vampire, the antiserum would attack and destroy all the chupa's venom in the vampire's bloodstream; venom that now resided in the vampire's blood cells, sustaining life and providing immortality.

Clint presumed that the lack of venom would result in the vampire's permanent demise, although without actually injecting it into a vampire, he couldn't verify that. Images of him injecting Lance flitted through his mind and were quickly followed by the image of Lance killing him when the antiserum proved ineffective. If he died before he perfected the solution, all would be lost.

Just then, a noise at the door drew his attention. Clint turned and saw the adult chupa drag herself into the room, Lance's blood still dripping from her mouth. He watched her walk across the room and settle down next to the baby. He fetched a bag of dog's blood and held it so she could drink from it, hoping it would dilute the effects of the human blood. He wasn't sure if it worked, but she seemed grateful for it.

Fatigue now beat at him, and he knew the time was near. He lay down beside the two chupas and absently stroked them, his thoughts turning to his daughter. He missed her and was sorry for the worry and heartache she had suffered because of him. When he'd seen her in Taribu, he'd not wanted to leave, but he'd been too afraid of what Lance would do to her if he had refused. Now he felt that his only hope of seeing her again lay in helping Lance—or in destroying him.

Though he couldn't see it, Clint sensed the sun rising in the sky and just before he lost consciousness, he felt the cool texture of stone beneath his fingers.

# Chapter
# 12

Lanie woke, glanced at the clock, and saw that it was already four in the afternoon. She was starting to feel like a vampire herself, sleeping all day and up all night. It wasn't a hard adjustment, she thought. She was already used to being up at night because of her work with the fire department.

Thinking of it, she realized that she needed to make a couple of phone calls. Climbing out of bed, she walked to the connecting doors. They were open a crack, and peeking into the other room, she spotted Mac still in bed. She didn't know how long he'd sleep, but she decided not to wake him. Instead, she closed the door to her room and crossed to the desk, where she found the room-service menu and quickly placed an order. She was starving and wasn't going to start another new "night" without something substantial to eat. As a last-minute decision, she ordered extra for Mac. Then she set about brewing a pot of coffee because she needed the caffeine rush to jump-start her brain.

She showered while it brewed, and by the time she was dressed and the coffee was done, her food had arrived. She signed the bill, tipped the delivery guy, and then sat down to enjoy a nice normal meal in silence. She didn't even turn on the TV, too afraid there'd be another story about what the media were now referring to as the "vampire" murders. If they only knew how close they were to the truth.

When she finished her meal, she called the library in Houston and talked to her boss, briefly telling her that there had been problems surrounding her father's death and she was now in Washington, D.C., helping to sort them out. Once again, her boss had been understanding and told her to take as much time as she needed, but Lanie knew her vacation time was running out. Pretty soon, she'd have to go back or risk losing her job. At least it was summer and there were enough students looking for summer work to help out, so the library wasn't suffering from her absence.

Next she called the fire station and talked to one of the guys. She told him an equally vague story and asked him to pull her name off the roster until further notice. He assured her that while things had been busy, they were managing. She promised to call as soon as she was back in town and hung up the phone.

Guilt hit her. They needed her help back home, and she was refusing to return because she wanted to stay here—where Mac and Dirk didn't need, or want, her help. Not that she could blame them. After all, what could *she* do?

She wasn't specially trained like they were—all she knew was first aid, fires, and research.

That was it! She found her father's laptop and set it up on the desk, plugging it into the data port. She called the front desk and made the necessary arrangements for accessing the Internet. She was soon so absorbed in her work that she didn't hear the connecting door open an hour later.

"What are you doing?"

She looked up and felt her cheeks burn at the sight of Mac standing in the doorway between the two rooms. He'd pulled on his jeans but hadn't bothered with either socks or a shirt, and Lanie struggled not to stare. He looked disheveled with his hair mashed down in places and at least two days' growth of beard covering his jaw. Lanie thought he'd never looked better.

"Hi." She glanced down at her screen, afraid he might see how much the sight of him affected her. "I wanted to help, so I thought I'd see what I could find on the Internet that might be of use."

"You did, did you?" He gave her a lazy smile as he walked toward her, and there was no hint of his earlier limp to mar his easy gait or the enticing motion of his hips. The memory of those hips pressed against her almost pulled a sigh from her.

As if sensing her thoughts, he came to stand behind her, resting his hands on her shoulders as he bent his head close to hers in order to look at the screen. Then he turned to her. "What did you find?"

She felt herself drowning in the depths of his eyes and had to blink several times in order to break the spell. "I'm sorry, what did you say?"

He smiled, and she sat enthralled as he leaned closer still. It was a gentle kiss, not meant to seduce or arouse— though it did both. Lanie closed her eyes and focused all her attention on the warm, tender feel of his lips, his tongue brushing against hers. After a moment, the kiss ended and he pulled back, licked his lips, and smiled. "Is that coffee I taste?"

"Yes." She managed a smile and pointed to the bar. "There's extra, if you'd like some. Also, I ordered room service earlier and took the liberty of ordering something for you as well. It's in the microwave."

He cocked an eyebrow at her, and she got the impression that he was pleased. He poured himself a cup of coffee, which she noticed he took black, and after he took a sip, he opened the microwave door and looked inside. Then he gave her a surprised yet pleased smile and pulled out his steak, bloodred in the center, with fries on the side.

"I wasn't sure what you'd want," she started to explain, but he cut her off.

"This is perfect. Thank you." He pulled out the plate, grabbed the extra set of flatware, and sat on the edge of her bed. It surprised her because she hadn't expected him to stay in there with her, but she found she liked it. She watched him cut a bite of steak and caught a glimpse of his fangs as he popped it into his mouth to chew. Seeing them added a touch of surrealism to what was already a bizarre experience for her.

"I thought I might be able to help you find where Burton and my father are staying," she said, trying to get her thoughts back on the right track. "I figured they'd have to stay somewhere during the day. In the movies, it's always a crypt or graveyard, but somehow I don't think that's where we'll find the modern-day vampire.

"So I did a search of the city's public records and real-estate listings for empty homes, apartment buildings, city buildings, warehouses—that kind of stuff. I then did a search on all news reports in the last couple of days covering unusual murders or anything having to do with blood. Interestingly enough, two hospitals have reported the theft of venipuncture, blood bank, and chemical lab supplies. I don't know if that's related or not."

He'd been cutting his steak and looked up at that bit of news, his brow furrowed. "Why would they steal supplies?"

"Assuming that my father is still more or less himself, despite being a vampire, then I can understand the chemical lab supplies. Dad is the type who'd want to know more about how the venom turns humans into vampires. That might also explain why they took blood supplies."

"Maybe." He shrugged, popped a fry into his mouth, and thoughtfully chewed before swallowing. "Anything else?"

"Not really. I've got the list of empty buildings. I thought that maybe tomorrow I could start visiting them."

"Absolutely not," he said without even looking up at her. "I don't want you looking for Burton on your own. Dirk and I have a plan. Believe me, we'll find him."

She'd expected this type of reaction and finished downloading her file and broke the connection to the Internet.

"So what *are* the plans for tonight?"

"The same as they were last night. Dirk will watch one while I watch the other. If we're lucky, we'll get there before Burton arrives, catch him in the act, and terminate him."

"Sounds good. What should I wear? Something dark?"

"You're not going," he said around a mouthful of steak, still not looking at her.

"Wait a minute. Last night—"

"Last night, I said you could stay. I'm not taking you with me to face Burton. It's too dangerous."

Trying to control her temper, she glared at him. "Fine. Then I might as well go ahead and start searching the empty buildings for where they're staying."

"No, you won't." Mac laid his flatware across his plate and, pushing off the bed, set the plate with partially eaten food on the tray holding her empty dishes. Then he turned to her, his gaze steely. "How long are we going to argue about your going out tonight?"

"How long do you plan to stand there and tell me what I can and cannot do?"

He drew in a deep breath and then let it out. "Wear dark clothes. I'll call Dirk for the address, okay?"

She smiled. "Works for me."

"Yeah," he muttered as he walked out the door. "You say that now."


An hour later, Mac and Lanie stood in the hallway outside of Smith's hotel room. They had no idea if the man was inside or not, but Mac felt certain that they couldn't just stand around in the hall all night. Someone was bound to ask them what they were doing and then call the cops if they didn't leave. Innocent bystanders were the last thing they needed, Mac thought.

He knocked on Smith's door and waited. There was no sound from the other side, which could have meant anything. For all Mac knew, Smith might not even be there.

Or, worst case, he was there and dead or dying. It was this last thought that gave him his greatest concern.

"What now?" Lanie asked, standing beside him.

"I go in. *You* wait here." The hall was empty, so Mac gripped the handle of the door and, using his newfound strength, forced the handle down and opened the door. The sight that met him told Mac they were too late.

The inside of the room was a wreck. The bed linens were strewn across the floor, and the curtains were ripped and torn where they hung. Even the dresser was knocked askew. The remains of the desk chair lay in pieces, and Mac wondered if Smith had used it to defend himself. There was enough blood around to know violence had taken place—a pool of it on the floor near the remains of the chair and more of it sprayed across the bed.

"Mac?" Lanie's voice came to him from the hallway.

"He's not here," Mac informed her.

"Meaning he's checked out or . . ." Her voice drifted and he answered her unspoken question.

"Yeah, Burton got him."

Across town, Dirk crouched behind the hedge of bushes running along the front of a house in a modest residential section. He was grateful the owners weren't home. The windows were blessedly dark, making the shadows between the house and the bushes, where he crouched, even darker.

He'd been waiting for almost two hours now and was beginning to think that Burton had chosen Mac's target to acquire tonight instead of his. It might be just as well if that was the case, he thought. Mac, with his newfound inhuman abilities, was the better match for a vampire. Of course, Dirk worried about what that made Mac. If he was turning into a vampire himself, then sooner or later Dirk would have to terminate him. It wasn't something he looked forward to.

A movement in the shadows next door caught his attention and Dirk focused on Harris's house. He knew Harris was home because he'd done a preliminary inspection and had seen his former team member watching TV.

The movement that caught his eye came again, this time from the far side of Harris's house. He debated on leaving his hiding spot but thought better of it. He didn't want to alert Burton to his presence, if that's who it was. So he continued to wait and watch.

Whoever it was turned out to be as patient as Dirk, because almost thirty minutes passed before anything happened. Finally, Dirk saw a dark figure emerge from the deep shadows. Dirk stared in amazement as Burton walked up to the front door as if he were paying a call on a neighbor. Dirk wasn't sure what he'd expected the vampire to do, exactly. Maybe something more sinister? Then he remembered that Burton and Harris were old friends, and Harris probably wouldn't think twice about inviting Burton inside.

As it turned out, that was exactly what happened. After Burton disappeared inside, Dirk considered moving in, but didn't. He saw a second shadow in the bushes. Thinking it might be Munoz, he decided to wait.

Straining to see into the dark, Dirk thought he saw the tip of a fin. He followed it downward until he saw the outline of the body. He recognized it instantly, although he'd never seen it like this before. Last time he'd seen the creature, it had been a stone figure in a cage—and presumably harmless.

Reaching for his phone, he called Mac, as per their agreement. "He's here," Dirk whispered when Mac answered.

"Roger—we're already en route. Don't do anything until I get there."

"I don't know how much time we've got. What's your ETA?"

"Five minutes, max."

At that moment, the front door opened and the creature moved toward it. Dirk knew he was out of time. "It's going down now. I can't wait." He disconnected with Mac shouting on the other end.

By now, the creature had disappeared inside the house and the door was closed once more. From inside, Dirk caught the sounds of a man's scream, and then all hell seemed to break loose. Pulling his gun, he raced for the front door. As expected, it was locked. He thought about smashing it down, but decided that the element of surprise would be ruined if once inside the house he had to go find which room they were in.

He ran around the house, glancing at the curtained windows as he passed, searching for the telltale shift in shadows that would indicate Burton, Harris, and the creature were on the other side.

He had to vault the fence to get into the backyard, but the open vertical blinds of the sliding-glass doors gave him a panoramic view of the chaos inside.

The creature held Harris in its clutches, and Burton stood nearby, watching smugly as it bit Harris's neck. The man must have put up a fight because blood was splattered across the room. There was even some on Burton, who wiped a drop from his face with a finger and then licked his finger clean.

Staying off to the side, Dirk moved toward the house until he could reach the handle of the sliding door. He pushed, but it didn't budge. There was only one other option and it had better work, because the creature was killing Harris.

Moving back into the yard, Dirk took a bracing breath and then ran straight at the sliding door, firing his gun as he did. The glass pane shattered just as he hurled himself through it. He immediately tucked his body into a ball and rolled, coming out of it with his gun leveled at Burton, who reacted with a bored kind of smile.

"Really, Adams. Such dramatics. What? Are you going to shoot me?" He laughed and Dirk fired off a shot. It struck Burton in the chest but seemed to have no more effect than to irritate the man. His smile vanished, replaced by a glare. Dirk fired a second time, aiming for Burton's head. He missed and quickly fired again. And missed again.

Then he realized that it wasn't his aim that was off. Burton was moving so fast that he was literally dodging the bullets. A feeling of dread hit Dirk. He was in serious trouble.

As Burton moved toward him, Dirk remembered something Mac told him. He looked around for a chair he could smash or a fireplace poker—anything that he could use to stake Burton through the heart, all too aware as he scanned the room of the creature sucking the blood from Harris's body. Dirk worried that his efforts were for nothing. Harris had stopped struggling, and his unnatural still-ness cast an eerie silence over the scene.

Dirk spotted the fireplace just as the creature dropped Harris's lifeless body to the floor. Dirk ran for it but never got there. From seemingly out of nowhere, Burton appeared in his path.

The first punch sent Dirk flying across the room, and in some small, still-functioning part of his brain, he mar-veled that the blow hadn't broken his jaw. He landed in a heap against the far wall, and then shook his head to clear it as he struggled to push himself to his feet.

He didn't get the chance. Burton dragged him up as if he weighed nothing and punched him in the side. Once again, Dirk went flying, his ribs aching as only broken bones can. This time, he'd barely made it to his knees before Burton was on him. After that, everything hap-pened so fast, Dirk didn't have time to defend himself.

"Adams, I thought better of you," Burton mocked, picking him up again. "How disappointing, but perhaps we can reform you."

Dirk landed at the feet of the chupacabra. He could only stare into the creature's glowing red eyes as it leaned down and grabbed him. The thought that he was dead barely registered before he felt two sharp fangs sink into his neck.

Mac's sense of foreboding added weight to his foot on the accelerator as he raced down the streets of the neigh-borhood until he found the house he sought. Beside him, Lanie had long since given up trying to caution him to safety.

He slammed on the brakes, threw the car in park, and was out the door, racing across the lawn toward the front door. He didn't even bother trying the handle—merely hurled his body against it and broke it open.

The scene that met him was worse than he'd expected. Harris lay dead at Burton's feet, and the chupacabra had Dirk in its claws, its teeth buried in his friend's neck.

# Chapter
# 13

M ac wasn't aware that he'd pulled his gun, but he immediately opened fire on the creature, being careful not to hit Dirk. The bullet ripped into the creature's side, causing it to pause and look up. Behind him, Mac heard Lanie run into the room and heard her quick intake of breath. Then, before he could shield his eyes, she'd turned on the overhead lights.

Deprived of sight, Mac grew acutely aware of a low thrumming in his head. He focused on it and several conflicting emotions hit him. Pure hatred and anger; a lust for death and destruction that warred with a weaker resistance and pain. Mac knew they weren't his own emotions, and as his eyes adjusted, he looked around the room.

Burton's face was a mask of fury as he stared at the creature, which seemed to simply be holding Dirk in its clutches, and Mac sensed its reluctance to attack. In a moment of sudden clarity, he realized that the emotions he felt were those of Burton and the creature. Somehow, he seemed to be sharing a psychic link with them, and as he tried to make sense of this discovery, he felt the urge to kill grow stronger. He saw the creature bend its head toward Dirk and knew that Burton was somehow projecting his own emotions onto the chupacabra, wearing down its resistance.

If Burton could do it, Mac thought, then he could as well. Focusing his thoughts, he urged the creature to resist, praying that he was using the link correctly.

Miraculously, he saw the chupacabra hesitate. A look of surprise crossed Burton's face. The small victory encouraged Mac, and he put more effort into his projections. It came easier the second time and the chupacabra, already reluctant, released Dirk's unconscious form, which fell to the floor.

At that moment, Burton looked around and his eyes fell on Mac, who smiled.

Burton's eyes grew wide in a moment of surprise, and then his look turned to one of pure hatred. Moving quickly, he crossed to Harris's body and picked it up, slinging it over his shoulder. Then Burton raced out of the house. Mac wanted to chase after him but knew he needed to stay and help Dirk, who lay deathly still.

"He needs to go to the hospital," Lanie said, already leaning over Dirk and checking his pulse. "He'll need a transfusion—I just hope it's not too late; otherwise . . ."

She didn't need to finish the sentence. They both knew what would happen if Dirk died.

"We can't call the ambulance here," Mac said, going over to the limp body of his friend. "Too many questions that I can't answer."

Lanie had stopped the bleeding, but Dirk's complexion was extremely pale, and Mac, with his hypersensitive hearing, could barely detect Dirk's heartbeat when he placed his head to the man's chest.

Mac lifted Dirk up into his arms, and Lanie ran ahead to open the back door of the car. She climbed in and then helped him get Dirk inside.

Mac drove like a madman, amazed that no one tried to stop him. He arrived at the entrance of the hospital's ER, and rather than wait for someone to come out and meet him, he pulled Dirk from the backseat and carried him inside.

The emergency staff wanted to know more about how his injuries were sustained, but thankfully were too busy to wait for answers that weren't forthcoming. They started a blood transfusion while Lanie and Mac were forced to wait in the outer lobby.

Two hours later, they were still waiting on word about Dirk's condition. Whether he lived or died, things would be different. If he died, Dirk would have to be staked, and Mac would be left to deal with Burton and the others on his own. If he lived, Lanie knew there was a good chance he would recover as quickly as Mac had—and be affected in the same way, or maybe even worse. The damage he'd sustained had been more extensive. The amount of blood the chupa had taken, and subsequently the amount of venom introduced into Dirk's system, was far greater than it had been for Mac. It made sense to her that his changes, too, might be more pronounced. She couldn't help but wonder what Mac would do if Dirk suddenly became part of the problem.

Another, more unsettling thought hit her. What if the evolution of changes in the two men didn't stop until they *both* became vampires? She'd be the only one left who knew of their existence. It would be so easy for Mac to slip into her room one night and kill her, before she even realized how far gone he was. Even if she fought for her life, it would do no good—he was so much stronger. She glanced at him out of the corner of her eye, wondering if it would even bother him to kill her. She thought that he cared for her, a little, but that was the human side of him—the side that was disappearing.

She had to share what she knew with someone, and Uncle Charles was the obvious choice. He knew the men and their capabilities, and because of his friendship with her father, the notion of vampires and chupacabras existing wouldn't be too far-fetched. Satisfied that telling Uncle Charles was the thing to do, she resolved to slip out the following day, while Mac slept. There were advantages, she thought, to being a plain old human.

Feeling better now that she had a plan of action, Lanie allowed herself to relax. She knew there was nothing more she could do for Dirk right now. She closed her eyes and felt the burn from having worn her contacts too long. Elsewhere in the waiting room, she heard the sounds of the triage nurses assessing incoming patients, the clerk at the front desk keying information into the computer, and the sounds of men and women praying, crying, and whispering to themselves as they awaited word on loved ones.

Outside, a siren's wail suddenly grew silent as the ambulance pulled up with its latest victim. Medical personnel shouted orders and Lanie opened her eyes, curious to see what was happening.

The person being rushed in on a gurney was coding. Doctors and nurses converged around him instantly, and the group disappeared through the doors into the back. A few minutes later, the EMT came back out. He stopped at the nurses' station, and his voice carried into the waiting room where Lanie caught five words that had her straining to hear the rest.

". . . lost a lot of blood."

"What happened?" Lanie heard the nurse ask.

"Heart attack. He's homeless. Someone found him in the alley."

"Probably alcohol-induced," the nurse said, sounding like it happened all the time.

"Maybe," the EMT said doubtfully, "only he didn't smell of alcohol. And he was carrying a hell of a lot of cash on him—almost two hundred dollars."

"Drugs, then?"

"Be my guess. We found recent track marks on him. Still, if he had a bad habit, you wouldn't think he'd have cash left over."

"Where does a guy like that get that kind of money?" the nurse continued. "Not begging. If he did, then I need to quit my job and start standing on the street corner, you know?"

"Some of his buddies said there was a place nearby paying them for blood. I've never heard of it before, and there's nothing over in that part of town except derelict old buildings, so maybe they were confused."

Lanie stopped listening and turned to look at Mac, who must have felt her gaze on him because he turned his head.

"You think buying blood from homeless men is the modern vampire's method of eating these days?" he asked.

"Maybe so. It would explain the theft of venipuncture supplies. But why? Burton doesn't strike me as the kind who worries overly much about killing his food."

"No, he's not," Mac agreed. "But he *would* be the kind to worry about leaving a trail of dead bodies that might lead me to him. In that event, he might consider an alternative means of getting blood."

Mac got up from his chair and went outside to talk to the EMTs who'd brought in the homeless man, while Lanie went to check on Dirk. They met back at the waiting room a short while later.

"The doctor says that Dirk is still in critical condition, but stable. If he got as much venom in him as you did, he'll probably be up and trying to get out of here sometime tomorrow." Through the window, Lanie saw the EMT Mac had talked to drive off. "Did you get an address?"

"Yep. The EMT refused to give it to me, but I was able to get the address from his log sheet while he wasn't looking. Feel like checking it out?"

She nodded, and after Mac gave his phone number to the head nurse with instructions to call if anything happened to Dirk, he and Lanie went outside, got in his car, and left.

The location where blood was being purchased was several long blocks from their hotel, but it seemed easier to walk there rather than drive through the presumably deserted streets and announce their presence.

Mac seemed reluctant to talk as they walked along, and Lanie soon found herself too breathless to speak. She didn't know if he realized how fast he was moving, but since she was able to keep up—breathlessly—she didn't ask him to slow down. In some respects, she was as anxious as he to get there and see if she could catch a glimpse of her father.

As they drew closer to the address Mac had "borrowed" from the EMT, Lanie noticed fewer people about and wondered if that was because of the area or the time of night. Even street thugs and the homeless had to sleep sometime, didn't they? Still, the farther they went, the more grateful she was not to be alone.

"What do we do when we get there?" she asked.

"That depends on what we find."

All around her, the buildings rose like silent, dark sentinels waiting quietly for them to pass into their lair. Lanie couldn't help glancing around nervously, feeling like eyes watched her from every direction. So busy was she, looking for potential surprises, that when Mac grabbed her arm, she cried out in alarm.

"What's the matter?"

He scowled and raised a finger to her lips to silence her, then he looked around, even studying the rooflines of the buildings around them. Seconds passed as they waited, and Lanie felt the tension grow inside her. They were standing in front of a building on a corner, and when Lanie moved to stand next to Mac, he put out his arm and herded her behind him.

Lanie finally heard the shuffling noise, but just as she braced for something horrible, she felt the tension in Mac ease as a homeless man appeared. His ill-fitting clothes were streaked with dirt and hung loose on his emaciated frame. She couldn't tell what color his matted hair was beneath his hat, and it was impossible to judge his age. When he saw them he stopped, a wary look crossing his face as he tried to back away, clutching something in his hand. Looking closer, Lanie saw that he held a twenty-dollar bill and she quickly glanced at his arm, looking for some sign that he'd recently given blood. His sleeves were down and she saw nothing. Unable to stop herself, she looked at his neck, afraid he might have made a direct donation, but although dirty, there were no obvious wounds.

"Easy, old man," Mac spoke gently. "We're not looking for trouble." He reached into his pocket and pulled out another twenty-dollar bill and held it up for the old man to see. "Just a little information."

The old man stared as if weighing the sincerity of Mac's offer. Finally he nodded.

"We're looking for the blood center. I understand it's around here. Do you know where it might be?"

"The mission?" The expression on the man's face turned worried. "You're not going to shut it down, are you?"

Lanie understood his concern. He didn't want to lose what was probably his only source of income, but she wondered if he realized vampires ran his *mission*. On the other hand, taking another look at his appearance and guessing what his life must be like, she thought he probably wouldn't care.

"I have business with the missionaries," Mac told him. "Can you tell me where it is?"

The man nodded and pointed around the corner in the direction from which he'd come. Mac thanked him and gave him the money. They waited until he'd shuffled down the street a ways, and then they rounded the corner he'd indicated. They'd gone only a block when Lanie noticed an increase in the pedestrian traffic. They continued walking, and it soon became obvious which building they sought because all the homeless seemed to be entering and leaving the same one.

"They seem to be doing a brisk business, don't they?" Lanie whispered to Mac, worried about the large number of people she saw.

"You wait here while I go in, and for God's sake, Lanie, stay out of sight. If you see Burton, Munoz, your dad, or anyone else who looks like a vampire come outside—don't follow them. Just watch and see which way they go."

He started to walk off, but she grabbed his sleeve. "Wait a minute. You can't go in there and fight them all by yourself. You don't even know how many there are."

He gave her that look she was beginning to recognize—the one that said he thought she was wasting his time with useless protests.

"Okay," she conceded. "But, for the record, I don't like your plan."

"Just stay out here so I don't need to worry about your safety as well as my own."

He seemed to be waiting for her to agree, so she swallowed her objections and nodded instead. "Don't get yourself killed, okay?"

His hard stare softened. He placed his hand briefly on top of hers and then he was gone.

Standing there, alone, she felt suddenly exposed. She glanced behind her and spotted a nearby entryway. Thinking it would provide better coverage than being out in the open, she went to stand in it.

She'd been there almost ten minutes when she got her first indication that something was going on inside the mission. There was a mass exodus from the building as the homeless hurried out. Visions of Mac fighting Burton and Munoz filled her head, and she struggled not to panic. Indecision created havoc with her ability to focus; she didn't know whether she should run to his assistance or run for help.

So preoccupied was she that she almost didn't see the shadowed form that flitted toward her and then away. She couldn't help but remember the way her father and Burton had looked on the security tape, and she was immediately struck with a sense of grave danger—like the small rabbit spotted by a pack of wild dogs. She fell back into the entryway and clutched the locked doorknob at her back, frantic for a way to escape.

If it had been a vampire, then why hadn't it attacked her?

She looked around and though she saw nothing, she couldn't get over the thought that it lurked nearby, waiting for an opportunity to attack her. Acutely aware now of every shadow and small noise that filled the night, it took all her self-discipline not to let her imagination run away with her. Feeling chilled to the bone, she absently rubbed her hands up and down her arms, trying to warm herself. Torn between fear and worry over Mac, she was near to screaming when he finally appeared in the doorway of the mission, looking unharmed.

Unable to suppress a small exclamation of relief, she ran to him and threw herself into his arms, wrapping her own around his waist, holding him tightly. His arms instantly enfolded her, and she felt his body tense as he looked around. "What's wrong?"

"Did you see it?" she asked. "Over there." She turned slightly, pointing to the spot where the shadowed figure had been. "Something was there. I swear it was."

"I believe you," he said and simply held her until she felt calm enough to leave the security of his arms. When she looked around, they were alone. The streets stood quiet and empty, and she felt a little foolish for the way she'd acted. "What did you find inside?" she asked, trying to divert his attention away from her.

He sighed. "Nothing. The place was clean."

She was confused. "Then why were all those homeless there?"

"I don't know. I went around the back way and when I got inside, the place was empty. I must have just missed the vampire who was there."

"What makes you so sure one was?"

"I felt it," he said simply.

"You mean, the same way you felt Burton at the reception?"

Surprise crossed his face. "Yeah, exactly like that. They must have known I was there in the same way."

"What now?" She'd had enough excitement for one night and was exhausted.

"We go back to the hotel."

"Good."

They walked side by side in silence. After about a block, Lanie glanced at Mac and noticed how wan and pale he looked. She hadn't noticed before and wondered if it was a trick of the lighting from the street lamps or if he was sick.

About to ask, the prickling of the hairs along her neck and the pervading sense that they were being followed distracted her. Not sure whether her imagination was working overtime or not, she glanced at Mac, but he appeared lost in thought. She resisted the urge to turn around, but as they continued to walk at their slow, leisurely pace, the feeling grew worse. There was definitely something out there.

"Keep walking," Mac said in a hushed voice, grabbing her arm when she would have turned around to look.

"There's someone there."

He didn't respond, but as they reached the end of the block, she heard the pounding of footsteps drawing nearer. Lanie and Mac whirled around at the same time, and while she could only stare in horror at the men racing toward them, Mac became a force in action.

He raised his leg in a back kick and planted his foot in the first assailant's chest. As that man fell back, Mac rammed the heel of his hand into the face of the second attacker. The third man had the good sense to hesitate after seeing the fate of his two companions, but was not smart enough to turn and run away. Instead, he came at Mac, emitting a loud roar as he swung his fists. All three men were of average height and looked street tough, but they were human—not vampires. Lanie almost wanted to laugh at the absurdity of it. A normal street mugging now seemed laughable.

Still, the attackers were unrelenting as they ganged up on Mac, who, Lanie thought, was enjoying himself. He met each blow with one of his own, and while he was grossly outnumbered, he seemed to be toying with the men.

She watched his eyes take on that reddish glow and his lips curled back, revealing his fangs. He slammed his fist into one man's jaw, snapping the man's head back with such force that he was unconscious before he hit the ground. It seemed to anger his two friends, because they rushed Mac together, but he was ready for them. When they lunged for him, Mac grabbed them both by the front of their shirts, yanked them off their feet, and slammed them against the side of the building and held them there, feet dangling in the air. Lanie looked on, afraid of what he might do next. The atmosphere around them suddenly changed, and the glow in Mac's eyes grew brighter as he cocked his head to one side and leaned forward. She saw him run his tongue over his front teeth and, in that moment, knew that he was about to bite the men and drink their blood. The men knew it, too, because in an instant, they went from aggressive attackers to frightened prey. Their eyes grew wide, and she thought she detected a slight shaking in one of them.

She had to do something.

"Mac, let them go." She forced herself to sound calm and steady. *No surprises or sudden movements*, she told herself. *Slow and easy.* "You don't want to hurt them. They're not worth it." She moved closer to him, praying that in this vampirelike state, he could still hear her. The eyes of the two men darted back and forth between her and Mac. They were clearly terrified and looking to her for help. She had half a mind to walk away and let Mac do whatever he wanted to them. She wasn't trying to save their worthless lives. She was trying to save what was left of Mac's humanity before it was completely lost.

Slowly, she laid her hand on Mac's arm, hoping her touch would help him focus on her and not on his desire to attack the men. "Please, Mac. Let them go." When he didn't respond, she tried another approach. "I want to go home, now. Please take me home."

As if he were trying to wake from a powerful dream, he turned to look at her. She offered him a small smile and watched the light in his eyes fade and his lips relax until the fangs were, once again, covered. "Can we go now?" She gave a small tug on his arm, and he gradually lowered the men until their feet touched the ground. She didn't try to remove his hand from the front of the men's shirts, but waited for him to do it. When he did, she let her hand slide down his arm until she could lace her fingers through his.

"Get out of here," she ordered the two men, her tone brusque. "And take your friend with you."

They didn't wait to be told twice, but bent over to grab their still-unconscious friend under the arms and haul him away. Lanie didn't give them another look. She had achieved her goal and prevented Mac from killing the three men, but now grew concerned for her own safety. Mac seemed barely under control to her.

She gave his hand a gentle tug to get him walking beside her, but didn't let go of him, praying she was doing the right thing. They reached the hotel without further incident, despite the fact Lanie couldn't shake the feeling that they were being followed. She was glad when they finally stepped into the lobby.

Once inside her room, Mac let go of Lanie's hand and silently headed for his own side. He was back to normal, as far as she could tell, but very subdued.

"Want to talk about it?" she offered, following him to the connecting doors.

Mac stared at her. "Were you a psych major in college? No. I don't want to talk about it." He knew he was being rude, but at the moment, he didn't care. He wanted her to leave him alone.

"Fine," she snapped, stepping back through the doors, mumbling under her breath. "Good night."

He saw the connecting door slam shut, heard and felt the impact of it hitting, and knew he should follow her to apologize, but Christ, he couldn't deal with it right now. He had to sort out what had happened tonight.

Lanie had been right to interfere, and he was grateful that she'd been able to stop him. It meant there was still a shred of humanity left in him, albeit a tiny shred, because he'd enjoyed fighting those men, and there at the end, he'd had every intention of killing them. He'd actually meant to pierce their necks with his fangs and draw blood. And the real horror was that he would have drunk their blood until he'd had his fill, and he would have enjoyed it.

Clint stood outside the hotel feeling lost—and amazed. The minute he'd felt the strange presence coming through the link he shared with Lance, he'd thought it might have been Hector, whom he hadn't seen since nightfall. As the presence grew stronger, however, he knew it was one he'd not felt before and he'd quickly packed up everything, sent the homeless away, and left the building, slipping outside to lurk in the deepest shadows, hoping to get a glimpse of this unknown intruder.

That's when he'd seen Lanie, waiting in the darkened entryway. He hadn't expected to see her again—much less here in Washington, D.C.

Drawn to her, he'd moved closer and then quickly left, moving with such speed that he would appear as little more than a shadow to her. He should have gone back to the lair, but he'd not wanted to leave her so soon, content with simply watching her.

He'd been surprised when the door to the mission opened and the man who'd confronted them in Taribu stepped out. Even more amazing was watching his daughter run straight into this man's arms. She obviously cared about him, and Clint felt the familiar weight of fatherly concern.

Curious, he'd followed them. When the street punks attacked them, Clint had moved closer, driven by a primitive urge to destroy the threat to his daughter. Then he discovered that his help was not needed. The young man with his daughter had reacted with surprising speed and strength in dealing with the attackers, and Clint would have left to return to his lair, reassured that his daughter was in good hands, had he not, at that moment, caught sight of the young man's fangs and glowing red eyes.

He was a vampire!

Instinctively, Clint had rushed forward to once again protect his daughter, but was brought short a second time when he saw her place a hand on the man's arm. Over the distance, he heard her gentle urgings and was further amazed when the man complied.

Filled with questions and concerns, he'd followed them all the way to the hotel where he presumed they were staying and stood there now, gazing at it, lost in a mire of speculation and unanswered questions. Finally, knowing that dawn lay not far off, he turned and left, carrying his bags of blood and the weight of his concerns.

When he reached the old building where he and the others were staying, he found Lance ranting about an incident that had occurred earlier that night when he'd gone to collect his latest recruits—Smith and Harris. Making matters worse, there appeared to be dissension among the newly arisen troops.

"I don't think we owe you shit," the man named Kinsley was shouting when Clint slipped into the lair. "I don't remember asking you to kill me."

"You'll do as I order," Lance bit out.

"Fuck you—you're not my commanding officer anymore, Burton. Get over it."

Lance said something more, but Clint didn't pay much attention as he moved through the lair to where the adult chupa rested. When he walked in, she didn't even lift an eyelid and his concern grew. He placed the backpack on the floor as Gem jumped onto his shoulder and greeted him.

"How are you, girl?" He gave her an affectionate pat and then set her on the floor where she went to squat beside the adult. "I'm going to help you," he promised the adult chupa, stroking her head and letting his hands trail along the huge fins on her back.

Getting up, he grabbed the backpack and pulled out two bags of dog's blood. He gave one to Gem and watched as she set to work, piercing the bag with her teeth. As she ate, he held the bag in front of the adult, who finally opened her eyes. He used his own teeth to pierce the bag, then held it so the adult's tongue could suck up the blood.

When both had fed, he lay down beside them, the seeds of a plan germinating in his head. The sound of the men arguing floated to him, and he knew Lance was too preoccupied with his recruits to notice Clint's thoughts coming through the psychic link. Clint smiled to himself. It was an oversight that Lance would soon regret.

# Chapter
## 14

A loud, piercing noise jerked Lanie rudely from sleep. Her heart racing, she reached blindly for the alarm and struggled to figure out how to turn it off, but the noise continued to blare, loud and irritating. On the verge of ripping the cord from the wall, she finally found the right button and blessed silence filled the room.

She fell back against the pillows, trying to remember why she'd set the alarm to go off so early. Then she remembered her plan to see Uncle Charles and forced her eyes back open. Getting out of bed would be tough, so she pulled back the covers and practically fell out, knowing that if she didn't, she might not wake up again until much later.

Stumbling across the room to her purse, she searched the contents until she found his phone number and placed her call. Within a few minutes, she had him on the phone.

"Lanie, my dear, how are you? Is everything all right?"

"Actually, Uncle Charles, things aren't all right. Is there any chance you could meet with me today? I'd like to talk to you."

"Of course. Let's see, it's almost sixteen hundred hours—how about meeting over dinner?"

"That would be great."

"Perfect. Shall I pick you up in, say, thirty minutes?"

She gave him the address, hung up the phone, and quickly showered and dressed. Thirty minutes later she was downstairs waiting for him when he pulled up, driving a gold-tone Humvee. She climbed in, appreciating the spaciousness of the vehicle, and exchanged polite, casual conversation with him as they drove to the restaurant. Several times when she looked at him, she was struck by his ageless appearance. She thought he must be in his late fifties, although he could easily pass for a man ten years younger. He reminded her of Sean Connery, both in looks and manner, and she wondered again why he'd never married. He was a very attractive man.

When they reached the restaurant, she discovered that he'd called ahead and a table had been prepared for them. He held the chair for her as she sat and then summoned the waiter over before taking his own seat.

"Lanie, what would you like to drink? Something stronger than tea, perhaps? No? Make that two." He dismissed the waiter, who rushed off to fill their order, and then politely waited for her to tell him what was wrong.

"I'm not sure how to begin," she said. "What I have to tell you seems so unbelievable, even to me, but it's very, very real."

"Try me. You'll find I'm more receptive than you think—after all, Clint and I were friends for a long time and shared many common interests."

It was true, but still she hesitated. "But this has to do with . . ."

"El Chupacabra?"

She stared at him in disbelief. "You knew?"

"Why do you think I called your father in the first place? Though no one else in the military recognized what we'd found in the jungle, I did. And I knew how hard Clint had worked to prove they existed. I thought he deserved to be the one to study them." He grew silent as he glanced down at his napkin. "I wish I'd known how dangerous they could be."

She reached out a hand to touch his. "Because of you, he got the chance of a lifetime. His death wasn't your fault." She took a deep breath and let it out slowly. It was time to tell him everything. "In fact, he's not really dead, exactly. More like he's undead." If she hadn't known him so well, she never would have noticed the slight widening of his eyes betraying his surprise. She rushed to get the rest of it out before she lost her nerve. "Please hear me out. I'm sure my father mentioned the possible connection between the chupacabra and the vampire?" He nodded, and she felt a moment of hope. "Well, that connection is real. When the chupacabra killed Dad and Lance, it converted them into vampires. I think it has something to do with the venom they secrete when they drink the victim's blood. It doesn't seem to have an effect on most animals. Once dead, they stay dead. But on humans . . . they come back to life."

She paused, expecting him to laugh at her or at the very least call her crazy, but he did neither. "Did you tell Mac about this?"

She grimaced. "Yes, and at first he didn't believe me."

Uncle Charles raised an eyebrow and appeared curious. "What changed his mind?"

"Oh, I think it was a combination of several things," she said facetiously.

"Like?"

"Like getting attacked by the chupacabra himself, followed by a run-in with Dad and Burton after they were supposedly dead, watching Burton kill a man by biting his neck, and then watching one of the dead researchers come back to life."

"Mac was attacked by the creature?"

"I'm sorry. We meant to tell you earlier."

"I'm sure." At that moment the waiter appeared with their drinks. He handed them menus and after a moment took their orders and left once again.

"Mac looked to be in good shape when I saw him the other night; he must not have been too seriously injured."

"Actually, he almost died."

"What?"

"I'm sorry, Uncle Charles, to be the one to break it to you."

"Maybe you'd better tell me all of it—and don't gloss over the rough spots, okay?"

She quickly told him everything that had happened since she first arrived in Taribu and found the chupacabra in the cage. The only time she paused in her story was when the waiter brought their food or to answer a question.

When she finished, he knew as much as she did, and while she felt relieved, he looked deeply troubled.

He reached into his pocket and took out his cell phone, quickly dialing a number. After a moment he spoke into the phone. "This is Admiral Winslow. You have one of my men there—a Dirk Adams. I'd like to check on his status." He waited a few minutes and as Lanie watched him, she was impressed again with his calm, cool acceptance of the situation.

"Yes, thank you," he said, breaking into her thoughts. "Can you connect me with his room? Thank you." There was a moment's pause. "Dirk? How are you doing, son? I just heard." There was the sound of a response on the other end, but Lanie couldn't catch what was being said. Finally he nodded. "Of course, we'll get you out as soon as we get a clean bill of health from the physician. No, I'm sure it won't take that long. Just sit tight. Try to relax."

Lanie heard the loud litany of protest coming through the phone's earpiece before Charles, smiling, disconnected the call. He replaced his phone and chuckled to himself. "That boy sure wants out of the hospital." Then he sobered. "There's no way he should have recovered that quickly. The doctor told me that by all rights he should be dead."

"It's the venom," she explained. "He got a lot of it."

"We'll keep an eye on him. Mac, too," he promised her. "I'd like to think they'll be okay, but if not, we'll handle it. You're not alone."

She gave him a grateful smile and then was startled when his phone rang. Judging from his expression and tone after he answered it, Lanie knew the conversation wasn't good. When he disconnected, she thought he looked tired.

"Bad news?"

"Yes. That was a friend of mine with homicide. They found Mark Kinsley's body."

"Where?"

"An abandoned building about twenty minutes from here."

"What about the others? Burton, Munoz, Patterson, Brown, and Harris? And Dad?"

He shook his head. "No sign of them."

Maybe her father was still alive, or undead, or whatever the correct term was. She hid her relief as an image of the researcher at the facility rose up in her mind. "The body will have to be staked."

He stared at her, and for the first time she wondered if he'd really believed her or had only been humoring her. As if he realized what she was thinking, he nodded, then folded his napkin and laid it on the table. "I'm sorry to cut our dinner short, but I have to go ID the body. I'll take care of the, uh, details." He removed several dollars from his wallet and tossed them onto the table. Then he took several more bills and held them out to her. "This should cover your cab ride back to the hotel."

"Keep it," she said, snatching the napkin from her lap and tossing it onto the table as she stood up. "I'm going with you. And we should probably call Mac and tell him to meet us."

"We'll call him on our way."

Once inside the Humvee, Lanie pulled out her phone before realizing that she didn't know Mac's phone number. She was about to call the hotel when Charles stopped her. "Might be better if I talked to him," he told her, pulling out his own phone once more.

The phone's volume was set so high, she heard the ringing as the call went through and then Mac's grumbling voice when he finally answered. He didn't sound happy about being awakened.

"Young man," Uncle Charles said in a deep, authoritative voice, "I'll thank you not to take that tone of voice with me."

There was sudden silence on the other end.

"That's better. Now, here is the situation." He briefly told Mac about the body being found and listened to Mac's reply. "Fine. Lanie's with me. We're already en route and will meet you there." He listened a moment and then smiled, although he kept his tone serious. "Not that it's any of your business, but we were having dinner. Yes, it was quite enjoyable, thank you. We'll see you there."

Charles put away his phone and glanced at her. "He was very upset."

"About Kinsley?" She'd forgotten that Mac used to be his commanding officer.

"Well, Kinsley, certainly, but I don't think that's what upset him the most." He smiled then but didn't elaborate, and Lanie didn't press the matter.

Fifteen minutes later they pulled up near the scene of the crime. Mac stood out front, looking worried, irritated, and paler than usual. When she joined him on the sidewalk, he shot her a look she couldn't interpret, but otherwise ignored her to address Uncle Charles.

"They won't let me in without you."

"Then let's go take a look."

The building loomed before them, about eight stories tall, Lanie guessed. It was made of that faded brownish-red brick that always looked weathered and old. Uncle Charles walked up the front steps and spoke to the uniformed officer guarding the entrance. A few minutes later, a tall, forty-something man appeared and waved them inside.

They stepped into the small foyer with mailboxes for each of the apartments lining the wall to the left and a door to the first apartment off to the right. Straight ahead and to the right was the staircase. The walls had been painted a dull institutional yellow that had long since grayed, and the hard linoleum floor was stained and torn in more places than not. Lanie found it depressing.

"What can you tell us, John?" Charles asked after introducing them to his friend Detective John Boehler.

"We got a report just before dawn of strange lights and noises. By the time a car got here, everything was quiet. A preliminary search of the building uncovered a body down in the basement. We don't know the exact cause of death yet—there weren't any obviously fatal wounds."

Lanie exchanged confused looks with Mac. The neck wounds of the chupacabra would have been hard to miss. Maybe they were wrong, and Kinsley's disappearance had nothing to do with Burton and the chupacabra.

"We also found lab equipment down the hall," the detective said, waving a hand in that direction. "It's too early to draw any conclusions, but it looks like someone was making drugs."

They went down the stairs and walked to the far end of the basement before the detective stopped. "The body is in the corner. My men have finished in here, so feel free to look around. I'd appreciate it if you'd share any thoughts you have concerning what might have happened. Every little bit helps."

Lanie knew perfectly well that they'd never tell the detective anything—it was better if no one else knew about either the vampires or the chupacabras.

They entered the darkened room, now lit with temporary lamps, and Lanie looked in the corner. She wasn't sure what she expected, but it wasn't to see a body contorted as if frozen in the midst of a violent seizure, eyes staring wildly, arms reaching out, fingers bent and curled, and legs twisted to the side.

She moved in for a closer look, conscious of Mac's and Charles's reactions—or the lack thereof. They'd known this man, had worked with him—what were they feeling? Their total lack of emotional response made her wonder just how many times they'd encountered death in their line of work.

She did her best to objectively view the scene before her, but the body's appearance puzzled her. As Detective Boehler had said, there were no obvious fatal wounds, but then, he'd not known what to look for. Stooping for a closer look, she saw that the two dark circles, where the chupacabra had bitten him, were now little more than faint marks on his skin. They'd no doubt healed when he converted, as Burton's and her father's neck wounds had.

Mac bent down beside her. "What would make him contort like this?"

"I don't know," she admitted, whispering. "Maybe there was something in his genetic makeup that reacted badly to the conversion." She stood up and addressed Detective Boehler. "Did you say that you'd found lab equipment?"

He nodded and gestured for them to follow. "It's down the hall here."

The minute she saw it, she knew her father had worked here. He'd been obsessive about how his lab should be set up—refrigerators in the back, test tube racks on the left, because he was left-handed, droppers and reactants on the right. He always kept things in the same order, no matter where he was or what he was working on—and in the freezer, she'd find . . .

She crossed the room and opened the top door of the refrigerator and looked inside. A thick coating of ice covered the inner walls, but otherwise it appeared empty. A wave of disappointment hit her and she started to close the door. That's when she saw it—a small folded white piece of paper, almost invisible against the ice.

"Lanie?" Uncle Charles asked from across the room. "Did you find something?"

She snatched the paper and palmed it before closing the door. She didn't want the others to see it. "Empty."

Lanie felt Mac staring at her, but she refused to look at him. "Did your men find anything?" she asked the detective.

"Nothing useful. A couple of spent bags of blood, plastic tubing, and a lot of questions."

It was obvious from looking around that there was nothing here that would tell them what her father had been up to, so they left the room.

They climbed the stairs in silence and retraced their steps down the hallway to the foyer, stopping once more before the front door.

"You'll call my office if you discover anything?" Uncle Charles asked.

"I will. Do you know if the deceased had family?"

"A brother. I'll call him and give him your number."

The detective nodded, and as they turned to leave the sound of someone hurrying toward them caught their attention.

Lanie turned and saw a uniformed policeman.

"Sir, we found something else. You might want to take a look."

Detective Boehler nodded, then shook hands with Uncle Charles, promising that he'd be in touch. They waited a heartbeat after he left and then followed him, even though they hadn't been invited.

This time, instead of going back down into the basement, they stayed on the first floor. When they reached the room the detective had disappeared into, they followed him inside, curious about what had been found. A statue of a man lay on the floor, spotlighted by the small amount of fading light filtering in through the window where a board was missing. Curious, Lanie and Mac moved closer for a better look.

Lanie gasped. The statue was an exact likeness of Munoz—so exact that it couldn't be a replica. Munoz had been turned into stone, and with the sunlight filtering in on him, it wasn't hard to guess what had happened. Now they knew what happened to vampires when they were exposed to the sunlight. Like the chupacabra, they turned to stone. The question that remained was, what happened when the sun set? Would Munoz come back to life?

She stared at it for a long time, then turned to Mac, who was standing beside her. "What if he wakes up?" she whispered. "It'll be dusk soon."

"Higgins, dust that thing for prints," Detective Boehler ordered, unaware of the danger.

Mac held out his hand. "Not yet." The detective looked like he wanted to ask questions, but then thought better of it. He nodded to the uniformed man who had come when he called, and the man remained standing off to the side.

Lanie wasn't sure how long they stood there, watching the statue, but it seemed to be forever. Someone behind them turned on a couple of high-beam flashlights so they could see after the sun completely set, and still the Munoz statue did not move. Finally, it was obvious to Lanie that Munoz was not going to be waking up—ever again.

Mac must have reached the same conclusion because he gestured for the man with the black case to come forward. The man knelt by the statue, took powder and brush from the case, and dusted the statue for prints. There wasn't a single one to be found. He shook his head and packed his gear.

"Send in a couple of guys to carry this thing back to the station," the detective instructed them as he left the room.

Two men arrived shortly and took up positions on each end of the statue, but when they tried to lift it, the stone crumbled in their hands, sending forth a small explosion of fine dust. Lanie grabbed Mac's arm, stunned, as she watched the dust settle. Next to her, Mac silently extracted his arm from her grasp, turned, and walked out.

With a final look at what had once been Munoz, Lanie raced after him.

Outside, the night air was warm, but not uncomfortably so as she stood on the front steps, looking for Mac. She spotted him a short distance down the street, pacing back and forth, and hurried to join him.

He stopped and dragged a hand down his face in obvious frustration. "Is that what I have to look forward to? Are these changes going to keep on until one day, I go outside—and turn to stone? That's some future. Put me in a park and let the birds crap on me—until the first hard rain, and then I crumble?"

"I don't think that's going to happen to you, Mac." But she wasn't sure, and he heard the doubt in her voice.

He swore. "I'm going back to the hotel."

"I'll go with you."

"No. I need to be alone. Let Winslow bring you back." He walked off, leaving her standing by herself.

It was some time later when she finally arrived at the hotel, carrying a small package. She'd said good night to Uncle Charles, who was on his way to the hospital to check on Dirk. Lanie would have gone with him, but she'd been worried about Mac. He hadn't been looking well lately, and she was concerned that he might be getting worse. She'd shared her concerns with Charles, and he'd suggested making a quick detour on the way to the hotel in order to make a small purchase. He'd thought it would be a good idea to offer it to Mac, although Lanie had her reservations.

Now she stood at the connecting doors, listening for movement on the other side. Hearing it, she knocked lightly and then entered when she heard him mumble.

She found him coming out of the bathroom, fully dressed but with a towel pressed to his face as if he were drying it. When he took it down, she gasped. He looked awful. His color was beyond gray, and his eyes had dark circles under them as if he'd not slept all day, though she knew that wasn't true.

"What do you want?" he snapped at her.

She gave him a saccharine-sweet smile. "My, we're in a good mood, aren't we?"

"Is there a purpose to your visit—other than to irritate me?" He leaned into the bathroom and tossed the towel on the floor.

"While it is my new life's goal to *irritate* you, I did come for another reason. You look like shit, by the way."

"Thank you."

She glanced around the room and noticed the partially eaten food sitting on the room-service tray. "Did you eat?"

"I tried."

She heard the resigned tone in his voice. "Problems?" From what she could see, the rare steak and vegetables looked like his normal fare.

"Nope. It went down almost as easily as it came back up."

She reached into the plastic bag she held, pulled out the contents, and held them out to him. "Here, maybe this will help."

He took it from her and, for a minute, his face remained expressionless. "More pig's blood?"

"No—human blood."

He stared at her, his expression hard and frigid. "And you thought, since I seem to have turned into a vampire, I might as well start drinking blood?"

"What I thought," she enunciated clearly, "is that if you got enough of the venom into your system, then maybe the reason you're feeling—and looking—like sh . . . so bad, is that you need blood. And knowing you found the pig's blood not to your taste, I thought maybe you'd prefer this."

"Because, of course, the monster in me needs to eat, is that right?" He tossed the bag into the bathroom, where it hit the wall and split open, blood splattering over everything. "Well, pardon me if I find that a little hard to accept right now."

Lanie gaped in shock as blood ran down the wall and onto the tiled floor. "A simple no thank you would have sufficed."

"What the hell did you think you were doing?" He took a step closer, and if he was trying to intimidate her, he'd succeeded, but she'd be damned if she'd let him know it.

"I was only trying to help."

"I think you've helped enough already," he sneered, stepping closer to her.

"Wh-what do you mean?" It took every ounce of courage not to back away from the waves of anger pulsing off him.

"What I mean is—thanks to your propensity for doing whatever the hell you want to and opening that cage door in the first place, my life, as I knew it, is over—forever. I'm *never* going to get it back."

Stunned by his accusation, she tried to open her mouth to say something, but no words would come. The truth of his statement hit her, leaving her breathless, and she barely registered that Mac's eyes were glowing dully and his fangs were bared. "I think you should leave now."

She nodded. "You're right. It *is* my fault, and if I could relive the moment and make it right, I would, but I can't. I'm sorry."

Hurrying into her room, she closed and locked the door behind her. Then she sank down onto the edge of the bed and took a deep, ragged breath as the full weight of her guilt and regret pressed in on her. He was right to hate her—she had ruined his life.

# Chapter
# 15

After a few minutes Lanie heard Mac leave. She wondered where he was going and then told herself that she didn't really want to know. When the phone rang moments later, she welcomed the distraction.

"Oh, hello, Uncle Charles."

"Lanie, what's wrong? You sound upset."

"No, I'm fine," she lied. "Is everything okay with Dirk?"

"Yes, he looks remarkably well for someone who practically had his throat ripped out."

"Good."

"The reason I'm calling is that I wanted to know how Mac took to our gift. Did he drink it? Did it help?"

Lanie sighed. "I'm sorry you went to the trouble you did, Uncle Charles. Not only did he not like it, he threw it against the wall. I just hope he remembers to wipe it up before the hotel kicks us out of here."

"Well, if they do, you can always stay with me. I'd be thrilled to have you."

"Thanks, I'll keep that in mind. Any suggestions on what to do about Mac? I'm afraid he might be seriously ill."

"I'll talk to him. Is he there by chance?"

Lanie felt the hurt of Mac's anger once more. "No, he left. I don't know where he went or when he'll be back."

There was a slight pause on the other end of the phone, but if the admiral noticed the quaver in her voice, he was kind enough not to say anything about it. "I'll find him and talk to him. Why don't you try to relax tonight?"

"Thanks. I think I will."

She hung up the phone and looked around the room, feeling out of sorts. She went into the bathroom to wash her face and felt better. Thinking a cold soda might taste good, she grabbed the ice bucket to go get ice when she suddenly remembered the note she'd taken from the freezer. Setting down the bucket, she reached into her pocket and pulled out the small folded scrap of paper. She opened it and read:

> D 1. yqf3 jqe3 0oqhw 59 o3qf3. og 8w
> eqht3497w.
> g3 dq43r7o. 28oo d9h5qd5 697 w99h.
> o9f3, eqe.

It took her tired brain a moment to make sense of the seemingly nonsensical characters, but then she recognized it for what it was—a game she and her father had played when she was growing up. It warmed her heart that he had remembered.

Going to the laptop, she studied the keyboard. *D 1* stood for "down one level"—it was the key to breaking the simple code. Knowing that, it didn't take long to transcribe the rest of the message by selecting the key one level below the letter or number in the message. When she finished, she read it.

*Have made plans to leave. LB is dangerous. Be careful. Will contact you soon. Love, Dad.*

The fact that he'd left a coded message for her told her that he'd not wanted Burton to know—which suggested to her that he wasn't a willing participant in Burton's schemes. Feeling better than she had been, she booted up her laptop and logged on to the Internet. Though she thought the chances were slim that she'd find one, she checked her e-mail in-box for a possible second message from her father. There wasn't one. Determined to not let that bother her, she continued to study the city's public records for anything that would help her locate where Burton might be hiding out.

An hour later a knock sounded on her door.

Getting up, she looked through the peephole and saw one of the hotel staff standing on the other side, an envelope in his hand.

"Yes?" she asked, opening the door.

"Lanie Weber?"

When she nodded, he handed her the envelope. "This message was called into the front desk for you a little while ago."

She thanked him and he disappeared before she could give him a tip. Curious, she tore open the envelope and inside found another message from her father—this one asking her to meet him. She grabbed her purse and ran downstairs.

"I understand you're giving the nursing staff a hard time," Mac commented, walking into Dirk's hospital room where he found his friend sitting in bed, looking very uncomfortable in a hospital gown.

"I told them I wanted out of here, and the doctors refused to discharge me. When I informed them that I intended to discharge myself, they took my clothes." Dirk glared at him. "Why would they do that, do you suppose?"

Mac smiled. "Probably because I told them to. I didn't want you to leave before I got here."

"What took you so long?"

"I had to make a quick stop at the morgue—a small matter to be seen to." When Dirk gave him a confused look, he explained. "They found Kinsley's body earlier today. He was dead—really dead, but I didn't want to take any chances, so I dropped by to stake him."

He held out the small workout bag he carried with him. "I brought you a change of clothes. Hope you weren't too attached to the old ones. I had them thrown out."

Dirk got out of bed and took the bag from him. He pulled out his IV and wasted no time ripping off the hospital gown to change clothes. Mac watched, amazed, wondering if his friend was even aware that he was moving unusually fast. It seemed the chupacabra venom had affected him, too, and Mac felt an odd sense of camaraderie—he was no longer the only one like this.

"How are you feeling?" he asked.

"I feel fine. Everyone around here is acting like I almost died, even though I keep telling them it was only a scratch." He touched his neck where the bandages covered his wounds.

"You really believe that?"

He looked at Mac, and for a moment, Mac thought he'd deny the truth, but Dirk was stronger than that. "No."

Mac nodded. "Believe me, I understand what you're going through—probably better than anyone."

Dirk sat on the guest chair across the room to put on his new shoes and socks. He didn't say anything until he'd finished, then the look he gave Mac was one of resigned acceptance. "So, I'm going to be like you?"

Mac merely cocked an eyebrow and smiled. "Not *going to be,* you *already are.*"

Dirk seemed to digest that, then slapped his hands on his knees as he stood up. "Okay—what now?"

Mac held out the Against Medical Advice papers. "Sign these so I can get you out of here, and then let's go talk to Winslow. He said he came by earlier."

"Yeah. He wanted to see how I was doing and offered to let me stay at his place."

"Good, I think you should."

They walked out of the room, stopping off at the nurses' station where Dirk turned in his self-discharge papers.

"What about you?" he asked as they walked toward the elevators that would take them to the first floor. "Winslow said he offered his place to you and Lanie as well."

"I don't know. I didn't get a chance to talk to her about it."

There must have been something in his tone because Dirk gave him an inquisitive look. "Trouble in paradise?"

Mac didn't feel like discussing it, yet found himself doing just that. "We had a fight." At Dirk's raised eyebrow, he went on. "She thought I wasn't looking well and brought me human blood to drink, thinking it might help." Even now, his stomach revolted at the memory.

"Why would she think you'd want or need blood?"

"Maybe because I bit her the other day and drank some of hers."

"What?" Dirk turned on him, a look of stunned condemnation and worry on his face.

"We were in bed, and in the heat of the moment . . . something came over me and I bit her."

"Did you hurt her?"

"No, I don't think so. She didn't act like she was hurt, but I could tell that the whole thing surprised her as much as it did me. But what's worse than biting her is that I drew blood and swallowed some. And damn it, Dirk, it tasted good."

Dirk grew thoughtful beside him. "But the blood she brought you today *didn't* taste good?"

"I don't know—I didn't try it."

"Weren't you curious?"

Mac shook his head, remembering how the sight of the blood had turned his stomach, making him almost as sick as the rare steak he'd eaten earlier that evening had made him. "Not in the least."

Dirk sighed. "That's a relief. I don't mind the glowing eyes or the fangs, but the thought of drinking blood doesn't appeal to me, you know?"

"Yeah." They hailed a cab to take them to the admiral's house and once they were on their way, Dirk asked him, "Are there any other changes I should worry about?"

"You mean, other than the whole lifestyle, sleep during the day, up all night part?" He shrugged. "I don't know. I'm not sure I've figured it all out yet." He gave Dirk a friendly slap on the back and smiled. "We'll figure it out together."

"This is it. You want me to wait?"

The cabbie's voice broke into her thoughts, and Lanie leaned closer to her backseat window so she could peer out. She wouldn't have thought a single town could have this many depressed and vacant buildings.

"Are you sure this is the right place?" She repeated the number, speaking distinctly, hoping he had misunderstood her earlier and her real destination lay in a safer neighborhood.

"This is it," he said, dashing her hopes. "Maybe you got the wrong address?"

"No," she answered resignedly. "I'm not that lucky." She looked out the window again, but saw no sign of her father.

"Maybe you could drive around the block?" she suggested, not wanting to leave the safety of the cab just yet. Maybe her father was running late.

"Sure, but the meter's runnin'." He put the car in gear and started forward at a slow pace. "This ain't that great a place to be hangin' out, day or night."

That seemed obvious to Lanie. "I'm supposed to meet someone here," she explained. She saw the driver's raised eyebrows reflected in the rearview mirror, but didn't bother to elaborate.

"Is that who you're meeting?" The cabbie's voice sounded hopeful as, a minute later, he pointed to a figure standing around the corner.

"Can you drive up to him, please?"

The cabbie rounded the corner, but as soon as they got closer, the man walked off, turning into the nearest alley. By the time the cabbie reached the alley entrance, the man was more than halfway to the other end.

"Your friend seems a little shy."

*Of course*, Lanie thought, mentally slapping her forehead. Her father wouldn't want anyone else to see him. She dug in her purse and pulled out a few bills, which she gave to the driver. "Would you wait for me, please? I won't be long."

He nodded, so she climbed out of the cab and started toward the figure waiting in the distance. The evening sky was slightly overcast, making it even more difficult to make out her father's features.

"Dad?" She hollered to him and raised her arm. It seemed to her that he hesitated before returning her wave, and that struck her as odd. Without consciously meaning to, she slowed her steps. Doubts crept in. Would her father ignore a lifetime of paternal instincts and ask her to meet him someplace dark and potentially dangerous?

She didn't think so. She wondered if she should return to the safety of the cab and glanced back, only to see taillights disappearing down the street. Alarm shot through her as she silently cursed the cabdriver.

The figure in the alley was moving toward her now, and she didn't recognize his gait. The thought that this might be Burton or one of his vampire recruits held her frozen in place. Was this how she would die? Her lifeblood drained out by a vampire?

No, she wouldn't die, a horrified voice in her head whispered. She'd come back as a deranged, bloodsucking fiend. It was this thought that finally broke through her paralysis.

Lanie knew that if she turned and ran, he would know she had discovered the trap and he would attack with such speed that she'd have no chance at all. Her only hope lay in letting him think she was deceived and then catching him off guard.

She moved forward at a snail's pace and pulled her purse to the front so she could slip her hand into it without taking her eyes off the vampire. Blindly, she groped around for anything she might use as a weapon. Her choices were depressingly limited.

Before she was ready, the man was close enough to see, and as she'd suspected, it wasn't her dad. Neither was it Burton, for which she was marginally grateful.

"Where's my father?"

"I'm afraid I don't know exactly." He made no effort to hide his fangs when he smiled. "I suppose he's still collecting blood, like he does every night for us."

"You sent that message to me?" She knew she had to keep him talking, to distract him as she subtly moved her hand to the other corner of her purse, touching and rejecting items.

"Yes. Burton wants you."

She stilled as the pronouncement soaked in. "Why?"

"I didn't ask."

"And if I refuse to go with you?"

He laughed, and it was an ugly sound. "Not an option."

It was the answer she'd expected, and as he reached for er, she made a final, desperate grab at the contents of her urse. Her hand closed around a small cylinder and she ulled it out, her finger already on the nozzle.

Her aim was true as she fired a stream of pepper spray irectly into his face. Caught off guard, he wasn't able to hield his eyes in time and received a large dose. Lanie mmediately darted backward as he stumbled toward her, ne hand over his eyes while the other reached out for her. lis violent stream of obscenities filled the quiet night.

Lanie turned and ran. She listened for sounds of pur- uit as she reached the street and looked around desper- ely for a cab. There were none, so she picked a direction random and ran. She knew she didn't have much time efore he came after her.

Racing along the next block, she passed another alley. lancing in, she came to an abrupt halt. An old trash umpster sat midway down. She looked to make sure the mpire wasn't already in sight, watching her, and then icked down the alley. She checked the doors of the ildings on each side of her, pushing open the ones that e could, hoping he would think she'd gone in one of em.

When she reached the Dumpster, she pressed her nds against the lid and lifted. A whiff of air escaped, and e almost choked on the foul stench. Bracing the lid up th one hand, she lifted the corner of her shirt and dragged roughly over the corner of the Dumpster so the cloth ught and tore. When she lowered the lid, a trace piece of

her torn shirt was barely visible, but it was enough. A former SEAL with a vampire's night vision should have no
trouble spotting it.

She glanced to the front of the alley and still saw no
sign of him, so she raced for the nearest unlocked door
and ducked inside.

Moving as silently as she could, she crept through the
building, groping her way through dark hallways, grateful
for what little light spilled in through the windows from
the street lamps outside. She kept her mind firmly focused
on finding the front door, though she was all too aware of
the soft scratching and scurrying noises around her.

After what seemed forever, she found it. Looking out
the side window, she leaned first to one side and then
the other, trying to see as much of the street outside as she
could. There was no sign of the vampire.

Then she heard a noise from the alley. It was the sound
of the Dumpster lid being thrown back. Knowing this was
her best opportunity, she opened the door as silently as
she could and took off running down the street. As soon as
she reached the next corner, she turned and kept going.

The name of the street seemed familiar. Reaching the
next corner, she turned again, remembering that there was a
residential area only a few blocks away. She was breathing
hard by the time she got there. Trying the door of the first
apartment building she reached, she found it locked.
Wondering what to do, she noticed the call box mounted
beside the front door. She pushed all the buttons, hoping
that someone inside would ring her in.

"Can I help you?"

She gave a startled cry and whirled around to see a
young man standing behind her. He wasn't the vampire.

but she shuddered to realize that she'd been so preoccupied pushing the buttons, she hadn't heard him come up behind her.

She swallowed, forcing her heart back into her chest, and gestured helplessly to the door. "I don't suppose you can let me in? I can't find my key."

"I don't remember seeing you around," the man said, not rudely or accusingly. "Do you live here?"

"I'm new." She practically held her breath and kept her expression innocent. Finally, he smiled and pulled out his key.

As soon as the door opened, Lanie hurried inside, glancing down the street as she did. So far, so good.

"Thanks again." She waved to the man as she hurried up the staircase, trying to act like she knew exactly where she was going. He started up the stairs behind her, and she wondered if he was following her. She decided to go up to the third floor and was grateful when he stopped on the second.

She walked down the hallway and let herself relax a little. She was fairly certain that she had lost the vampire. Taking out her phone to call Mac, she hesitated as his words from earlier played over in her head. Asking Mac for help was the last thing she wanted to do. She considered calling Uncle Charles or a cab, but didn't want to put someone else's life in jeopardy with the vampire lurking just outside. When it was closer to dawn it would be safe to leave, and that's when she'd call someone to come get her. It wasn't a great plan, but it was a plan.

Putting away the phone, she walked back to the stairwell. If the vampire came after her, one or two good kicks against the old wood banister and it would break into stakelike pieces. Satisfied that she wasn't completely without a weapon, she sat on the stairs, leaned against the wall, and pulled the ever-present novel from her purse. Flipping to the last page she'd read, she settled in for the long wait.

"Come on in, boys," the admiral invited Mac and Dirk, leading them through the large open foyer, past the great room, and down the hall to a set of large double doors. He opened them, and Mac found himself inside the admiral's study.

The hardwood floor was polished to a high gleam, and a large Oriental rug covered the center of the room. The walls running the length of the study were floor-to-ceiling bookcases, and opposite the door, a huge mahogany desk stood facing them. Two burgundy leather chairs with a small table between them faced the desk, and on the wall behind it, on each side, were two large windows looking out on well-lit, manicured lawns and a swimming pool.

Displayed on the wall behind the desk, between the windows, was the largest collection of knives, daggers, and swords that Mac had ever seen. Taking a look around the room, Mac saw that here and there were glass display cases containing additional swords. In the center of one of the bookcases was another glass case holding all the admiral's military medals.

"Is all this authentic?" Dirk asked from where he stood examining what looked to Mac to be a samurai sword.

"Yes, it's all authentic."

"This must have cost you a fortune," Mac said quietly, wondering where the older man got his money.

"Most of these I inherited," the admiral replied. "Although I have managed to add a few pieces to the collection over the years." He walked to the far side of the room where a waist-high display cabinet stood and looked down through the glass. "This is my favorite."

Mac walked over and looked inside the case where he saw a most unusual sword. The pommel appeared to be silver-plated, and engraved on the side was a man's head with eyes of embedded rubies and fangs protruding from an open mouth. It looked suspiciously like a vampire. The hilt of the sword curved outward and back, acting as a hand guard, and the blade, forty-some-odd inches by Mac's estimate, gleamed under the display lamp.

"This, gentlemen, is a sword that has been in my family for many generations." The admiral pulled a key chain from his pocket, selected a key, and opened the locked case. He lifted the sword out lovingly, but when he went to offer it to Mac for a better look, the blade slipped and he winced, drawing back his hand and dropping the blade.

With lightning-fast speed, Mac grabbed it, not letting it hit the ground, then turned to the admiral, who cradled his injured hand as blood pooled in his palm from the cut in the padding beneath his thumb.

"Damn," he muttered. "I must be getting clumsy in my old age."

Mac stared at the blood, mesmerized by it. When he finally looked up, he found the admiral watching him closely and suddenly felt as if he were being tested. Irritated, he looked over at Dirk and found his friend also staring at the blood. As if feeling his gaze, Dirk looked up and their eyes met.

"What's going on, Admiral?" Mac demanded. "You're not that old or clumsy, but you're a little transparent. That was no accident, so what's up?" Suspicion furrowed his brow. "Lanie told you we were vampires, is that it? And you wanted to see how we'd react to the sight of blood?"

Rather than look embarrassed, Admiral Winslow smiled. "Something like that."

"Maybe we should get a rag or something," Dirk suggested, "before you bleed all over the rug here."

The admiral didn't move but studied each man in turn with the same keen, assessing look Mac had seen many times before during his SEAL years. It was a look he knew well—and respected.

"For generations, my family has guarded a secret so sacred that we never speak of it aloud. It has been passed down from father to son in a secret ritual. Now, when I die, since I never married or had children, it is at risk of being lost forever—unless I choose a successor." He glanced at each of them and smiled. "I had thought it would be impossible to find someone worthy of this responsibility, but now, it seems, I've found two such individuals."

"Admiral, maybe you'd better sit down. I think you might have lost more blood than you realize," Mac suggested.

"Do you trust me?"

The question took Mac by surprise and looking into the admiral's eyes, he knew the older man didn't want an automatic response. He wanted honesty, and so Mac took a moment to think about it. Across from him, he knew

Dirk was asking himself the same question. Did they trust him?

Finally, he nodded. "Yes."

"With your life?" the admiral pressed, sounding very serious.

"With my life," Mac responded, equally serious.

The older man looked at Dirk for his response, and there was no hesitation. "With my life," Dirk replied.

"Then trust me now," the admiral replied. "Kneel before me."

Mac exchanged another look with Dirk, but they both did as instructed. The admiral stood before them, his eyes shining bright with an emotion Mac couldn't identify.

"I give this gift freely that you may understand," he intoned, raising his cut hand above them. "Open your mouths." As Mac watched in stunned disbelief, the admiral tilted his hand and allowed blood to run into his mouth. Unsure what to do, Mac held it there, refusing to swallow. The admiral turned to Dirk and did the same thing.

"What is freely given must be freely accepted. You have only faith and trust to guide your decision. To accept, all you have to do is swallow my blood." Up to this point, Mac thought the admiral sounded like he was reciting passages from a ritual. Now his tone changed. "There's no shame in spitting out the blood. I only ask that you spit it out in the trash can by the desk, rather than on my rug. Blood is rather difficult to get out."

It was the moment of truth, Mac realized. Everything in him longed to spit out the blood, reject the monster within, yet he hadn't lied to the admiral. His was not a blind trust; it was one carefully weighed and measured.

Would he walk into the pits of hell for this man? An image of Lanie appeared before him, and he was shocked to realize when it came to people for whom he'd lay down his life, she now was first in his thoughts.

Distracted by the discovery, a trickle of blood slipped down his throat. Rather than find the taste repulsive, he found it quite palatable.

He felt a growing warmth in his hand and looked down at the sword he still clutched. The heat seemed to be coming from the pommel. He gripped it tightly and vowed to himself that if his trust was misplaced, then his last act would be one of vengeance.

He swallowed the blood.

# Chapter
# 16

I mmediately Mac felt the blood coursing through his body and it infused him with a vibrant energy. His senses grew sharper, and the lethargy that had weighed him down for the last several nights disappeared. The sword in his hand pulsed, and he looked down to see the ruby eyes of the face glowing brightly.

He heard Dirk's quick intake of breath and turned to see a bemused expression that, he thought, mirrored his own. When he glanced up, Mac saw the admiral smiling broadly. He gestured to the sword and then to Dirk, so Mac passed the weapon to his friend, who held it reverently. If possible, the rubies shone more brightly.

"I imagine you both have several questions," the admiral finally said. "Let me wash away this blood, and then we'll talk."

Mac and Dirk rose to their feet as he walked out of the study, and for several seconds they simply stood there. Mac thought he might be in a state of shock, because something significant had occurred here, but he had no clue what it was.

"This can't be good," Dirk muttered. "But what a rush."

Mac couldn't have agreed more. Trying to give himself time to collect his thoughts, he walked around the study, examining the other weapons. When the admiral finally joined them again, both men turned to him expectantly. He reached for the sword, taking it from Dirk's hand. The rubies in the pommel faded to a dull red.

"She's a beauty, isn't she?" He stroked the gleaming blade with a loving touch, then turned and smiled at each of them. "How do you feel?"

"Depressingly good," Mac replied truthfully. "Before now, I hadn't thought of myself as a vampire."

The admiral laughed. "You're not a vampire—either of you."

"But we drank your blood," Dirk replied.

"Only because I asked you to—freely given and freely accepted. A true vampire doesn't ask. He—or she—takes by force because they need the blood to survive. You do not."

Mac and Dirk exchanged looks. "Why do I get the feeling that you know more about all this vampire stuff than you're letting on?" Mac asked.

"You're right. I've not been completely forthcoming, but please understand, until this afternoon, I didn't realize the full situation or the extent of your involvement."

"Lanie."

The admiral nodded. "But you mustn't be upset with her, Mac. She was worried about you both, and it was right for her to come to me. Vampires and chupacabras have been around for hundreds, maybe thousands, of years.

Usually, we're able to keep them under control, but every now and then, a situation arises that must be dealt with."

"Who's *we*?" Mac asked.

"My family. We are responsible for finding the changelings—and for the sword." He raised the weapon higher, drawing their attention to it. "The inscription here on the blade is written in an ancient language that has been all but lost over the ages. Loosely translated, it reads: *When the sword finds the slayer, death on winged horse shall fly. Let justice prevail.*" He opened the hand around the hilt so they could see the emblem on the side. "You saw the rubies glow when you held the sword? It hasn't done that in almost a hundred years. That was the last time the sword was held by a true slayer."

"Slayer of what?" Mac was pretty sure he didn't want to hear the answer.

"Vampires."

He rolled his eyes. "Please. You're telling me that *you're* a vampire slayer."

"No. I'm merely the Keeper of the Sword. Only changelings can be slayers."

"Do you know how crazy this sounds?" Dirk asked.

"I would imagine not as crazy as it would have *before* you knew vampires existed."

Mac had to give the admiral credit for that one. "I'm almost afraid to ask, but who are these changelings you keep talking about?"

The admiral smiled and gave them each a pointed look.

Dirk shook his head. "Oh, no. You can't be serious. What is a changeling, anyway?"

"Half vampire and half human."

Mac felt a chill run down his spine. "I thought you said we weren't vampires."

"You're not. You're half vampire. The chupacabra, when it attacked you, injected you with enough venom to convert you. You've noticed the changes in yourselves."

"So what are you suggesting? That we go around looking for Burton and other vampires, with swords strapped around our waists?" Dirk asked, incredulous. "No offense, but are you crazy?"

The admiral merely cocked an eyebrow, as much as saying yes. Dirk swore.

None of it made sense to Mac, but there was one part of what had just happened that bothered him the most. "If we're not really vampires, why did you ask us to drink blood?"

"Blood that is freely given and freely received has the power to energize and heal the changeling. The key is life. Blood is essential to life. Unlike the vampire, who was human and then died before turning, a changeling doesn't die. Therefore, they are creatures of life, not of death. Because blood is a gift of life, the changeling who drinks it is imbued with the life force."

As far as surreal explanations went, it was consistent with all the others he'd heard, and Mac shelved it away for later consumption. "What if we'd been real vampires?"

The admiral's expression turned carefully blank. "As Keepers, my family has, for centuries, taken an herb that only we grow. We call it *la fleur de vivre*. It absorbs quickly into the bloodstream and lasts for twenty-four hours. It's the only thing we've found to be effective against vampires."

Mac didn't like the way the admiral avoided giving a direct answer to his question, so he asked it again. "What if we'd been real vampires and swallowed your blood?"

"Then you'd be dead—permanently dead."

Clint sat alone in the empty building, having finished collecting blood for the evening and sent away the last homeless blood donor. He looked at the fresh bag in his hand and with a resigned sigh bit into it, feeling more like a monster than a man.

As much blood dribbled down the side of his mouth and chin as down his gullet. Normally, he would have squeezed the contents into a cup first, but there was something satisfying about the feel of his fangs piercing the plastic bag. It was like piercing human flesh, which he was reluctant to do in reality. While the notion of drinking blood no longer bothered him, he didn't like harming innocent people.

The night of his rising haunted him still, and he found little solace in knowing that he'd been unable to control himself or that Lance had done most of the actual killing. Once Clint realized what was happening, he'd done nothing to stop it, which only added to his sin. He was grateful that during the days, his sleep was dreamless.

Shaking off the memory, he brought his thoughts back to the present. He hadn't stopped Lance that fateful night, but he had no such excuse now. He'd overheard Lance talking to the others; knew their plans. The lives of more than a few researchers were now at stake, and Clint knew he had to do something. He went over his plan once more in his head and then, satisfied that he'd thought of every contingency, finished drinking the blood and tossed the bag into the corner. He wouldn't be back.

At his feet, Gem stared up at him, her eyes a brilliant green, reflecting her contented state. He picked up the spent bag of dog's blood and tossed it over beside his own. "You like that?" He smiled and gave her head a loving pat. She hadn't grown at all over the last six months, and he was beginning to think it took chupacabras decades to mature—which meant the adult was quite old.

"She should be treasured," he mumbled to himself as he stood and packed all the blood into his backpack. "Are you ready to go?" he asked the small creature as he struggled into the shoulder straps. At his words, the baby chupacabra leaped into the air and landed on his shoulders, where she preferred to ride.

Slipping into the night, Clint blended with the shadows and made his way back to where Lance had established their new lair, taking a slightly different route than he normally did. He made one stop along the way, at a vet's clinic, where he made a "purchase," leaving behind enough money to pay for the items he took.

As he rehearsed what he needed to do, he was struck with a peculiar sense of déjà vu—hadn't he done something similar just the other night?

Both Harris and Kinsley had proved resistant to Lance's command and his plans, but it was Kinsley who had opposed Lance openly, making him the perfect candidate for the experiment. Clint knew that Lance would miss him least. He'd hated to take a life, but it had been important to test the antiserum without Lance's knowledge, so Clint had gone to Kinsley just after sunset, catching the man as he first rose. He'd injected the man before he knew what Clint intended to do, and by the time he reacted, it was too late.

As the antiserum destroyed the venom-filled cells of his body, the seizures had been immediate—and clearly painful. It was over in minutes, leaving Kinsley dead. Clint enjoyed a private victory—the antiserum worked!

Lance discovered the body later but had been so preoccupied that morning, no doubt concerned about Hector's continued disappearance, that he'd not given Kinsley's demise much thought. In fact, Clint thought Lance had taken the news of Kinsley's death surprisingly well.

The new lair loomed ahead of him, and Clint went around to the back of the building where he could sneak into his lab without having to see the others. The adult chupacabra was there, waiting for him. She'd grown so weak that she could barely stand, much less attack, and so Lance had been leaving her alone.

She raised a weary eyelid when she saw Clint. *Feel bad.*

"I know."

*Dying.*

He knew that, too, and hated that he'd not been strong enough to prevent it. He had a plan now, but the most he hoped to achieve was to free the adult long enough to give her a place where she could die in peace—he knew he couldn't save her.

Once again, he'd failed to protect those he cared for, and he found himself thinking of his daughter, longing for things that could not be.

Setting his backpack on the floor at his feet, he reached inside and pulled out the vial of drugs and the large syringe he'd taken from the vet's office. He pulled the protective cap off the needle and drew several cc's of medicine into the barrel. He had no idea how much of the tranquilizer he'd need and worried that too much might kill her instantly, rather than simply knock her out.

He eyed her again, judged her to be about the size of a small pony, and drew a little more of the drug into the syringe. When he finished, he went back to the adult.

"You'll have to trust me on this," he told her. "He'll never let you go." He saw her gaze flicker to the baby beside her and felt a warmth and fear through the link. "I'll take care of her," he promised. "I won't let him have her." For a moment, creature and vampire studied each other, and then very slowly and deliberately, the chupacabra blinked her eyes in assent.

Clint offered a silent prayer, on the off chance that heaven still heard him, and injected the drug into her. Morning was approaching, and he had just enough time to dispose of the drug and syringe before Lance came strolling in. He found Clint sitting on the floor with the two creatures. Lance stared at them with disgust and then snorted.

"Weber, sometimes I think you like those creatures more than you like people." He left the room never having spoken a truer word.

Tired from an evening spent talking to the admiral, Mac and Dirk returned to the hotel together. The first thing Mac noticed when he walked into his room was that Lanie was not in hers. He'd become so attuned to her—

the sound of her breathing, the tempo of her heartbeat, the scent that was hers alone—that he noticed when she was absent.

He remembered the harsh words he'd spoken to her earlier, and a part of him was afraid she'd left for good. Stepping through the connecting doors, he swept the room with his gaze, verifying what he already knew. She wasn't there. He tried to tell himself that she'd run out for a quick errand and would be back soon, but it was still dark outside and that argument seemed unlikely.

"Problems?" Dirk asked from the other room.

"She's not here."

As he stood surveying the room, under the irrational hope that she'd materialize out of thin air, he heard the shuffle of paper and then Dirk's muttered oath.

"I think you'd better take a look at this."

Mac hurried into the other room and saw Dirk standing by the door, holding an open envelope and a note.

"I found this in the corner. It must have been pushed there when we opened the door."

Mac looked at it, then swore.

*I have her. Burton.*

An address was scrawled across the bottom.

Checking the time, he saw that it was almost sunrise. "I have to go get her," he announced.

Dirk, looking tired, already had his hand on the door. "Let's do it."

Mac studied his friend. Dirk had been attacked the night before and was not fully recovered. How wise was it for him to exert himself so soon when the night had already proved so trying?

Still, Mac knew that if the situation were reversed, he'd insist on going, so he didn't try to talk Dirk out of it. Rather, he welcomed the company. If Burton had Lanie, he needed all the assistance he could get.

They took a cab to the address on the note and found themselves in front of an old hotel, located on the corner of derelict central. It was a dilapidated ten-story structure that had rotted or missing boards on the doors and windows.

Mac and Dirk did a quick surveillance of the area while approaching, alert for signs of the trap they knew they were about to walk into. When they were certain they weren't being watched, they walked to the back of the building to find the rear entrance.

They found the one that led down into the basement, which was where Mac felt sure they'd find Burton. Without windows, it was the safest place for vampires, so it made the most sense to hold Lanie there.

Checking their guns, they opened the door and stepped inside. With every step, Mac prayed that he would find Lanie alive and unharmed.

Lanie arrived back at the hotel, numb with exhaustion from a night spent in the apartment building. Some of the residents went to work at dawn and after calling for a cab, she'd followed them outside, hoping there was safety in numbers. Now, all she wanted to do was sleep.

Opening the door to her room, she was struck by the silence. She'd been sure that Mac would have returned from wherever he went. It suddenly occurred to her that maybe she'd been naive to think he would get over his anger and hurt with her. Concerned, she walked into his room and saw that it was empty.

She started back toward her side, resigned to wait for him, when she noticed the paper and envelope lying on the desk. It looked just like the note she'd received earlier that evening, the one that had sent her hurrying out into the night—into a trap.

She picked it up and read it. Icicles of fear pierced her heart as she realized that Mac had raced off into danger— to save her. Wishing she knew Mac's cell phone number, she went to the phone and dialed the number to the hospital instead, asking to be connected to Dirk's room. He would know what to do.

Her fear grew to panic when she was told that he had checked out hours ago. Quickly she phoned Uncle Charles, but hung up when she reached his answering machine. She was on her own.

Their search of the basement was thorough and fast because it was empty. Refusing to leave until he'd checked every room and closet, Mac and Dirk proceeded to the next floor.

By the time they'd searched it, the sun was peeking over the horizon, and tendrils of light filtered through the cracks of the boarded windows. Mac struggled up the next flight of stairs. The coming of dawn had brought with it a lethargy that made him feel as if his bones were made of granite. Behind him, he heard the labored breathing of Dirk and knew his friend suffered similarly. When they reached the door to the next floor, Mac opened it and stepped through, looking up and down the hallway as he caught his breath.

"Should we split up?" Dirk asked, coming to rest beside him.

Mac considered the suggestion. They could cover more ground if they did, but Burton was evil, not stupid. Splitting up was too dangerous. "No."

Mac led them to the right, stopping to look inside the first room, which was missing a door. It was obviously empty, but there were back rooms that had to be searched. Dirk pulled his gun and stood off to the side while Mac moved forward cautiously.

He pulled open the door and ducked inside the room, but it was empty. He moved on to the next one, repeating his actions on down the hallway, his anxiety and concern for Lanie growing as each successive room proved equally deserted. He forced himself to move faster. If something happened to her . . .

He refused to finish the thought and headed down to the other end. Once again, they checked each room, and when they found the last one empty, both men silently resigned themselves to climbing the flight of stairs to the next level.

This floor had suites, which meant fewer rooms to go into, but more places to stash a hostage—or lay a trap. By now, Mac was having trouble stifling the doubts and recriminations flooding his mind. He should have sent Lanie home when he had the chance. She would have been safe then. Why had he let her stay?

He knew the answer to that, and it made the fear that she might be hurt that much more intense. He clinched the grip of his gun tighter, feeling the sting of his nails biting into his flesh where his hands overlapped.

Finished with the second floor, they continued on to the third, and then the fourth. It was rapidly becoming apparent that Lanie was not in the building. Still, he couldn't leave without knowing for sure, so they continued on.

Suddenly an explosion that rocked the entire building forced Mac and Dirk to their knees. Plaster from the ceiling and walls crashed down around them, sending up a fine haze of powder. Mac didn't know if it was caused by accident or sabotage, but either way, they needed to exit the building immediately. Already, he smelled the acrid scent of burning plaster and wood, and knew a fire raged below them.

"Get out of here," he ordered Dirk.

"Not without you. Let's hurry and check the rest of this place."

Mac knew not to argue. By the time they checked the last room on the floor, Mac realized that he and Dirk were in trouble. Despite the doors sealing off each floor of the stairwell, the halls were filling with smoke, making it hard to breathe and almost impossible to see. The temperature inside the building had risen so that the oppressing heat worked in concert with their fatigue until every step seemed to require herculean effort.

For the first time, Mac doubted whether he and Dirk would get out alive. Beside him, Dirk, still weak from his attack, stumbled and fell to his knees.

"Man up, soldier. This is no time to quit." Mac gripped Dirk's arm and pulled him to his feet, but it cost him precious energy he couldn't spare. Both men bent over, trying to catch their breath and avoid the thickest smoke, which rose to blanket the ceiling just above their heads.

"We've got to get out of here," Mac said, his voice hoarse.

Dirk nodded and the two took several steps toward the stairwell, their feet like leaden weights, but already Mac saw they couldn't go down that way. Smoke seeped up from below.

The next explosion knocked them both to the floor.

The temptation to stay down was too great. Glancing at Dirk's still form, Mac was afraid his friend might already be dead, and his mind filled with images of Lanie. He knew now that if she'd been in the building, she, too, must be dead. The thought brought a sharp pain to his chest. He had failed her.

The urge to fight for his own survival died. If Lanie was gone—if he'd never see her again—then what was the point of going on? Better to have no life at all.

# Chapter
# 17

*I'll see you soon, baby.*

    At least, he hoped he'd see her in the afterlife—hoped that he'd lived with enough honor to deserve to see her—and then silently chuckled as his mind conjured an image of the two of them, dressed in white gowns, perched on the edge of a billowy cloud, talking—because God knew, the woman always wanted to talk about something.

Even now, he heard her voice in his head, calling his name.

Before him, the smoke swirled and a form appeared within its midst, moving toward him. An angel, come to bear him home. He closed his eyes and felt only relief because if an angel was coming for him, then maybe he wasn't destined for the pits of hell after all.

When next he dared look, she was closer, one hand covering her nose and mouth, the other outstretched, beckoning him.

His eyes stung from the bite of the smoke, but he forced them open, wanting to see her face. Slowly the image became clearer, and he found himself staring into a pair of familiar blue eyes. She was a mirage, a final boon from God.

"Lanie?" he croaked, his voice rough.

"Mac? Are you hurt?" She ran her hands intimately over his chest and arms, checking for signs of injury, and it gradually occurred to him that this was no mirage. This was flesh-and-blood Lanie. She was alive—and she was here, with him.

The realization was a shot of adrenaline straight to his heart. Suddenly he found the energy and strength he'd lacked before. He gripped her shoulders with both hands and pulled her to him in a fierce, near desperate embrace. "I'm sorry for everything I said earlier," he croaked.

He felt her arms tighten around him as she nodded against his shoulder. "It's okay. We'll talk about it later."

He wanted to laugh out loud, but his throat hurt too much. Instead, he released her and then bent over to check on Dirk.

"Is he dead?" Lanie whispered in the unusual quiet.

"I don't think so. Not yet." He shook Dirk and got a small response.

"Mac, we have to hurry," Lanie urged him. "That fire is right below us, and it's burning fast. We don't have much time."

"Help me get him up."

Mac got to his feet and then reached down to grab one of Dirk's arms while Lanie took the other. Together they pulled him up and he opened his eyes. Mac noticed that once Dirk focused on and recognized Lanie, he seemed to rally. As a group, they moved into the last room on the hall and headed for the window. Looking out, Mac met a grim sight. The fire escape that should have led them to safety was little more than a rusted, tangled web of metal, barely hanging from its last remaining anchor several stories below.

"Let's try the other side," he suggested. With Lanie between the two men, her arms around each, supporting them as needed, they moved back out into the hallway and hurried to the opposite side.

They'd taken only a couple of steps past the stairwell door when Lanie pulled the men to a stop. She motioned for them to stay put while she moved forward slowly, testing each step with her foot before placing her weight on it and taking another. After several tentative steps, she backed up and repeated the process off to first one side and then the other. Finally, she returned to Mac's side

"The whole floor's spongy," she announced, gesturing to the expanse of hallway before them. "I think the fire's coming up directly below here. It's not safe. We need to find another way out."

Mac saw her gaze travel upward and knew what she was thinking. They couldn't go down, but they could go up. Unfortunately, there was no way to know if the fire had leaped over a floor and burned up there as well.

Still supporting Dirk, Mac started for the stairs, intending to lead the way. Lanie stopped him.

"I'll go first," she shouted. He shook his head, but she cut him off. "Mac, *this* is what I do. I'll go first."

He didn't like it, but she was right. This was her area of expertise, so he nodded and let her go before him. With the possibility of grave danger ahead, it was one of the hardest things he'd ever done.

They headed straight for the top floor, hoping they'd find a way down. When they reached the door to the roof, Lanie touched the back of her hand to it, checking the temperature to make sure a blazing inferno didn't lie on the other side.

A second later she put her hand on the knob, but when she tried to turn it, nothing happened. She tried again, with the same result. It was locked. She cast a worried glance at Mac and he knew what she was thinking—with a locked door before them and a raging fire burning toward them from below, they were trapped.

But they weren't dead yet. With Lanie standing next to him, looking at him with such despair in her eyes, he knew he couldn't give up. He felt the monster that he tried so hard to keep suppressed lurking beneath the surface and gave it free rein, feeding it the anger and frustration he felt.

His vision took on a reddish tone, nearly blinding as he picked up patterns of heat all around. Of their own accord, his lips started to curl and his fangs began to show. He heard Lanie's gasp and felt Dirk tense beside him. He shot his friend a look and saw him waging his own personal war.

"Let it out," Mac snarled.

"I don't know if I can control myself," Dirk admitted, his glance touching on Lanie.

Her eyes widened at the implication. Mac knew that if Dirk couldn't control himself, then Lanie was in as much danger from him as she was from the fire. Even now, the structure of the building was compromised. If they didn't get onto the roof soon, they could very well fall through to the floors below.

"We have no choice," he said, addressing them both. "I won't let you hurt her." He held Dirk's look as the other man considered his words.

Then he grabbed the knob of the door and on his nod, he and Dirk threw their weight against it. The door crashed open and they ran outside into the warm morning sunlight.

Mac and Dirk instantly flung their hands up to shield their eyes as Lanie ran to the edge of the roof and looked over the side. Mac, still adjusting to the brightness, squinted as she ran along the entire perimeter, looking over the edge at intervals.

He walked over to stand beside Dirk, and they looked down at the roof of the building next door. A small alley, about fifteen feet wide, separated the two buildings. As he stood there, calculating the odds of the idea forming in his head, Lanie joined them.

"We're going to have to jump," he announced.

"Mac, it's ten stories to the ground," Lanie protested. "We won't survive."

He shook his head and pointed to the building next door. "It's only a one-story drop to the next building."

Lanie looked down at the alley that loomed as wide to her as the great Rio Grande and knew she was dead. Maybe Mac and Dirk, with their SEAL training and chupacabra-enhanced abilities, could make that jump, but there was no way she could.

She saw Mac look at Dirk, who gave a solemn nod. Then Mac turned to her. She didn't realize she'd been shaking her head until Mac cupped the sides of her face with his hands. Any other time, she might have been frightened by the eerie red glow of the eyes looking deeply into hers, but behind that light was intelligence, concern, and the confidence she so desperately needed at this moment.

"I'm not going to let you die." He infused the words with such self-assurance, she found herself almost believing him.

In the distance, she heard the faint wail of a siren and hope sprouted. "Do you hear that? We don't have to jump."

"They're too far away, Lanie."

"No. They'll be here soon. They'll have ladders." When he looked doubtful, she hurried on. "You don't even know if you'll make it. You're weak from the sun."

"This isn't the first time we've faced overwhelming odds under the worst possible conditions," Mac told her, referring to himself and Dirk. "We'll do what it takes to get out of this alive—all of us."

At that moment, the building rumbled beneath them and they heard a loud crashing noise. Lanie knew then that Mac was right—there was no more time. Below them, the floors were collapsing. It wouldn't be long before the entire building followed.

"Go!"

She turned at Mac's shout and saw Dirk start running. Lanie saw no sign of hesitancy as he approached the edge of the building and leaped off. Her heart felt as if it went with him. For several seconds he hung in the air and then disappeared from sight. Hardly daring to breathe, she rushed to the edge, praying she wouldn't see his dead body sprawled on the ground in the alley below.

Amazingly, there on the roof of the other building stood Dirk, looking winded and weak, but still alive. She felt Mac's hand on her arm and allowed him to pull her to the opposite side of the roof.

"I can't do this." She waved a hand at the opening. "It's too wide."

"That's why I'm going to carry you."

"What? No," she protested. "I'm too heavy."

"Not for me. Now, climb on." He turned so his back was to her and bent down.

From the vibrations of the roof beneath her feet, Lanie knew she really had no other choice. The building was about to cave in. Grabbing hold of Mac's shoulders for support, she hopped on his back and wrapped her legs around his waist.

Then, before she had time to adjust, Mac was up and running. She felt his muscles working under her legs as he raced across the roof, and then suddenly he gave a great leap and they were airborne.

Fear ripped a scream from her, and she clutched his neck in a near stranglehold, afraid she would fall. For a few seemingly endless moments, the yawning opening of the alley was the only thing beneath them, and Lanie felt the pull of the street far below. Then everything sped up as the roof of the other building rushed to meet them.

They hit with such a jarring impact that Mac stumbled and almost fell. Dirk rushed to them and lent a steadying hand as Lanie loosened her grip and slid off Mac's back. For several seconds, all she could do was stand there, trembling, amazed that they had made it.

Then, as the shock wore off, she turned to Mac, over-come with emotion, and hugged him tightly. His arms enfolded her in a way that was growing both familiar and comfortable.

"Let's go home," she heard him whisper.

They walked several blocks without speaking much, and then caught a cab to take them the rest of the way to the hotel. Mac kept his arm around Lanie the entire time, but she didn't mind. She'd come too close to losing him.

As she rode in the backseat, sitting between the two men, she remembered the notes left for them. "We need to find a new place to stay," she told the men. "Who knows what Burton will send next?"

Mac leaned forward slightly to give her a quizzical look. "Where were you earlier?"

"Sitting in an apartment stairwell halfway across town, waiting for the sun to come up." She quickly explained, ignoring the look of reprimand he gave her when she mentioned running out to meet her father. His features darkened further when she told them how she'd escaped the vampire. "Then I waited until dawn, went outside to find out where I was, and called a cab," she finished. "When I reached the room, I found the other note and knew you and Dirk were walking into a trap. I tried to get there in time to warn you—I'm sorry I was late."

He gave her a squeeze. "I thought you were dead."

"I thought we all were," she admitted. "I was standing in the stairwell when the first bomb went off. I knew I could only go up from there, so I prayed you both were above me."

They reached their hotel, but rather than approaching the front desk as Lanie expected, Mac led them to the elevator.

"Aren't we going to at least see about getting different rooms?"

"Look at us, Lanie. We'll be lucky they don't kick us out, much less give us new rooms."

He was right. They looked like drunks who'd rolled around in the soot. Their faces and clothes were streaked with the black ash from the burning building and they smelled of smoke.

"I think we'll be okay during the day," Mac added as they stepped onto the elevator and rode it in silence to their floor.

As soon as they entered the room, the two men ambled over toward the bed, looking like they could barely stand. She was afraid they'd fall asleep, soot, smell, and all.

"Wait. Don't sit down," she hollered as Dirk approached the bed. "Mac, do you have any clean clothes?"

He stared at her as if he had a hard time processing her words, but then nodded.

"Good, get two sets." She figured he and Dirk were close enough in size and build that his clothes would fit Dirk. She watched Mac rummage in his duffel bag in the closet, coming up with two sets of boxers and jeans, which he held out to her.

She took them and put one set in Mac's bathroom and another in hers. "Okay, before you two drop, go take a shower and put on the clean clothes. Leave the dirty ones on the floor."

Mac looked like he wanted to laugh at her taking charge, but didn't have the energy. Instead, he glanced at his bathroom and then at the connecting doors. "You take this one," he said to Dirk, pointing to the bathroom in his room. "You can crash here."

Dirk nodded.

"I'll shower in here."

Ten minutes later she was sitting in the desk chair when Mac walked out wearing nothing but a towel. He looked tired, clean, and his skin had a bright, healthy glow from the heat of the shower.

"You can take your shower now." His husky tone brushed over her.

"Thanks." She stared at him, a little surprised he wasn't wearing the clothes she'd put in there. Expecting him to go into his own room, she wished him a good night. "Hope you sleep well."

"I plan to," he replied, walking to her bed.

"What are you doing?" she asked when it appeared that he was about to take off his towel and climb under the covers.

His hands froze at his waist. "Taking off my towel."

"You're sleeping in *my* bed?"

"Very observant of you."

"Where am I supposed to sleep?" She wondered if her voice sounded as breathless to him as it had to her.

"There are two beds, Lanie. One in here and one in there. I'll let you decide." His hand began to undo the towel, so she dashed into the bathroom, quickly shutting the door. There was only so much excitement a girl could take.

She took a long shower, giving herself plenty of time to relax and think about all that had happened—and to delay the moment when she had to walk back into the room. Finally, when her skin had pruned, she knew she couldn't put it off any longer. She shut off the water and stepped out. Taking the last towel, she dried herself and then realized that she hadn't brought in a change of clothes. She wrapped the towel about her body as best she could and prayed that Mac had already fallen asleep.

She cracked open the door and listened. When she heard the sound of steady, deep breathing, she stepped out and tiptoed across the room to her duffel bag. A glance at Mac's face took her breath away. Once again, she was struck by all that virile masculinity in *her* bed.

She dug through her bag until she found a T-shirt to wear. It was her last one, and she knew she'd have to do laundry soon. She carried it back to the bathroom to change and briefly considered sleeping in the tub, but how silly would that be?

She stepped out and stood at the connecting doors, looking at Mac's sleeping form in one bed and Dirk's in the other. It would serve Mac right, she thought, taking a step toward the other room, if she went to sleep with Dirk.

"Don't even think about it." His deep voice rumbled; a warm caress on a chilly night.

"I thought you were asleep." Embarrassed, she turned to face him.

"No. I was waiting for you."

"You were?"

"Yeah." He flipped back the bedcovers beside him. "Come here."

Her gaze locked on his, and she walked to him as if drawn. Self-consciously, she climbed in beside him, all too aware that beneath the covers, he was totally bare.

She lay stiffly, waiting as he pulled the covers up over her. Beside her, Mac turned to face her, stretching out his lower arm and then pulling her into his embrace.

"Relax, baby," he whispered, drawing her close so that her head rested in the crook of his chest and arm. "I just want to hold you."

He closed his eyes then and gave a contented sigh. Soon, the rhythm of his breathing grew deeper and slower so that Lanie was slightly surprised, and disappointed, to discover that he really had fallen asleep.

She was trying to decide if she felt insulted or not, then realized that she was too tired to care. She let herself relax and snuggled closer. Nightmares of the fire, her desperate search for Mac, and the nearly crippling fear that they'd all die failed to surface, and she slept better than she had in a long time.

Clint noticed the difference as soon as he rose the next evening. The psychic bond that linked him to the others was so faint, it was barely detectable—but it was still there and Clint breathed a sigh of relief. *She* was still alive.

He rose and turned to see Gem standing over him, watching him. When their eyes met, Clint noticed the little one's eyes seemed cloudy and troubled. Standing, he rubbed the stiffness of the cold floor from his limbs and then went to check on the adult. Normally, she would be awake by now, but this morning Clint found her still in her stonelike state. He didn't have time to smile because at that moment Lance burst into the room, clearly upset.

"What the hell is going on?" he demanded, just before his gaze fell on the stone chupacabra. His eyes narrowed as he shot Clint a look. "Why isn't it awake?"

"I'm not sure, but I think she's dead."

Lance appeared shocked at the pronouncement, and he went up to the creature and laid a hand against the cool, hard skin. He stood that way for a moment and then let his hand fall back to his side. "Damn it. I wasn't done." His eyes flickered to the baby, and Clint stepped into his visual path to distract him.

"She isn't big enough to convert a human into a vampire."

"How long before it is?"

"Based on her rate of growth over the past six months, I'd guess in about twenty years."

"Twenty years?" Lance's mouth dropped open. "You're kidding me, right?"

"No."

"Great, just great. How many vials of the adult venom do you have?"

"Just one," Clint lied.

"Give it to me—and the synthetic stuff you've been working on!"

Clint didn't have to mask his concern. "It's still unstable."

"I don't give a damn. Give me what you have. It'll have to do."

Reluctantly, Clint took the two vials from his backpack, carefully avoiding thought of the third vial, and handed them to Lance, hoping he'd have a chance to get them back later. Though the synthetic venom wasn't perfect, he felt it was close enough that it might be able to convert a dead human to a vampire—for a while. That made two more possible recruits for Lance's growing army.

"We'll have to proceed with the team we have in place," Lance said, crossing over to the cooler where the blood was stored. He pulled out several bags before heading for the door. "You'll need to collect more bags while we're gone." He glared at Clint one final time and then stormed out, calling to the other men as he went.

The order put Clint in a quandary. He didn't want to leave the adult unattended, but if he didn't collect blood, Lance would know he was up to something and frankly, despite going behind Lance's back, Clint was afraid of what the man would do to him.

He grabbed Gem and his backpack, and after leaving several bags of dog's blood on the floor in case the adult woke while he was gone, he left.

He made good time to the collection site where he found a small gathering of homeless men and women waiting for him. He worked quickly, not taking the time to chat with everyone.

Four hours later, when he had enough blood to satisfy Lance, he packed up everything and hurried back to the lair, hoping that no one had arrived before him and found the chupacabra awake, which he prayed she was. He couldn't possibly move her by himself.

When he reached the lair, he noticed that the others, thankfully, had not yet returned. Eager to check on the adult, he rushed into his room and stopped short, his jaw falling open.

The three bags of dog's blood were empty, and the adult chupacabra was gone.

# Chapter
# 18

Lanie woke to the sound of a slow heartbeat and it took her a moment to realize it wasn't her own. It seemed to come from just beneath her ear and as she focused on the sound, she noticed the soft springiness of chest hair and hard muscle beneath her cheek.

The events of the early morning came rushing back to her and she cracked open an eyelid, confirming what she'd almost hoped had been a dream. She was lying with her head on Mac's chest. Worse still, sometime while they'd slept, her shirt had ridden up around her waist and now her bare hips were pressed intimately against Mac's completely nude form.

Heat flooded her face at the predicament, and she tried to figure out how to get out of bed without waking him. When she felt his hand gently caress her back, she realized it was too late. Her mind desperately sought a way to escape this embarrassing situation, and she held perfectly still.

"I know you're awake," he said softly, his voice barely above a whisper.

"I, uh—no, I'm not."

His soft laughter was a low rumble beneath her ear, making her realize how much more comfortable he seemed to be at this moment than she. It made sense, she thought. He'd probably been in bed with hundreds of women, whereas her experience was limited to a few extremely forgettable episodes.

"You're thinking too hard," Mac whispered, putting a finger under her chin and tilting her head up until she was looking into his face. Slowly, he dipped his head toward her and she held her breath, suddenly worried about things like bad hair, no makeup, and—morning breath. "Stop it," he softly chastised, his warm breath fanning her face seconds before his lips touched hers.

All thoughts vanished as her entire consciousness narrowed to focus on his lips, which, like the man, were firm and demanding. She was hesitant at first, but as the kiss grew more intense, so did her response. It seemed that her very essence centered on the feel of his body against hers and when he pulled at her shirt, she willingly allowed him to rid her of it. She almost moaned aloud when they came together again and she rubbed against the soft hairs of his chest.

For several long minutes, he held her head and simply kissed her; long, thorough, devouring kisses. Then his hand was at her shoulder, caressing a trail down her arm until he cupped her breast, molding her fullness. She felt her nipple harden beneath his palm and when he rolled it between his fingers, her breath caught from the sheer pleasure of it. With a groan of impatience, he pulled her on top of him so that her breasts hung heavy in his face. He laved the tip of one nipple before taking it into his mouth to suckle.

Each tug on her breast sent tremors shooting to a point low in her belly, and when she felt his erection against her upper thigh, she shifted so he was between her legs. The tip of his shaft teased the sensitized flesh at her entrance and she squirmed, needing to feel him inside her. As if sensing her need, he grabbed her hips and held her in place as he thrust up into her. The sensation of him filling her almost sent her over the edge. Her hands clutched at his shoulders as shudders spread through her.

She rose up slightly with her knees, letting him draw partway out before lowering herself, ever so slowly, exulting in the thick fullness of him. She started to rise again, when her world suddenly tilted and she found herself on her back with Mac cradled between her legs, staring down at her.

"Sorry, baby. My turn to drive." With one hand braced on the mattress by her head, he used the other to hold her to him as he drove himself into her, over and over, each thrust more powerful than the last.

If she'd been able to form a coherent thought, words like *primitive* and *animalistic* might have come to mind, but she was well beyond thinking. He held her mercilessly and with unrelenting urgency took her until the wave of emotion that had been building inside her crashed in a tidal wave of sheer ecstasy, ripping a small cry from her throat. She clutched Mac as if he were a lifeline and still he continued his pounding rhythm. Though she would have thought it physically impossible, the tension inside her built again.

With her attention focused on the myriad of sensations coursing through her, she was barely aware of Mac's warm breath on her neck. The first scraping of his fangs against her highly charged skin elicited the purest form of erotic pleasure she'd ever felt and at the first prick of her flesh, she gasped as the white-hot flames threatened to consume her.

"Oh, God. What have I done?"

Lanie teetered on the edge of what promised to be the greatest sexual experience of her life and couldn't understand why Mac had suddenly grown still. "Please, don't stop," she begged, clutching at him.

"I hurt you." His body shook with the effort not to move.

"No, you didn't." She wanted to cry or scream. "Don't stop. Oh, God, *please* don't stop."

"You don't understand." He sounded desperate. "I wanted to bite you. I wanted your blood."

He held himself above her, muscles quivering, and Lanie saw the determination in his face, as well as the desire burning brightly in his red glowing eyes.

She faced a moment of truth. She could tell him to stop and he would, or she could trust her life to his ability to control himself. Taking his head between her hands, she pulled him down until their lips were inches away. "I trust you." The gentle kiss she gave him was in stark contrast to the tumultuous emotions inside her.

Still he hesitated. "Lanie, I don't think I can . . ."

"It's okay," she whispered, looking up into his face. She knew that she'd never be with another man like him. This experience might have to last her a long time—maybe a lifetime. She wanted him so badly at that moment that she couldn't play fair. She thrust her hips up against him, driving him farther into her. The light in his eyes grew suddenly wild and he growled, grabbed her to him, and resumed their lovemaking with heightened intensity until, once again, she felt she was teetering on the edge of a great precipice.

When his mouth fell against her neck and his fangs pierced her skin, it was more than she could take. She screamed as her world shattered into a million brightly burning stars.

In the next moment Mac thrust into her one final time and his own primal cry joined the echo of hers.

Slowly, the tide ebbed and they lay there, spent and exhausted. Lanie smiled as Mac trailed kisses along the side of her neck before rolling off and pulling her to him so she lay tucked against his side.

For several seconds neither spoke, then Lanie said the first thing that popped into her head. "Wow."

Beneath her head, she heard and felt the soft rumble of Mac's chest. "I have to admit, it was pretty incredible."

"You didn't hurt me, you know." She wasn't sure if she could tell him that the bite had been just the opposite. Rather than painful, it had been wonderfully erotic, but she was curious how it made him feel. "What was it like—drinking my blood?"

"It was like drinking from a fountain of pure energy. One that tastes like the sweetest nectar." He paused before continuing in an almost reverent tone. "I've never felt so alive."

His admission confused her. "If drinking blood makes you feel that way, then why did you throw away that blood I brought you?"

"Because for some reason, Lanie, it's only your blood I want. But don't worry, love—I'll never take it without permission. I promise."

At that moment, their door burst open with a loud crash. Suddenly alone in bed, heart racing, Lanie clutched the sheets to cover herself and wondered what the hell was going on.

Mac stood between her and the door, somehow managing to have rolled out of bed without getting tangled in the covers. From somewhere close-by, he'd retrieved his gun and held it aimed at the intruder. Lanie thought he looked very intimidating, despite being totally nude. From the connecting door across the room, Dirk appeared, also holding a gun, but thankfully wearing jeans.

For several long minutes, no one moved. Because Mac obstructed her view of the intruder, Lanie leaned to one side—and then promptly wished she hadn't. She'd never been so embarrassed in her life and wished that she could simply disappear.

Judging from Dirk's expression and stance, he looked ready to pull the trigger and ask questions later. Afraid both he and Mac would open fire at any moment, Lanie knew she had to do something. Her options were limited by her state of undress, and so she did the only thing she could.

"Mac, Dirk. I'd really appreciate it if you wouldn't shoot my father."

Mac had never quite found himself in this type of situation before. By the look in the creature's eye, Mac knew the vampire was there to kill him. Whether it was because Burton had sent him or because he'd found Mac sleeping with his daughter, Mac didn't know.

Whichever it turned out to be, Professor Weber was at a decided advantage—being dead already—but Mac wasn't going without a fight. Weber had caught him with his pants down, literally, and he felt his own temper flare and fought to keep it under control.

He waited for Weber to make the first move, determined that the man wouldn't harm Lanie. As he and Weber studied each other, Mac became aware of a steady litany of curses issuing from the bed and an unexpected spark of amusement shot through him. Most women would have cowered under the covers, but not his Lanie. Even now, he heard her struggling to get out of bed.

"Lanie, stay there," he ordered, afraid she might step into his line of fire.

"I am not sitting here while you go all Buffy the Vampire Slayer on me. If either of you shoot my father, you'll have me to deal with." Mac heard the thud of feet hitting the floor and knew she'd gotten out of bed. She moved into his peripheral vision and he noticed that she'd managed to wrap the sheet around herself. She also clutched his jeans in one hand and shoved them at him.

"You might want to put these on. The people in the hall are beginning to stare." He didn't move, wanting to see what the vampire was going to do.

Lanie finally gave an exasperated huff and turned to her father. "Hello, Dad. I'm really glad you decided to visit, but couldn't you have knocked first?" She gestured helplessly at the door hanging from only its top hinge.

As she rambled on, Mac noticed Dirk's nod toward the door and dipped his head once to acknowledge the message. He kept his gun trained on Weber as Dirk slipped into the room, lifted the door, and fit it back into its frame.

Fortunately, Mac thought, passersby were too stunned at seeing a nude man holding a gun to notice anything unusual about the man with his back to them.

Lanie continued to stand there, glaring first at Mac and then at her father. "Really," she said, disgusted. "This is too much. Dad, stop snarling at Mac."

"I heard you scream," her father gritted out between clinched teeth, his anger still quite evident.

"You didn't hear me scream," she denied.

"Hell, the whole hotel heard you scream," Dirk muttered from off to the side.

"See?" the professor bit out, sounding vindicated, and Mac made a mental note to shoot his friend later.

He saw Lanie's cheeks turn pink and a look of dismay cross her face. She sank into the desk chair and out of the corner of his eye, Mac saw her lower her head into her hands, muttering, "Oh, God. This is not happening."

"Knowing you were keeping company with a vampire, I naturally assumed you were being attacked," Weber continued. "And when I get in here, that's exactly what I find."

"Nonsense," she scoffed. "Mac would never do anything to hurt me." She said it with such conviction that Mac felt humbled.

"Your neck is bleeding," her father pointed out indignantly.

"Yes, but as you can see, I'm fine."

"I don't know why you feel you need to protect him, Lanie, but I know what I saw. He had you on the bed—"

"*In* bed, Dad. We were *in* bed. And he wasn't attacking me."

The professor's tirade suddenly stopped, and the look on his face changed to one of horrified disbelief as comprehension finally dawned. Mac thought he might have been safer before, when the man thought he'd attacked his daughter.

"You slept with him?"

"Who slept?" She gave an unladylike snort. "Sorry, it's a line from a movie." She took a deep breath. "Okay, Dad, *you* need to calm down." She stood up and walked over to Mac, poking him in the arm. "*You* need to get dressed, and don't shoot my father. Now, if you will excuse me, I'm going to shower and dress. When I come back, we can all sit down and have a nice little chat."

To the amazement of all the men there, she went to her duffel bag, pulled out clothes, and walked through the connecting doors into the other room.

"Lanie," her father shouted after her, "I'm not going to forget what he did to you." His threat sounded dire, and Mac prepared himself for the worst.

Lanie's laugh surprised them. "That makes two of us. Wow!"

Mac heard the bathroom door close, soon followed by the sound of the shower. The three men faced one another, in a standoff.

"That is the most unusual woman I have ever run into," Dirk muttered from the other side of the room.

"You have no idea," the professor muttered, and Mac thought he detected a spark of amusement replace some of the irritation in the eyes that locked on his. "But you do, don't you?"

Mac nodded. "Yes, sir. And I'd never do anything to hurt her—you have my word of honor on that."

The professor let out a sigh. "I suppose your word means something to you?"

"Just because we served in the same military unit, don't let Burton color your view of the rest of us," Mac said. "Honor and integrity still mean something to most of us."

For several seconds he felt as if he were a fleck of something interesting under the professor's microscope, as closely as the man studied him, but then the professor nodded. "It's clear that my daughter cares for you greatly, and she is, usually, an excellent judge of character." The older man's shoulders slumped a little, as the fight seemed to go out of him. "I didn't come to hurt anyone."

Mac didn't lower his gun. He believed in honesty and integrity, but over the years, he'd developed serious trust issues. "Why did you come?"

"I came to see my daughter."

Mac shook his head. He wasn't buying it. "Try again, and if you lie, I'm going to shoot you—not once, but as many times as I have live rounds. Past experience tells me I'll only need eight."

The professor's already pale complexion grew more so. Mac didn't think this man of science was used to such displays of violence—although the last week had probably given him a good introduction. "I did come to see my daughter, but I knew you'd be here. I know you're after Lance—and me," he quickly added when Mac gave him a pointed look. "I came to offer a trade—my life for information about Lance and his plans."

"Why should I trust you?" Mac asked.

"Because I have nothing to gain and everything to lose if Lance survives. I don't know what he was like when he was alive, but now he's psychotic—and if he gets a chance, he'll kill me."

"Why?"

"I was developing a synthetic venom for him because he was killing the adult chupacabra with his constant abuse. They don't attack humans by choice—only out of fear or when forced."

Mac nodded, remembering the war of emotions he'd picked up between the creature and Burton at Harris's house.

"The adult was dying. I wanted to get her away from Burton so she could find a quiet place to pass. I had a plan."

Mac was curious. "What was it?"

"I tranquilized her so that when the sun went down, she was slower to come to life. When Burton found her, she was still stone, and I told him that she'd died. He didn't stop to question it." The professor paused, and Mac noticed a frown crease his forehead.

"But something went wrong?"

The question seemed to startle the older man. "Yes. I had to leave the adult alone for a while. I'd hoped she'd be safe if everyone thought she was dead. I was going to take her out into the country, where she could pass in peace, but when I got back to my lab—she wasn't there.

"At first, I thought Lance had done something with her, but later, when he came into the lab, he wanted to know what I'd done with the body." The professor took a deep breath. "I told him that I had disposed of it, but the truth is—I don't know where she went. I'm almost positive that she wandered off on her own to die, so in the end, I guess it's all the same.

"Anyway, I knew if I stayed around, Lance would demand I make more of the venom so he could continue to convert his former unit members into vampires. With me gone, he's limited to the two vials he has—no more."

"Those two vials and anyone he feeds off of," Mac pointed out.

The professor looked surprised. "The people we kill when we feed rise up as vampires?"

Mac and Dirk exchanged stunned looks. "Didn't you know?"

"No, I'm afraid I didn't. I thought it might be possible, but I never had the opportunity to experiment."

"One of those researchers you killed rose up, and though it was difficult to tell at the time, Lanie thinks that he might have been more monster than human, so to speak."

"Well, yes. That makes sense," the professor continued analytically. "Second-generation effect. The venom probably loses something each time it gets passed on. Oh, dear." His eyes took on a distant look. "I wonder . . ."

"What?"

"Lance took up the practice of forcing the adult to feed from him every night. With each new infusion of venom, he grew stronger. Any vampire he created now . . ."

He left the sentence hanging, and Mac didn't like the implications. "How many has he killed himself?"

"I don't know. There were the homeless men when we first arrived. Hector had just awakened and needed to feed, although I think Lance killed at least one of them himself."

"I staked them," Mac said.

"Oh. Good. We started collecting blood from the homeless after that, rather than kill them. It became our primary food source. Lance ordered all of us to drink exclusively from the bags, but he'd go off on his own at night, disappearing for hours. I have no idea what he did during those times."

*Great*, Mac thought. They'd have to watch the news for stories of strange deaths—at least for a few days. He looked over at Dirk and caught his eye. He raised the jeans in his hand and waited for Dirk's nod. Without taking his attention off the professor, Mac stepped back and set his gun on the desk while he pulled on his jeans. Once dressed, he breathed easier. Picking up his gun again, he addressed the older man. "You said you had some information?"

"Yes." The professor looked at the desk chair just past Mac. "Would you mind if I sat down? This pack can get heavy after a while."

Mac nodded, backing away to allow the professor room to walk. As he passed by him, Mac noticed movement in the backpack.

"What's in there?" He was instantly alert.

"Nothing dangerous," the professor hurried to assure him. He slipped the pack from his shoulders and lowered it gently to the floor. "This is Gem, the baby chupacabra," he explained, unzipping the top and reaching in.

Dirk hurried across the room to stand beside Mac.

"She won't hurt you," the professor said when he noticed that neither of them had relaxed their stance.

"You'll have to forgive us if we seem doubtful," Mac said. "Our experience with chupacabras hasn't been good."

At that announcement, the professor's head snapped up and he studied them both carefully. "Really?"

"Yes, we both had run-ins with the adult."

"You were both attacked?"

"Yes."

He nodded. "That explains it."

"Explains what?" Dirk asked.

"Why I can feel your thoughts and emotions through the link—we were all created by the same creature. Although," he added ruefully, "I misinterpreted that last burst of emotion I picked up from you."

Mac knew he had to be referring to the moment when Mac had bitten Lanie, but he wasn't about to explain it to her father. "There is one difference between us," he pointed out. "We were attacked, but never actually died."

The professor looked confused. "But I saw you in the alley where those three men jumped you. I saw your speed and strength; your eyes and fangs." His eyes took on an unnatural red glow. "The thought of those men attacking my daughter made me so mad, I wanted to feel their flesh against my mouth, tear out their throats, and drink their worthless blood until I'd consumed every drop. And if I couldn't do it myself, I was glad to have you do it for me."

Mac felt a moment's confusion. Those had been his exact thoughts and feelings that night. Or had they? Was it possible that the professor, much in the same way Burton had controlled the chupacabra, had transmitted his emotions to Mac? It seemed more than likely, and a weight lifted from him. Perhaps he wasn't a monster.

"If you're not vampires," the professor began, interrupting Mac's thoughts, "then that would make you—?" He paused as his eyes took on a gleam of excitement. "So the legends are true. Does Charles know?"

"About us?" Mac nodded. "Yes—and he knows about you as well."

Just then the creature, no doubt tired of being ignored, pushed up against the professor's hand. As he lifted it out of the backpack, Mac got his first look at the baby chupacabra. It reminded him of the statue sitting on his sister's desk back home—only larger. She called it a Desk Guardian, in the form of a ceramic gargoyle.

Thinking of Sandra, he reminded himself to call her and let her know he was all right—and prayed that it wasn't a lie.

The professor sat on the desk chair and the baby jumped up to land on his shoulder, where it sort of hunkered down and perched. "If you wouldn't mind," he said, looking at both Mac and Dirk, "I'd really like to know more about your attacks and how the changes came about."

Mac and Dirk exchanged looks and shrugged. Neither could see the harm in telling him, so they each described their attacks. His interest seemed to be more scientific than anything else.

Finally, Lanie appeared in the doorway between the two rooms. Her hair was damp, but Mac thought she had never looked more beautiful to him. He quickly had to rein in thoughts of shared showers before he became too distracted to pay attention to her father. Even now, Mac felt Weber's eyes on him and when he glanced at the man, he saw a father's concern for his daughter.

Just then, Lanie caught sight of the small chupacabra and gave a cry of delight as she reached out to stroke the small creature's head, as her father had done moments earlier.

"Her name is Gem," he told her. "Isn't she something?"

Lanie looked up and Mac saw the smile that passed between father and daughter. There was such warmth in it that he felt an unfamiliar pang of jealousy. When Lanie turned and shared that smile with him, the resulting jolt of surprise and joy caught him off guard. Before he knew what he was doing, he'd reached out to scratch the creature's head.

For several minutes, Mac stood by and watched as Lanie acquainted herself with Gem. The professor told her all about the creature's feeding habits and needs. It was as if he was leaving his pet with her while he went on vacation and it occurred to Mac that, perhaps, he was doing exactly that.

"Professor Weber, you said you were interested in a trade?"

The professor's face grew somber, and he gave Mac a solemn look. "I overheard Lance talking to the other, uh, men last night. He said he'd talked to his contact, and funds had been transferred to his account."

Beside him, Dirk swore. The news wasn't entirely surprising. Last year's ambush had no doubt been funded by the same contact for the same purpose—Lance's greed.

"I don't suppose you know what their plans are?"

The professor nodded. "They're going to Camp David. They talked about how easy it would be for them to slip past all the security."

Mac and Dirk exchanged looks. Things had just taken a serious turn for the worse. Mac had no doubt that Burton and his special-ops team of vampires would do just as they boasted. They probably could slip right past security—elusive shadows, undetectable and deadly.

"Who's the target?" he asked, though he already knew the answer.

"The President of the United States."

# Chapter
# 19

Lanie gasped and felt her world tilt off kilter a little more. Chupacabras, vampires, and now possible terrorist actions? Her life used to be so safe, stable, and uneventful. What was running into a burning building compared to all this? *Boring.* "I don't understand," she heard herself saying. "Why would he go after the President?"

The three men looked at her with similar expressions, making her think the answer was obvious but she was too dense to figure it out. Then they all answered at once.

"Power."

"Greed."

"Money."

"But he's a vampire," she protested. What did the undead need with any of those things?

"Being dead didn't change him. Burton has always been the type of person who's never satisfied," Mac explained. "He constantly wanted more, whether he deserved it or not. That's a good part of why he never succeeded in the military. It was all about him, not what was good for the unit or the country."

"When he couldn't get what he wanted by working inside the system, he decided to work outside of it," Dirk added. "I would imagine that he's tired of doing it piecemeal and is going straight for the brass ring."

"But the President? Why go after him?"

"Because he can," Dirk said. "He has the abilities."

"Think what would happen to our country if the President was shot at his private retreat," Mac continued. "No one would feel safe anymore. Plus, rumors are that the Vice President's health isn't good. He has a weak heart. If they assassinate the President, then the strain of taking over could kill the Vice President as well, thus taking out the top two levels of leadership and placing the U.S. in an extremely vulnerable state. Which of our enemies wouldn't pay a fortune for that to happen?"

What they said made sense. "We have to stop him."

"*We* will," Mac said firmly. "*You* will stay out of it."


Thirty minutes later, Lanie sat listening to her father describing, again, everything he'd overheard Lance planning. This time, Uncle Charles was there to hear it.

He'd come as soon as Mac had phoned him. When he first arrived, Lanie had expected to see a heartfelt reunion between him and her father, but Charles had acted wary, making her father shift nervously under his close scrutiny. After several tense moments of uncomfortable silence, her father had tentatively held out his hand to congratulate his old friend—something about a family legacy and understanding what it meant—and that seemed to ease the tension on both sides.

Then they'd all sat down to listen to what her father had to say. When he finished, the admiral, Mac, and Dirk retired to Mac's room to figure out their next course of action, leaving Lanie and her father alone. It was the first time she'd had to really focus on him; his death and current state weighed heavily on her mind.

"What's it like to be . . . ?" She wasn't sure how to put it, but her father seemed to know what she meant.

"Undead?"

She smiled. "Yeah."

"Well, the speed and strength are nice." He chuckled. "I was never particularly strong or athletic growing up, so it's a nice change."

"What about the blood?"

He shrugged. "The blood doesn't bother me. It's what I need now to survive. My body craves it." His tone, which had been analytical and light, grew serious. "I don't like killing to get the blood, and to the extent that I don't have to, I won't. What worries me is that, each day, the thought of killing grows less daunting. It's like being a member of the undead somehow affected my soul—my ability to respect life and the living. I'm afraid that one night I'll rise and be the monster in the horror stories, unable to remember what it was like to have a conscience. I can easily see where someone of, let's say, questionable moral fiber would become a real threat if ever he, or she, were to become a vampire."

His words chilled her. "You mean someone like Lance Burton."

"Yes, exactly. I hope they're able to stop him," he said, nodding to the other room. He stood then and pulled her to her feet, enfolding her in his arms. "I have missed you so much these last several months."

"I missed you, too." She hugged him close. "When they told me you were dead, I—" Her voice cracked. "I'm so sorry for not spending more time with you."

"Hush, child. There is no need for regrets. I couldn't have asked for a finer daughter. While this is a strange existence to be sure, it is not horrible—yet. However, I find the lure of human blood a temptation that wears on me, and I'm afraid that sooner or later, I will slip and become a danger to those around me—even you. So, I've decided to remove myself before anything like that happens."

Lanie gasped, looking up at him. "You're not thinking about killing yourself, are you?"

"You mean, permanently?" He gave her a sad smile, but shook his head. "I haven't the courage, but I won't stay here."

"Where will you go?"

"I think back to the Amazon. I want to find Guberstein's village. It would be the find of a lifetime."

"But no one knows where it is. You could be in the jungle for years, looking, and never find it."

"Then it's a good thing I'm immortal."

She tried to smile at his joke, but it was too hard. He was leaving, and she'd never see him again, unless . . . "I'll go with you."

He rested his cheek on her head. "No. I think not. You're still human, and it wouldn't be safe. Besides, unless I'm mistaken, I think your young man might want you to stay."

*Her young man.* As far as she knew, Mac still blamed her for the accident that changed him into something he hated. Their lovemaking had been about a warm body in the right place at the right time. Nothing more—at least, not to Mac. Sooner or later, she would return to Houston, alone, having lost the two men she loved most dearly in life.

It was the first time she'd allowed herself to form the thought, but once it was there, she knew it to be true. She loved Mac. The realization made anticipating the future without him that much harder.

"I have to go." Her father's voice broke into her thoughts. He released her and turned to where the baby chupacabra rested on the bed. He lifted the creature into his arms and held her, stroking her head and neck with great affection. "I want you to take care of Gem for me," he told Lanie. "I'm not as talented at evading Lance and his men as they are at tracking. If he wants Gem, she's safer with you and Mac than with me."

Lanie reached out and stroked the little chupacabra's neck. "Will you be in touch?"

"If I can, I'll contact you—I promise. There are a couple more things—before the others come back." He put the chupacabra back on the bed and retrieved his backpack from the floor. From inside, he pulled out several bags of blood and set them on the small desk. "Dog's blood, for Gem." Then he took out a small bundle of cloth, which he handed to her. "This is for you."

"What is it?" She took it from him and unwrapped the cloth to find a small glass vial and a syringe, like the kind used by diabetics.

"Venom and antiserum." He held up the vial of colorless liquid. "This is the last vial of real chupacabra venom. I took it from the adult a few days ago. As I'm sure you're aware, there are some remarkable healing powers in this venom—if we could just figure out how to re-create and harness them. To do that, though, you'll need to find a reputable biochemist with a good lab. But be warned, Lance has two vials that he intends to use, I'm sure, to create new recruits."

She nodded as he placed it back in her palm and picked up the syringe filled with amber liquid. "This is the antiserum. It attacks and destroys all the cells containing venom—in essence, killing the host. I had an opportunity to test it. It's painful, fast—and lethal to vampires."

Lanie thought back to the body they found, horribly distorted, at the abandoned apartment building. "Kinsley," Lanie said softly.

Her father nodded. "It's not something I'm happy about, but it needed to be tested." He paused and gave her a significant look. "I think it will work equally well on changelings, should you find you have the need."

"Changelings?" It wasn't an expression she was familiar with, but when her father looked pointedly toward the connecting door, she understood. "Oh, I don't think—"

Her father closed her fingers around the syringe and vial before covering her fist with his hand. "Just in case you need it, okay?"

She nodded. "Okay." Rewrapping the package, she tucked it into the middle of her duffel bag. She turned around, and the expression on her father's face told her their time together was at an end. He gathered her into his arms once more and hugged her, placing a kiss on her head. "It's not good-bye, Lanie, my sweet. More like see you later. I'll contact you as soon as I can, but until then, you be careful, okay?"

She nodded into his chest, the tears she'd held off so long now flowing freely down her cheeks. "I love you, Dad."

"As I love you." His arms tightened around her briefly. "Tell Charles that I said . . . see you later." Then he was gone and she was alone in the room.


"How do you know they won't attack tonight?" Lanie asked an hour or so later, sitting at the foot of the bed in Mac's room. The admiral had left, and she and Mac were waiting for Dirk to return from running several errands.

"Mainly because the President isn't due to arrive at Camp David until tomorrow night," Mac said in a clipped tone from where he sat by the desk.

Now that they were alone, she was disappointed that he'd made no move to recapture their earlier closeness. She tried not to dwell on it, though, because she knew he had other things on his mind.

"I thought the newscaster on TV said he was already there."

Mac shot her a look and she instantly felt foolish. It hadn't occurred to her that the media might be fed misinformation.

"So what's the plan?" she asked, trying to change the subject.

"Admiral Winslow will call in a few favors and get a warning to the Secret Service about this potential threat. We're not telling the FBI, or any other agencies, because we don't want the whole world to know that vampires exist.

We'll have to deal with it quietly. In about six hours, after we've had some sleep, Dirk and I will fly to Camp David, where we'll meet with the Secret Service and offer our assistance. By my estimate, we should arrive an hour before sunset with enough time to set up. I don't think Burton will do anything before then."

"What can I do to help?"

Mac's jaw tightened as he gave her his full attention, his expression unreadable. "Go home."

His words cut like a knife, and she couldn't help staring at him, her face slack with surprise. "I . . . I don't want to go. I want to stay here." *With you.* She sounded pathetic, but didn't care.

"You got to see and talk to your father, so you have no reason to stay."

She opened her mouth to argue, but he held up his hand to silence her. "Let me be blunt. I don't want you to wait for me, Lanie. For God's sake, just go home."

She felt numb from head to toe. *Go home? But I love you,* she wanted to scream, but the words remained unspoken.

Finally, she found a shred of dignity. Pushing herself off the bed, she went back to her room. Every part of her wanted to slam the connecting door as hard as she could and scream at the top of her lungs, but she wouldn't give in to it. Instead, she grabbed her duffel bag and tossed it, perhaps too forcefully, onto the bed. She fumbled for the zipper, hurt and anger nearly blinding her.

"Lanie," Mac's deep voice rumbled from the connecting doorway. "I'm sorry if I . . ." He paused and panic filled her.

*Oh, God. Don't let him apologize for not loving me.* "No, you're absolutely right. It wouldn't have worked out." She kept her attention focused on packing. "Besides, I need to get back to Houston. I have"—*no one*—"people waiting for me."

She shut up, at risk of rambling to fill an otherwise awkward silence. Without looking at him, she crossed to the dresser, where she took her dirty laundry from the drawer and dumped it on the bed.

"Lanie, I—" At that moment there was a knock on the door, and Mac went into his room to open it.

With quick, angry movements, Lanie folded a dirty shirt and stuffed it into the bag, hearing Dirk's voice from the other room. There was a brief exchange of words, too soft for Lanie to catch, and then Dirk came bustling through the connecting doors, hauling a small dog carrier with him.

"I brought you a present," he told her, stopping short when he saw the open duffel bag. "Are you going some-where?"

"Home—apparently." She muttered the last word under her breath.

Dirk's surprise seemed genuine, and she felt better knowing that the two men had not conspired against her. Dirk wasn't stupid, though, and after a quick glance back at Mac, he seemed to understand. "When do you leave?"

"I don't know. I haven't—"

"You're on the one o'clock flight."

She waved a hand at Mac but addressed Dirk. "Well, there you go. I'm on the one o'clock flight." She gave him a too-bright smile, then pinned Mac with an accusing glare before wadding a pair of pants into a ball and shoving them inside the bag.

She was as mad at herself as she was at Mac. *Love*, she scoffed. Who was she kidding? Love happened in fairy tales; it wasn't real. Oh, but the pain of it was, she thought, knowing that somehow, she'd have to get over this and move on with her life.

If only it was that easy.

She saw Dirk glance back and forth between her and Mac before setting the small carrier on the floor by the dresser. "I thought this carrier would make a nice bed for Gem," he said. "I guess it'll make a good travel carrier as well."

"Thank you." She gave him a grateful smile and then crossed to the closet, ignoring Mac, who stood watching her from the open doorway. There weren't many clothes hanging up, so fortunately she was able to grab them all. As she started back to the bed, she noticed one of the items in her hand was the dress from the night of the reception. She pulled it out from the other clothes and held it up. She loved the dress, but there was no way she could ever wear it again and not be reminded of Mac. She gave him a pointed look and, very purposefully, walked back to the closet and hung it up.

She resumed her packing, ignoring the two men, doing her best to look busy. Luckily, they returned to Mac's room just as she ran out of things to pack.

Lanie didn't even try to listen in. Instead, she plopped herself down beside the duffel bag and took a deep breath. At some point, as she sat there, the hotel staff came to replace the door. They went about it as if it were no more unusual than bringing fresh towels. Lanie thought that might have something to do with the admiral's sizable financial contribution.

By the time the hotel staff left, her anger had worn off, leaving only hurt in its wake. A small gurgling sound caught her attention, and she looked around to see the small chupacabra amble over to her.

"Hey, girl," she said softly, rubbing the smooth, hairless hide of Gem's neck. "You know what it's like to lose a loved one, don't you?" She thought of the adult creature, by itself, alone and dying. "I guess it's just you and me from now on." She tried to look at Gem objectively. "I don't suppose my neighbors will believe me if I tell them you're a new breed of South American kangaroo?" Maybe she should consider moving out to the country, she thought.

Rising from the bed, Gem still in her arms, Lanie grabbed a bag of blood from the desk. She carried Gem into the bathroom, placed her in the tub with the bag, and waited as the little chupacabra drank. When Gem was finished, Lanie rinsed away the spilled blood and then carried her back into the bedroom.

There was little left for her to pack, so rather than finish immediately, she opened her curtains and sat down in the corner armchair. Gem hopped into her lap and, as Lanie began stroking her head, emitted a soothing purring noise. Together, they watched the sun rise.

The sound of the phone ringing woke Lanie sometime later, and muscles stiff from having slept at an awkward angle, she had trouble getting out of the chair to answer it. In her arms she still clutched Gem, now looking like a rather large gargoyle statue. Setting her down on the bed, she reached for the phone.

"Hello?"

"Ms. Weber? This is the front desk with your wake-up call," the too-pleasant voice on the other end of the line replied.

"My what?" Lanie was confused.

"Your wake-up call. Mr. Knight placed the request a couple of hours ago. He said you had a plane to catch. We have a car ready to take you to the airport where, I'm told, there is a ticket waiting in your name. Will you need a bellhop to help with your bags?"

It took several moments for Lanie's foggy brain to register what she was being told. Mac had taken care of everything. She guessed he didn't want to take any chances that she would stay. Well, no worries there. "No, that won't be necessary. I've changed my mind and decided to stay."

"Oh." The woman's worried tone concerned her.

"Is that a problem?"

"Well, it's just that your room has already been reassigned to someone else." The woman was clearly flustered.

"You rented my room to someone else? Who?"

"I'm sorry. We're not at liberty to say."

Lanie stared at the wall, doing her best to bring her emotions under control. "Okay, look, that's fine. Do you have any other rooms available? I'll take one of those."

Immediately the woman's tone brightened. "Yes. I can put you on the fifth floor."

"Great."

"I'll need a credit card."

"I'm on my way down."

She hung up the phone, feeling irritated yet defiant. She wasn't going to let Mac force her to leave. Digging in her purse for her "emergencies only" credit card, she pulled it out, feeling victorious. Just let *that man* try to tell her what to do, she silently challenged. She'd stay as long as she damn well wanted to—or at least as long as she could. She held the card up and studied it, as if she might find the amount of her remaining available credit balance stamped somewhere on the surface.

Surely there was enough for one night, and that's all she'd need to make her point. She grabbed her key card and went down to the lobby. It didn't take long to register, and with the key to her new room in hand, she returned to the old one to begin transferring her few belongings.

She did a final check of clothes and toiletries and was about to close her duffel bag when her eyes strayed to the closet—and the dress still hanging inside. Exasperated with herself, she went over and got it. "This does not mean I'm keeping it," she argued to herself. "I'm simply going to hold on to it until I've had a chance to consider the matter and make a less-emotional decision." She folded the dress and placed it on top of the other clothes. "Besides, I can always throw it out later."

She looked around the room once again and saw there was nothing left to pack, so she zipped up her bag. She pulled her father's suitcase and laptop from the closet and stood them next to her duffel bag and purse. Next, she picked up Gem, now looking like an exceptionally large paperweight, and placed her inside the carrier, closing the door.

She was ready. She looked about, trying to decide the best way to carry all her things, when there was a knock at her door. Her first thought was that the balance on the credit card hadn't been enough. She grabbed her wallet, just in case, and then opened the door.

The impact of a fist hitting her jaw sent her flying backward. Pain shot through her as she landed on the floor. She quickly scrambled back to her feet, trying to make sense of who was attacking her and why. The man, who clearly wasn't the bellhop, didn't seem interested in providing explanations as he moved rapidly and hit her once more. This time she fell against the TV, knocking it askew.

When she straightened and tried to run for the other side of the room, he tackled her to the floor and pinned her. She struck at him with her fists and kicked her feet, desperately trying to get away, but to no avail.

She opened her mouth to scream but never got the chance. She saw the fist coming at her and felt the pain. Then there was nothing.

Mac and Dirk had left while Lanie was sleeping. Mac had made arrangements to get her to the airport, fighting the urge to wake her and explain how he really felt. Only the unknown of the future kept him from doing it. If he and Dirk couldn't find Burton, or couldn't kill him, then they'd never be safe. He didn't want her constantly having to look over her shoulder, which was the life he had ahead of him if he failed tonight. It would be better for her to hate him and get on with her own life.

With thoughts of her roiling through his head, Mac had been poor company for Dirk. Now, hours later, they sat on the tarmac of the airfield at Camp David, watching the sun set on the horizon and waiting for the Secret Service to escort them to the main facility. From there, they'd spread out and look around for signs of Burton and his men. With luck, the Secret Service had taken Admiral Winslow's instructions seriously and secured the President. Meanwhile, a look-alike was being flown in shortly, in hopes that they could still flush out the would-be assassins.

His thoughts returning to Lanie, Mac wondered what kind of future they might have had together. He wasn't the same man he was when he'd started this adventure. Maybe it would be better if he *didn't* try to see her again. Returning to fly charters was out of the question, unless he took only the night flights. It was something he'd have to discuss with Keith and Sandra.

Slowly, Mac realized that Dirk was talking to him. "What?"

"I said, as soon as we get back, I'll move my stuff into Lanie's room—or rather my new room—and then we can decide what to do about Winslow's offer." He paused a moment. "Do you think he was serious?"

"About joining his task force? Probably."

Dirk gave a soft chuckle. "*Joining* the task force, hell, man, we *are* the task force."

It was true. The admiral's idea was to create a task force, funded by his family fortune and operated secretly. Its main objective—to track down and kill vampires.

"Are you seriously considering it?"

Dirk thought about it. "Yeah, I think I am. What about you?"

"I don't know," Mac admitted. "Maybe. There are some things I need to take care of first."

Mac didn't specifically say Lanie's name, but he knew Dirk understood. The way he'd left things with her, he wasn't sure she'd ever want to see him again.

He felt his mood sinking lower still and drew on years of discipline to drive thoughts of her from his mind. Now wasn't the time to let emotions get in the way.

"Showtime," he said when his phone rang. He pulled it out and then felt his heart lurch when he glanced at the caller ID.

"Lanie? Is everything all right?"

"Sorry, old man." Burton's laughter greeted him. "She can't come to the phone right now. She's a bit tied up."

# Chapter
# 20

I f you harm her in any way," Mac warned, filled with an impotent rage. "I'll—"

"What?" Burton mocked. "You'll kill me?"

"Where is she, Burton?"

"She's here—in my bed. I can well understand the attraction, Knight. In fact, I'm not sure that I'll grow bored with her as quickly as with the others." He laughed again, and it took everything in Mac not to react.

"I want to talk to her," Mac bit out. "Now."

There was a moment of silence, and then Lanie came on the line, sounding faint—and frightened. "Mac?" Her voice cracked when she said his name and he longed to hold her; to protect her.

"I'm here, baby."

"I'm sorry, Mac."

"Be strong, Lanie. I'm coming to get you."

"No, don't," she begged. "Save the Pres—"

There was the sound of a slap, followed by Lanie's

small cry, and Mac's grip on the phone tightened until he thought it might break.

"If you want to see your girlfriend again," Burton said, coming back on, "then you'll meet me—tonight."

"Where?"

"Tell him where we are, sweet thing," Mac heard Burton say. "He'll never believe me if I tell him."

Lanie's voice, sounding strained and defeated, came back on the line and she gave him a D.C. address. Mac swore beneath his breath. Burton had never left town.

"Got it?" Burton asked, back on the phone.

Mac glanced at his watch and did some quick math. "It'll take me a couple of hours to get there."

"I'm sure we'll find a way to keep ourselves amused until you arrive."

The phone went dead, and Mac gritted his teeth tightly together, trying to get his emotions under control. Finally, he forced himself to take a deep breath and relax. "He's got Lanie." Quickly he told Dirk everything.

"No problem," Dirk said. "You fly the plane back and take care of Lanie and Burton. I'll stay here and deal with the assassins."

"You know it's a trap."

"Sure, but for which one of us? Burton's not even here, and we both know he's the bigger threat. Chances are, he's not alone. Worst case for me is that I've got two or three vampires to find and take out. Piece of cake. You, on the other hand . . ."

Mac nodded. He didn't need Dirk to spell out the dangers for him.

"Be careful." Dirk reached into his pocket, pulled out a set of keys, and tossed them to him.

"You, too." They shook hands and Dirk climbed out. Mac waited until he saw his friend standing clear of the plane before starting the engine. He called in the change of flight plans as he taxied down the short runway, and by the time he reached the end and lifted into the sky, he'd received clearance.

The trip back to Washington, D.C., was the longest of his life. Thoughts of what Burton was doing to Lanie persecuted him, and it seemed that the plane couldn't fly fast enough while the clock, counting down the minutes of Lanie's life, ticked loudly in his head. He'd never felt so powerless in his life.

Finally, Andrew's Air Force Base came into view, and Mac landed without incident. Soon he was in Dirk's car, racing toward the warehouse where Burton supposedly waited with Lanie. He didn't park right out in front, hoping to preserve some small element of surprise. They might be expecting him, but they didn't know exactly when he was arriving.

He walked around the warehouse, keeping to the shadows, wondering how he could get in without being detected. There were no windows on the sides or rear of the warehouse, and it seemed that his only choice was going to be to storm the front doors. Then he spotted the metal rungs, attached to the outer wall in back—a type of fire escape.

He climbed them to the roof where he found an access door to the inside, rusted and deformed by age and neglect. Grabbing the handle, he pulled it open as quietly as he could. It still creaked, but he hoped that any vampires waiting inside hadn't noticed.

Stepping inside, he paused to take in his surroundings. There were no lights on, but with his excellent night vision, that wasn't a problem. He stood in the middle of a big open loft and, from below, caught the faint rumble of voices.

Moving quietly, he followed the sound and soon found himself standing at the edge of an upper landing that opened to the floor below. The place reminded him of what once might have been a mechanic's shop because old engine parts and empty oil cans littered the ground floor. Off to one side was a long mound of dirty oil rags, and on top of that, tied and gagged, was Lanie.

"What's taking him so long?" Mac heard Harris ask.

"Be patient," came Burton's terse reply. "He'll be here soon enough."

"Maybe you got it wrong," Harris continued. "Maybe—"

"Shut up," a third voice hissed.

Mac took a deep, silent breath. There were at least three vampires down there, which left two still unaccounted for. They could be here, or they could be at Camp David. He'd know which soon enough.

He'd brought his gun, but didn't have enough bullets to decapitate all of them. *Damn.* He should have come better prepared, he thought, looking around for a pipe or forgotten tool, anything that could be used as a weapon. On the floor of the loft there were only wire cables, a few wood pallets, scattered trash, rat droppings, spiderwebs, and dirt. Not much to work with.

As he considered how to break the pallets into stakes, he caught the barest whisper of a sound. He whirled around just in time to face a charging vampire. Mac had only time to recognize him as Smith before the impact of

Smith's tackle carried them both to the floor. Mac knew he was stronger than most humans, but he was astounded at how much stronger Smith was. It put Mac at a decided disadvantage.

He closed his mind on his self-doubt. There was no room for it in battle.

Within seconds, Smith, hissing like a wild animal, had him pinned to the ground and had turned his face into a punching bag. Mac was barely aware of the shouts from below and knew the others were on their way up to join the fight. There was no way he could fight them all.

Bucking violently, he managed to catch Smith off balance. Shoving him off, Mac scrambled to his feet. As soon as Smith stood, Mac began his own assault, repeatedly hitting the man's face and stomach. He knew that if he slowed down, gave the vampire any opening at all, he'd be in serious trouble.

The fight moved dangerously close to the edge of the loft where wire cables threatened to entangle Mac's feet with each step he took. Sounding much too close, he heard the other vampires running up the stairs. He was out of time.

Diving for the floor, he tucked and rolled past Smith, catching the vampire off guard. When he came up, he had a cable clutched in one hand. Without pausing, he looped it around Smith's neck and then shoved him off the platform.

The thin cable became a noose around Smith's neck as his falling body pulled it taut. The noose tightened, slicing through the vampire's neck as easily as a wire cutter sliced through cheese. Smith's head flew off in one direction, eyes still open wide in surprise, while his body fell, lifeless, to the floor below.

Mac had no time to enjoy his victory because Burton, Harris, and Brown were there, stalking him, spaced far enough apart that he had a difficult time keeping an eye on all of them at once.

"What are you going to do now, Knight?" Burton taunted.

Brown was the closest, so Mac dealt with him first. Pulling his gun, he discharged a full clip into the man, even as the other two rushed him. The impact of the two hitting him sent the gun flying out of his hand, but out of the corner of his eye, he noticed that there was little left of Brown to worry about.

It was Mac's last victory. With both Burton and Harris attacking him, he was soon overpowered. They beat him until he could barely hold up his head, and the cuts from their sharp teeth and nails bled freely.

Consciousness came and went as they carried him downstairs and tossed him onto the pile of rags beside Lanie.

His eyes swollen almost shut, he struggled to open a lid enough to see. Her complexion was sallow, except for the bruises starting to darken her cheeks and jaw. The fear in her eyes tore at him, and Mac felt a murderous rage well up inside him at the sight of her abuse.

"Well, this is certainly a moment to be savored," Burton gloated, hovering just inside Mac's range of vision. "Unfortunately, I'll have to postpone the pleasure of killing you for another night. I have a few loose ends to tie up."

He turned to Harris. "Go dump what's left of Smith and Brown outside where the sun can turn them to stone. Then take these two to the lair. And, Harris—I want them alive when I return. I've waited a long time to kill Knight. I won't be robbed of the moment."

He stared at Mac with bared fangs and ran a tongue over their gleaming points. "Victory will taste so sweet. Now, if you'll excuse me, I must go see an old *friend*." He spit out the word *friend* as if it tasted bad. "I'll be sure to give the admiral your regards—right before I rip out his throat."

Laughing, the two vampires left, leaving Mac and Lanie alone.

"Baby, are you all right?" Mac croaked past his bloodied lips, knowing it was a stupid question but needing to ask it anyway.

Lanie nodded. "I'm sorry you had to come for me."

He forced himself to sit up, though it cost him dearly, and struggled to get close enough that he could reach the ropes binding her arms. "I'm going to undo these, and then I want you to leave." He paused to take a breath and found her shaking her head.

"No way. I'm not going without you."

If he'd had the strength, he would have groaned. "Now is not the time to argue. Just do as I say. Please?"

"You can't ask me to leave you," she begged. "Come with me. I'll help you."

He worked at the knots, his fingers bruised and swollen, almost too numb to function. The loss of blood from the cuts he'd sustained made him feel light-headed and it took several tries, and the last of his energy, to finally get the knots undone. He fell back on the pile of rags and closed his eyes, the thought of death almost a welcomed relief. "It's me they want," he said weakly. "As long as they have me, they won't go after you."

He rolled his head toward her and cracked open one eyelid again. She was busy untying the bindings around her ankles. Soon she had those off as well.

"Okay," Mac mumbled. "Get out of here and call the admiral. Tell him Burton is coming." *He'll know what to do.*

She didn't move, and he grew desperate. Didn't she realize that Harris would be back any second?

Her brow furrowed for a moment, as if she waged a great internal debate, and then she pulled her hair away from her neck and tipped her head to one side. "Bite me."

Mac would have raised an eyebrow if he'd had the strength. "Excuse me?"

She scooted closer so she could lie down, putting her neck within easy access. "You know—feed off me. It's the only way we both have a chance of getting out of here. Please, Mac. You remember how you felt when you took my blood earlier. It gave you energy. It might revive you."

He rolled over on his side so he could see her better, wanting to push her away. All too well he remembered the revitalizing energy and strength that came after he'd taken her blood. It had been incredible, but he'd not been in such desperate need. Now he was weak, near death. What if he lacked the control to stop?

Seeing the fear in his eyes, she placed her hand lightly against his cheek. "I trust you."

Her words left him dazed, barely noticing when she pulled his face to her until his mouth was pressed against her neck. The intoxicating lure of her pulse beneath his lips sealed her fate.

He pierced the tender skin with his fangs and let her life-giving blood fill his mouth. Once again tasting the sweet nectar, he swallowed and felt new strength and energy coursing through his body. It was ambrosia to a starving man, and he lost himself in the sensation.

How long he drank he wasn't sure, but the fear of hurting her overrode the pleasure of drinking and he forced himself to stop. He licked the traces of blood from her neck, feeling incredibly good. When he turned to thank her for her gift, her face looked paler than before, and her eyes were closed. Instantly, his euphoria was replaced by the horrible fear that he'd somehow misjudged how much he'd taken.

"Lanie, look at me. Are you okay, baby?"

Her eyelids fluttered open and she smiled weakly up at him. "Wow," she whispered.

He smiled back, relieved, and kissed her forehead. At that moment he heard Harris return. Mac waited until the man came closer and he could see that Burton was not with him. Then Mac rose to his feet.

Harris's eyes went wide in alarm when Mac lunged at him. He put up a good fight, but Mac had the benefit of his energy boost. In a macabre dance, they moved about the warehouse floor, exchanging blows, each trying to wear down the other. They had drawn even with the outer door when Harris ducked a punch from Mac and raced outside, disappearing into the night.

Mac let him go and returned to Lanie, who still lay on the pile of rags. She hadn't moved. Worried, he stooped to pick her up and carried her to his car. When he set her in the passenger seat, she opened her eyes. "We have to go back to the hotel."

"No way. I'm taking you to the hospital."

"No, there's no time. Take me back to the hotel—I have something there." She paused before going on. "You'll need it . . . to save Uncle Charles."

He hesitated. For once, his course was unclear.

"Please, Mac. You're the only one who can save him."

A few minutes later, Mac opened the door to Lanie's hotel room. It was still in shambles from when Lanie had fought off her abductor.

"He hired someone to kidnap me," she said, as if reading his thoughts. "He came while I was packing." She gave a helpless gesture. "The sun was out. I wasn't expecting trouble." She spoke slowly as if she were having a hard time catching her breath. "He took me to the warehouse and we waited for the sun to set. He thought he'd get paid. Instead, Burton killed him."

Mac felt no remorse for the kidnapper. He got what he deserved. They moved into the room with Mac supporting her as she stumbled along, her gait unsteady. Near the chest of drawers, in the travel carrier on the floor, the baby chupacabra moved about, restless. Mac ignored it as he helped Lanie across the room. He started to take her to the bed, but she motioned to the desk chair instead.

"Look in my duffel bag," she told him, not making an effort to get it herself. He lifted the bag onto the bed and, digging around, soon found the small wrapped bundle.

"Be careful," she warned as he unfolded the layers of cloth. "There should be two items in there—a vial and a syringe. You want the syringe."

"What's in it?" He held it up to the light and examined the clear, amber liquid.

"It's antiserum. According to Dad, it's fast-acting, extremely painful, and lethal when injected into vampires." She hesitated. "And changelings, so don't accidentally stick yourself with it."

Mac nodded, knowing why she'd not told him before. Her father had given it to her for protection—against him, if need be. He couldn't blame the man for that.

He put the syringe in his pocket and then turned to Lanie. She was looking worse. "I'm calling an ambulance."

"No—I'm fine. You have to hurry. Since Uncle Charles didn't answer the phone when you called from the car, Burton must already be there."

Knowing she was right, he gave her a quick kiss and left.

"I love you," she whispered, watching him leave, a single tear escaping to run down her cheek. Fate could be so cruel. To find love too late . . .

Inside the carrier, Gem rattled the cage door, clearly irritated with being locked away all night, but Lanie didn't have the energy to let her out. She was cold and tired—so tired. All she wanted to do was lie down and sleep.

But she couldn't. Not yet. There was something she needed to do first. She pulled out paper and pen from the middle drawer and started to write. There was so much she wanted to say, but in the end, the message was brief.

When she finished, she left it on the desk and crossed to the bed. It took almost more strength than she had to climb under the covers, and though she pulled them up to her neck, she still started to shake. She let her mind wander to thoughts of Mac, praying he'd be okay. When sleep finally beckoned, she closed her eyes and surrendered to it.

The front door to the admiral's house stood open, and Mac didn't bother looking for another way in. The main room showed signs of a struggle and Mac followed the blood trail to the study, where he found Burton sitting at the desk. He didn't look the least surprised when Mac walked in, leaving Mac to wonder now if maybe Harris's running away had been not an act of cowardice, but rather a strategic retreat, in keeping with a carefully orchestrated plan.

Mac didn't like the feeling that he'd been played. Walking into the study, he saw that books had been haphazardly knocked off the shelves and imagined it had happened when the admiral's body had been slammed against the bookcases. The display cases holding the various daggers and swords lay shattered about the room and their contents hung from the ceiling, tips embedded in the wood.

Admiral Winslow lay prone on his stomach off to one side, his head bloodied. Mac couldn't tell if he was alive or not, but resisted the urge to go to him. First, he needed to deal with Burton.

"Interesting choice you made," Burton said casually, playing with a letter opener. "I would have bet on the woman, but perhaps your relationship wasn't as close as I'd assumed." He glanced over at the admiral and shook his head. "He put up a good fight. Oh, don't worry. He's still alive—barely." He turned back to look at Mac.

"What about Lanie? I know you fed off her to regain your strength. Was she still alive when you left her?"

"Unlike you, Burton, I don't have to kill when I take blood. Lanie will be fine."

Burton looked first surprised and then pleased. "She didn't tell you, did she? Impressive. She's obviously stronger than I thought."

Mac felt confused. "What are you talking about?"

"Lanie's blood donation to you was not her first this evening. In fact, it wasn't even her second or third. When I finished, I honestly wasn't sure if she'd live long enough for you to *rescue* her." He showed mock concern. "Did you have to take an awful lot? I mean, the human body can't afford to lose too much."

"You're lying," Mac growled, suddenly filled with doubt. "I saw her neck—there wasn't a mark on it."

"Well, there wouldn't be, would there? I find the *upper* femoral artery to be so much more—enjoyable—when feeding on women."

# Chapter
# 21

Unable to listen to more, Mac leaped over the desk, going for Burton's throat. The weight of their bodies sent his chair toppling backward and they crashed to the floor. Mac delivered a blow to Burton's face before the vampire hit him, knocking him back. Mac quickly climbed to his feet and, driven by an unrelenting fury, went after Burton again. They exchanged blows of inhuman strength that sent vampire and changeling, in turn, hurtling through the air until they smashed into the bookcases lining the walls.

The surge of energy Mac felt after receiving Lanie's blood quickly ebbed under Burton's constant assault. In the back of his mind, he worried about Lanie, fearful that Burton might have told him the truth and she lay dead or dying back at the hotel. Desperately, he fought, but Burton's strength and energy far exceeded his own.

Picking himself up off the floor from where Burton had recently thrown him, Mac charged. His reaction time was too slow and Burton sidestepped him, bringing his arm down on Mac and smashing him to the ground.

Burton rolled him over until he lay on his back, fighting to stay conscious while Burton straddled him, sitting on his chest, pinning him to the ground.

"You put up a good fight," Burton gloated. "Just not good enough. Before I kill you, let me tell you what I'm going to do to all the people you care about. First, I'm going to finish off . . ."

Burton rambled on, but Mac had stopped listening. His hand was resting on the floor beside his hip and he felt the small bulge of his pocket. *The antiserum.* The trick was getting it out without Burton noticing.

"Whoa," Burton mocked when Mac suddenly bucked his body, extracting the syringe as he did. "I guess there's a little fight left in you, isn't there?"

"More than you know." Mac snapped off the protective cap of the syringe and stabbed Burton in the hip, injecting him.

Burton lurched away but didn't get up as he twisted to see what had stuck him. When he saw the syringe, he pulled it out and held it up. For a minute, he looked confused, and then comprehension dawned.

He winced as the first of the antiserum coursed through his body, then Mac saw the muscles along his neck spasm. Burton shut his eyes as a look of pain distorted his features. Mac held his breath, unable to do any more than that, and waited for the serum to end Burton's life.

The look of pain on Burton's face gradually faded and was followed by one of intense concentration. That, too, quickly vanished as he opened his eyes and sighed with relief.

"Was that the best you could do? The professor's anti-serum? Surprised that I know about it? Please. Do you really think he was capable of thinking of it on his own?"

Mac stared up at him in horror, slowly realizing that his ace in the hole, the antiserum, hadn't worked.

"Planting the suggestion was easy," Burton continued. "I'll admit that it took a little more of a compulsion to get Weber to test it on Kinsley, but well worth the effort. What's the matter, Knight? Confused? Let me explain it to you.

"Every time the chupacabra kills, it injects more venom. I've not died once, Knight. I've died *five* times. That's five times as much venom and recuperative powers. This little injection isn't powerful enough to hurt me." He tossed the syringe over his shoulder.

The expression on his face changed from one of amusement to one of pure hate, and Mac knew he was counting the last of his time alive in seconds. Garnering his energy for a last desperate attempt to get free, Mac twisted his body, trying to dislodge Burton, but the vampire didn't budge.

"Give it up, Knight. You lose. I've anticipated every move you could make. You can't kill me."

In his twisting, Mac had seen something familiar out of the corner of his eye, too far away to reach. Stretching out his hand, he yearned with all that was in him that he might be given one last chance. Suddenly something warm, hard, and metallic smacked into the palm of his hand.

"There's one thing you didn't anticipate," he said, closing his fingers around the hilt and swinging his arm upward. "Let me introduce you to the Vampire Slayer."

The sword sliced cleanly, leaving no evidence of a wound for several long seconds. Then blood began to seep, forming a necklace of red around Burton's neck. Then the body was roughly shoved aside, and Mac heard the sick thud of Burton's head hitting the floor somewhere out of his range of vision. He looked up and saw the admiral standing there, beat up and shaken, but very much alive. He extended a hand down to Mac and helped him to his feet.

Mac, still clutching the sword in one hand, turned with the admiral and together they studied what was left of Burton. Neither spoke at first.

"Death Rider," the admiral finally said conversationally, as if he were commenting on the weather.

Confused, Mac gave him a questioning look.

He gestured to the sword. "The sword is called Death Rider—not Vampire Slayer."

Mac held it up and saw the ruby eyes of the etched vampire's face blazing brightly in the pommel, blood clinging to an otherwise gleaming blade, and he rolled his eyes. "Whatever." He handed the admiral the sword and raced out of the house.

Mac broke land-speed records getting back to the hotel. He'd tried several times to call Lanie on the phone and when she didn't answer, he tried the hotel's front desk. The young man he spoke to assured him that they would send someone to Ms. Weber's room immediately and would call an ambulance if necessary. He thought he heard something about the fifth floor as he disconnected and when he called back, no one answered the phone.

There was no ambulance out front when he reached the hotel. He hurriedly parked the car and raced to the rooms they shared, a litany of prayers running through his head asking that she be alive; that Burton had lied, despite the ring of truth he'd heard in Burton's tone.

Throwing open the door to the room, Mac spotted Lanie's still form in bed. He rushed to her side and pulled back the covers, but she didn't move. Her eyes were closed and she was so pale, even her lips had lost their color.

Undoing the fastening of her pants, he peeled them down her hips, needing to know the truth, no matter how it turned out. Four sets of bites lined her inner right thigh, and knowing how forcefully Burton had to have bitten her in order to reach the artery buried so far below the surface of the skin, Mac wondered why the bruising was not worse than it was. Until he realized that there'd not been enough blood left in her body to form much of a bruise. He and Burton had taken it for their own selfish purposes, but at what cost to her?

"Lanie, baby, can you hear me?" He shook her gently, praying she was only unconscious. She didn't stir. Across the room, the young chupacabra rattled its cage door, trying to get out, but Mac ignored it as he placed his fingers against Lanie's throat and felt for a pulse. Nothing.

"Oh, God. Please, baby, don't be dead. Don't be dead." Growing desperate, he held his finger under her nose, waiting to feel the soft brush of her breath against his skin. When he felt nothing, he placed his head on her chest to listen for a heartbeat. He heard only the pounding of his own pulse and roared in silent denial of the truth.

She was gone.

The full horror of it hit him and he gathered her to him, holding her as he'd wanted to hold her earlier that day, his guilt more than he could take. He'd killed her. He'd killed her emotionally when he'd rejected her earlier, and now he'd killed her physically. And the irony was that he loved her more than life itself—would gladly have traded his life for hers. He'd wanted only to protect her—and instead . . .

He laid her back on the bed, gazing upon her face, so peaceful now, until the pain of loss bent him double to the floor. And though he had no memory of ever having cried before in his life, he wept there in the room.

A long time later, he gradually became aware of the chupacabra's near-violent behavior in the cage, and he forced himself to go to it, a kindred spirit in pain. As he passed the desk to reach its cage, he saw the note Lanie had left him.

> *Dearest Mac, I'm sorry that I didn't tell you about what Burton did to me. I knew you wouldn't take the blood you needed had you known. If you are reading this note, then you are safe, Burton is dead, and it was all worth it. There is something I want you to know and I'm sorry to have to tell you in a note, but I love you—with all my heart. If I had to do it all again, knowing the consequences in advance, I would, with no regrets. If you have some small affection for me, I beg you to do me one last favor. Stake me—and let me stay dead. I do not wish to become a vampire. All my love, Lanie.*

He read it through again, his mind numb. Learning that she loved him, as he loved her, only made the heartache that much worse. He clinched his hand into a fist, resisting the urge to put it through the wall. He loved her. He loved her so much, he wanted her to come back, even as a vampire, but did he love her enough to let her stay dead? With a resigned sigh, he walked through the connecting doors to his room and pulled a stake out of his bag. He *did* love her that much.

Returning to Lanie's side, he raised the stake high, but when he would have stabbed her through the heart, he couldn't. Not yet. There was a little time left, he thought, before she'd rise. He sat beside her and held her hand, gazing upon her face, so lifelike despite its chalklike pallor.

Behind him, the chupacabra set up a horrific screaming and Mac realized that if he didn't do something to pacify it, someone would come to check on the noise. He didn't think he could explain why he was alone in the room with a dead woman and an alien-looking creature.

Unsure what to do, he raised the latch on the door. Immediately the chupacabra charged out of the cage and before he could even react, it raced past him. When he turned around, he was struck with a new horror. The creature was bent over Lanie's neck, biting her.

Though logic told him that she was beyond pain, he roared with anger and rushed at the creature, intending to knock it away. His hand pulled back, ready to deliver the blow, but he paused when the baby looked up and stared into his eyes, filling him with a startling sense of hope and well-being. Caught off guard, he lowered his arm.

Confused by both the creature's actions and the strange feeling washing over him, he lost the urge to kill and decided to put the small creature back into the carrier until he was thinking more clearly. When he took a step toward the bed, however, it growled at him, baring its fangs. Surprised, Mac quickly stepped back. For several minutes, he stood in a quandary over what to do. He tried to grab it again, but the creature wouldn't let him get any closer to Lanie's body. It stood beside her, a sentry guarding precious treasure.

As the night's adrenaline rush ebbed, fatigue pulled at him. Knowing the chupacabra would be stone in a few hours, he decided to wait until then to put it back. Crossing to the large armchair, he sank into it and closed his eyes, wanting to escape the pain of his reality, if just for a little while. Later, after the sun came up, he'd finish what needed to be done and somehow find the strength to say a final good-bye to Lanie and stake the woman he loved.

From deep within his dreams, an angel's voice called to him. He recognized her voice and was filled with such longing that he never wanted to wake. The need to be with Lanie, to feel her touch, to hold her, was so intense that he imagined the soft feel of her lips against his. Then they were gone and he didn't know how to bring her back. "Don't go," he begged, his voice little more than a choked sob.

"I won't," her soft voice came to him, and he felt a light touch on his arm. "Not if you don't want me to."

"Never again," he said. "Promise me."

"Never again." The whispered words caressed his face just before he felt the pressure against his lips again, this time more insistent and much less—dreamlike. Stunned, he opened his eyes—and nearly fell out of his chair. Lanie stood smiling down at him, looking tired and pale, but alive.

He jumped up and pulled her to him, holding her tightly, afraid that if he let go, she'd vanish into thin air, merely a figment of his tortured imagination. Not normally a devout man, he offered up several silent prayers of thanks. "I thought I'd lost you. It's a miracle that you're alive. It's . . ." He dropped his arms from her as if burned and stepped away. "Stay back."

She cocked her head to one side and frowned. "Not exactly the response I was hoping for, especially after such a warm beginning."

"I'm sorry," he said, edging closer to the desk where the stake lay. "It's just that—you're dead."

She smiled and Mac felt his gut tighten. He let his hand fall back to his side. She was beautiful and he loved her so. If she *was* a vampire, he prayed she'd forgive him, because now that he had her back, he'd never be able to stake her.

"I don't think I'm dead," she said, interrupting his thoughts. "I don't think I ever was. I heard you come back, but I couldn't move. Everything sounded so far away. I remember being cold, so cold." She wrapped her arms around herself, and Mac didn't know if she was still cold or simply reacting to the memory.

"There was a searing pain seeping through my body as if it rode my bloodstream, leaving darkness and death in its wake. I was being consumed, and I knew that if it didn't stop soon, I would die—or worse." She gave an embarrassed laugh. "I guess that sounds crazy, doesn't it?"

Mac wasn't so sure, but he didn't say anything, letting her go on.

"Then I heard Gem," she continued. "It was like she was crying to me, begging me to hold on. There was a pressure at my neck. It didn't hurt, exactly. It felt more like warmth and sunshine, spreading through me, easing my pain, and chasing away the darkness. After that, I think I fell asleep. When I woke up a little while ago, I saw you sleeping in the chair."

He took a step closer to her, fighting the hope swelling inside him. "Then you're not a vampire?"

Lanie placed her hand against his cheek, letting all the love she felt for him show in her eyes. She'd felt so helpless lying there in the bed, unable to move or respond to anything going on around her. When she'd heard him weeping, she'd longed to hold and comfort him, just as she wanted to do now because he looked lost and confused. "No, I'm not a vampire." She smiled. "I don't even think I'm like you and Dirk. I'm just me, only more anemic than normal." At that moment, her knees buckled, and he helped her into the chair as a wave of dizziness washed over her.

"Are you all right?"

She waved a hand dismissively. "Just feeling a little weak still. How's Uncle Charles?"

"He's fine, I think." Mac furrowed his brow. "I sort of left him in a hurry."

She nodded. "And Dirk?"

"I don't know. I haven't heard from him."

"How are *you* doing?"

He shrugged and his expression turned worried. "Honestly? I don't know. I'm so afraid I'll blow it again." He knelt before her and took her hands in his, gazing at her with such raw emotion, her heart ached for him. "I don't know if you can ever forgive me for what I did to you. I wouldn't blame you if you can't, but I want you to know this—I love you. More than I've loved anyone in my life."

Lanie felt suddenly breathless. She wanted to believe him so badly. "Are you sure?"

"Lanie, when I thought you died, *I* died. I know I said and did things earlier that hurt you. I didn't mean them. I thought it would be easier for you to leave if you were mad at me."

"Next time, just tell me to go away, okay?"

He gave her an astounded look. "Would that have worked?"

She smiled. "I doubt it."

He looked surprised at her answer, and then his smile turned into a chuckle.

"I love you," she said. "I understand why you did what you did." She bent her head close to his and kissed him.

"Will you marry me?"

His whispered question caught her off guard. "Are you sure that's what you want?"

"I've never been more certain about anything."

Her heart soared. "Yes, I'll marry you." He stood and when he pulled her into his arms, her gaze wandered to a spot behind him, on the bed.

"What about Gem?"

He leaned back so he could see her face. "What about her?"

"What will we do with her?"

He smiled, dropping his forehead to hers. "We'll keep her, of course. I have a very warm spot in my heart for that little creature," he admitted. "I think we have her to thank for saving your life. Wherever we decide to live, she'll have a home with us."

Now everything was perfect, she thought. "Do you know how much I love you?" she asked softly.

"It can't possibly be more than I love you." He pulled her close, enfolding her in his tight embrace. "Now let me hold you, Lanie," he whispered. "Because I never thought I'd be able to again."

# Epilogue

The next several days passed in a whirlwind of activity. Mac and Lanie had a private wedding, and though she would have preferred that her father walk her down the aisle, she was content to have Uncle Charles do the honors. The admiral had made a swift recovery from his encounter with Burton, and Dirk had returned the next day. His night had been uneventful.

Two vampires, Harris and Patterson, remained at large, but no one thought they'd be foolish enough to draw attention to themselves, although sooner or later, they would need to be found. That's where the soon-to-be-retired Admiral Winslow's private task force came in. Privately funded, Uncle Charles had some notion that Dirk, Mac, and Lanie would help him on his quest to search for and eliminate the threat of vampires all around the world. Special concessions were given for Professor Weber, as Mac refused to hunt his father-in-law.

"How are you feeling, Mrs. Knight?" Mac asked as he pulled the car out of the admiral's driveway.

Lanie knew the question had double meaning. There'd been no negative side effects to either Burton's or Mac's bites and Lanie didn't think there would be, but she knew her husband would continue to worry. It was his nature, and she loved that he cared so much about her. "I feel just like my old self, a mere human mortal, only happier. Much happier." She leaned across the center console and they exchanged a quick kiss. It was so nice to be able to do that anytime she wanted, Lanie thought, a contented sigh escaping her lips.

She thought back to the first two days following her abduction. She didn't know why the baby chupacabra's venom would have such healing powers while the adult's could turn a human into a vampire or a changeling. Maybe the venom changed as the animal matured. She didn't know and wished again that her father were around. He might have been able to discover the answer. Now, they might never know, and it made her think of all the unknowns that lay ahead of them.

"Are you sure you want to do this?" she asked Mac, studying his profile as he drove. They were going back to Houston for a brief stay. Long enough for Mac to visit with his sister and sign over his half of the charter business to his partner and brother-in-law. Lanie was going to quit her job and sell her house, because they were moving in with the admiral for an unspecified period of time.

"Yeah, I'm sure. What about you?"

"Up all night; sleep all day? Yeah, I'm okay with that, as long as I'm with you," she said honestly.

He took one hand off the wheel long enough to give hers a gentle squeeze. "That's good, because I'm never leaving you or sending you away again."

"Promise?"

"Scout's honor."

Lanie laughed. "You were never a Boy Scout."

He gave her a roguish smile and a wink. "It's a good thing, too. Otherwise, Dirk would have gotten that suite of rooms you like so much at the admiral's house."

Dirk was offered an early retirement option, thanks to a few strings the admiral was able to pull and he, too, was moving in with the admiral. They would be one big, happy vampire-hunting family, and Lanie couldn't have been more pleased. She was going to put her computer and research skills to use helping them. After all, everyone on the new task force couldn't go around killing vampires.

She glanced in the backseat where Gem, still in her stone phase, rested inside the carrier. Lanie was eager to learn more about the chupacabra so she'd have much to share with her father when he contacted her, as she knew he would.

Looking out the window, Lanie watched the scenery pass by. The bright orange sun was beginning to set, and already the shadows were growing darker. Up ahead was the Capitol Building, its dome roof glowing in an otherwise fading light. On the edge of the roof, an object caught Lanie's eye, and as they drove past the building, she turned her head to get a better look at it.

A lone gargoyle sat there, looking over the city. Sure she'd been mistaken, Lanie turned around in the seat to get a better look, but by then the sun had set and the gargoyle was gone.

# About the Author

**Robin T. Popp** grew up watching *Star Trek* and reading Nancy Drew, Robert Heinlein, Sharon Green, and Piers Anthony. She loved the daring and romantic exploits of heroic characters on grand adventures in otherworldly places. It wasn't long before she wanted to write such tales to share with others. Though she was forced to take a thirty-year detour through the real world—which certainly wasn't without its share of adventures—armed now with two master's degrees, a full-time job, and a family, she has taken the first steps toward realizing her original dream of becoming an author.

*Too Close to the Sun*, a futuristic romance published in July 2003, was her first novel. *Out of the Night* is her second novel and represents her first foray into another of her favorite alternate realities—the realm of vampires.

Robin lives southwest of Houston, Texas, with her husband, three kids, three dogs, two frogs, one rabbit, and a mortgage. She is living the American dream.

More
Robin T. Popp!

Please turn the page
for a preview of

*Seduced by the Night*

Coming soon from

Warner Books.

# Chapter

# 1

On an otherwise still and silent night, the faint noise and gentle breeze barely registered with Bethany Stavinoski, whose thoughts were focused elsewhere. On her way to the office, she walked another half block along the deserted city sidewalk before it occurred to her that a woman alone at night should be more cautious—and alert.

Spinning around, she half expected a mugger or vagrant to leap at her. She felt both relieved and a bit foolish when she saw that she stood alone. The only other person in sight was a man leaning against the inside wall of a building's doorway, half a block behind her. The feeble glow of the nearby street lamp touched only the outer half of him, leaving the rest to be swallowed by the darkened entryway. His features were unclear, and a trick of the poor lighting gave his eyes a reddish glow. He wore a long black duster over equally dark clothes. With one leg bent at the knee so he could brace his foot against the wall, he smoked a cigarette, appearing both unhurried and extremely dangerous.

Having just come from that direction, Bethany wondered why she hadn't noticed him before. Now, as she watched, he took the cigarette from his mouth to exhale, and his lips lifted in a slight smile as he tipped his head in a subtle greeting. Afraid that her staring might be misconstrued as something more than simple curiosity, she turned and hurried away.

*That's right, sweet thing. Be very afraid.* Dirk Adams watched the look of apprehension cross the young woman's face just before she turned and walked off. He raised his hand, bringing the lit cigarette to his mouth and took a long drag before slowly exhaling the smoke.

He waited until she disappeared around the corner before flicking the cigarette to the street, where he watched the tip flare briefly as it bounced and rolled away. It wasn't even his; Dirk didn't smoke—not anymore.

"Thanks for the loaner," he said conversationally, turning to the creature he held pinned to the door by the neck. "But you know? They just don't taste as good as they used to. Probably just as well. Those things'll kill you." He smiled at his own joke as he studied the creature, more monster now than the twenty-something man it used to be. "I don't suppose that matters to you, though."

"I'm . . . going . . . to . . . kill . . . you," the creature choked out past the constriction of its throat, sounding harsh and wild. "You can't . . . stop me."

Sharp, clawlike nails raked across Dirk's hand, and he winced at the pain. It hurt like a son of a bitch, and he felt his anger rise but didn't loosen his grip. Instead, he let his lips curl back in a snarl.

For a moment, the creature's eyes widened in surprise as it looked at him, then renewed its struggles. Dirk hesitated to do what had to be done, hoping to get some useful bit of information while there was a modicum of coherent thought left in his captive. "Where are Harris and Patterson? Where is the lair?"

"Go to hell," it spit back.

"Right." Dirk pulled a small dagger from its sheath beneath his duster and drove it into the vampire's heart. "Save me a seat."

Bethany anxiously glanced up and, seeing the familiar shape of the Van Horne Technologies Building ahead, breathed a sigh of relief. It wasn't a large building, only four stories in height, but it was home—more so than her apartment, lately. She'd worked there as a research biochemist for almost five years and enjoyed what she did. There was an inherent order to doing research that appealed to her. She liked her life neat, organized and, most important, uneventful.

She reached the door of the building and swiped her ID tag. The doors immediately opened and she crossed the lobby to the security desk, her footsteps ringing loudly in the silence. Bethany found it curious that the guard was not at his post, but assumed he was making his rounds. She signed the after-hours register, noticing her assistant's signature on the line above, and couldn't help worrying what havoc Stuart was wreaking in her absence. The thought sent her hurrying for the elevators.

Stepping inside, she pushed the button to the fourth floor and as the elevator began its ascent, she thought about her latest project. It had her baffled, but she was determined to rise to the challenge, even if it meant running a battery of timed tests that dragged her into the lab at all hours of the night.

She'd questioned Miles Van Horne about who had commissioned the project to analyze the plant extract, but he'd remained stubbornly closemouthed. It wasn't that she expected the CEO to divulge that information to just anyone, but she was not only the researcher in charge of the project, she was his . . . *fiancée*.

The word rolled around awkwardly in her mind, and she tried to view the very recent change in their status from a strictly analytical perspective. She had been dating Miles for almost a year now, and although she'd considered it unwise to date the boss, he had been charmingly persistent.

Miles was quite a bit older than she, and their physical relationship was more PG-13 than R, but that seemed to suit them both. They never mixed business with their personal lives, and she thought it unlikely that she'd find anyone else as supportive of her research and the crazy work schedule she kept. Add to the equation Miles's wealth and status, and the end result was that she could do a whole lot worse.

She'd made the right decision in accepting his proposal, she told herself, running her thumb over the band of the two-carat, emerald-cut diamond solitaire perched on her ring finger. All in all, theirs was the perfect relationship. So when he'd suggested they get married, why had she hesitated?

A soft voice whispered the answer in the back of her head, and she silently scoffed at herself. *Love? Please.* She was far too realistic to believe in that fairy tale. A score of disastrous relationships before Miles flickered through her mind. No, this was a good practical match.

As the elevator stopped on the fourth floor, Bethany forced herself to mentally switch gears and glanced at her watch. *Damn.* She was running late, and knowing Stuart, he'd started without her. She wondered, not for the first time, if she should talk to Miles about the man. Maybe if Miles understood just how incompetent Stuart was, he'd . . . he'd what? Fire Stuart? Bethany sighed. She didn't want to be responsible for someone losing their job.

Resigned to working with the man for now, she opened the door to her office and saw the light on in the lab beyond—Stuart hard at work, no doubt. Yeah, that was a laugh. *Please don't let him have started the next phase of the experiment*, she silently prayed.

She stashed her purse in her desk drawer, grabbed her lab coat off the nearby rack and, shrugging into it, hurried through the connecting doorway.

"Stuart—?" She came to an abrupt halt and felt her heart lurch. Her lab resembled the aftermath of a tornado.

Beakers lay shattered about the room; reagents ran across countertops and dripped on the floor where puddles already formed. Stands that had held flasks and tubing in place now lay strewn about in broken pieces. Everything was ruined—all of her hard work, flushed down the proverbial toilet.

And Stuart was conspicuously absent.

She felt anger burning inside and fought to control it. Had he done this? There was no question that the man hated her. He'd practically accused her of sleeping her way to the department manager position. Maybe this destruction was yet another childish act of professional jealousy. Well, this time, he'd gone too far.

Hurrying back into her office, she grabbed the phone and called the front desk. There was no answer and she hung up, her irritation growing to include the absent guard as she next punched in Miles's cell number. He picked up on the second ring, but she didn't give him time to say a word, launching immediately into her tirade.

"Everything is ruined, absolutely ruined. I'm going to have to start all over again. I can't believe he'd do such a thing—"

"Who?"

"Stuart! He destroyed everything. All of my work on this project is now strewn across the floor. I still have my notes, of course, but really! Is this his idea of working together? How could he—?"

"Bethany!" Miles's raised voice stemmed the flow of angry words. "Slow down and tell me what's going on. Are you all right?"

She took a deep breath, trying to bring herself under control and then, speaking more slowly, told him what she'd found.

"Okay," he said when she finished. "I'm on my way. Don't touch anything. I'll be there shortly, and then we'll decide if we need to call the authorities or not. If Stuart is responsible, I'll deal with him. Just in case he's still around, though, I'd feel better if you called Frank to come wait with you."

She felt another stab of annoyance at the mention of the missing guard. "I tried. He's not at his desk."

"He's probably making his rounds. Go down to the lobby and see if he's back, but first call me back on your cell phone. I want to be in touch with you the entire time."

Bethany hung up, grabbed her cell phone from her purse, and headed for the elevator. She knew the phone wouldn't work once the doors closed, so she waited until after she reached the ground floor to place the call. Though she'd grown accustomed to the silence of the office after hours, now the quiet took on an ominous quality.

"Okay, I'm downstairs," she told Miles when he answered. She crossed to the front desk and looked around. "Frank's still not here. Let me check the monitors to see if I can find out where he is."

She walked behind the desk and sat in the chair, studying the images from the various security cameras throughout the building. "No, I don't—wait, I think I see something." She studied the controls, finding the ones that would change the angle and zoom of the lens. Adjusting the camera's view, she took a closer look. "Oh, God."

"Bethany, what is it?"

"I found Frank."

"Good. Tell him to get his ass back to the desk where it belongs."

"I can't. He's dead."

Dirk hauled the body of the dead vampire from the back of his SUV and slung it over his shoulder. He didn't have to carry it far, only about ten yards to the "dump" pile. He threw it on top of the bodies already there and then studied the sight. Six vampire-corpses—and he'd been responsible for bringing in four of them. The numbers bothered him because he knew that tomorrow, there'd be more. It almost seemed like lately, Harris and Patterson, the two Primes, had been engaging in some orgiastic feed-fest.

Dirk gritted his teeth and searched the pockets of the latest victim, looking for some form of ID to hand over to Detective Boehler. Their ally in the police force was getting good at making up stories to cover the inexplicable deaths that seemed to be growing in number.

Dirk's hand closed around the vampire's wallet and pulled it out. In with the credit cards and driver's license was a photo of the man beside an attractive young woman and a little girl. Closing the wallet, he shoved it into the pocket of his duster and glanced toward the back of the mansion he called home. The admiral would need to know so that another anonymous donation could be made to a grieving family.

With one final task remaining, Dirk returned to the SUV and retrieved the rolled blanket in the backseat. He took it out, holding it carefully, and placed his hand against one end. There was a brief hum of energy and then a warm pommel hit the palm of his hand. He wrapped his fingers around it, and pulled the long, gleaming sword from the scabbard inside the blanket. He placed the blanket and scabbard back in the car and held the sword up, admiring how the blade glinted in the moonlight. It was the Death Rider sword, used to slay vampires, and only a changeling—half vampire, half human—could wield it and command its full power. There were only two changelings in the entire D.C. area, hell, in the entire United States. Dirk was one of them. As he held it, the pommel grew warm in his hand and the ruby eyes of the vampire's head, etched in the side gleamed a bright red.

He went to stand before the pile of bodies and not for the first time, wondered what would happen if he pulled the dagger out of a vampire's heart. Would the body rise again? His cell phone picked that moment to start buzzing, and he glanced at the caller ID before answering it. "Yes, Admiral?"

"John Boehler called. There's been another killing. He thought we'd want to take a look. I saw you drive by the house—are you almost done?"

"Yeah. I'll be right there." Dirk put away the phone and stared at the sight before him. Tomorrow, the sun would turn the pile of corpses into a stone mass that the first stiff wind would then reduce to dust. Only one last task to perform.

Raising the sword high, he brought it down in one swift, smooth stroke. There was no blood as the head hit the ground with the muted thud that Dirk had grown accustomed to. With a grim countenance, he tossed the head back on the pile and cleaned the blade of his sword on the dead man's clothes.

There were moments when he liked being a Death Rider—this was not one of them.

Elsewhere in the city, Kent Patterson wiped the blood from his mouth as his meal slumped to the ground, already forgotten. Patterson had fed until he could consume no more, yet the hunger would not abate. It clawed at him until anger and irritation rode him relentlessly. He considered tasting one of the other humans chained to the wall, their fear a cloying scent in the otherwise rancid atmosphere of his lair, but a sound from the outer chamber distracted him.

His converts had returned and Patterson was eager for the prize they'd brought him. Patterson, ever resourceful, had a plan—one that included personal wealth and power. The success of his plan, however, depended on the biochemist they'd kidnapped for him, and with whose help—given willingly or coerced—Patterson would become a major player in the lucrative underground world of drug trafficking.

Immortality did not come cheap, but it *could* be bought.

Now that he had all the time in the world, Patterson intended to enjoy every minute of it.

He stepped through the door and gazed upon the frightened young man in a white lab coat, held suspended by his arms between the two underlings. Patterson suspected they retained their grip on the young man more to support him than to keep him from bolting. The irony here was that it was not the young man who should be the most frightened.

"What the hell is this?" Patterson bellowed, causing the two lesser vampires to stumble back.

"It . . . it's the biochemist you wanted," the braver of the two responded.

"No," Patterson said, his voice sounding deceptively calm. "This is not the biochemist *I* wanted. This biochemist is a *man*." He raised an eyebrow as he looked first at one underling and then the other, as if daring them to refute the obvious truth. "Where is the woman?" If it were possible for the two vampires to grow paler, they did.

"We went to the lab as instructed, but he was the only one there."

"Then. You. Failed." Patterson spit out the words, making sure the disciples fully appreciated the extent of his displeasure. Their hold on the prisoner grew tentative, as if they would leave him there and return immediately to the lab. *Imbeciles.* "You can't go back now. Your incompetence has put me in a difficult situation. I'll have to find another way to get what I want." He turned to go back into his chamber.

"What do we do with this one?"

Without turning, Patterson waved his hand in a dismissive gesture. "I don't care. Drain him if you like."

"Wait!"

Patterson stopped and looked back at the young man who was either braver, or more foolish, than Patterson had expected. "You wish to say something?"

The young man swallowed visibly and took a deep breath. "You want Bethany Stavinoski, right? I can help you get her."

# THE EDITOR'S DIARY

*Dear Reader,*

Whether it's a deliciously naughty rogue or a creature that only comes out at night, a little danger never hurt anyone. So jump right into our two Warner Forever titles this September and feel your heart race.

Once a rake, always a rake, according to Miss Meredith Merriweather in **A LADY'S GUIDE TO RAKES** by **Kathryn Caskie**. That's precisely why Meredith is engaged to a very nice but dull man. But to save other women from heartbreak, she's devised a plan to tempt the most notorious reformed rake in all of London, the devilishly handsome Alexander Lamont, by using herself as bait. Her goal: to teach him a lesson and document her findings. But when they are caught in a rather scandalous situation in a very public park, Meredith's plan backfires and Alexander's father demands that Alexander marry her. So this reformed rake must come out of retirement and seduce the lovely temptress with every roguish trick he knows. But can he win her heart? New York Times bestselling author Sabrina Jeffries raves "this delightful confection will charm and beguile you—don't miss it!" so grab yourself a copy today.

I'd like to introduce an irresistible new voice to Warner Forever, **Robin T. Popp**. In her exhilarating novel **OUT OF THE NIGHT**, the author offers a twist on the paranormal with a combination of vampires, changelings, and an action-adventure romance. Feisty heroine Lanie Weber isn't afraid of danger. As a volunteer fire fighter, she knows she can survive anything and come out on top. So when her father suddenly goes missing, she flies to the heart of the Amazon jungle to find him. But nothing can prepare her for what's to come. Strong and sexy Mac Knight has agreed to help Lanie find her scientist father. But when they arrive at the research lab, Mac and Lanie find five dead bodies and a bloodsucking creature only believed to live in legends. When the creature attacks Mac, leaving bite marks on his neck, Lanie fights to keep him alive. Though he's exhibiting more vampire characteristics as time passes, Lanie can't disguise her own hunger for him. But can she save both Mac and her father before it's too late?

To find out more about Warner Forever, these titles, and the authors, visit us at www.warnerforever.com.

With warmest wishes,

*Karen Kosztolnyik*

Karen Kosztolnyik, Senior Editor


P.S. Fate takes a hand in these two irresistible novels: Wendy Markham delivers the touching and charming story of the quintessential bachelor who avoids marriage at any cost and the beautiful bride-to-be who's out of time—and a groom—in BRIDE NEEDS GROOM; plus Diane Perkins tells the heart wrenching story of woman who's duty-bound to the gravely ill man who saved her from an undesirable marriage then abandoned her in THE MARRIAGE BARGAIN.

*Want to know more about romances at*
*Warner Books and Warner Forever?*
*Get the scoop online!*

## WARNER'S ROMANCE HOMEPAGE

Visit us at www.warnerforever.com for all the
latest news, reviews, and chapter excerpts!

## NEW AND UPCOMING TITLES

Each month we feature our new titles
and reader favorites.

## CONTESTS AND GIVEAWAYS

We give away galleys, autographed copies,
and all kinds of fun stuff.

## AUTHOR INFO

You'll find bios, articles, and links to personal
Web sites for all your favorite authors—and
so much more!

## THE BUZZ

Sign up for our monthly romance newsletter,
and be the first to read all about it!

# Kitty and the Midnight Hour
## CARRIE VAUGHN
### (0-446-61641-9)

Kitty Norville is a midnight-shift DJ for a Denver radio station—and a werewolf in the closet. Her new late-night advice show for the supernaturally disadvantaged is a raging success, but it's Kitty who can use some help. With one sexy werewolf-hunter and a few homicidal undead on her tail, Kitty may have bitten off more than she can chew . . .

❧

## Everyone Loves *Kitty*

"I relished this one. Carrie Vaughn's KITTY AND THE MIDNIGHT HOUR has enough excitement, astonishment, pathos, and victory to satisfy any reader."
—*New York Times* bestselling author
Charlaine Harris, author of *Dead as a Doornail*

"Fresh, hip, fantastic—Don't miss this one, you're in for a real treat!"
—L.A. Banks, author of
The Vampire Huntress Legends series

"You'll love this! This is vintage Anita Blake meets *The Howling*. Worth reading twice!"
—Barb and J.C. Hendee, coauthors of *Dhampir*

❧

*About three things I was positive.*

*First, Edward was a* **vampire.**

*Second, there was a part of him
that thirsted for my* **blood.**

*And third, I was in* **love** *with him.*

❧

# ANNOUNCING *TWILIGHT*
the stunning debut of
# STEPHENIE MEYER
that will have you up all night,
riveted until dawn.

❧

OCTOBER 2005

Megan Tingley Books    Little, Brown and Company
www.twilightnovel.com